COOKIES AND SCREAM

A COOKIE CUTTER SHOP MYSTERY

COOKIES AND SCREAM

VIRGINIA LOWELL

WHEELER PUBLISHING
A part of Gale, Cengage Learning

Farmington Hills, Mich • San Francisco • New York • Waterville, Maine
Meriden, Conn • Mason, Ohio • Chicago

GALE
CENGAGE Learning

LIBRARY OF CONGRESS CATALOGING-IN-PUBLICATION DATA

Lowell, Virginia.
  Cookies and scream / by Virginia Lowell. — Large print edition.
    pages cm. — (Wheeler Publishing large print cozy mystery)
    ISBN 978-1-4104-7702-6 (softcover) — ISBN 1-4104-7702-9 (softcover)
    1. Murder—Investigation—Fiction. 2. Large type books. I. Title.
  PS3612.O888C68 2012
  813'.6—dc23   2014047574

Published in 2015 by arrangement with The Berkley Publishing Group, a member of Penguin Group (USA) LLC, a Penguin Random House Company

Printed in the United States of America
1 2 3 4 5   19 18 17 16 15

A12006 434183

For Viki and Bob

ACKNOWLEDGMENTS

I am truly grateful for the support, encouragement, and guidance of so many talented people, especially my wonderful editor, Michelle Vega, as well as Robin Barletta and the skilled copyeditors at Berkley Prime Crime. As always, my family and friends have propped me up when I needed it and kept me more or less sane. I am grateful to Sherry Ladig for her sharp eyes and her amazing range of knowledge. A special thanks to Carolee Jones, who shared with me her stories and writings of life aboard an Australian cruise ship. And to Tom Colgan: Thank you for believing in me so many years ago.

CHAPTER ONE

As soon as she flipped on the lights in The Gingerbread House, Olivia Greyson sensed something was wrong. She felt certain the store was not as she had left it six days earlier, when she'd abandoned Chatterley Heights to escape the unrelenting heat of early August in Maryland. Spunky, her little rescue Yorkie, snoozed in her arms, exhausted by hours spent protecting his backseat domain from the other cars whizzing past.

Olivia closed her eyes and listened to her store. She identified Spunky's light snoring, the faint humming of the overhead lights, and the air conditioner purring on a low setting. Olivia heard the faint, comforting tinkling of cookie cutter mobiles as the whispering air jostled them. Could she have picked up a subliminal sound coming from the kitchen? Olivia envisioned a colony of mice methodically munching through un-

9

opened bags of sugar and flour before balancing their diets with meringue powder. She didn't see any evidence of water seeping under the kitchen floor, but what if a pipe were about to burst? Great, now she'd probably dream about swimming through a flooded store to rescue drowning cookie cutters. She could almost hear their little metallic cries for help.

Get a grip, Livie. After so many hours of driving, mostly in the dark, she was too tired to think clearly. She should have gone straight upstairs to her apartment, but after nearly a week away from her beloved Gingerbread House, she'd craved a peek inside the store before falling into bed.

Spunky stirred in her arms. Olivia glanced up at the beautiful, unreliable Hansel and Gretel clock on the wall, which put the time at about 2:40 a.m. If Spunky woke up and realized they were home, he would want to go outside for a run. Olivia hoped to be in bed before that happened. On the other hand, she needed to check the entire store, or she would dream about hulking gingerbread monsters bent on destroying their bakers.

If only Del were back in town, sitting in his office at the Chatterley Heights Police Department. But no, Del had to rush off to rescue his former wife, Lisa, leaving the town without a sheriff. Okay, that wasn't fair. Deputy Cody was filling in as acting sheriff. Besides, Olivia understood why Del felt compelled to help Lisa. She was filing for divorce from her abusive third husband, and Del was worried for her safety. Of course, Lisa's third husband had also been her first husband. He'd been abusive then, as well, yet Lisa had divorced Del to remarry him. Olivia shook her head to clear it. Del's ex-wife was his problem, and he would handle it with his usual calm intelligence. *I hope.*

Spunky lifted his head and whimpered groggily. "We'll go upstairs soon," Olivia whispered. "Just a quick look around the store and then to bed." As she rubbed Spunky's silky ears, Olivia scanned the sales floor, hoping to identify the source of her vague discomfort. The glass-door cabinet, which usually held vintage and antique cookie cutters, was empty, as she had left it. Less valuable cutters, arranged on tables and in mobiles, remained on display. Olivia hadn't wanted the store to look unoccupied while she was out of town. She poked her head into the dimly lit cookbook nook, where the shelves of cookbooks looked organized and neat. No bodies slumped in

11

the two stuffed easy chairs.

Olivia took a few tentative steps farther into the store, where her gaze landed on a shelf loaded with colorful sparkling sugars. The display didn't look quite right. She walked closer to get a better look. The small, clear plastic containers all stood upright, labels facing forward, as they should. However, they were no longer arranged by color in neat little clusters. It looked to Olivia as if someone had knocked the sugars off the shelf and hastily replaced them. The holiday reds and greens were grouped together, a display no Gingerbread House employee would dream of creating during a sweltering August. What if it made customers feel hotter and crankier?

Normally, Olivia wouldn't be alarmed by a messy shelf; customers often picked up items to examine more closely, then plunked them down willy-nilly. But the store had been closed and locked up tight for a week, since much of Chatterley Heights had fled town to avoid the heat. Maddie Briggs, Olivia's friend and business partner, wasn't due back for a couple of days. Maddie and her new husband, Lucas Ashford, were celebrating what they called their "Honeymoon, Part Two" by hiking in Monongahela National Forest. Olivia's mother had dragged her unenthusiastic stepfather to a retreat in the Pocono Mountains. Bertha, the store's head clerk, and Mr. Willard were visiting historical sites in the Johnstown-Altoona area. As for Olivia, she and Spunky had escaped for a week to a rented cabin in the Finger Lakes.

Spunky began to squirm in Olivia's arms, awake now and eager to investigate his domain. She lowered him to the floor. With terrier single-mindedness, the little guy scurried among the display tables and over to his chair near the large front window. Satisfied that no interloper had invaded his territory, he checked the store perimeter. He paused to sniff the sales counter. Following a scent, Spunky rounded the counter and disappeared behind it. Olivia heard him growl, and her heart rate kicked up a notch. Had a burglar found a way inside the store and tried to open the register? Olivia had left the register empty, of course. Their more valuable vintage and antique cookie cutters were locked away in a hidden wall safe in the Gingerbread House kitchen.

"Uh-oh," Olivia whispered. "I'd better check on those cutters." At the sound of her voice, Spunky reappeared and trotted toward her. "Okay, Spunks, you may come along with me to the kitchen. The store is

13

closed, no one is baking cookies, and the Health Department will never know." Just the same, Olivia scooped Spunky into her arms in case he found an irresistible scent and decided to roll in it.

Olivia felt a moment of disappointment when she opened the kitchen door and no burst of lemon cookie dough greeted her. The kitchen felt lonely without Maddie's exuberant presence. Olivia missed seeing her friend's flour-coated red hair bounce in time with the music piping through her earbuds. On the other hand, having some quiet time alone in The Gingerbread House sounded lovely. *As long as our most valuable cookie cutters are still safe.*

Spunky wriggled in Olivia's grip. She knew he wanted to explore the kitchen while he had the chance. She relented and released him. Besides, she'd need both hands to move the battered antique spice rack she had hung on the wall to mask the safe. Spunky took off like a pup on a sugar high. He raced around the kitchen, jumped onto a chair to reach the table, then leaped over to the counter. The whole room would need a thorough sanitizing before they could begin baking again. On the other hand, Spunky was having such fun, and the kitchen was overdue for a scrubbing, anyway.

As Olivia approached the wall safe, her anxiety intensified. She held her breath as she lifted the spice rack off its moorings. The safe door was closed and locked. Olivia placed the spice rack on the worktable and took a calming breath, as her yoga-obsessed mother had demonstrated to her more times than she cared to count. Nevertheless, Olivia's staccato heartbeat didn't subside until the lock clicked, and the door opened to reveal a safe filled to capacity with cookie cutters.

Olivia's instant relief turned to sudden confusion. Before leaving town, she had secured the store's most valuable cookie cutters, which had left the safe about half full. Now the safe was packed so tightly there wasn't room for even the tiniest of fondant cutters. When Olivia tried to extract one cutter from the pack, the others began to shift. Fearing an avalanche, she grabbed the loose cutter and slammed the safe door shut.

"Wow," Olivia whispered as she stared at the metal shape in her hand. She'd never seen it before. She sat at the kitchen table, under the light, to get a better look. Clearly the heart-shaped cutter was handmade, shaped from tin and soldered to a brace. The tail of the heart was long and thin. The cutter and its brace looked worn, but the piece was in excellent condition. Olivia guessed it to be a genuine antique, possibly a hundred or more years old. Something about the design made her wonder if it might be German in origin. *I'll have to check with Anita.* Though she and Anita Rambert, owner and manager of Rambert's Antique Mall, were frequent rivals in the pursuit of valuable antique cookie cutters — and not always in a friendly way — Olivia trusted Anita's superior expertise.

"Now I'm sorry I sneaked home from vacation early." Spunky trotted over in response to Olivia's voice. "I wish Maddie were here." Maddie and Lucas had been part of the first wave to leave Chatterley Heights, so it couldn't have been Maddie who put the mysterious cutters in the Gingerbread House safe. She might know who had done so, but then why wouldn't she have called to forewarn Olivia? Maddie was congenitally incapable of keeping a secret, especially when it concerned a collection of potentially valuable cookie cutters.

Spunky leaped onto the chair next to Olivia and yapped. "I know," Olivia said. "You've been cooped up in a car for hours, and now you want to go for a run. Only here's the problem: It's three a.m. I'll lay out a couple of puppy pads for you when we go upstairs, okay? I promise we'll run tomorrow, by which I mean today, only much later. Mother has spoken."

Spunky tilted his fluffy head, fixed Olivia with achingly sad brown eyes, and whimpered.

"You heard me." Olivia opened a kitchen drawer and slid the unfamiliar cookie cutter under a pile of napkins to keep it out of sight. Spunky jumped from the chair to the counter, where he flopped down and rested his head on his paws. "Oh, don't look at me like that, you pathetic creature." She lifted Spunky into her arms and headed toward the kitchen door. The tired pup nestled against her chest. "Come on, kiddo, let's get some sleep. Tomorrow we'll take a nice, long run in the park. Then we will track down the source of those mysterious cookie cutters. I just hope that, for once, no one has been murdered."

CHAPTER TWO

Olivia awakened to sunshine, heat, and a phone ringing next to her ear. She groaned and slid her head under the pillow. When the ringing stopped, Olivia lifted the pillow. After a few seconds of reorientation, she remembered she was home from vacation and sleeping in her own bedroom, which was hot and way too bright. She had been so exhausted she'd neglected to adjust the air-conditioning or pull down the blinds.

Spunky lay curled at the foot of Olivia's bed. He lifted his head, ears perked, and waited to see if his mistress was serious about getting up. When she turned on her side and closed her eyes, Spunky snuggled deeper into the covers.

The cell phone rang again. Olivia considered throwing it across the room, but that would require effort. She managed to fumble for her phone, flip it open, and mumble an irritable greeting, all without lifting her head.

"Livie? Sounds like you had a bit too much merlot last night."

Olivia struggled to focus her mind. "Constance? That you?"

"That me," said Constance Overton, sole proprietor of the Chatterley Heights Management and Rental Company. "You cut your vacation short, I hear."

"Yes, I'm aware of that," Olivia said. "How did you know?"

"You sound crabby, so I'm guessing you got in fairly late. To answer your question, several citizens reported spotting your unmistakable PT Cruiser this morning between two and five a.m."

"I got back just after two." Olivia attempted to sit up. She failed. "Did you wake me up to report that the entire town of Chatterley Heights knows I'm back? Am I supposed to be amazed? Or is this yet another attempt to punish me for stealing your boyfriend in high school, which, as you well know, I did not do."

"*Really* crabby," Constance said with her throaty laugh. "No, Livie, I did not call to torture you, though it's always such fun. I have some information you will need quickly. We decided it wasn't necessary to bother you on vacation, and Bertha didn't

19

want to leave you a note, in case . . . well, Bertha felt responsible for the store's safety, since she was the last staff member to leave town. So she thought it more prudent, given the circumstances, to wait until she returned to town, rather than leave a note for you on the counter. However, you came home early, so the responsibility falls on my competent, yet shapely, shoulders."

"Bertha? Information? Hold on a sec." Suddenly, Olivia felt wide awake. She swung her legs out of bed so fast that Spunky yapped at her. "Constance, does your information have anything to do with cookie cutters? Specifically, a wall safe filled to the brim with amazing antique cutters I've never seen or even heard about before?"

For once, Constance sounded surprised. "You checked your safe in the middle of the night? Why? I mean, were you simply being cautious?"

"Hard to explain, and it doesn't matter. Tell me what's going on." Olivia held the cell to her ear while she gathered clean clothes with her free hand.

"Long, yet fascinating story," Constance said. "Have you had breakfast? No, of course not. I'm at Pete's Diner. My meal hasn't arrived yet. Get here in ten minutes; we can eat and talk."

"Spunky really needs a run. He's been cooped up in a car."

"Well, run him through the park and over to Pete's. I'm confined to a wheelchair, after all. Spunky can be my companion dog and sit on my lap."

"Are you sure Pete will be okay with — ?"

"Nine minutes and forty-five seconds. Step on it."

Olivia arrived at Pete's Diner in just under twelve minutes, after the world's fastest shower and a run with Spunky through the town square. They had stopped only once, at the statue of the town's founder, Frederick P. Chatterley, memorialized forever in an attempt to mount his patient horse. Frederick P., as the portly gentleman was called by affectionate and amused townsfolk, was a popular destination for the Chatterley Heights canine community.

Olivia held Spunky tightly against her chest as she entered Pete's Diner. Pete had cranked up the air-conditioning to its highest setting. The welcome coolness swirled around Olivia, carrying the delicious scents of strong coffee, bacon, and freshly baked cinnamon rolls.

Constance Overton, lovely as ever, sipped coffee in her usual spot, which gave her the

21

best view in the diner. Pete had installed a special table, higher and wider than usual, to accommodate her wheelchair. As Constance greeted Olivia with a regal nod of her head, a lock of wavy blond hair brushed her cheek. Constance looked cool in a pale blue silk blouse with short sleeves that revealed her slender, muscular arms. Her crystal-blue eyes held a hint of amusement as she watched Olivia struggle to hold on to five pounds of excited, wiggly Yorkshire terrier.

"There's no need to crush the poor guy," Constance said. "Pete has given permission for Spunky to sit with us, as long as he's with me. So hand him over."

"If you say so, but keep hold of his leash." Spunky went eagerly into Constance's arms and nestled on the soft shawl covering what remained of her lap after a serious automobile accident had taken her legs. As a real estate and business agent, Constance had become quite wealthy. Olivia wondered if she had investigated the possibility of prosthetic surgery to help her become more mobile, but she wasn't comfortable bringing up the topic. Though the two of them had smoothed over their high school animosity and become friends, Olivia felt there would always be a distance between them.

She wasn't sure why.

Ida, a waitress at Pete's Diner since well before Olivia was born, shuffled over to their table. "Heard you were up driving till all hours," Ida said. "If your mother were in town, she'd have something to say about that."

"My mom always has something to say," Olivia said, "although I don't always understand what she's talking about."

Ida rattled a cup and saucer on Olivia's place mat and filled it halfway with coffee. "I'm not surprised. Kids never listen. They go off and do whatever they want. Next thing you know, they want to put you in a home, never mind you've been working for more than sixty years. You want your usual?"

"Um, sure," Olivia said. "I'll have the scrambled —"

"Scrambled eggs with cheese, two strips of bacon, and toast. My memory's sharp as it always was. Kids. . . ." Ida shook her head vigorously, loosening a thin strand of iron-gray hair from her tightly wound bun. She ignored it.

As Ida trudged toward the kitchen, Constance grinned at Olivia. "I knew you'd never make it here in under ten minutes, so I told Ida to hold my breakfast until you arrived." Constance reached into a leather

23

pouch attached to her wheelchair and extracted a file, which she handed to Olivia. "Take a look at this," she said. "It's a partial list the owner sent me before her arrival in Chatterley Heights. The full list is in my safe. I will give you the original when we meet with her. I'll keep a copy."

Olivia wanted to ask who this mysterious "owner" was, but her interest in the cutters themselves got the better of her. She opened the file and began to skim through the first of several typed pages. They were mostly antiques, as far as she could tell from the descriptions. Someone must have done a great deal of digging to uncover the history of each cutter. Olivia spotted a listing for a German tin cutter in the shape of a thin-tailed heart. "I think I saw this cutter," Olivia said, pointing to the listing. "She tried to get away when I opened the Ginger-bread House safe, but I captured her. She's hidden in a drawer. I managed to slam the safe door shut before the whole pack of cutters could escape."

"My, my," Constance said. "Cookie cut-ters are like little people to you, aren't they? Rebellious little people, it seems."

Olivia laughed. "They are usually quite well behaved, although I can't vouch for their behavior when I'm not around." Flipping to the second page of the list, she said, "Okay, so this is a long list of rare antique cookie cutters. They all originate in Europe, as far as I can tell. But there are many more cutters listed here than could possibly fit inside my little safe."

"The rest of them are secured in the more substantial safe in my office," Constance said. "I'm sure you realize how valuable these cookie cutters are."

"Oh, I realize that all right." Olivia felt light-headed with excitement. "Most are quite old, some more than two hundred years. I've read about similar cutters, but I haven't heard that anyone has spotted them in decades. I assumed they had all been snatched up by private collectors. Apparently, I was right."

Constance leaned across the table to see the list. She smiled when she saw where Olivia was pointing. "Bertha and I went through that whole list and put the most valuable items in my safe. That cutter was one of them."

"Because your safe is so superior to mine?"

Constance grinned. "Now, now, this is not a contest."

Ida arrived at their table and plunked down their breakfast plates. Olivia felt torn between avid curiosity and a growling stomach. Curiosity won. "Okay, Constance, put down the fork. What's going on here?"

Constance's laugh sounded rich and husky, with a hint of triumph. "This has been fun," she said, "but I suppose I should take pity on you and spill the story." She took a quick bite of her scrambled eggs before reaching back into her leather pouch for a manila envelope. "Chatterley Heights has a new permanent resident," Constance said as she opened the envelope. "She arrived last Saturday, the very day you left on your vacation. Her name is Greta Oskarson." Constance extracted a photo and handed it to Olivia.

While she nibbled a slice of bacon, Olivia studied the excellent photograph of an attractive middle-aged woman wearing an off-the-shoulder ball gown. The pale blue satin of the gown appeared to match perfectly with the woman's icy blue eyes. "This is our new resident?" Olivia asked with astonishment. "Are you sure she came to the right place?"

Constance almost choked on her coffee. "It's true, Chatterley Heights hasn't hosted many fancy dress balls since the days of Frederick P., but I guarantee Greta came here on purpose. I asked her for a photo for my files. Greta insisted that's the only one she could come up with on short notice. It's about a decade old. At the time, she was married to Count Something-or-other. Her fifth marriage, she said. She'd started off with a count when she was eighteen, and I think there was yet another count somewhere in her marital history. Maybe two. I don't know, I lost count of Greta's counts. I really wasn't terribly interested until she began to discuss her waxing and waning fortune. She appears to be fairly well off at the moment, since she was able to purchase a home outright. However, she worries about her financial future, probably because she experienced some rough patches in the past. Now Greta has come home to retire, which is where you —"

Ida materialized at the table, wielding a pot of fresh coffee. "Well, I'll be," Ida said as she snatched the photo out of Olivia's hand. "That's Greta Oskarson, all dolled up. She doesn't look like that now, does she? If she's smart, she won't show up in here again. I might accidentally spill hot coffee on her." Ida left before her startled listeners could ask what she meant.

"This just gets more and more interesting," Constance murmured as she spread raspberry jam on her toast.

Olivia added cream and sugar to her coffee and settled back in her chair. "Okay, Constance, I think you'd better start at the beginning. Who is Greta Oskarson, and why would she want to retire in little Chatterley Heights instead of, say, the Côte d'Azur? Her name sounds vaguely familiar, but I've never seen her before, at least as far as I can remember."

Constance polished off her toast and washed it down with coffee. "Greta left Chatterley Heights long before you were born. Greta's name might seem familiar to you because Clarisse probably mentioned her. Greta would have been a few years older than Clarisse, but they bonded over their shared passion for cookie cutters. Both of them had become avid collectors."

Olivia no longer winced at a casual reference to her murdered friend, Clarisse Chamberlain, but she still felt the loss. "So Greta grew up in Chatterley Heights? And she left at eighteen to marry a count?"

"Correct, more or less," Constance said. "I think she ran off to Europe at eighteen and found her count after she got there. She was a bit vague about the order of events."

"But . . . Clarisse would have been younger than eighteen, and I know for a fact she didn't start collecting cookie cutters until her early twenties, after she married Martin." Olivia picked up the photo and studied it. Greta Oskarson did not look the least bit familiar to her.

Constance opened a small quilted bag, decorated with embroidery, and withdrew a handful of bills. "Breakfast is on me. Business has been good lately. And I need to get back to it. I have a lot of work to do before the weekend; Saturday and Sunday are busy days for realtors."

"Thanks for breakfast, Constance, but you can't have told me the whole story about Greta and her cookie cutters. I want every last detail."

As if on cue, Ida appeared again with her ever-present pot of coffee. She filled their cups and left without a single acerbic comment.

"Drink up and listen," Constance said. "Greta contacted me before she left Europe because she wanted to buy a small house in Chatterley Heights. At that time, she said nothing to me about her background or about cookie cutters. She really is serious about settling down here. She has had her fill of fancy dress balls and rich counts, or so she says. She longs for a quiet life. When Greta heard about Clarisse's murder, she said she was saddened and disappointed.

Greta and Clarisse had corresponded for some years, and once again when Greta was thinking about coming home. It was during their more recent correspondence that Greta heard good things about you from Clarisse."

"I'm surprised Clarisse never mentioned Greta to me," Olivia said. "Why would Greta want to move back here?"

"I'm getting to that," Constance said. "I found her a charming little house on the north edge of town, just a block from the Chatterley Mansion. It's actually not far from the Chamberlain house, but now . . . Well, it would have been perfect, if Clarisse were still alive. However, Greta liked what she heard about the house I found for her, and she bought it sight unseen. Yes, I'm that good. She sent most of her belongings ahead, but she carried the cookie cutters with her from Europe. She took a ship over from Europe so she wouldn't have to part with her collection during the journey."

Olivia drained her coffee cup. "Most people have no idea that cookie cutters can be valuable to collectors. Still, it was wise of Greta to keep an eye on her collection."

"Indeed," Constance said. "Greta has some money, as I mentioned. However, she's counting on the value of her collection to provide her with that extra bit of security in the retirement she envisions for herself. So she wants to sell those cookie cutters for as much as possible, as quickly as possible. When Greta first arrived in Chatterley Heights last Saturday, she made straight for The Gingerbread House. She wanted to talk to you at once. She says she trusts you, and only you, to handle the sale of her collection for her, even though she has never met you in person. Don't ask me to explain it."

"Thanks."

"Don't mention it." Constance smiled. "Mind you, I didn't say she was wrong. But to continue, Greta found The Gingerbread House closed up tight on a non-holiday workday. She didn't realize that Bertha was on her way to the store to make sure all was well before she and Mr. Willard left for their getaway. Greta was quite upset to find no one there, so she went straight to my office. She was dragging along her entire cookie cutter collection."

"Ah," Olivia said. "At least I understand how part of the collection ended up in your safe."

"Exactly. However, even my safe could not hold all of them. I knew Bertha hadn't left town yet, so I called her cell. When I found out she'd gone to The Gingerbread House to make sure it was all locked up, I sent Greta right over. Somehow Bertha managed to cram the remainder of the collection into your little safe." Constance glanced at the bill for breakfast, counted out exact change plus tip, and left it on the table.

"And Bertha didn't leave me a note because . . . ?"

"Because she was feeling paranoid." Constance reached into a quilted pocket attached to her wheelchair and produced a small mirror. A glance at her hair and face seemed to satisfy her. "Bertha was afraid someone might realize the store was empty, break in, and find the note," Constance said. "If this intruder was looking for something valuable to steal, cracking the safe might sound like a good idea. Bertha figured she'd be arriving back home about the same time you did, so she could tell you about the collection then. She didn't realize that you, too, might be paranoid. It never occurred to her you'd come home early and open the safe the instant you arrived, never mind it was the middle of the night." Constance wheeled herself back from the table's edge. "I have to say, Livie, I'm surprised. I can't imagine what on earth possessed you to check that safe."

Constance directed her state-of-the-art

wheelchair toward the diner door before Olivia could respond. She wasn't sure she really could explain. Maybe it wasn't important. Surely Greta Oskarson must have accidentally knocked over the little containers of sparkling sugars while she was waiting for Bertha to secure her cutters in the wall safe. Greta might have picked up the sugars out of curiosity and put them back on the shelf without thinking about it. She wouldn't have known how to arrange them properly.

"Almost forgot," Constance said, twisting her head to look back toward Olivia. "Greta wants to meet with you as soon as possible to discuss selling her collection. She doesn't assume you will buy it, of course, but she refuses to consider anyone else to handle the whole process. As you will learn soon enough, Greta is a woman who expects to get her own way. However, she can't meet with you today. No one expected you to be back so soon, so Greta went to DC to select a few pieces of furniture for her new home. I will contact you sometime tomorrow to arrange a meeting."

With a sense of relief, Olivia added another dollar to the tip and pushed back her chair. Bertha, Maddie, and her mom would be back in town soon. She would again have her friends and family around her, ready to offer ideas, support, and unsolicited advice. Meanwhile, Olivia intended to take it easy while she had the chance. She had nothing to worry about. The mystery of the cookie cutter–crammed safe had been solved. She could kick back and relax for the remainder of her first real vacation since she opened The Gingerbread House.

CHAPTER THREE

Once word spread through Chatterley Heights that Olivia was back in town, her solitude evaporated. After breakfast with Constance Overton, Olivia walked Spunky back to their Queen Anne home to find her porch occupied by two of her least favorite people: Binnie and Nedra Sloan. Binnie cared only about her newspaper, *The Weekly Chatter,* and her niece, Nedra — or Ned, as she preferred to be called. Ned, who rarely spoke, provided the *Chatter*'s non-verbal elements, such as embarrassing photographs. Binnie took care of the verbal part, and not in a kind way. She also lacked any dedication to truth in journalism, though she called it "going after the essence of a story." Olivia often felt like Binnie's favorite target.

As soon as Olivia climbed the steps to her front porch, Ned's camera started to flash. Olivia ignored the intrusion and let

Spunky's snarling express her opinion.

Ned, stick thin and always in motion, snapped photos nonstop, while Binnie lounged on the comfortable porch rocking chair, her pencil and notebook ready for action. Binnie's stout figure was encased, as usual, in men's cargo pants and, in deference to the heat, a beige T-shirt. Her numerous pockets bulged and sagged from the weight of her news-hunting tools, which included spare pens, notebooks, a simple cell phone, and an old plastic recorder. Although she hosted a blog, her irritating adjunct to *The Weekly Chatter,* Binnie never touched a computer. She wrote the fibs and left the electronic wizardry to Ned.

As Olivia inserted her key into the front door lock, Spunky yapped and struggled to free himself from her tight grip. Olivia had hoped to slip inside before Binnie had a chance to bombard her with insulting or accusatory questions, but no such luck.

"Ned, get a good shot of that nasty animal," Binnie said. "He is baring his teeth and snarling. We'll need a photo for the paper and, of course, our evidence file."

Binnie was forever trying to prove that Spunky was dangerous, but so far her accusations had never been taken seriously. Olivia shoved the front door with her shoulder, clenching her teeth to keep from reacting to Binnie's taunts. The door stuck. *This blasted heat. . . . Temper, Livie, temper.* If she could just get into the foyer before . . . Olivia pushed the door again, harder; it shifted slightly.

"So, Livie," Binnie said, "our sources tell us you've gotten your hands on yet another priceless bunch of old cookie cutters. Naturally, our readers are wondering if this valuable collection will end up belonging to you, like the last one did. Care to comment?"

Olivia focused on her breathing as anger threatened to engulf her. Binnie might possibly be the world's worst reporter, but she had a knack for nasty insinuation. Olivia warned herself not to take the bait. Clarisse Chamberlain, Olivia's dear friend and mentor, had owned a phenomenal collection of cookie cutters. After Clarisse was murdered, Olivia had been stunned to discover that she'd inherited Clarisse's collection, along with a generous monetary gift. Binnie Sloan, ever the opportunist, had hinted strongly in both *The Weekly Chatter* and her blog that the inheritance had given Olivia a powerful motive to kill Clarisse.

Olivia pressed her shoulder against the front door and felt it give. The door scraped against the jamb. One more push, and it should open. She'd only have to slide through and slam the door behind her, and she'd be safe. Del always insisted he'd be glad to arrest Binnie if she refused to leave The Gingerbread House's grounds. Unfortunately, Del wasn't around. Maybe he would never return. As a wave of sadness distracted her, Olivia loosened her hold on Spunky. The feisty little dog, sensing his mistress's distress, wriggled out of her arms and hit the ground running. He charged toward Binnie Sloan, growling like a mama bear protecting her cub. Or so Olivia imagined.

Binnie backed awkwardly across the porch. She grabbed Ned's elbow and tried to pull her toward the front steps. Ned pulled away from her aunt and kept her camera trained on Spunky. Ned leaped sideways as Spunky lunged at her skinny legs. Trapped against the porch railing, Ned hoisted herself up and over, landing on her backside in the grass.

Olivia tried to snatch Spunky before he could bolt off the porch after his prey. She missed. Olivia almost felt sorry for Ned, who struggled to her feet, clutching her camera to her chest as if it were an infant. Defeated, Ned wobbled across the lawn to join her aunt on the sidewalk. Glaring in

Olivia's direction, Binnie shook her fist with such violence that she backed off the curb onto the street. An oncoming car blasted its horn at her.

Spunky halted at the sidewalk as if he knew he'd reached the property line. He paced back and forth on the lawn, yapping ferociously as he guarded the perimeter. Binnie and Ned stayed put.

Olivia heard a clapping sound nearby and realized they were not alone. No fewer than five passersby had paused at a safe distance to watch the action. They were applauding Spunky. Olivia felt so proud, she almost wished she'd given birth to the little guy herself. She did wonder, though . . . were puppies born with claws?

From the look on Binnie's face, not to mention the redness of her plump cheeks, she was now beyond enraged. She extended her right arm, pointed toward Olivia with what looked like a pencil, and shouted, "I'll get you for this."

Sudden quiet followed Binnie's threat. Even Spunky stopped barking, though he growled off and on. A child's voice broke the silence. "Mommy, Mommy, look!" The girl's thin arm pointed in Binnie's direction. "It's the Wicked Witch of the West!"

"Spunky, my boy, you are a prince among pups." Olivia tossed him an unprecedented third treat from the box she kept in her apartment kitchen. "However, we must face reality," she added as she moved the treat box out of sight. "Binnie Sloan will not rest until she has both our hides hanging above her fireplace. I wish Maddie were here. But never mind, Spunks, you and I will lock the doors and spend a quiet, yet pleasant, day puttering around inside The Gingerbread House. I'd love to get a closer look at those antique cookie cutters crowding our wall safe, but that will have to wait. I need to reorganize the sales floor displays first. Then we can play."

Olivia and Spunky headed down the hallway to the bedroom. Despite her recently installed air-conditioning, the room felt stuffy. Ignoring her unmade bed, Olivia took a quick shower and changed into white shorts and a T-shirt, the only clean clothes she could find. She had intended to finish unpacking and get a jump on the laundry, but even the thought of those chores made her feel hot . . . and bored.

For some time, Olivia had wanted to

redesign the layout of the sales floor. Of course, she could always ask Maddie to come up with a plan. Maddie would generate numerous ideas with lightning speed and no concern for time and expense, although they'd be wonderfully creative. However, Maddie was out of town, and Olivia wanted to see where her own imagination might take her.

"Come on, Spunks, let's go back downstairs to the store." Olivia nearly tripped over her little Yorkie as he shot between her ankles in his rush for the door. In case Constance called to set up a meeting with Greta Oskarson, Olivia grabbed her cell phone and slid it into her shorts pocket. As she locked the apartment door behind them, Spunky bounded down the staircase ahead of her. Every day she reminded herself that the convenience of living above her business was well worth her hefty mortgage for the roomy Queen Anne. She marveled that the house had once served as a mere summer cottage for a wealthy Baltimore family. It was larger than her childhood home, where her mother and stepfather still lived.

When she joined Spunky in the downstairs foyer, Olivia found a pile of mail on the tile floor. By now, all of Chatterley Heights, including its post office staff, would know she had come home early. Binnie would have spread the news on her blog. Sam Parnell, mail carrier and town gossip, had undoubtedly been one of the first to find out. A devoted follower of *The Weekly Chatter,* Sam's nickname, Snoopy, was well earned. He could twist the tiniest, most innocuous of details into scandalous gossip. He had probably rushed right over to the store as soon as he could, hoping to pick up a rumor-worthy morsel he could flesh out during his mail route. Perhaps Sam had already heard all about Olivia's breakfast meeting with Constance, which meant he would be angling for a promising tidbit about Chatterley Heights' intriguing new resident, Greta Oskarson.

Olivia hadn't heard the doorbell ring earlier. She must have been in the shower when Sam arrived. She was grateful to have avoided him. However, after missing his chance to pick up some fresh gossip from Olivia, Sam must be feeling frustrated. He would be back.

Olivia released Spunky and scooped up her mail before she unlocked the door to The Gingerbread House. Spunky burst through the open door, his nails clicking on the tile floor. Olivia flipped on the lights and smiled at the sight of her little guardian, ears twitching as he performed his daily, corner-to-corner inspection of the store's sale floor. It was good to be home.

As he'd done the night before, Spunky paused to sniff the floor near the shelf that held the display of decorating sugars. Olivia's contented mood dimmed. She'd nearly forgotten her discovery of the oddly disarranged sparkling sugar display. Spunky seemed even more intrigued by the scents under the shelf than when he'd first detected them. Olivia dropped her mail on an empty display table and joined him. "What is it, Spunks?"

Spunky whimpered. He knew Bertha well, so Olivia guessed he'd picked up a stranger's scent. Olivia squatted down next to him. "Want to know what I think?" she asked. Spunky tilted his head at her. "I think our mysterious new resident must have knocked over the sugar display while Bertha was busy stuffing all those cookie cutters into our wall safe. That's all. You will meet her soon, and then you will recognize her scent. So there's nothing to worry about, little one, though I appreciate your protective instincts."

Spunky yapped only once, but with an edge, as if he weren't quite convinced but was willing to wait and see.

43

"You have every right to feel irritated." Olivia sat cross-legged on the floor, and Spunky crawled onto her lap. "A stranger came into the store while you weren't here to guard the place, and that isn't right. On the other hand, I don't think she's dangerous, only clumsy. Anyway, I'm sure we'll meet her soon, so she won't be a stranger for long." Her explanation seemed to satisfy Spunky. He leaped out of her lap and renewed his inspection of the sales floor.

Olivia rolled to her knees and stood up. It made perfect sense that Greta Oskarson had accidentally knocked over the sparkling sugar display. Although Olivia had to wonder . . . Where was Bertha when this happened? Was she alone in the kitchen as she wedged all those valuable cookie cutters into the store safe? Why? Was she afraid Greta might learn the safe's combination? Wouldn't Greta have wanted to ensure her cutters weren't damaged as Bertha packed them into such a small space? But this was useless speculation. A few disarranged sparkling sugars did not mean murder and mayhem were waiting in the wings. Never mind, Olivia told herself, Bertha would be home in a couple of days to clear up the confusion. Meanwhile, it wouldn't hurt to leave the sugars as she'd found them.

As Olivia entered the store kitchen, Spunky scooted past her before the door closed. "Don't get used to this, kiddo," she said. Spunky ignored her and got to work at once. Olivia ground coffee beans and awakened Mr. Coffee from his vacation slumber. While the coffee dripped into the pot, Olivia searched the refrigerator for cream. She found an unopened container and checked the expiration date. "I've got one day to drink this up," she said. "It's a demanding job, but I'm up to it."

"Okay, now for the fun part," Olivia said as she fixed herself a cup of coffee and settled at the little kitchen desk where she usually reconciled receipts at the end of her workday. She dug through the desk drawer to find a small notebook and a working pen. "I have my tools, Spunks. Let's go envision a stunning new sales floor." To avoid interruptions, Olivia left her cell phone on the kitchen counter.

Spunky followed his mistress back to the sales floor. Apparently, he had lost interest in the mystery of the sparkling sugars, preferring to curl up on his favorite chair, where he held court daily whenever The Gingerbread House was open for business. Certain customers stopped by the store several days a week just to see Spunky. Of course, they rarely passed up the free decorated cookies. Spunky seemed to understand that he and Olivia would be on their own for the day, so he settled down to nap.

Hoping to trigger redecorating ideas, Olivia stood in the middle of the sales floor and turned a slow circle, then another. Nothing. She tried again, more slowly, giving herself time to notice the display tables and how they were arranged. Before leaving town, Olivia had removed all valuable baking items and cookbooks, and she'd left them out of sight in the locked storage room. About half the tables were empty, or nearly so. At once Olivia identified a problem she'd never considered before: all of the round, metal display tables were identical. She'd purchased them in a batch from a store that specialized in commercial furniture. The stark, utilitarian style looked anachronistic in her wonderfully quirky, nineteenth-century house. Maybe she could find round, embroidered tablecloths to cover a few of them. She might want to replace the others with similar-size wooden tables, perhaps a few antiques if they were in good condition and affordable. Or maybe she could —

The front doorbell made Olivia jump.

Spunky leaped to his paws and growled. "It's okay, Spunks," Olivia said. "Everyone we know is out of town, so it's probably Binnie coming back for the kill. Or Snoopy Sam. We'll ignore it." Spunky poked his head under the arm of his chair, which allowed him to watch the Gingerbread House porch through the store's large front window.

"Attaboy," Olivia said. "You keep those nasty intruders at bay while I mentally reorganize the sales floor." Holding her pen and paper, Olivia stood near the front of the store. She wanted to see what customers saw when they entered. The sales floor looked crowded with tables and mobiles, but wasn't that part of its charm? The Gingerbread House was supposed to feel like . . . well, like a fairy tale. *Maybe what it needs is even more —*

Olivia's peripheral vision caught movement on the porch outside the front window, followed instantly by Spunky's warning yap. "Oh no, not Binnie again," Olivia said as she turned the front doorknob. "If I have to order her off my property, I will. That woman is —" Spunky's yap lost its fierce edge and sounded excited. Olivia spun around to see a petite figure standing at the

47

front window, peering into the store.
"Mom?"

CHAPTER FOUR

Ellie Greyson-Meyers waved to her daughter and pointed toward the front door. By the time Olivia had crossed the foyer and unlocked the outside door, her mother was waiting for her. Ellie looked cool and relaxed in dusty pink shorts and a matching T-shirt. "Hello, dear," she said. "You look surprised."

"Uh . . . weren't you and Allan booked at a spa until Monday?"

"A retreat, dear. I wouldn't be caught dead at a spa unless it stressed exercise and adventure, which is what the retreat was supposed to offer."

"But it didn't?"

"I'll be glad to share every detail, Livie, if you'll invite me in. I assume you've cranked up your air-conditioning?" Ellie's long gray tresses were gathered into a braid, which she lifted off her neck. "I'm about to melt into a puddle."

"Oh, sorry, Mom." Olivia stood aside to let her mother enter. "The foyer is still hot, but the store has cooled down fairly well." She closed and locked the front door, while Ellie scooted into The Gingerbread House.

Spunky jumped off his chair and trotted over to greet Ellie. "I've missed you, too, little one," Ellie said as she scooped him into her arms. With Spunky snuggled against her shoulder, Ellie gazed around the sales floor. "It looks so barren and sad in here," she said. "Shall I help you put it together again?"

"Too much energy, Mom. Anyway, I'm thinking about changing the display to make it more enticing. I'm not sure what that means yet."

"That's easy, dear. Make it more whimsical. You might consider a dollhouse designed to look like a fairy-tale gingerbread house, and you could decorate it with cookie cutters. Maybe put a witch and little cookie cutter children inside."

"Wouldn't that terrify the real children?"

"I doubt it would bother the children," Ellie said, "but I suppose their mothers might object. Mothers can be so overprotective these days. Well, you could simply have children playing in the yard. It would be fun to decorate the house for every holiday, especially Halloween."

Although the idea sounded delightful, Olivia thought about the work involved in creating and maintaining such a display. "Why do I suspect you are taking a class on dollhouse construction?"

With a wistful sigh, Ellie said, "There is no such class, at least not within a reasonable distance from Chatterley Heights. I'm afraid I've taken every class available to me, many of them more than once. The supply has been dwindling."

"Mom, you sound bored. I've never heard you sound bored before." Olivia headed toward the kitchen. "You need coffee and a cookie. I'm afraid the cookie will come directly from the freezer. Maddie hasn't been around to bake a fresh batch."

"A frozen cookie sounds perfect," Ellie said. "Shall I put Spunky back on his chair?"

"Bring the ferocious beast with you," Olivia said as she held open the kitchen door. "No baking is going on in this kitchen until Maddie returns."

"Your health code violation is safe with me." Ellie settled at the kitchen table and snuggled Spunky on her lap.

Olivia poured fresh coffee into two cups and took a plastic container from the freezer. "Maddie baked a batch of lime cookies before she left town. She said the flavor sounded cool to her. Since the cookies are currently frozen, I'd say she was right." Olivia opened the container and offered it to her mother.

"Yum," Ellie said as she bit into her cookie. "It's like eating frozen limeade right out of the can."

"Okay, Mom, explain yourself. Why did you and Allan come home early from your retreat? Was it really that disappointing?"

"It became less disappointing once I'd explained to the retreat leaders how their approach could be made more effective and interesting." Spunky sighed in his sleep as Ellie stroked the silky fur on his back. "However, I had a strong intuition that you were going to need me, so I told Allan we should leave. I think he was grateful, given how quickly he packed his bag."

"I'll bet. I imagine he whimpered when you dragged him to that retreat." Olivia's self-employed stepfather's greatest love — after her mother, of course — was creating Internet businesses. "Why did you think I might need you?"

"It was intuition, dear, not an actual thought. Intuition is hard to explain."

"Really? Mom, I came home early only because I ran out of books and got bored, not because I was in dire need of my mother's assistance. And I found out about Greta Oskarson and her cutter collection about an hour ago, and I don't need your help with that. Intuition? I think not." Olivia felt rather pleased with herself.

Ellie smiled in her otherworldly way. Without a word, she selected a second cookie, took a delicate bite, and closed her eyes as she chewed. "Such a lovely flavor," Ellie murmured.

Olivia took a gulp of her coffee, which tasted faintly of lime. "Okay, Mom, I'll bet you came back early because someone called and told you about Greta Oskarson and her cookie cutter collection. Am I right?"

"Nearly right," Ellie said, chuckling. "In fact, three people called to tell me all about Greta's return. She has caused quite a stir."

"Let me guess," Olivia said. "One call had to come from Polly Franz. She's got a great view of the town square from her second-floor office at the food bank."

"And Polly has such powerful binoculars," Ellie said. "She knows I count on her to keep me informed."

"Then there's Ida," Olivia said. "People tend to ignore waitresses, so Ida hears all sorts of juicy gossip at Pete's Diner. She always passes it on to you because, as everyone knows, Ida adores you. You are the daughter she never had. Polly is her main competitor."

"Competition can be so helpful, don't you think? Although in this instance, the two of them cooperated. Polly spotted a well-dressed, statuesque stranger visiting all the stores on the square. It was Greta Oskarson. When Greta stopped at Pete's Diner for a bite to eat, Polly called Ida to find out who she was." Ellie reached for the carafe and divided the remaining coffee between their two cups. "This is fun," she said. "And who did my third call come from?"

Olivia hesitated. Chatterley Heights contained plenty of gossips, but who else might have called her mother right away? "Maybe Struts Marinsky? She isn't a big gossip, but Jason might have mentioned that Greta wanted me to broker the sale of her cutter collection." As soon as Olivia uttered her younger brother's name, she knew she was wrong. Jason Greyson worked as a mechanic at the Struts & Bolts garage, but he paid no attention to town gossip unless it had to do with cars or free food. "Never mind," Olivia said. "I have no idea who the third call came from."

"Two out of three is an excellent score."

Ellie patted her daughter's hand. "Maddie called me. She and Lucas are heading home, by the way. Aunt Sadie called Maddie with the news about Greta Oskarson."

"Maddie . . . of course, I should have known." Olivia had lived in Baltimore for ten years, and, as Maddie often pointed out, her small-town gossiping skills had suffered. "I'll bet Maddie is practically exploding with excitement about Greta's cookie cutter collection. But Mom, I still don't understand *why* you rushed back home."

Ellie pulled her long braid over her shoulder, unraveled it quickly, then began rebraiding. Olivia recognized the behavior; her mother was worried. Olivia started another pot of coffee. While Ellie unbraided her hair a second time, Olivia took the remaining frozen lime cookies from the freezer.

"Something is bothering you, Mom. What is it?" Olivia refilled their cups with coffee and delivered the cookies to the kitchen table. Her mother didn't appear to notice. "Earth to Planet Mom," Olivia said.

"What, dear? Oh, thank you, you're a mind reader," Ellie said as she reached for a cookie.

"No, I am most definitely not a mind reader." Olivia added cream to both coffees.

"I'm dying to know what you're thinking. Your face has been going through all sorts of interesting contortions, but no actual words have come from your mouth."

Ellie maintained silence long enough to finish her braid and secure it with a pink band. "After Maddie called me, I called Sadie," Ellie said. "Not many people are aware of this, Livie, but Greta Oskarson has a . . . a history. Many years ago, Clarisse told me what she knew about Greta's past, and it was disturbing. That's why I called Sadie Briggs. I thought she might know more than anyone about Greta's background. I was right. You know what dear Sadie is like; she wants to believe the best about everyone. However, even Sadie felt uneasy knowing you and Maddie would be involved in the sale of Greta's cookie cutter collection. Though, of course, she would never interfere. She kept saying that her information was secondhand and, anyway, people change."

Ellie lapsed into silence. When she reached for her braid, Olivia grabbed her hand. "Hasn't your hair been tortured enough? Tell me what you learned about Greta from Clarisse and Sadie. If I'm to help Greta sell her cutter collection, I need to know if her 'history,' whatever that means, will be a problem."

"Yes, I realize that, Livie. Otherwise, I would never breathe a word of this. So much of it is hearsay." Ellie bit into her cookie and visibly relaxed. "I never really knew Greta when she lived in Chatterley Heights. She is at least ten years older than I am, so I would have been a youngster when she left for Europe. I was given to understand that she had been accepted by the Sorbonne in Paris. A few years later, when I was a young teen, I remember learning that Greta had married a wealthy French count, which sounded terribly romantic. That was the last I heard of her until a few years ago when Clarisse and I met for lunch one day."

"When was this?" Olivia asked.

"While you were living in Baltimore, but not long before you moved back home."

Olivia thought back to her return to Chatterley Heights, after her divorce from Ryan. She had arrived with a brand-new business degree and a dream. Olivia had always wanted to open a store that specialized in anything and everything connected to cookies. Clarisse Chamberlain, an experienced and very successful businesswoman, had encouraged Olivia to reach for her dream, which led to the purchase of her Queen

Anne house and a business partnership with her childhood friend, Maddie Briggs.

Thinking back to her many long conversations with Clarisse, Olivia said, "It's odd; I don't remember Clarisse ever mentioning a Greta Oskarson. Yet according to Constance, Greta insisted that she and Clarisse had bonded over a mutual fascination with cookie cutters."

"Oh dear," Ellie said as she nibbled on her cookie. "I must have a chat with Constance as well."

"About what, exactly?" When her mother didn't answer, Olivia added, "Mom, you're scaring me."

"I'm sorry, Livie, I'm just preoccupied. I wish I'd maintained my old contacts in the FBI and the CIA. Although perhaps I could reconnect —" Ellie laughed when she saw the expression on Olivia's face. "I'm sorry, dear, I didn't mean to terrify you. Here's the scoop: Clarisse told me that Greta's French count — her first count, that is. I heard there were more, though I assume they didn't all perish under mysterious circumstances — anyway, Greta's first husband died barely a year after their wedding. The count — I'm afraid I've forgotten his name, if I ever heard it, Count Number One, let's call him — he and Greta were alone together on their yacht, supposedly enjoying a romantic cruise off the coast of France, when the count somehow wound up in the water. He drowned. Clarisse read a newspaper article about the incident. Apparently Greta was hysterical, quite devastated. Of course, she was a lovely and highly intelligent young woman . . . and I'm sure the investigating officers were men."

Olivia dipped a frozen cookie into her coffee and let it dissolve in her mouth as she mulled over the implication in her mother's account. Rich older man, pretty young wife, no apparent witnesses. "Weren't the authorities at all suspicious? I mean, Del is male, but a pretty face wouldn't cloud his investigative instincts."

"A different time, a different culture, Livie. According to Sadie, this wasn't the only troubling incident she'd heard about from Greta's past." Spunky stirred on Ellie's lap, and she stroked his back until he quieted.

Olivia checked the clock above the kitchen sink. "It's nearly one o'clock. I'll spring for lunch at the Chatterley Café if you'll fill me in on everything you've ever heard about Greta Oskarson."

"I'll do my best." Ellie rubbed Spunky's ears to awaken him. "I wish we could take

Spunky along."

"He has been spoiled quite enough for one day. Pete let him come to breakfast with Constance and me, and now he thinks the Gingerbread House kitchen belongs to him. He'll be impossible to live with for months." Olivia scooped up her snoozing pup and led the way into the store. "I'll leave him on his chair. If he wakes up, he can watch out the window."

Spunky barely stirred as Olivia and Ellie entered the foyer. While Olivia locked the store, Ellie opened the front door. A blast of hot air infiltrated the space. "Ugh," Olivia said. "I really hate letting that awful stuff get inside."

"Thanks a lot," said a familiar voice behind Olivia. She turned around to find her best friend since age ten, Maddie Briggs, standing on the porch, key in hand. Maddie's sunburned cheeks were redder than the curly hair that puffed around her face. Olivia gave silent thanks for her own blush- and burn-resistant skin. Her wavy auburn hair, on the other hand, invariably went limp in humid weather.

"Maddie, dear," Ellie said. "How lovely. We were just heading to the Chatterley Café to discuss Greta Oskarson and her cookie cutter collection."

"Then my timing is, as always, perfect," Maddie said. "I'm glad I asked Lucas to drop me off here as soon as we arrived. I had another long, long phone chat with Aunt Sadie while we were driving home. My cell phone finally ran out of juice, so I drained Lucas's, too. I have much to tell, and time is short. Let's get cracking."

CHAPTER FIVE

The Chatterley Café was emptier than Olivia had ever seen it, probably because the heat had driven so many Chatterley Heights residents to mountains, lakes, or oceans. Ellie requested and was granted a prime booth far away from the kitchen. Normally the servers at the café were perky to the point of insolence, but the young brunette who took their orders for lemonade and cold sandwiches looked as if she needed a nap.

As the waitress dragged herself toward the kitchen to deliver their order, Olivia's cell phone rang. She glanced at her caller ID and answered at once. "Constance?"

"I heard from Greta Oskarson and told her you'd returned early," Constance said in her clipped voice. "She wants to meet with you this evening to discuss strategies for selling her cookie cutter collection."

Olivia groaned. "Constance, it's hot, I

drove straight back from Upstate New York, I've had only a few hours sleep. . . . I'd much prefer to meet with Greta tomorrow, and I don't mean first thing in the morning."

"Greta is very insistent," Constance said. "She is a strong-willed woman, used to getting her way. I advise you to suck it up and meet with her this evening."

A surge of anger gave Olivia renewed energy. "Constance, you of all people ought to understand that a successful business-person takes control of a negotiation. She does not shrivel up and cave in to unreasonable demands from a prospective client. I can carve out time to meet with Greta tomorrow, late morning or early afternoon. If you prefer, I will tell her myself." A moment of silence followed Olivia's ultimatum. Maddie and Ellie grinned at her.

"Whew," Constance said with a light laugh. "I wouldn't want to go up against you in a courtroom. You go, girl! I'll relay your message to Greta, minus the hard edge. It'll be fine." Constance hung up her cell without saying good-bye.

Olivia flipped her phone shut and relaxed against the back of the booth.

"Wow, talk about assertive," Maddie said. "I guess all that money you spent on business school wasn't entirely wasted."

"Livie has always had her assertive moments, even as a toddler," Ellie said quietly. "Although in those days they were called tantrums."

"No comment." Olivia lifted her menu to cover her face.

"Uh-oh," Maddie said.

"Come on, Maddie, don't take Mom seriously, you know how she —"

"No, I mean 'uh-oh,' as in 'look who is heading right toward us.' It's Anita Rambert, and she has that barracuda aura about her."

Olivia lowered her menu and peered over the top. Sure enough, Anita Rambert's gaze never left Olivia's booth as she wove through the crowded restaurant. Anita was always on the prowl for rare and valuable items to offer collectors. Antique cookie cutters were high on her list. Although she sold many vintage cutters of lesser value, any serious collector knew that the truly rare finds would never make it to the sales floor; they were usually snapped up in private sales. For these special antique cutters, Anita conducted bidding wars among select customers.

"She is definitely heading toward our table," Olivia said, "which means she knows about Greta Oskarson's cutter collection, and she wants to get her hands on it. I should have anticipated this."

Maddie slid down in her seat. "How? You only just found out about Greta's collection. Knowing Anita, she has probably heard rumors about it for years. She is obsessed with antique European cookie cutters. I'm thinking this could get scary."

"I'll have to put her off until I've had time to assess Greta's collection, but even then . . . Anita is a tough bargainer." Olivia didn't add that Anita's success and stunning beauty gave her unshakable confidence. She usually got what she wanted.

"And I repeat," Maddie said, "Anita is scary. I mean, look at that linen outfit she's wearing. Not a wrinkle in it. She is superhuman."

"Nonsense, you two," Ellie said, using what her family called her "mother voice." "Anita Rambert is a perfectly reasonable adult. Livie, not ten minutes ago you demonstrated your ability to stand up to pressure. I'm quite certain you can handle Anita." Ellie lowered her voice as Anita entered hearing range. "And if that doesn't work, you can always throw a tantrum."

"Really, Mom? No deep breathing to cleanse and center myself?"

65

"That goes without saying." Ellie straightened her spine and put on a smile. "Anita, how lovely to see you. Won't you join us for lunch?" Ellie slid aside and patted the seat. "We haven't had a chance to chat in such a long time."

Anita hesitated only a fraction of a second. Olivia suspected she was calculating whether sitting down would enhance or diminish her power advantage. "I really can't stay long." Anita leaned against the side of the booth, forcing Olivia to shift sideways and look up at her.

The brunette waitress, looking wearier than ever, appeared at the table holding a menu. "I'll bring an extra chair," she said as she offered the menu to Anita.

Anita ignored the menu. "I'm not staying." She took a step back from the booth.

"Okeydokey," the waitress said. She shook her head as she walked away. Olivia decided an extra-large tip was in order.

Anita crossed her arms and impaled Olivia with her piercing black eyes. "We need to talk at once about the Oskarson collection," Anita said. "I have private buyers who are impatient to bid on the more valuable cutters, so it's important to move quickly." Anita checked her watch. "I can carve out some time in about an hour. I'll meet you

66

at The Gingerbread House. You can transfer the collection to my care at once, and I'll contact my customers as soon as I determine the value of the pieces. Now, I'll leave you all to your breakfast."

"I'm afraid that won't be possible, Anita." Olivia's voice sounded breathy, so she paused to calm herself. "Greta is out of town today. I haven't had a chance to meet with her, let alone determine how she wishes the sale of her collection to be handled. She might want to hang on to certain favorite cutters. Once I've had time to inspect the entire collection and estimate its value, I will decide the best way to sell it, or parts of it."

Anita's dark hair caught the light and glistened as she shook her head impatiently. "I know this business," she said. "I've been conducting long-distance auctions for years, and I'm very good at it. I have the contacts, I know what they want, how much they can be convinced to pay . . . even their weak spots. Nothing personal, Olivia, but you run a little shop where you sell a few insignificant vintage cutters and some cookbooks. Can you honestly say that you are the better choice for selling the Oskarson collection?"

Olivia didn't look toward Maddie and Ellie, but she felt their tension in the silence around the table. In the distance, Olivia noticed the young waitress watching their table as if she sensed all was not well. Olivia forced herself to hold Anita's gaze for a few seconds before she said, "Yes, I believe I am the better choice, for one excellent reason."

Anita did not respond, though she arched her sculpted eyebrows in a clear expression of disbelief.

"I've worked with you before, Anita, and yes, you are good at what you do. You've brokered many lucrative sales for scores of collectors. And you yourself have become wealthy in the process, haven't you?" Olivia stated the question as a fact. "You take a healthy cut of the proceeds, more than I suspect your customers realize. Greta Oskarson and Clarisse Chamberlain were once close friends. As you well know, Clarisse was a very dear friend of mine. And she was murdered."

Anita checked her watch and sighed. "If you're going to —"

"I'm not finished," Olivia said. "Greta wants to sell her antique cutters to help fund her retirement. Because of Clarisse, Greta feels she can trust me to help make that happen. I intend to earn that trust. I'll do my homework, consult experts, whatever it takes to sell her collection for the highest price possible. And I will not be taking a cut of the proceeds. I'll be doing all this to honor Clarisse." Olivia hadn't meant to decline payment, but she wasn't sorry it popped out.

As Anita's lips parted slightly, Olivia noticed a dot of bright red lipstick on an otherwise perfect front tooth. It made Anita seem a bit more human . . . a tiny bit.

With a dismissive flip of her hand, Anita said, "Up to you. It's hard to believe you have a business degree, with such a naive attitude. However, it's your future foreclosure, so don't say I didn't warn you." Anita turned her back and wove among crowded tables toward the front of the Chatterley Café. The eyes of numerous male customers followed her fluid movements.

"How sad," Ellie said.

"You gotta hand it to Anita Rambert," Maddie said. "She knows how to make an exit."

"I'm stuffed," Maddie announced as she pushed aside her empty breakfast plate. "But I don't regret a single bite. The Chatterley Café makes the best eggs Florentine I've ever tasted. I wish I knew their secret."

"Butter," Ellie said. "Lots of butter."

"Now I wish I didn't know." Maddie drank the last of her coffee. "On the other hand, I'm proud to report that Lucas and I hiked nearly every day last week, and I have the muscles to prove it . . . and the blisters, too."

"Not me," Olivia said. "Spunky and I took walks in the woods, but mostly we sat in the shade while I read out loud. It seems Spunky is a mystery fan. He did get a bit nervous when I read Miranda James to him, though. I think he's afraid I'm planning to adopt a cat that's four times bigger than he is."

The waitress arrived with a carafe of coffee and a fresh pitcher of cream. She left both on the table. "Take your time," she said. "The lunch rush is finally done." She sighed and left.

Maddie refilled cups and passed the cream. "Drink up. I have much to recount about Greta Oskarson, as told to me by Aunt Sadie, who knows practically all and never makes stuff up."

"What would we do without Sadie," Ellie murmured.

After checking the nearest booths, all of which were empty, Maddie leaned in closer and lowered her voice. "Aunt Sadie does know a lot, but even she can't decide if

Greta is a crook or merely a victim of unfortunate circumstances."

"So *many* unfortunate circumstances," Ellie said.

"Like what?" Olivia asked. "You're killing me here."

"Keep it down, Livie," Maddie whispered. "Okay, here's what I've found out so far. Ellie, feel free to jump in if I'm getting it wrong." Maddie fortified herself with a gulp of sweet, milky coffee. "Greta burned through six marriages, starting with a guy named Count de . . . I don't remember, but it was something French. Anyway, he was fabulously rich, seventy-five years old, and in poor health when they tied the knot."

"How convenient," Olivia said.

Maddie snickered. "Not quite convenient enough. Marriage to the lovely Greta dramatically improved the count's health . . . until the drowning incident, that is."

"Weren't the French authorities the least bit suspicious?" Olivia asked. "I find that tough to buy. How many of her subsequent husbands were rich, elderly, and frail?"

Maddie grinned. "All of them."

"And how long did they survive after marrying Greta?"

"Oh, from about four to sixteen months," Maddie said. "Greta was questioned follow-

71

ing each death, but she was never arrested. Technically speaking, all her husbands were found to have died of natural causes. And who knows, maybe they did. They were all pretty old."

"And rich," Olivia added.

"It's not as if Greta should have felt impatient. She had access to their wealth while they were alive, and Aunt Sadie said Greta never lacked for younger companionship. However, none of those men came under suspicion, either."

Olivia topped off her coffee. "Greta didn't ever marry any of those younger men?"

"Nope, not according to Aunt Sadie. She married only rich, older men." Maddie frowned. "I'm wondering, though . . . Greta's six husbands were incredibly wealthy, and she inherited their fortunes. Why hasn't she retired to a villa on the Riviera or somewhere equally swanky? Why come back to little old Chatterley Heights and buy a small house that's worth less than Aunt Sadie's? Why sell her cookie cutter collection to help finance her retirement? Where is all that money?"

"All excellent questions," Olivia said. "From what Constance told me, it seems Greta spent her money freely. She probably needed to replenish her cash flow periodically."

"Greta did grow up in Chatterley Heights," Ellie said. "Perhaps she felt more comfortable returning to her humble roots."

"Humble roots?" Maddie sounded miffed. "Aunt Sadie didn't tell me about any humble roots. Although my cell did conk out before she had finished revealing all."

"They are no secret," Ellie said. "Greta's father grew up in Sweden, one of eight children in a poor family. He emigrated as a young man to make a better life for himself. He learned carpentry and was quite skilled, as I recall, but he had a bit of a drinking problem. Greta's mother was the daughter of Swedish immigrants. I didn't know either of them. I do remember that they both admired the Swedish actress Greta Garbo, which is how our Greta got her name."

Olivia snickered. "It sounds as if our Greta had some serious acting skills, too. All those rich, old husbands . . . you can't convince me she married for love. Maybe she had the right idea."

Ellie frowned as she watched her daughter gather her pancake remains into a neat pile shaped like a coffin. "And how is Del doing, Livie?" Ellie asked. "Has he shared more with you about his situation?"

"Not much." Olivia picked up her knife and sawed the pancake coffin in half.

Maddie bounced to attention. "Are you telling me Del is still helping that crazy ex-wife of his?"

Ellie reached across the table and patted Olivia's hand. "You're upset, I can tell."

Olivia shrugged one shoulder, and said, "I don't mind that Del is helping Lisa. She's in a frightening situation . . . which she brought on herself, but never mind. What irks me is that Del has called me exactly twice, and our conversations were brief . . . almost impersonal."

"And you are afraid he is falling, once again, for his ex-wife?" Ellie said.

Olivia shrugged, then nodded.

"Del isn't that stupid," Maddie said. "This conversation requires more coffee. Maybe some fresh raspberry sherbet." She slid out of the booth and held her empty cup in the air. A new server materialized at once, filled their cups, and took their orders for sherbet. "I love this place," Maddie said as she resettled next to Olivia and reached for the cream. "Now, fill me in. When Del called, did he say anything about what's going on? How much danger is Lisa in? Or is she just playing the damsel in distress to get Del back?"

"I wish I knew," Olivia said, cradling her steaming cup in her hands.

Ellie plopped her elbows on the table as if she were about to deliver a lecture. "I don't know Lisa," she said, "but I do know Del. He won't fall for a damsel-in-distress act. Given what I've heard, Lisa is in real danger from her abusive husband, and divorcing him is unlikely to end that danger. I suspect Del is very busy trying to keep Lisa safe during the divorce proceedings. Once those are finished, he'll want to get her as far away from her ex-husband as possible."

Olivia felt a sliver of hope. "I hadn't thought about that," she said. "That won't be easy, and it sounds . . . scary."

"And it will take some time." Ellie squeezed Olivia's hand. "The last thing Del would want to do is involve you in any of this. He might very well be trying to keep you safe, too."

Olivia shivered, and not because of the air-conditioning.

"On the plus side," Maddie said, "we can take comfort in the fact that we are in Chatterley Heights, and Lisa lives in some little town in western Maryland, so there's a bunch of miles between us. I'd be more precise, but I don't do numbers. Even if Del has Lisa safely hidden, she'll still have to appear for divorce proceedings and so forth, so he wouldn't send her here to escape from her ex." Maddie frowned into her coffee cup. "At least, not right now. Maybe after the divorce is —"

"Livie, dear, won't it be interesting to meet Greta Oskarson?" Ellie asked, smoothly changing the subject. "From everything I've heard, her collection of antique cookie cutters is impressive and quite valuable. What fun that she chose you to help her sell it."

Olivia ate her last bite of sherbet, paid the bill, and left a generous tip. As she reached for her cell phone, it began to play "Too Darn Hot" sung by Ella Fitzgerald. "I'm guessing we're about to find out when I'll be meeting Greta to start the process," Olivia said as she flipped her phone open. "Hi, Constance, what's up?"

"Tomorrow morning, eleven a.m.," Constance said. "That's when Greta Oskarson agreed to be at my office for our meeting. Bring the cookie cutters stored in your safe. I heard Maddie's back in town; you can bring her along if you wish. And your mom, too. Ellie has a way of calming the atmosphere. Does this meet with your approval?"

Olivia winked at Maddie and her mother. "Perfect. Thanks, Constance. We'll be there." Olivia flipped her phone shut and relayed the message to Maddie and Ellie.

"This will be fun," Maddie said. "I'll whip up some cookies for the meeting."

"Good idea," Olivia said. "Oh, and Maddie? When did Ella Fitzgerald sneak into my cell phone?"

Maddie grinned. "When you excused yourself to visit the ladies' room. And I can't take full credit. Ellie chose the song. Aren't you glad we're all together again?"

"I'll get back to you on that." Olivia slipped her phone into her shorts pocket. "Mom, Maddie and I need to pick up some baking supplies. How about coming with us? Then we can all return to The Gingerbread House together. I want to tap your voluminous knowledge of Chatterley Heights and anyone who has ever lived here."

"I wish I could, Livie, but I've scheduled several private yoga sessions. The first one starts in fifteen minutes, and the second is tomorrow at nine a.m. It was lovely to get out of town, but I had so little time to keep up my practice. I feel . . . disjointed."

"If you say so, Mom." Olivia led the group to the restaurant's front exit.

"However, I'll come to the store right after yoga tomorrow morning," Ellie said as she stepped outside. "I'd love to accompany you to your meeting with Greta. I'm so curious to find out if the rumors I've heard about her are true."

"Do you mean about her marriages," Olivia asked, "and how they ended?"

Ellie remained quiet. Her hazel eyes flicked around the park as if she were searching for an answer. With a slight shake of her head, she said, "No, dear, I wasn't thinking about Greta's marriages, though they do bring questions to my mind. I was referring to much earlier rumors." Ellie stood on tiptoe and gave Olivia a one-armed hug. "I'll see you after yoga tomorrow, dear. We'll talk then." With a distinct sense of unease, Olivia watched her mother's tiny figure head across the park.

CHAPTER SIX

"Ugh. It must be a million degrees out here," Maddie said as she trudged up the front steps of The Gingerbread House. "Lugging all these bags of groceries doesn't help. Livie, you did crank up the air-conditioning in The Gingerbread House, right? Because I really need to bake. Oh, and I forgot to mention, I had another great idea while you and your mom were discussing yoga. It will require lots of baking, which is fine with me as long as the air-conditioning holds out."

"And your idea is?" Olivia prodded.

Maddie plopped down on a porch rocking chair to wait while Olivia dug out her keys. "I think we should host a store event for Greta Oskarson," Maddie said. "You know, like an official welcome to Chatterley Heights. We weren't planning to reopen The Gingerbread House until Tuesday. Tomorrow is Saturday. We could hold the event tomorrow afternoon, maybe about one o'clock. I'll have today and tomorrow morning to bake while you put the store together again."

Olivia hated to give up her last hours of vacation leisure. "One p.m. sounds tight to me. We're meeting with Constance and Greta at eleven a.m. Also, I'll need some time to think before our meeting."

"You'll have plenty of time to think, I promise. I'll do practically all the preparation. And a two-hour meeting is an eternity. We'll have to plow through Constance's agenda, whatever that is, plus the oohing over Greta's fabulous cutter collection. If we get everything set up for the event before we leave for Constance's office, Greta could come back here with us. Constance, too, for that matter. Please, Livie?"

"All right," Olivia said. "A store event would be a great way to introduce Greta to Chatterley Heights, and it would help us spread the word about the sale of her cutter collection."

"Uh-oh, what if Anita Rambert shows up and tries to corner Greta?" Maddie asked. "Geez, she might even try to convince Greta that you don't have enough expertise to sell her collection."

Olivia chuckled. "I'm not too worried.

Greta sounds more concerned about trust than expertise. Anyway, all we have to do is put Mom to work at the event. She can pass the word, ever so gently, that Anita tends to jack up prices so she can take a substantial cut of the profits on private sales. Many collectors already know that, anyway, though they'll put up with it if they can't get what they want through another agent."

"Ooh, and let's not forget to ask Constance for help," Maddie said. "She isn't fond of Anita, and she isn't as gentle as your mom."

When Olivia opened the front door, cool air spilled out from the foyer. She stepped gratefully inside. Maddie followed, slamming the door behind her. The inner door to The Gingerbread House opened at once, and Bertha Binkman's plump, cheerful face peeked out. "I thought all that noise might be you two," Bertha said. "As soon as I saw Spunky in his chair by the window, I knew you'd beaten Willard and me back home. My goodness, you must be so hot and tired after carrying those heavy bags. Here, let me take one. Come on in out of that dreadful heat. By the way, I didn't have anything to do, so I gave the kitchen a good scrubbing." Bertha locked the door behind them and bustled off toward the kitchen.

Spunky hopped to all fours on his chair as Olivia passed, hoping to be allowed in the kitchen again. "Sorry, kiddo," Olivia said. "The kitchen is sanitized, and we'll be unpacking food, so you can't come with us. It's back to guard dog duty for you." Spunky curled into a ball on the chair's woven seat and closed his eyes. "Or you could just take a nap," Olivia added, laughing.

While Bertha and Maddie stocked the kitchen shelves, Olivia switched on her laptop. She was hoping Del might have emailed, since he'd been stingy with his phone calls to her. As the computer awakened and yawned, Olivia helped Bertha tote the bags to a storage cupboard. "What brought you home early?" Olivia asked. "Don't tell me you and Mr. Willard had a tiff, because that would destroy my fondest illusions."

"Oh my, no," Bertha said with her husky laugh. Olivia noted with relief that Bertha's laughter no longer triggered a gasping fit. Since she and Mr. Willard had begun "seeing one another," as Ellie put it, Bertha's weight had gradually descended to what her doctor called "a healthy range." She was now merely on the plump side, which was fine with Mr. Willard.

"Dear Willard and I had such a lovely time

visiting museums and historical sites, but we were ready to come home. I must admit, we were both so curious to see Greta Oskarson." Bertha hefted a sack of flour onto a high shelf and brushed off her hands on her apron.

"Did everyone know about Greta's arrival except me?" Olivia was beginning to feel left out.

"Now, Livie, I'm sure your mother intended to call you as soon as she heard about it, but everything happened so quickly. Ellie was most concerned about finding out all she could about Greta, especially after Sadie Briggs called her. That's really why Ellie called me: because I'm old enough to remember Greta. I didn't know her well, of course, but I'd certainly heard about her, mostly from dear Clarisse. They were friends off and on, you know."

"Off and on?" Olivia asked. "Did something happen to make Greta and Clarisse stop being friends?"

Bertha's forehead puckered as she opened a bag of sugar and set it on the worktable for Maddie, who was impatient to begin measuring cookie dough ingredients. Bertha lined up the remaining sugar bags on a low shelf, and said, "I do hate to spread old gossip, because you never know . . . I suppose it's possible that Greta has come back to make amends. Maybe that explains why Sadie thought she seemed genuinely sorry to hear that Clarisse had passed away."

Make amends? Olivia tried to avoid gossip, but Greta was about to become her client. She wanted to know what she might be facing. Olivia heard the whir of the stand mixer. Maddie's attention seemed focused on the flat beater as it moved around the bowl, blending flour, sugar, and butter into cookie dough. "Bertha," Olivia asked quietly, "did Greta hurt Clarisse in some way? Why would she need to make amends, all these years later?

Bertha's thin white eyebrows shot up as if the question startled her. "My goodness, Livie, for the usual thing, of course. She had an affair with Martin."

Olivia gasped at the same moment the mixer stopped. "Are you sure? Because —"

"Are you kidding?" Maddie abandoned her half-mixed dough. "Clarisse's husband? *That* Martin? Why haven't I heard about this? I don't believe it, not for a moment. Clarisse and Martin were totally, absolutely devoted to one another."

"Now, now, Maddie," Bertha said in her firm, yet motherly tone. "I know you're only just married and all, and Lucas is a fine

84

young man, no doubt about that. I'm sure he'll be loyal as the day is long. But anyone can stray. If that happens, it doesn't mean the marriage wasn't good to begin with, and . . . well, sometimes a couple can weather the storm and feel even closer."

"Bertha, I'm confused," Olivia said. "Clarisse was several years younger than Greta. I heard that Greta left the country at eighteen, so Clarisse would have been about fifteen. She hadn't even met Martin. If she and Greta corresponded from separate continents, how could Martin have. . . ." Olivia remembered a long-ago talk she'd had with Clarisse about raising children. Although Clarisse and Martin had built several lucrative businesses together, the burden of child rearing had fallen upon Clarisse. She'd hired Bertha to help, but she hadn't wanted to abandon her boys to a full-time nanny. Clarisse had genuinely wanted to be a mother. So she'd stayed home when the family businesses required travel. "Martin sometimes flew to Europe, didn't he?" Olivia asked. "Clarisse mentioned that to me maybe a year before she was . . ." The memory of Clarisse's murder invaded Olivia's thoughts less frequently now, but it still hurt. "I remember Clarisse seemed to regret never having traveled to

Europe."

Bertha snorted. "Her regret went a lot deeper than that. There she was, staying home with her little boys because they both had chicken pox, and Martin goes traipsing off to Europe by himself. He didn't have to go, mind you. The trip was supposed to be part business and part vacation for him and Clarisse. I was planning to stay with the boys. Then they got sick, and what with Clarisse being trained as a nurse, she decided she should watch over them. I know she was hurt when Martin wouldn't postpone the trip until the boys were well."

"I'd do more than feel hurt if Lucas did that to me," Maddie said. "I'd punch him in the nose. Hey, do you suppose Martin decided to go to Europe alone because he was already carrying on with Greta? Maybe they'd been writing each other and planning how to get together."

"Maddie, my friend, you're making my head hurt," Olivia said. "I doubt Martin would have planned to take Clarisse with him if he intended to meet up with Greta once he got there. Anyway, I'm fairly sure Martin couldn't have predicted his sons would get chicken pox."

Maddie's green eyes sparkled like emeralds, a sure sign her imagination had burst its constraints. "Maybe he knew chicken pox was going around. Or maybe . . . you know, Clarisse and Martin's biggest company dealt with medical supplies, plus they had all those drugstores. What if Martin got his hands on some chicken pox serum or something, and then he —"

"Maddie, please stop, I beg of you." Olivia nodded toward the abandoned stand mixer. "Don't you have dough to mix, roll, cut, and bake?"

"You never let me have any fun." Maddie tried to pout but started laughing instead.

"Oh, you two," Bertha said. "I never know when you're joking around."

Maddie turned her back on the mixer. "I am now shifting into serious mode. If Martin had an affair with Greta, even a brief one, it isn't really very funny. So did he confess and all was forgiven?"

"If you want my opinion," Bertha said, "there's a type that strays, and then there's men like Martin. He adored Clarisse and loved his boys, but he lived to build up those businesses. Couldn't be bothered with the rest. I believe Martin went off to Europe because it was about business to him, plain and simple." With a sad smile, Bertha said, "I remember when Martin and Clarisse would throw parties to entertain buyers and such like. Clarisse was a charming hostess. She kept everything going smoothly, while Martin . . . well, he didn't like to socialize. He'd smoke like a bale of hay on fire and talk business all evening. Never talked to the wives or girlfriends, didn't even look at them. When the conversation turned more personal, Martin would excuse himself and go to his study. Just like that. Clarisse would carry on until the party ended."

"Didn't Clarisse resent having to do all the people work?" Maddie asked. "Not that it would feel like work to me, except for the talking business part."

"Oh my, no." Bertha sighed. "Clarisse loved it all."

"Well, I'm convinced," Maddie said. "Greta must have initiated the affair. Martin probably didn't have a clue until it was too late."

Olivia smiled to herself. Clarisse had been her friend, older and wiser, but she'd also provided a strong mentoring presence. Olivia was convinced that everything she had accomplished since her return to Chatterley Heights wouldn't have happened if she and Clarisse had never become friends. Would Martin have risked losing her? On the other hand, Olivia knew from painful experience that marriage was far more complex than a business partnership . . . or even a good friendship.

Olivia glanced at the clock over the kitchen sink. "We'll probably never know what really happened all those years ago. Clarisse and Martin are gone, while Greta has re-appeared, bought a house, and intends to settle in Chatterley Heights. I'd like to start out on the right foot with her, especially given she has asked me to handle the sale of her cookie cutter collection. I'm thinking it would be a good idea to keep the story of Martin and Greta to ourselves."

With a dramatic sigh, Maddie said, "Oh, I suppose you're right. I'm amazed it isn't common knowledge already."

"I haven't thought about that episode in years," Bertha said. "I'm not one to gossip. It's so destructive, and you never really know where someone else has been."

Olivia tried to feel reassured, but she was afraid the story would be all over town five minutes ago.

By early evening, Olivia had dusted all the shelves in the Gingerbread House sales area, as well as every item on those shelves. She'd left the disturbed sparkling sugar display as she had found it in the early morning hours. Neither Maddie nor Bertha had mentioned noticing anything amiss. Olivia wasn't deeply concerned about how or why the colored sugars wound up out of order, but she couldn't let it go, either. The puzzle niggled at her.

Olivia had begun arranging items on the display tables when the snow and the holiday season popped into her mind. *Why?* Autumn certainly wasn't nipping the air, since the outdoor temperatures were stuck in the nineties. Olivia glanced back at the shelf of cookie decorations, where the jars of red and green sparkling sugars were still clustered together, ready for holiday baking. Maybe that accounted for her flash-forward in time.

As Olivia worked her way closer to the sales counter, the luscious aromas drifting from the kitchen grew stronger. Maddie had begun the baking phase, and Olivia realized at once why she'd thought of the holidays. She smelled cloves and . . . was that cardamom? An interesting choice, cardamom. Delicious, too, though a little went a long way. Why would Maddie choose cardamom-flavored cookies for a summer event? Unless . . . of course, Greta's family was Swedish. Leaving a display table partially arranged, Olivia entered the kitchen and walked into a cardamom cloud laced with tangerine. Maddie was removing two octagonal shortbread molds from the oven.

"Maddie, wow, you made shortbread. You must be feeling well rested. Shortbread is labor-intensive. I think it's better when the batter is kneaded by hand, but I can never get it to work right. Either it comes out too dry, or half the dough sticks to the mold when I try to pop it out."

"Aw shucks, nothin' to it," Maddie said. "Shortbread takes a bit of practice, that's all. I've certainly dumped my share of failures into the garbage, but eventually your fingers get the feel of it. This recipe is sort of an experiment, so I make no promises. I wanted something productive to do while my lebkuchen dough is chilling in the freezer."

"*Lebkuchen?* Do I detect an ambitious Germanic theme here, Maddie?"

Maddie's tangle of red curls looked as if they'd lost a skirmish with a flour bin. "I should take vacations more often. I got way too much rest, so I'm bursting with excess energy."

Olivia recognized the maniacal glint in Maddie's bright green eyes. "Does this mean you'll be up all night baking? If our event is tomorrow afternoon, you don't have much time. And now that I think of it, doesn't lebkuchen take several days to make properly?"

"Technically, yes." Maddie opened the freezer door and pointed to a covered bowl. "I found a recipe that shortens the process. The dough stays in the freezer for about four hours, maybe a bit more, till it firms up. Then I'm supposed to scoop out the dough and bake the cookies right away, while they are really cold. I've never tried it before, so I have no idea if it'll be wonderful or dreadful. But no worries. Bertha should be back soon with supplies, in case we need to repeat a recipe or two. Or more. I've got bunches more cookie recipes to try."

"Try?" Olivia trusted Maddie's baking skills, but . . .

"This is such a kick," Maddie said. "Remember your mom mentioned that Greta's parents emigrated from Sweden to Chatterley Heights? And her father had a crush on Greta Garbo, so he insisted his daughter be named after her? Which probably explains why she moved to Europe and married all those counts and so forth. Anyway, I didn't get a chance to tell you that Aunt Sadie said Greta also spent a lot of time in Germany and Sweden, and she even married a Swede or a German or maybe one of each." Maddie shrugged. "I got a bit dizzy listening to all the marriages Greta lost, one way or another, although she did seem to have a gift for ending up with the money. Anyway, now that we're hosting a store event to welcome Greta back home, I thought it would be fun to offer cookies that represent some of the places she has lived."

"But, Maddie, isn't it a bit risky to try so many experiments right before an event?"

"Hey, do I ever express the slightest doubt about your ability to reenvision your business plan? Heck, I don't even know what that means, yet I've put my personal financial future in your hands. Let me do the creative baking; that's what I do best. You run along and, I don't know, do something brilliantly businesslike."

"Yes, ma'am," Olivia said. Maddie had brewed a fresh pot of coffee, so Olivia fixed herself a cup and returned to the sales floor. When she had finished cleaning and reorganizing the display areas, she settled into a cozy stuffed chair in the cookbook nook to study the list of cookie cutters in Greta Oskarson's collection. Almost at once, Spunky joined her.

"Hey, there, Spunks. It isn't as much fun on the sales floor without your adoring fans, is it? Come on, there's room enough for both of us." Olivia patted the large chair's

93

seat, and Spunky jumped up beside her. After completing a couple of tight circles, he snuggled next to her.

"It doesn't get much better than this." As Olivia turned her attention to the cookie cutter list, her cell phone rang. It was her mother. Olivia considered letting the call go to voice mail, but she couldn't quite do it.

"Livie, I'm so glad I caught you." Ellie did not sound like her normal unflappable self. "I'm down the street at the BookChat Bookstore. I was just picking up a book for my nineteenth-century novel group, and I was wondering if I could drop by the store in ten minutes or so."

"Sure, Mom. You sound harried. Is everything okay?"

"What? Wait a moment, dear." Ellie's muffled voice came through her cell as she talked to a companion. "Sorry, dear, I have someone with me, so there will be two of us coming to see you. We're just —" The line went dead.

Olivia waited several moments for her cell to ring again. When it didn't, she settled back in her soft, roomy chair to wait for Ellie and her talkative companion to show up. Gently massaging Spunky's back, Olivia read through the list of Greta's cookie cutters. Olivia had picked up some knowledge of antique and vintage cookie cutters, but she hadn't heard of most of the items on the list. The ones she did recognize were newer and probably less valuable. The collection was predominantly European in origin. Olivia was better versed in early American cookie cutters. Anita Rambert was the most knowledgeable antique cookie cutter expert around, but Olivia didn't dare share the list with her. Olivia wished there were someone she could talk to, someone who wasn't trying to get her hands on Greta's collection.

The porch doorbell rang, and Spunky's ears perked to attention. "Down, boy," Olivia said. "It's just Mom and whoever is making her act so unlike her always serene, composed self."

Spunky growled and yapped.

Olivia slid her arm around Spunky's middle and held him against her side. "Better stick with me, kiddo. No ankle nipping allowed, although I'll make an exception if Binnie is out there." When Olivia entered the foyer, the doorbell rang again, twice. That wasn't like her mom, who was known for her otherworldly patience. Olivia tightened her hold on Spunky, just in case. . . .

Olivia was reaching toward the front door when she heard a sharp knock. She opened the door to find a tall, sturdily built woman with her fist raised to knock again. Olivia guessed her to be about forty. The woman barged into the foyer, barely missing Olivia, who hopped out of the way. Ellie followed, casting an apologetic glance at Olivia.

"It's too blasted hot out there to stand around," the woman said.

Olivia had to stop herself from apologizing for both the weather and her own unforgivable slowness. Instead, she turned to her mother for explanation.

"Livie, dear, I'd like you to meet Allan's cousin, Calliope Zimmermann," Ellie said with strained enthusiasm. Her unspoken message was clear: this is your stepfather's kin, so be nice, no matter what.

Calliope charged through the open door and into The Gingerbread House. "I told you, Ellie, call me Cal, not Calliope," she snapped. "It might be my name, but that doesn't mean I have to use it. Stupid name, it makes people think I'm a carousel, which isn't even the same thing. I'm supposed to be named after some obscure Greek goddess, but most people are too ignorant to know that."

Olivia suppressed a giggle as she envisioned a brightly painted wooden horse with Calliope's stern, sullen face. Come to think of it, she did have a rather long nose. *Now, now, Livie, don't get snarky. It'll only backfire.*

"Cal it is, then," Olivia said. Ellie shot her a look of gratitude. "So, Cal, what brings you to Chatterley Heights? Are you visiting Allan?"

"Allan? Ha! All that man does is vegetate in front of his computer screen." Calliope gazed around the sales floor with a tight frown, as if she found Olivia's profession no more defensible than Allan's. "I've decided to move here for good," Calliope said. "Allan acts like a bump on a log, but he's about the only family I've got left. The climate here is dreadful, of course, but maybe winter won't be so bad."

"Where were you living before?" Olivia asked.

"All over the place." A faraway look softened Calliope's pale blue eyes, and she almost smiled. "I spent a lot of time in Europe, on the move, exploring here and there. I don't like to be tied down. Makes me feel trapped. But everything good comes to an end, so here I am. Can't be helped."

Her curiosity piqued, Olivia glanced toward Ellie, who shrugged.

Calliope examined the ceiling as if she were looking for cracks. "Quite a big place you've got here," she said. "You've probably got some spare rooms to rent. Ellie said you live upstairs, and I smell baking, so you must have two kitchens."

"Oh no, Callio . . . I mean, Cal," Ellie said. "The kitchen belongs to The Gingerbread House, which occupies the entire ground floor. Olivia and her business partner, Maddie, run a cookie catering business in addition to this store. Olivia does live upstairs in a *small* apartment, which she shares with her sweet dog." Sensing an implied threat to his territory, Spunky growled.

"Well, Allan made it quite clear I wasn't welcome to live with you two, never mind the empty bedrooms." Calliope walked over to the cookbook nook entrance. "You could put a double door right here, and you'd have a nice little apartment to rent out. The extra income might help keep this place afloat."

Olivia had vowed to remain on her best behavior, but this was too much. "The Gingerbread House is quite a successful business," she said. "I don't need any help to keep it afloat, thank you." Olivia saw her mother's hazel eyes widen, just for a moment, before her right eye winked.

With a shrug, Calliope said, "Well, let me know if you hear about a place. Someday

I'll get a little house of my own, but it doesn't pay to rush into those things. Meantime, I can't live on the streets, can I?" She stared at Olivia, who noticed her eyes had a tendency to bulge.

"Of course not, Cal," Ellie said. "Allan and I have said you are welcome to stay with us for a week or so while you're looking for a place of your own to rent. Meanwhile, we'll introduce you to Constance Overton. She is an excellent realtor. I'm certain she can find exactly what you're looking for, and in record time."

Olivia decided she wanted to be there when Constance and Calliope met. It promised to be entertaining. Olivia put her money on Constance, but not by very much.

CHAPTER SEVEN

After a quiet Friday evening stretched out on her living room sofa, studying Greta's cookie cutter list, Olivia found herself snoozing. To wake herself up, she turned on the television and surfed the Internet on her laptop, searching for information about the most interesting cutters on Greta's list. Olivia was trying to confirm the cutters' origins, which might give her clues to their value. She hoped to assess their market value without consulting an expert. Anita Rambert would have been a helpful source of information, but she wanted those cutters too badly. Who wouldn't? So far, Olivia hadn't found much beyond some bits and pieces, which she'd printed out. Spunky curled up beside her and began to snore softly. A nap sounded tempting. She closed the lid of her laptop and joined Spunky.

When Olivia awakened, early morning sun filtered through the thin living room curtains. Her nap had lasted through the night. She was still on the sofa in her apartment living room, but now Spunky was curled on her stomach. His furry head popped up in response to a faint animal cry from the television, where Olivia had left Animal Planet on low volume. Through slitted eyes, Olivia watched as a female orangutan fed pudding from a spiky bowl to her hungry infant. *No, that can't be right.* Spunky hopped off the sofa as Olivia hiked up on her elbow to see the television better. "That's got to be some type of fruit," Olivia said. "Mom would know."

Spunky stiffened and growled at the television screen. "Don't even think about it," Olivia said. "You can't catch a squirrel, and you wouldn't know what to do with it if you did. Those creatures are way bigger and stronger." Spunky's ears twitched, but his eyes never left the screen. "But then, who am I to dash your dreams?" Olivia groaned as she sat up.

The list of Greta Oskarson's antique cookie cutters lay on the living room rug, next to the sofa. On the coffee table, the laptop's "on" light winked at Olivia. When Frank Sinatra began to croon "Summer Wind," Olivia patted the pile of papers to find the small lump that was her cell phone.

She glanced at the caller ID before answering. "Maddie? Did you get some sleep? Where are you?"

"Where else but downstairs in the kitchen, finishing a monumental baking project? The lebkuchen turned out well, if I do say so . . . at least after the first batch, which I had to dump. I also made a batch of springerle cookies."

"Mom used to make those," Olivia said. "I think she stored them for several days before she declared them edible."

"I appreciate your delicately stated concern," Maddie said, "but these are soft springerle cookies. They don't need to age. Aunt Sadie used to make them for me when I was a kid."

"Of course she did. Sorry for doubting you." Olivia yawned. "I need coffee, and then I'd better grab a shower."

"I should hope so. Meanwhile, I'm about to start deep-frying the rosettes. I should be done with those before we leave for our meeting with Constance and Greta. Then I'll have completed the baking, unless I get another brilliant idea. I sure hope the air conditioner cools down the store before the event starts. How is your research going?"

"Slowly." Olivia began pushing her papers into a pile. "I wish I could find a disinterested expert to talk to about this collection. I'm concerned about giving away too much information."

"Yeah, every serious collector will want to bid on those cutters," Maddie said. "Better to start the bidding outrageously high and see what happens. Or here's an idea, why don't you talk to Aunt Sadie? She knows lots about antique cutters, and her intentions will be honorable."

"Excellent idea. I'll call — Hang on a sec, Maddie. I think my kitchen phone is ringing." Olivia moved too quickly and stubbed her toe on the coffee table leg. Stifling a cry, she limped into the hallway as the answering machine kicked on. "It's Del," Olivia said into her cell phone. "I can hear his voice leaving a message." She reached her kitchen doorway as Del was signing off. "Missed it," Olivia said. "He just hung up."

"Why wouldn't Del call your cell?"

"Because you were hogging it. Del was probably sent to voice mail." Olivia sank onto a kitchen chair and rubbed her throbbing toe. "Or maybe he figured I'd be in bed, and he just wanted to leave a message. I'll check in a minute."

"You will check now," Maddie said. "And don't you dare hang up on me. I want to know what's going on with that man. Hold your phone near the answering machine so I can get the gist."

"What if the message is personal?"

"Then hold it closer," Maddie said. "I have a vested interest in your future happiness."

"Uh-huh. Okay, here goes." Olivia pointed her cell toward the answering machine and hit "play."

"Livie, it's me." Del's voice sounded rushed. "Can't talk long, but I wanted to check in and let you know I'm okay. Listen, things have gotten hairy around here. I don't have time to fill you in completely, and maybe that's for the best. Just don't worry about me. Try not to get too irritated with me, either." Del's light chuckle made Olivia realize how much she missed him. "I wish I could call and talk to you every day, but . . ." Del's voice faded, as if he'd turned aside to talk to someone nearby. "I need to go, Livie, but I wanted to warn you that Lisa's husband hired an investigator to follow me, so it's hard to keep my calls private. I miss you, Livie. Remember that."

"I don't care if it is only a few short blocks to Constance's office," Olivia said, sweeping her bangs off her forehead. "They will be blisteringly hot blocks. We are driving. This heat is making me crabby."

"No kidding," Maddie said. "Mind you, I've been baking in a hot kitchen, so I'm not objecting to an air-conditioned car."

"Nor am I." Ellie had tied her long tresses into a wavy ponytail. With her slender, petite figure, she looked like a gray-haired teenager.

Olivia unlocked the doors of her PT Cruiser and stood aside as the trapped air escaped. She felt sorry for the painted gingerbread figures that gamboled over the blistering heat of the car's metal exterior. "Give me a second to get the AC going." Olivia grimaced as she slid onto the hot front seat. She cranked the air conditioner to its highest setting, hopped out of the car, and slammed the door. After about thirty seconds, Olivia said, "Okay, let's go. We have two minutes to get to the meeting on time."

Constance Overton owned the Chatterley Heights Management and Rental Company, located a block west of the town square. The thriving business had recently taken over an entire building, displacing a dentist who had wanted to retire anyway. Constance had hired a male office manager named Craig, a well-built young man with brown eyes and dark, shoulder-length hair held neatly with a band at the nape of his neck.

Craig greeted Olivia and her party with an offer of iced coffee. "Constance will be just a moment," Craig said. "She is settling a few details with her client, Ms. Oskarson." He gave them a quick smile and returned to his desk. Olivia wasn't surprised that Constance had hired someone both efficient and attractive.

Craig had barely awakened his desktop computer when the intercom buzzed. He sprang to his feet and said, "Constance will see you now." He held open the door for the women and followed them into the office.

"Ah, Craig," Constance said. "Please copy this list and give the original to Olivia on her way out."

Craig took the pages and closed the door noiselessly as he left.

Four large, solid armchairs with tall backs formed a semicircle facing Constance's desk. Greta Oskarson was reputed to be a tall woman, yet Olivia could see only her long, pale hands resting on the broad arms of one of the chairs.

Constance sat behind a walnut desk that Olivia recognized as an antique, though she wasn't sure what era it represented. Maddie would know; lately, she'd been delving into the study of antique furniture. Constance's previous desk, also an antique, had been large, but this one was twice its size. The bottom half of Constance's custom-made motorized wheelchair was hidden behind the desk. Only the top part of the wheelchair showed: an antique mahogany rocking chair with carved roses across the top. Behind Constance, Olivia knew, was a cushioned back decorated with embroidered roses.

"Wow, Constance," Maddie said. "You must be raking in the bucks. When did all this happen?" She turned in a circle to admire the stunning room, entirely renovated.

Olivia shot her friend a warning glance, but Maddie ignored it.

Ellie put an arm around Maddie's shoulders and herded her toward the chairs. "Thank you for including us, Constance," Ellie said. "I've been longing to see what you've done with this old building, and I must say it's impressive. So lovely, and yet comfortable."

"I like it," Constance said, unruffled. "Maddie, is that a bag of cookies I see in your hand?"

"Hm?" Maddie smoothed her free hand along the corner edge of a mahogany bureau bookcase as she passed by it. "Gorgeous," she said with a sigh. "It's Georgian, isn't it?"

"Correct," Constance said, casting an amused glance toward Greta's chair. "I believe we were discussing cookies, Maddie?"

"I adore cookies." Greta's rich contralto voice flowed through the room like molten chocolate. She stood and turned around to face Maddie, gripping the top of her chair as if she felt unsteady. "Especially cutout cookies," Greta added, "although I consider all cookies to be gifts of the gods."

No one spoke for several seconds. Olivia found herself mesmerized by Greta's presence, which her photo had not captured. She was taller than Olivia, who at five foot seven towered over her four-foot-eleven-inch mother. Greta might be as tall as six feet, though her long, slender neck and the pure white hair piled on her head might make her seem taller than her actual height. While some women might slump a bit to look smaller, Greta stood ramrod straight. Her crystalline blue gaze shifted from Maddie to Ellie, landing finally on Olivia.

Ellie recovered first. She held out her hand toward Greta, who took it with a slight grimace, as if the gesture caused her pain. "I am delighted to meet you," Ellie said, quickly releasing Greta's hand. "Welcome home. And yes, Maddie has indeed brought cookies to celebrate your return. Maddie is a wonderful baker. She and my daughter, Livie, run The Gingerbread House together."

"Livie. . . ." Greta turned toward Olivia. "I've heard all about your store. It sounds delightful. Dear Clarisse mentioned you in her last few letters to me. I look forward to working with you on the sale of my cookie cutter collection. I hate to let go of it, but. . . ." Greta's Gallic, one-shouldered shrug reminded Olivia of her own time in France, during her junior year in college.

Maddie handed her bag of cookies to Constance, who immediately buzzed Craig and told him to bring a plate. He appeared at once, as if he kept kitchenware in his desk drawer.

"Everyone, sit down," Constance said as soon as Craig had left the room. "You're giving me a crick in my neck."

Greta sank back into her armchair, and Olivia chose the chair next to her. Ellie sat next to her daughter. As soon as Constance had selected two cookies for herself, Maddie appropriated the plate and held it for Greta.

"They look so lovely," Greta said. "How

109

can I choose?"

Maddie laughed. "No need to choose. Try them all."

Greta took one rosette. "These have always been one of my very favorites," she said in her mellifluous voice. "My mother used to make them. Thank you, my dear." She took a tiny bite, holding her hand under the rosette to catch the powdered sugar.

After taking a lebkuchen for herself, Maddie left the cookie plate on the edge of Constance's desk. She flopped onto the last empty armchair, kicked off her shoes, and sat cross-legged. "Yum, if I do say so myself," Maddie said as she bit into her cookie.

"By all means, make yourself comfortable," Constance said, grinning at Maddie. "Now, let's get to work."

"Ooh, before we forget," Maddie said, "we only have" — she checked her cell phone — "about an hour before we all need to get back to The Gingerbread House. Livie and I have prepared a scrumptious cookie feast, and we plan to open the store for a couple hours so folks can stop by to officially welcome you to Chatterley Heights, Greta. I baked some rare treats, just for you. Or is that bragging?"

"I have heard about your baking prowess, so I think not," Greta said. "However, I do tire easily, and I've already had a demanding day. I'm afraid two hours might be too much for me. Perhaps your guests could send their greetings through you?"

Maddie looked stricken and was, for once, silent. Olivia understood. Neither of them had considered the possibility that Greta might turn down an opportunity to meet new neighbors and reconnect with old friends over cookies and coffee. Olivia turned to her mother with a silent plea for help, but Ellie did not respond. She was watching Greta, a little worry frown between her eyebrows.

It was Constance who rescued the cookie event. "You know, Greta," Constance said, "a cookie event strikes me as the perfect way to spread the word about your remarkable cookie cutter collection. As you explained to me, many of the cutters are quite rare and valuable, but hardly anyone knows about them. You've already been in town for nearly a week, so you really don't need to introduce yourself. But if you could talk up those cookie cutters and how special they are, I'll bet people would start to covet them. Olivia could really jack the prices up, at least at first. As a businesswoman — and a hardheaded one, as I think everyone will agree — I see this as a rare opportunity to add substantially to your retirement fund."

Greta hesitated, as if giving careful consideration to Constance's reasoning. Olivia tried to sweeten the pot. "I understand your need for rest, Greta," she said, "but I doubt our event would be nearly as exhausting as you think. We'll have a comfortable chair for you, and the three of us will run interference to keep people from talking your ear off."

"You can count on us," Maddie said. "We know who the babblers are, and we aren't afraid to stuff cookies in their mouths."

When Greta smiled, Olivia watched Maddie's face light with pleasure. Greta had the ability to convey her appreciation in a way that seemed personal. She was able to make even a virtual stranger feel special. Olivia began to understand how Greta had charmed so many sophisticated, wealthy, and much older men into bequeathing their fortunes to her. And yet, she had a guarded air, as if she were keeping her true feelings to herself.

Greta's gaze shifted to Olivia, and her smile faded. "Very well," Greta said, "I'll be delighted to attend your cookie event. I do need to warn you, though. In the past, a few people in Chatterley Heights were rather unkind to me. I do not wish to make their reacquaintance. I remember too well how difficult it is to avoid others in a small town, but I am determined to try. I am too old now to tolerate cruelty or betrayal."

"Nor should you tolerate such treatment," Ellie said quietly. "Nor should *anyone.*" The emphasis was subtle, and Greta didn't appear to have noticed it.

Olivia glanced at her companions. Constance, her eyes alert between narrowed lids, studied Greta's face. Maddie's pale eyebrows hiked up high, as if she were thinking, *What just happened here?* Olivia had the same question. She sensed that her mother's words conveyed a restrained yet firm warning, directed at Greta.

Constance's crisp, businesslike voice broke the silence. "Let's move on to the cookie cutter collection, shall we? I have most of it here in my safe. Livie, did you bring the rest?"

Olivia retrieved her bag from the floor beside her chair. "Right here," she said. "Greta, I'll need to know as much as possible about the origins of these cutters, and there doesn't seem to be much information available. I'd rather not ask too many questions of antiques dealers. Some of them might undervalue the cutters in order to acquire them cheaply."

"I understand," Greta said as she reached toward the rug for the thin leather briefcase leaning against the side of her chair. She opened the case and removed a large manila envelope, which she handed to Olivia. "These notes should help you considerably," Greta said. "You see, my second husband gave me his deceased wife's collection. It was much smaller then, of course, but the cookie cutters intrigued me, so I decided to add to the collection. It became rather an obsession, I'm afraid. I was much younger then, and I was thinking about children, which spurred my interest. And, as I've confessed, I love cookies."

Olivia was aching to open the packet and examine the information Greta and her late husband had compiled. As if she'd read Olivia's mind, Greta said, "Go ahead, take a look. As you'll see, my husband wrote the earlier notes. As an international financier, he was most curious about the value of the cutters. Many of them are rare finds and nearly priceless."

Olivia drew out the notes and scanned the first page quickly. They were written in a mixture of French and English. "Some of the cutters appear to be incredibly old," she said. "How on earth did you obtain them?"

"Oh, we always kept our eyes open," Greta said.

Maddie grabbed the first page from Olivia's hand. Skimming through it, Maddie said, "Yikes. Some of these cutters must have been unearthed at archaeological digs. Have they been authenticated?"

"Indeed, most of them have," Greta said. "My husband consulted experts, as you'll see from the second set of papers. He died before the task could be completed. I continued to collect cookie cutters for many years after his death, and I did my best to continue the authentication process. All this was decades ago, of course, when collecting antique cookie cutters wasn't as popular as it became later. Then the truly valuable cutters began to disappear into private collections, most of them here in the United States."

"Given the value of this collection," Constance said, "I think it should be kept in a secure storage facility. The Chatterley Heights National Bank maintains such a facility not far from here, and I have already made arrangements with them. Since I now have the entire collection, I will deliver it and bring you the keys, Livie. There will be one key for you, Livie, and one for Greta. That way you two can examine the collection as needed while you develop suggested prices."

One glance at Maddie's face told Olivia she wasn't the only one about to explode with excitement at the thought of poring over such a promising collection. She genuinely hoped Greta wasn't a serial husband killer. That would definitely mar the thrill of handling genuine antique cookie cutters, not to mention the satisfaction of dispersing them back into the world. Maybe she could buy one or two cutters herself if she dipped into her inheritance from Clarisse Chamberlain. Clarisse would have approved.

Clarisse . . . had she truly forgiven Greta for her affair with Martin? Olivia had begun to regret her quickness to offer her services for free. However, since she'd never before brokered a collection sale, she would chalk it up to experience. Greta said she had corresponded with Clarisse until shortly before her death. Clarisse, Greta claimed, had praised Olivia's business acumen and honesty, which was why Greta had chosen her to handle the sale. It sounded like something Clarisse would do. It also sounded too good to be true.

Olivia gave herself a mental slap upside the head. Don't overanalyze your good fortune, she told herself. And don't expect disaster. The chance to work with Greta's fascinating collection promised to be one of the high points of her life, and she intended to enjoy it to the fullest.

CHAPTER EIGHT

Olivia, Maddie, and Ellie stepped out of Constance's cool office into blistering heat. Olivia checked her cell phone and discovered it was already noon. Their welcoming cookie event for Greta Oskarson was due to begin in one hour. The meeting with Greta and Constance had lasted far longer than Olivia had anticipated. Thank goodness Constance had volunteered to transport Greta to The Gingerbread House before the event.

Olivia challenged the strict Chatterley Heights speed limit and arrived at The Gingerbread House in record time. She parked her car on a side street off the square, where an old oak tree offered deep shade. Maddie and Ellie were opening the car doors before Olivia could turn off the engine. "I caught sight of the Gingerbread House porch," Maddie said. "It is crammed with people. We'd better take the alley and slip in through the kitchen door."

They backtracked half a block to the alley entrance. Olivia wasn't concerned about encountering a customer in the alley, but she worried that Binnie and Ned might be hanging around near the store's back door, which led directly into the kitchen. Ned had a habit of snapping photos nonstop to keep her victims off guard. Inevitably, some of the photos were less than flattering. Binnie always chose the most embarrassing examples to post on her blog, using captions such as: "Olivia Greyson sneaks furtively through the alley behind her store. What is she hiding this time?"

Maddie had her back door key ready. She didn't bother to knock before she unlocked and shoved open the alley door, which tended to stick in the heat. A startled cry came from inside the kitchen. Maddie froze. Olivia and Ellie slipped past her to find Bertha and her distinguished "gentleman friend" embracing. Olivia couldn't help herself; she giggled. Aloysius Willard Smythe, known as Mr. Willard to nearly everyone, winked at Olivia over Bertha's shoulder.

Bertha twisted around, clutching Mr. Willard's wispy upper arm. "Goodness, you three, you scared the living daylights out of me." In the past, Olivia would have worried that the older woman's reddened cheeks meant an impending asthma attack, but Bertha's breathing sounded normal . . . if a trifle rapid.

"I'm so sorry we startled you," Olivia said. "We didn't mean to burst in on you, but when we noticed all those people on the porch, we decided to sneak in through the kitchen. Has the crowd been well behaved, more or less?"

"Oh my, yes, they've been polite. I let Willard come in early, and everyone stepped aside to let him pass. I think they're all just curious about Greta Oskarson and hoping to get a cookie before they're all gone."

"Moreover," Mr. Willard said, "I believe our own local press corps had not yet arrived, so courtesy and reason prevailed." Mr. Willard's grin dispersed waves of thin wrinkles around the corners of his mouth. Everything about Mr. Willard was thin, even his eyebrows, but his frail appearance was deceptive. When confronted with a legal dilemma, his long years of experience as an attorney and his laser intellect were unbeatable. Bertha was the only one who dared refer to him merely as "Willard."

"Our meeting with Constance took much longer than I'd anticipated," Olivia said, "but it was worth the time. I'll fill you both in on the details later. Right now I want to be sure we're ready to open the store on time, more or less. Constance and Greta will arrive here together, and you know how Constance is about promptness."

"Don't you worry now," Bertha said. "The Gingerbread House is nearly ready for a wonderful event. Dear Willard helped me carry out the heaviest trays, so the rest should be easy. Goodness, those cookies look so interesting, and they smell delicious. Maddie, you are a wonder."

"Shucks, twern't nothin'," Maddie said as she cracked open the kitchen door to peek into the store. "Wow. Livie, Ellie, you've got to see this." She held the door wide.

The Gingerbread House had never looked so enchanting, Olivia thought. Bertha had outdone herself, with Mr. Willard's help, in a very short time. She had decorated many of the display tables with tableaus representing fairy tales. Olivia admired two scenes, in particular. One showed a witch peering through the window of a gingerbread house at two small children. On another table, covered with a lake-blue cloth, four ducklings swam in a circle around a lovely swan. All of the figures were cookie cutters. "Everything looks wonderful," Olivia said.

"However, we aren't done yet. Let's get moving."

With so many hands to help, the store was ready with twenty minutes to spare. Olivia considered opening early, but the guest of honor hadn't yet arrived.

Ellie frowned as she peered through the front window. "I'm worried Greta and Constance might have to force their way through the guests on the front porch."

"Constance has a plan," Olivia said. "She'll bring Greta in through the kitchen, if necessary. I'm more worried about how they'll get to the store. As far as I'm aware, Constance wheels herself all over town. I've never seen her drive. Well, she must have a specially equipped car. I hope so, anyway."

"Oh, Livie." Ellie sighed. "You do need to work less and get out more. Do you remember Irv and Louisa?"

Olivia narrowed her eyes at her mother. "I get irritable when you use non sequiturs. Is this leading to one of your lengthy and excessively detailed stories? Because —"

"Irv and Louisa owned a farm south of town," Ellie said. "When you were a child, Louisa used to sell eggs and fresh vegetables door-to-door. You saw her often."

Olivia shrugged. "Sorry, Mom, I just don't remember. We're running out of time, so if there's a point to this . . ."

"There is, Livie. Two points, in fact. First, if you paid more attention to your surroundings, especially the people, you might be quicker to understand human behavior. However, you have me to do that for you, so I'll move on to point number two." Ellie gave Olivia's arm a maternal pat. "A year or so before you moved back to Chatterley Heights, Louisa was the victim of a hit-and-run accident while she was delivering fresh eggs to the Chatterley Café. The morning cooks at the café heard the accident and ran outside, but no one got the license plate number or remembered what the vehicle looked liked. Well, naturally they were all so upset about Louisa that they didn't think to . . . Livie, dear, don't scrunch up your eyes like that. You will wrinkle. What was I saying? Oh yes, Louisa was badly injured and could no longer walk. They had no medical insurance, so Irv and Louisa had to sell their farm to pay her medical bills. Now they live in town, in an apartment. It's little but really quite sweet, and they do seem happy."

It took all the self-discipline Olivia possessed to keep from glancing at the clock. She told herself that her mother's stories, pointless and interminable as they might

123

seem, always had a purpose. If only she would get to it faster. . . .

"Irv and Louisa had enough to live on," Ellie said, "but they were used to being active. They wanted to do more than sit around and watch television." She glanced at her watch. "Relax, Livie. Everything is ready for the event, and I predict that Constance and Greta will arrive momentarily at the alley door. Bertha will let them in."

"I can't believe I'm encouraging you, Mom, but what on earth do Ed and Louisa —"

"Irv and Louisa, dear."

"What do *Irv* and Louisa have to do with Greta and Constance?"

"That's an excellent question," Ellie said with the merest hint of triumph in her voice. "You see, Irv and Louisa desperately wanted to be out and about — they so loved their drives in the country — but Louisa was in a wheelchair and she needed other equipment, for breathing and so forth. Constance offered to make the payments on a specially made van for their use if, in return, Irv would pick up Constance, along with her wheelchair, and drive her whenever and wherever she wanted to go. Within reason, of course."

Behind Ellie's back, the kitchen door opened, and Bertha poked her head out. "Constance and Greta just arrived," Bertha said. "Constance wanted me to give this to you right away." She handed Olivia a small key ring with one key. "She said it's for the secure storage vault. Should I bring Greta and Constance out here?"

"Not just yet," Olivia said as she took the key. "The crowd on the porch will see Greta through the front window, and I want to make sure she is mentally prepared."

Once Bertha had returned to the kitchen, Olivia said, "Nicely played, Mom. The timing of your Harve and Louisa story was perfect."

"*Irv* and Louisa."

"Sometimes you drive me crazy," Olivia said, "but there's no denying your unique genius."

Ellie took her daughter's arm and guided her toward the kitchen door. "Now, Livie, I meant what I said earlier. The more closely you observe human behavior, the better honed your instincts about people will become. Such a useful skill." Ellie paused near the kitchen door. "I'm worried about this afternoon," she said.

"Really? Why?"

With a slight shake of her head, Ellie said,

"I'm not sure. There's something about —"

The kitchen door burst open, and Bertha appeared. "We *really* need you in the kitchen, Livie. Maddie doesn't know what to do."

"What —" Olivia felt herself being pushed and pulled into the kitchen, where she found Maddie and Constance doing their best to convince Greta not to bolt for the alley door.

The kitchen phone was off the hook and emitting loud, irritating beeps. Olivia reached toward the receiver, but Maddie snatched it away. "Don't hang it up." There was a hint of hysteria in Maddie's voice. "We've been getting calls."

"I did not come here to be mocked and threatened." Greta's rage was evident in her clenched jaw and flushed cheeks.

"What's going on? What calls?" Olivia glanced at her mother, who shrugged.

"From Binnie," Maddie said. "We've hung up on her twice, but she instantly calls back. She keeps spewing nonsense about Greta's past. As usual, Binnie is hiding behind those 'anonymous sources' she finds under rocks."

"How does Binnie even know we are here?" Olivia sank onto a kitchen chair.

"Who knows?" Maddie said. "I suspect she has winged minions with cell phones."

Olivia sighed, and said, "Greta, on behalf of the entire town of Chatterley Heights, I apologize for Binnie Sloan's existence. She is deluded enough to believe it's acceptable to make up facts, as long as they create a sensational story. Believe me, the best way to handle Binnie is to ignore her. Better yet, laugh at her. We will laugh with you."

The flame began to fade from Greta's cheeks. Ellie pulled over a chair and offered it to Greta, who sank into it. "You are wise beyond your years," Greta said. "I had hoped that returning to the town of my birth would free me from all the envy and the wagging tongues, but I see now that I was idealizing my childhood. I was happy then, and protected. I was perhaps a bit spoiled by loving parents." Her wistful smile softened her features. "I had hoped to erase . . . But one cannot go back in time." She straightened her spine. "But one can go forward, I hope." Greta had spoken so softly that Olivia wasn't sure she had understood.

Shortly, The Gingerbread House would open its doors to the public for the first time in over a week. The crowd had expanded, now filling the porch, the steps, and much of the front lawn. The Chatterley Heights communication network had performed at peak efficiency to spread the word about the cookie event Olivia and Maddie had thrown together to welcome Greta Oskarson back home. Olivia noticed a number of unfamiliar faces, which told her how well the news of the fabulous antique cookie cutter collection about to go on the market had spread. Olivia felt almost as nervous as when she'd watched her first customers explore the newly opened Gingerbread House. She wanted everything to look and taste perfect.

Olivia's excitement took a hit when she glanced at the front window and saw Binnie Sloan's round face sneering at her. Next to Binnie, a camera pressed against the window, hiding Ned's thin, pinched features.

Maddie emerged from the kitchen holding aloft a large tray piled high with rosettes. Glancing toward the window, she said, "Ah, the vultures descend. I'm not referring to the guests, I hasten to add." Maddie turned her back to Binnie and Ned as she centered her tray on a small table. "Aunt Sadie's embroidered tablecloth is perfect," she said. "I love the way the gingerbread boys and girls are playing ring-around-the-rosy along the edge. Aunt Sadie is a creative genius, and I'm not just saying that because we share significant DNA." A sharp rapping sound made Maddie frown toward the window. Ned snapped her picture.

"Speaking of shared DNA . . ." Olivia watched as Binnie slapped her ever-present notebook against the window so she could jot something down. "I can't wait to see what she says about us on her blog."

"We really, really need a heavy curtain for that window," Maddie said. "I'll ask Aunt Sadie to make one for us. I'm thinking along the lines of a thick tapestry."

Olivia felt her cell phone vibrate in the pocket of her light linen pants. She resisted the urge to answer it, and the vibrating stopped. As Olivia rearranged a display of royal icing mixes, her cell vibrated again. She checked the caller ID. "It's Del," she said. "I'll take it in the cookbook nook."

"I'll load up the last couple of tables with goodies," Maddie said as she headed toward the kitchen. "Then we'll be ready to throw open the doors and let the festivities begin."

Olivia's cell phone had stopped vibrating by the time she reached a private corner in the cookbook nook. She flipped it open and found that both calls had been from Del. Olivia hesitated. She so wanted to talk to Del, but that might take a while. She wanted to give him her full attention.

Once more the phone in Olivia's hand

began to vibrate. Del, again. Now she was worried. She answered at once. "Del? Is everything okay?"

"Livie, I'm so glad I finally caught you." Del sounded breathless. "Are you alone?"

"Well, in a manner of speaking."

"Does that mean 'yes' or 'no'?" Del asked.

"Yes, I'm alone in the cookbook nook at the moment, but there are zillions of people waiting to come inside. We're hosting a cookie event to welcome Greta Oskarson back to Chatterley Heights. What's going on?"

"Listen, Livie, I can't talk for long, but I wanted to let you know . . . there's been a development here."

"Is Lisa all right?"

Del hesitated for a second. "Lisa is okay, technically speaking, but . . . Livie, please don't tell anyone what I'm about to say. It'll get out soon enough, but I'm trying to keep it quiet as long as possible."

"Del, you're scaring me." Olivia poked her head outside the nook entrance. She drew it back quickly as the kitchen door opened.

"There's nothing for you to worry about," Del said. "However, the situation here has become more . . . complex. It looks like I won't be back home for a while. The Twiterton sheriff will be handling Chatterley

Heights emergency calls until I return."

Olivia was surprised by the depth of her disappointment. "I thought you'd found a safe house for Lisa," she said, "and that the divorce would soon be final. What's left? Are you worried that the investigator Lisa's husband hired might follow you and find Lisa's safe house? You can't become her permanent bodyguard."

"The investigator is no longer a problem, and Lisa won't be needing a permanent bodyguard." Del's voice sounded grim. "But she does need a good criminal defense lawyer. Last night Lisa shot her almost-ex-husband. He's dead."

"Wow."

"Yeah, wow. Listen, Livie, I have no idea how this will play out. From the information I've gotten so far, it isn't slam-dunk self-defense."

"But the husband was abusive, wasn't he?" Olivia asked.

Del groaned. "Don't ask me why, but Lisa agreed to meet with him alone. She didn't tell anyone. He managed to get out on bail, but she would have been okay, I think, if she'd just stayed put in the safe house. Lisa says she just thought he'd be more reasonable about the divorce if he didn't feel so 'hounded' by police and so forth. So *she* called *him.* Between you and me, I think she still has . . . had feelings for him. I don't get it, but that was my impression. Lisa is . . . complicated."

Complicated . . . that's one word for it. "Where did she have this meeting?"

Del's sigh was audible. "In a bar, unfortunately. Lisa knew full well the man had a drinking problem, but she thought he'd 'mellow out' better with a drink. Like he'd ever mellowed out in his life. Drinking only made him more violent. Lisa knew that."

Olivia heard another sigh and then silence. "Del?"

"I'm here."

"So what comes next? Will Lisa be charged with murder?"

"Don't know yet. He was drunk, with a history of physically abusing Lisa, so there's that on her side."

"Del, Lisa's husband was a strong, violent man. Why wouldn't the police assume self-defense?"

"He was shot in the back," Del said. "The gun was registered in Lisa's name. She claims he'd taken it away from her months ago, but she can't prove it. Besides, he'd been in jail for some time, and he didn't have a permanent address, so where would he have been keeping the gun? It wasn't on his person when he was arrested for trying to break in to Lisa's apartment."

"So it's her word against a dead man's," Olivia said.

"Worse," Del said grimly. "The gun itself was wiped clean, but Lisa's prints were on the bullets."

CHAPTER NINE

After her unsettling conversation with Del, Olivia checked the time on her cell phone. She had only a few minutes to spare before the store event for Greta was due to begin. Olivia longed to sit down with Maddie over coffee and cookies to discuss what Del had told her, but there wasn't time. Just as well, Olivia thought. She had promised to keep the information to herself.

Olivia entered the kitchen, where she found Maddie, Bertha, and Ellie standing near the refrigerator, quietly discussing last-minute logistics for the afternoon. Ellie cast frequent glances toward Greta, as if she were keeping watch. Greta sat perfectly still, her hands folded in her lap. Next to Greta's chair, Constance sat in her wheelchair in stoic silence. On the surface, everyone appeared calm, but Olivia sensed it was the kind of calm that came before or after a storm.

Greta inclined her head toward Constance. "I once had blond hair like yours." Greta sounded wistful. She smoothed her white hair back from her face. "That was long ago, of course."

"Now, now," Ellie said. "Constance would be the first to admit that she has her hair touched up, wouldn't you, Constance?" Ellie's own long tresses, proudly gray, hung in loose waves down her back.

"If you say so, Ellie," Constance said.

Olivia felt as if she'd walked into the middle of a scene in a play. The characters were trying to act natural, while their body language and tones of voice screamed tension.

Maddie picked up a tray of cookies. "It's showtime, troops," she said as she pushed the kitchen door open with her posterior. "Bertha and I are putting out these last trays of, if I may brag, my delightful and delicious cookies. Then we'll unlock the doors and let the ravenous throng burst through."

"Greta, would you prefer to wait in here a bit?" Olivia asked. "It might be less overwhelming if you were to appear once the guests are occupied with cookies and coffee."

"Nonsense," Greta said. "I am quite used to being in the public eye." She rose to her

135

feet and squared her shoulders. Greta's gray silk suit must have been tailored to show off her tall, slender figure. Her erect posture and expertly applied makeup shaved at least a decade from her actual age.

Olivia began to wonder if her mother might actually be right about the benefits of regular exercise and clean living. Luckily, she had no time to think about it. "I'll open the doors," Olivia said. "As always, I'll leave it to Maddie to monitor the refreshments."

Maddie smirked. "Because you know I'm not above smacking a few greedy hands if they try to grab more than their fair share. Not naming any names, of course, but a certain member of the local press comes to mind."

"And my brother," Olivia said.

"Ah, Jason," said Maddie. "I have but to glare at him, and he cowers. Anyway, I promised him some of the leftovers, so he should be motivated to make sure there are some."

During her lighthearted interchange with Maddie, Olivia had noted that Greta's tight expression never relaxed. It occurred to Olivia that Greta might feel anxious about encountering someone, or perhaps several someones, from her past.

■ ■ ■ ■

Half an hour into the Gingerbread House welcoming event, Olivia finally began to enjoy herself. Greta appeared to have relaxed into her role as hometown girl returning to her place of birth. The crowd of local guests dwindled steadily as folks satisfied their curiosity about Greta, while they sated their sweet teeth. So far, Anita Rambert had been conspicuously absent. In fact, Olivia hadn't spotted a single antiques dealer among the guests, though she'd recognized several serious collectors.

Maddie's cookies were a huge hit, especially the cardamom tangerine shortbread. Luckily, Maddie had anticipated demand for the fragrant wedges, so she'd returned to the store kitchen before dawn to bake more. Bertha, too, had arisen early to make a backup batch of her delectable chocolate-chip oatmeal cookies. Olivia noticed that a small tray of lovely, brightly colored marzipan flower shapes had appeared on a table. She assumed her mother had created the rich almond confections, using her treasured collection of tiny fondant cutters. Ellie knew how to make all sorts of exotic treats, having taken every craft and cooking class within a fifty-mile radius.

Olivia noted with smug relief that Binnie Sloan couldn't seem to wrench herself away from the treats tables. Her notebook and pencil were nowhere in sight as she snatched up cookies with both hands. Olivia didn't kid herself that mere sweets could neutralize Binnie's acidic nature, but at least they were distracting her for the moment.

"This is going surprisingly well, isn't it?" Constance's deep, clipped voice came from behind Olivia, who spun around so suddenly she nearly lost her balance. "Your mom was right about you," Constance said with a snicker. "Balance is not your strong suit."

"So she keeps telling me," Olivia said.

"Come on, let's find a corner." Constance skillfully maneuvered her wheelchair to achieve a full turn in the tight space. "I scouted out the cookbook nook. It's fairly quiet at the moment." Without waiting for an answer, Constance headed toward the front of the store. Olivia followed.

As they reached the cookbook nook, a young couple emerged, leaving the room empty. The cozy area had once served as the dining room for the nineteenth-century Queen Anne house. The large arched entrance connected the cookbook nook with

138

the Gingerbread House sales floor, yet the room had a quiet, secluded feel. Constance wheeled herself toward a corner where two armchairs invited shoppers to relax with a cup of coffee and a cookbook. Olivia settled in a soft, deep chair next to Constance's parked wheelchair.

"I love it when I get to look down on you," Constance said. "It almost makes up for not being able to flop down in an armchair anymore. However, that's not why I brought you here. We need to confer."

"Is something wrong?" Olivia asked.

"Not wrong, exactly . . ." Constance frowned as she stared through the arched opening into the main store. "It's a funny thing. Most everyone in town is used to me being in my wheelchair. It took a while, but I'm matter-of-fact about the whole situation, so folks start to feel more comfortable around me."

"Plus you're smart and gorgeous," Olivia said.

"You forgot rich," Constance said with a grin. "However, my point is that sometimes folks who don't know me stare at me as if I'm an exhibit, or they ignore me as if I'm invisible. They don't even notice that I'm gorgeous, let alone how smart and expensively dressed I am. On the other hand, some folks who know me well — like you and Maddie and Ellie, to name three — treat me more or less the way they would if I were still able to walk."

"Oh, I don't know about that," Olivia said. "I'm probably nicer to you than I would be if the accident had never happened. Of course, you're a nicer person than you were then."

Constance tossed her long, silky hair in a gesture of impatience. "Do you mind? I'm trying to make a point here."

"I take back the part about you being nicer."

"Good," Constance said. "My point is this: sometimes I hear things that maybe I wouldn't hear if I were standing upright, rather than sitting in a wheelchair."

"You mean like gossip?" Olivia's interest quickened. Constance wouldn't bother with gossip unless it was important.

Constance nodded. "Specifically, gossip about our guest of honor. Not the usual stuff, either. I've heard all about her numerous wealthy husbands and their suspiciously similar deaths. All of which, by the way, I'm perfectly willing to believe, having met the lady. I overheard something about twenty minutes ago, soon after the initial crowd crammed into your store." Constance paused as if she were listening. "Peek in to the sales floor and see if anyone seems close by and a little too curious."

Olivia walked to the cookbook nook entrance and leaned against the edge as if she were taking a casual count of the visitors. No one seemed to notice her. "All clear," Olivia said as she sank back into her armchair.

Constance spoke softly. "I found this very disturbing, even more so than a string of dead husbands. I heard someone, a female voice, say under her breath something about Greta abandoning a child. At least, that's what it sounded like. I didn't turn my head to get a look at the woman for fear I'd frighten her away, but I got the impression she might have been muttering to herself."

Olivia remained silent for some seconds as she digested Constance's story. "I suppose I shouldn't be shocked," Olivia said. "If she really did do away with one or more husbands, even if she was simply giving nature a little push, then I suppose it's a short step to abandoning a child." The emerging picture of Greta portrayed a self-obsessed woman with little or no conscience. *Does that image square with my sense of Greta so far? Hard to say, but maybe.* "Greta does strike me as fairly secretive,"

Olivia said. "I keep wondering why she really returned to Chatterley Heights. Small towns are terrible places to hide."

"Yes," Constance said, "and isn't that lucky. If what I overheard is true, my guess is that sooner or later someone — I'm betting on your mom — will find out about it."

Maddie appeared at the entrance to the cookbook nook. "Livie, were you planning to make an appearance anytime soon? Because now would be good. Not to panic you or anything, but things are getting a little weird."

With a quick glance at Constance, Olivia asked, "Weird how? Is Binnie acting up?"

"I wish it were that simple," Maddie said. "If it were Binnie, I could just stuff a cookie in her mouth. No, it's Greta . . . or maybe Olaf started it. I only know that Greta got all high and mighty and flounced off to sulk in the kitchen. Well, she didn't exactly flounce. She isn't really a flouncer. It was more subtle than that."

"I'm glad to hear it," Olivia said. "Are you talking about Olaf Jakobson? I wasn't aware he and Greta knew each other. Why was Greta upset with him?"

Maddie flopped into the empty armchair next to Olivia. "Oh, you know what Olaf is like. His foot is permanently stuck in his mouth. I think it's because he's so spoiled by his vast wealth. Anyway, that's Aunt Sadie's theory. I don't really know Olaf very well; he's so much older than we are."

"Olaf Jakobson," Constance said, "is not the most sensitive of human beings. He hired me to sell one of his summer homes, and I ended up firing myself. I couldn't convince him to be reasonable. He wanted an outrageous sum for the house, even though he'd let it deteriorate. I had a buyer who wanted the house, was willing to put some money into it, but he wanted the price to come down because of its poor condition."

"I'm guessing Olaf wouldn't budge on the price," Olivia said.

"Not one dollar," Constance said. "And he was arrogant about it. Normally I'm fine with a touch of arrogance. I can relate. But Olaf is . . ."

"A rich jerk?" Maddie suggested. "Obnoxiously entitled?"

Constance threw back her head and laughed. "I was thinking 'stubborn and not very bright,' but I'll add your contributions to the mix."

"What did Olaf say that upset Greta?" Olivia asked.

Maddie curled her legs underneath her

and settled into her chair. "I only heard part of what Olaf said. Something about Greta having to sell her worldly possessions because she'd made such a huge mistake. The last thing he said was, 'I'll bet you're sorry now.' "

A young couple peeked inside the cookbook nook. They left when they realized the comfortable chairs were occupied.

"We should get back to our guests soon," Olivia said. "Maddie, aren't Greta and Olaf about the same age?"

"I think so," Maddie said. "I could ask Aunt Sadie. Is it important?"

"Probably not," Olivia said. "Right now I'm just curious, but the more I observe Greta's personality, the more I wonder if working with her on the sale of her collection is such a good idea. I'd like to know what I'm in for. Meanwhile, I think I'll go have a friendly chat with Olaf Jakobson."

As the three women emerged from the cookbook nook, the young couple reappeared along with as many cookies as they could carry. The woman gave Olivia a sheepish grin as she slipped past and headed straight for the deep armchairs.

"I'll replenish the trays," Maddie said as she headed toward the kitchen.

"I'll help empty them." Constance aimed

her wheelchair toward the refreshment tables.

Olivia spotted Olaf Jakobson near the large front window, where Maddie had loaded a table with a variety of cookies. Olaf downed a rosette as he listened to a woman who looked unfamiliar to Olivia. The woman's long, blond hair swung over her shoulder as she spoke. Olaf edged closer to her.

"People are so interesting, aren't they?" Ellie's voice startled Olivia, who stumbled sideways.

"No more comments about my balance," Olivia said. "I wouldn't ever lose it if everyone would stop sneaking up on me."

"Of course not, dear. Although I didn't actually sneak up on you. You were watching so intently." Ellie inclined her head in Olaf's direction. "Do you know the young woman talking to Olaf?"

"Not a clue. She looks about my age, but I don't remember her from high school." Olivia looked down on her tiny mother. "I suppose you know all about her."

"Not *all,* dear, but some," Ellie said. "She didn't grow up here in Chatterley Heights, so you wouldn't have known her from high school. I suspect she is about your age, early thirties, though she claims to be twenty-five. She lives in Baltimore. Her name is

Desirée. Such a lovely name, don't you think?"

"Who names a kid Desirée?"

"Someone prone to romanticism, I imagine," Ellie said.

"Okay, who did name her? What's her last name? What is she doing here? And why is she enduring an extended conversation with Olaf Jakobson, of all people?"

"Livie, dear, I don't know *everything*. I had a brief chat with Desirée, during which she shared her first name and place of residence. She did mention that she is single, and she is thinking about moving to a small town. I'm afraid that's all I can tell you."

"You're losing your touch," Olivia said.

"I was interrupted by your stepfather's cousin." Ellie looked to her right, where Calliope Zimmermann was engaged in a spirited conversation with Binnie Sloan. Binnie jotted rapidly in her little notebook.

Olivia groaned. "I hate to imagine what Calliope is saying, but I'm sure I'll find out from Binnie's next edition of *The Weekly Chatter* . . . or this evening on her blog. I need to stop myself from reading that blasted blog."

"It is best to know your enemy's strategy," Ellie said.

"If I must," Olivia said. "Meanwhile, tell me what you know about Olaf. Maddie told me he said something to Greta that sent her off in a huff."

"First I need a cookie," Ellie said. "Oh look, here comes Maddie with a full tray." She looped her arm through Olivia's elbow and pulled.

Maddie saw them coming and paused to wait for them. "Hey, you two look hungry. These are the last of the cookies, so you'd better grab with both hands."

Olivia limited herself to one lebkuchen and one small slice of cardamom tangerine shortbread. "Tangerine is good for me, right?"

"Absolutely, Livie." Ellie selected a larger shortbread slice and a soft springerle cookie. "I do love decorated cutout cookies," she said, "but it's lovely to have such interesting international flavors." She bit the point off her shortbread wedge. "Hmmm."

"I baked nearly all night," Maddie said, "but it was so worth it. It was cardamom tangerine shortbread that got Greta over her squabble with Olaf." Maddie pointed with her head toward the shelves holding cookie and royal icing mixes, where Greta listened to a middle-aged woman. The latter seemed to be doing all the talking.

"Did you find out what the squabble was really about? What was the huge mistake Greta made that Olaf thought she was being punished for?" Olivia asked.

"Hang on a minute." Maddie swapped her cookie-laden tray for an empty one on a nearby table. She returned with a shortbread wedge. "It might be a while before I have time to make these again," she said. "Okay, here's the scoop. Although Greta isn't the type to confide, she was mad enough to grumble in nearly complete sentences. What I got from her grumblings was that she and Olaf knew each other long ago and didn't part on the best of terms. I'm guessing that Greta spurned his advances, or something like that, because it sure sounded to me like Olaf was trying to get back at her for something personal. I mean, why else would he be so angry with her after all these years?"

"That sounds like a lot of supposition," Olivia said.

"Well, if you want to be all Perry Mason about it." Maddie bit off the point on her shortbread wedge and took her time chewing it.

"It is a reasonable supposition, though," Ellie said. "It does sound like Olaf. I know he can carry a grudge for eons. My friend

Frannie told me a story many years ago. After his first divorce, Olaf took Frannie out for dinner, and halfway through the meal he proposed to her. He just blurted it out. Frannie thought he was joking, so she laughed. Olaf got red in the face and stalked out of the restaurant. Frannie had to pay for the meal. It was quite an expensive restaurant. At least five years later, right after Frannie lost her first baby, she was having breakfast with her younger sister at Pete's Diner. Olaf walked in alone. He went right up to her table and told her, in front of her sister, that she looked old and haggard, and he hoped she was sorry for what she'd done."

"Ouch," Olivia said.

"I'd have punched him in the nose." Maddie popped her last bite of shortbread into her mouth.

With an innocent smile, Ellie said, "As it happens, Frannie's sister stood up and slapped Olaf across the face."

"How deeply satisfying," Olivia said, "but didn't Olaf then take revenge on Frannie's sister?"

"I doubt it." Ellie brushed some crumbs off her hands. "You see, Frannie's sister is married to Pete. As I'm sure you remember, Pete was once a prizefighter, and a good one. He still looks like he could hold his own in the ring. Well, Pete was standing nearby and witnessed the entire exchange. He escorted Olaf out the diner door. Frannie told me she heard Pete advise Olaf to keep his distance from his wife because she had a mean left."

"Did you make that up?" Olivia asked, while Maddie doubled over with laughter.

"Not a word of it."

"Speaking of Olaf . . ." Maddie nodded discreetly in the direction of the large front window. Greta stood straight and rigid, her arms hanging at her sides. Bouncing up and down on his toes, Olaf poked his finger toward Greta's face. "That's one angry dude," Maddie said. "Should we rescue her?"

"I believe Greta can take care of herself," Ellie said.

"I wonder what Greta did to Olaf years ago," Olivia said, remembering the story her mother had just relayed. "Any ideas, Mom?"

"I'm afraid so," Ellie said. "I was hoping it was all water under the bridge, since Olaf has married more than once since . . . You see, Greta and Olaf were once engaged to be married. It was so long ago, over fifty years now. They were both quite young. So odd. . . ."

"I don't know," Olivia said. "From your story about Frannie and her sister, I gather that when Olaf feels he has been wronged, he never forgives or forgets."

"Yes, and that's what is so odd," Ellie said. "You see, Olaf is the one who broke off his engagement with Greta. That was one of the reasons Greta left for Europe. As I recall, it was your Aunt Sadie, Maddie, who told me the story."

"Do you know why Olaf broke off the engagement?" Maddie asked. "And why would he say that *Greta* made a terrible mistake?"

Ellie shrugged her slender shoulders. "Greta could be difficult in those days. Yes, her parents adored her, but they also expected a great deal of her. That wasn't fair, of course. Greta's mother's family emigrated from Sweden before she was born, and her father was a Swedish immigrant. Greta's parents weren't well-to-do; they barely scraped by, but they were determined that their bright, beautiful daughter should marry well and rescue the family from poverty. Olaf Oskarson, on the other hand, was the son of Swedish immigrants who managed to become wealthy in America. Although from what I understand, they had been well off in Sweden, too. When Olaf broke off their engagement, Greta's parents were convinced she had done something to drive him away. And who knows, maybe she did. I can't honestly say that I wouldn't have done the same."

By late afternoon, the Gingerbread House's air-conditioning had begun to lose its battle with the intense afternoon heat. The number of event attendees had dwindled steadily once the cookies disappeared. Olivia finished ringing up the last sale and silently declared the close of their welcoming event for Greta Oskarson. As soon as the final guest had left the store, Olivia locked the front door of her Queen Anne.

When Olivia reentered the store, she saw her mother and Maddie helping Greta into the cookbook nook. Greta's slow pace worried Olivia, so she followed behind them. Ellie, who was far stronger than her wispy figure implied, guided Greta to an armchair and steadied her as she lowered herself into it. Greta relaxed against the soft chair back and closed her eyes. Olivia, Maddie and Ellie exchanged quick, concerned glances.

Greta opened her eyes and said, "Please don't worry about me. I've had these spells before, most often when I'm overtired. After all, I am not young anymore. When I was a young woman, I could spend the entire day racing from shop to shop and then dance until dawn." Greta rested her head against the back of the armchair. "But those days are only a memory."

"Could I bring you some coffee?" Maddie asked. "Or perhaps a cold drink?"

"Yes, coffee, thank you. I'll rest for a few moments and then, if you like, we could go over the list of my cookie cutters. I'd be glad to answer any questions you might have." With a wan smile, Greta appeared to relax into the armchair. She leaned her head back and closed her eyes again.

Maddie and Ellie headed toward the kitchen to make coffee, but Olivia, noticing Greta's hunched shoulders, lingered behind. She grew more concerned as Greta's long, thin fingers tightened her grip on the padded arms of her chair.

"Greta," Olivia asked softly, "are you sure you're not feeling ill?"

Greta's eyelids shot open. "What? No, no, I'm feeling fine. A bit tired, that's all." She sat up straighter and laced her fingers together in her lap. "I never used to get tired. Now . . . I suppose no young person ever expects to get old." Greta gazed up as if anticipating a response, but Olivia didn't know what to say. "There was a young woman at the event this afternoon," Greta said. "She was a natural blonde, I believe . . . a light, delicate color. Most unusual. She was quite lovely and vivacious. She spoke for some time with Olaf Jakobson. Perhaps you could tell me her name?"

"I know who you mean," Olivia said, "but I'm afraid I've never seen her before."

"She looked vaguely familiar to me," Greta said. "Such distinctive hair . . ."

Olivia had noticed a slight hesitation before Greta spoke Olaf's name. "You and Olaf once knew one another, didn't you?" Olivia eased into the empty armchair next to Greta.

After another moment of hesitation, Greta said, "Yes, when we were both young. Olaf has aged considerably, but it seems his personality hasn't changed."

Olivia sensed Greta was struggling to keep her emotions from showing. She was doing a good job. Olivia couldn't tell if she felt angry or sad or simply exhausted. "Weren't you and Olaf friends at one time?" Olivia asked.

"Friends?" Greta pondered the question. "I suppose we were, for a brief time." With a light laugh, she added, "It's hard to believe, but when we were quite young, Olaf used to come over to my house to bake cookies with my mother and me. Olaf loved to press cookie cutters into the dough. He did it rather violently."

Olivia was stunned into temporary silence. She had not expected to hear Olaf and cookie cutting mentioned in the same sentence.

Greta glanced sideways at Olivia. "Perhaps you've heard that Olaf and I were engaged to be married? This was decades ago, of course. Yet Olaf still harbors a grudge against me. You see, I broke off the engagement." Greta's expressive shrug struck Olivia as staged. "Olaf would never admit this, of course, but I ended our engagement because of his disturbing obsession with wealth. Even his interest in cookie cutters was more about their monetary value than their intrinsic worth. Why, he once asked my mother if she'd had her great grandmother's cookie cutters appraised."

"Olaf asked that kind of question as a child?" Olivia tried to imagine, as a child, even thinking of such a thing. "How did your mother handle that?"

Greta shrugged again. "Oh, I think she laughed and said the cookie cutters had been in her family for generations, which made them invaluable to her . . . something like that."

"How did your parents feel about your engagement to Olaf Jakobson?" Olivia asked.

Greta shrugged again. "They were against it, of course. They cared more about my happiness than they did about the Jakobson family wealth. But enough of that. I'm still curious about the young woman Olaf was talking to for such a long time. I can't help thinking I've seen her somewhere before. Although, despite her peculiar hair, that type is rather common, so perhaps she simply reminds me of scores of other young women."

"My mom spoke with her," Olivia said. "I think her first name is Desirée, but I'm afraid that's all I can tell you."

Greta nodded but said nothing in response. She stared in silence at her own interlaced fingers. Olivia couldn't see enough of her face to tell, but she was fairly certain that Greta was smiling to herself as she leaned against the back of her armchair and closed her eyes once more.

As Olivia walked toward the kitchen, she recalled her mother's assertion that it was Olaf who had broken off the engagement, and that Greta's parents had been upset with her. Was Greta lying about who ended the engagement? Or had she perhaps engineered the breakup? Given Greta's apparent self-involvement, she might lie to save face. Olivia found it interesting that Greta seemed so determined to discover the identity of the young woman Olaf had talked to during the cookie event. Perhaps Greta hadn't truly let go of her anger with Olaf for ending their engagement. Was Greta jealous? Or had she enjoyed watching Olaf make a fool of himself over an attractive woman less than half his age?

Leaving Greta in the cookbook nook, Olivia joined Maddie and Ellie in the Gingerbread House kitchen. "Let's let Greta rest for a few minutes before we bring her coffee," Olivia said as she poured herself a cup. "It's odd. I don't remember seeing Anita Rambert here. Did I miss her?"

"Nope," Maddie said. "I was watching for her." Maddie finished filling the dishwasher and pushed the "on" button.

"I was, too," Ellie said. "In fact, I didn't see any antiques dealers at the event. I do hope they aren't going behind your back. Much as I hate to think such a thing, I wouldn't put it past Anita to try to convince Greta to show her the collection or at least the list. Anita is persuasive. She could easily argue that you aren't experienced enough to handle the sale of such a valuable collection, Livie."

"Well, good luck to her." Olivia took a pitcher of lemonade from the refrigerator and poured three glasses. "The one and only original list is locked safely away in our little wall safe, and I have, on my person, our key to the storage vault that holds the collection. I gave Greta her key soon after she arrived for our cookie event."

"Not to be a worrywart," Maddie said, "but would you mind checking to make sure the key hasn't walked away?"

With an exaggerated sigh, Olivia reached inside the neck of her loose cotton top.

"What the . . . ?" Maddie threw back her head and laughed. "You hid the key in your bra? I should have remembered from high school. That's where you hid your boyfriend's . . . um." Maddie shot a sideways glance at Ellie.

With an indulgent smile, Ellie captured a strand of her long hair and began twirling it around her finger. "Never mind me, girls. Remember, I was once in high school."

"But Mom, that was way, way back in the sixties, before the discovery of fire."

"Now, Livie, I think you're a bit confused about the course of history, especially the history of relationships. Members of your generation are enjoying the freedoms that my generation created." Ellie tossed back her hair. "And don't you forget it."

"Yes, Mother." Olivia pinned the vault key back in its hiding place. "Now, I vote we take a look at that list while we give Greta a chance to rest," Olivia said as she lifted the antique spice rack off its wall hook to reveal the wall safe. She spun the combination and opened the door. "Et voilà." Olivia removed a small sheaf of papers from the safe. She handed them to Maddie for a first look.

Maddie eagerly scanned the pages. Halfway down the second page, she paused, looking puzzled.

"Come on, Maddie, this isn't funny. That's the list of Greta's antique cutters, right?"

Maddie's head jerked up. "Hm? Yes, this is Greta's list, only . . . didn't Constance give you Greta's original list? Because this looks like a copy. See, there's some shading along the edge that looks like what happens when the original is a little smaller than the paper it's being copied onto."

Olivia lifted the pages out of Maddie's hand. "I see it," she said quietly. "I don't know, we looked at the original when we met with Greta at Constance's office, but maybe Constance gave us a copy, just to be on the safe side. I could ask her."

159

Maddie shrugged. "It probably doesn't matter. We can always trade the copy for the original. Should I drop in at Constance's office on my way home, Livie?"

Olivia didn't answer. The apparent mix-up took her mind back to her late night return to The Gingerbread House from her vacation. She had found some of Greta's cookie cutter collection crammed into the kitchen safe. She'd also found the disorganized display of colored sugar sprinkles, implying that Greta had been roaming the sales floor instead of keeping watch over the disposal of her valuable cutters. Why wasn't Greta with Bertha in the kitchen, making sure her cutters were safely stored and well protected? Had Greta been feeling ill? But then why would she be wandering around the sales floor, aimlessly picking up items, as if she didn't care what happened to her precious collection?

"Livie, you look like you might explode," Maddie said. "What's going on?"

Olivia blurted out the entire story of her return home, including her discovery of the sugar sprinkles. "I'm probably making a big deal out of something totally innocent," Olivia said, "but it just seems odd."

"Hang on, girlfriend," Maddie said. "I already know the answer to that one. It was indeed Greta who was waiting in the store. Bertha told me that Greta felt tired and wanted to sit in the nook while the transfer was made. I didn't know about the sparkling sugars, but it makes sense. Greta probably got bored waiting for Bertha, so she started picking things up and looking at them. Bertha said she was relieved that Greta wanted to stay out in the nook. She doesn't like having anyone near the kitchen when she opens the safe. I told her not to worry. I mean, what was Greta going to do, steal her own collection?"

"It isn't out of the question," Ellie said. "If the collection was insured, that is. People do sometimes steal their own valuables in order to collect the insurance money. Or they hire someone else to do it."

Olivia glanced toward the safe, located in a section of the wall toward the back of the kitchen. She'd ordered it placed there so the body of the safe would protrude into the storage room, which always remained locked unless she or Maddie opened it to restock. They both were careful to lock the door again as soon as they'd finished.

Still, the sugar display was near the kitchen door. If Greta had cracked the kitchen door open to peek inside, she could have watched Bertha opening the safe. Bertha would have been faced sideways and working the combination with her right arm, which would have blocked her peripheral vision. However, it was unlikely Greta could have made out the combination easily. Unless . . . Whenever Bertha performed a task that consisted of several parts, she had a habit of whispering the steps to herself.

As Olivia was about to recount her thoughts to Maddie and Ellie, she realized the flaw in her thinking. Why would Greta go to the trouble of learning the combination to the store safe and then allow her cutter collection to be transported to another, more secure safe to which she'd been given a key?

Olivia gave up. Not every unexplained phenomenon pointed to crime. Most likely, Constance had accidentally given her the copied list rather than the original.

"Never mind," Olivia said. "Let's bring Greta her coffee and go over the list with her." Carrying a tray holding four cups of steaming coffee and a plate of cookies, Olivia led the way to the cookbook nook. She stopped short at the entrance, waiting for the others to catch up. "Looks like we took too long," Olivia said. "Greta has left."

"She was feeling tired," Ellie said. "Maybe she went home to rest."

"Or maybe," Maddie said, "Greta was standing outside the kitchen door, listening to us question her honesty."

CHAPTER TEN

Lemon blended with the fading scents of cardamom, cloves, and anise as Maddie whipped up her second batch of cutout cookies. Her first batch had been rolled, cut into daisy shapes, and chilled in the refrigerator. One sheet had nearly finished baking.

Olivia paused over her own, less tasty work to breathe in the sweet citrus fragrance. "I never get tired of lemon," she said. "It's good to be home."

"I'm with you," Maddie said as she removed the cookie sheet from the oven. "Even if it is a million degrees near the oven."

"You aren't going to bake all night, are you?" Olivia pushed aside the unpaid bills and leaned back in her chair. "It's Saturday evening. Don't you want to get home to Lucas? You don't qualify as an old married couple until you've been hitched at least a year."

"Really?" Maddie slid another sheet of unbaked daisies into the oven and closed the door quickly. "Is that how long it took you and what's his name?"

"That was different. Ryan was a resident in thoracic surgery. There was no honeymoon period."

"I'm not surprised." Maddie pointed her spatula toward Olivia. "Ryan studied heart surgery because he didn't have one of his own, right?"

Olivia chuckled. "That was cruel and . . ." More quietly, she added, "And possibly close to the truth."

"To answer your nosy question," Maddie said, "Lucas decided to do inventory tonight. I think he relaxed too much on vacation. He says he needs to lift heavy objects to get his muscles back in shape." Maddie switched on the oven light to check her cookies. "Just like I need to bake or I lose the knack."

"Not likely." Olivia stood and stretched toward the ceiling. Twisting to check the clock over the sink, she said, "I need to take Spunky for a walk before it gets too dark. If you're still at it when I get back, maybe we could do a bit of computer research."

"My favorite game, next to cookie baking," Maddie said, "but why?"

"It's probably nothing. I'm just uncomfortable about a few things."

"Like why Olaf and Greta hate each other, and who really broke off their engagement?" Maddie slid the sheet of baked cookies onto cooling racks. "I doubt the Internet would have anything much to say about that little puzzle."

"I was thinking more about who attended our event for Greta, and who was conspicuously absent." Olivia ran her fingers through her tangled hair. Maybe she could sneak in a shower after her walk with Spunky. She doubted Maddie would head home until well past midnight.

"Are you referring to Anita Rambert?" Maddie asked. "I figured she didn't see the point in coming. We'd have watched her every move to make sure she wasn't stealing potential customers for Greta's cutters."

"Not just Anita," Olivia said. "No antiques dealers were there, and only a few serious collectors. You'd think they all would have been curious about Greta's collection. I thought we'd be fending them off all afternoon."

Maddie's empty cookie sheet clattered as she dropped it on the table. "Uh-oh. Maybe

166

Anita hatched some sort of plot to take over the sale. Maybe she has been organizing the other collectors into a customer-hijacking gang."

"I wouldn't have put it quite so melodramatically. I don't know, I just feel . . ."

"Uncomfortable," Maddie said. "I get that. I'm starting to feel that way, too. You go walk Spunky, and I'll finish up this batch of cookies. Oh, and take a shower before you come back to the kitchen. Your hair is sticking out, in a sad, limp sort of way. Once it starts falling in your face, you won't be able to concentrate. I'm only thinking of your comfort."

"Thanks so much," Olivia said, laughing. "You're a true friend."

When Olivia opened the door to her upstairs apartment, Spunky was not there to greet her. Usually he made a leap for the door. Olivia headed quickly toward the living room, where she found her pup curled up on the sofa. Spunky lifted his head; that was the extent of his greeting.

"Hey, Spunks. Are you feeling all right?" Olivia sat next to him and rubbed his ears. "The apartment is warmer than I thought it would be," she said. "I know you don't like to get cold, but maybe you're a bit over-heated?" Spunky rolled on his back as if his belly needed air.

Olivia wasn't sure if she should be worried. Spunky hadn't been in the store for the event, so he couldn't have sneaked any of the spicy cookies. She nestled the little Yorkie on her lap. Maybe she ought to check with Gwen and Herbie. They owned the Chatterley Paws animal rescue farm outside of town, and both were veterinarians. She checked the time on her cell phone. "It's nearly eight p.m.," she said. "Herbie answers their crisis number until nine on Saturday nights. I think we'd better make a little visit to the vet, Spunky."

As soon as Olivia uttered the word "vet," Spunky leaped out of her lap and yapped.

"Oh, I see," Olivia said. "You hear 'vet' and suddenly you're feeling much better."

Spunky wagged his tail and trotted toward the kitchen. When Olivia didn't follow, Spunky turned around to face her and flopped down on his belly. He settled his chin on his outstretched paws, tilting his head slightly.

"Very cute," Olivia said, "but you'll have to try that con on someone else." She knew Spunky had been born in a puppy mill, from which he had escaped by digging under the fence. He'd spent several months

168

begging food from soft-hearted Baltimore residents until a Yorkshire terrier rescue organization captured him.

Rather than rush to comfort her pet, Olivia relaxed against the sofa back. "And don't bother to trot out that exaggerated limp, either. I'll see right through it." Spunky had sustained a paw injury during his run for freedom, and he wasn't above feigning a limp when he wanted extra treats.

Spunky sensed defeat. With one longing glance toward the kitchen, he padded over to Olivia and joined her on the sofa. She rewarded him by rubbing his ears. "Okay, no trip to Chatterley Paws. How about a walk instead? I know it's hot, but we can take it easy. We don't have to run. In fact, I'd be grateful if we didn't."

Spunky perked up when he heard the word "walk." He jumped down from the sofa and headed toward the front door of the apartment, where his harness leash hung on a hook. Olivia followed. The little guy waited patiently as his mistress secured his harness and locked the apartment door behind them.

The heat walloped Olivia when she opened the front door of the Queen Anne, but Spunky didn't seem to mind. He hadn't been outside since morning. Pent-up energy propelled him across the porch, and Olivia stumbled as she tried to keep the leash from slipping out of her grasp.

"Hey, slow down," Olivia said. "If I fall, it'll probably be on top of you. Trust me, you don't want to risk that." She wrapped the leash around her hand.

Olivia let Spunky choose the route for their evening walks. He usually loved a good run through the park, but he hesitated when he saw a rowdy group of high school boys tossing a football. Spunky stayed on the sidewalk and led Olivia down Park Street to the northwest corner of the town square. Near the Chatterley Café, he stopped to sniff the air. Olivia gazed longingly at the park, shaded from the setting sun by large, dense trees, but Spunky had other ideas. He led his mistress past the park and continued west for two more blocks. They had reached Apple Blossom Road before Spunky paused again to sniff the air.

When Spunky turned left on Apple Blossom Road, Olivia remembered. "One of your very favorite fire hydrants is on this street, isn't it, Spunks?" Also, there were numerous old oak trees for shade, so Olivia followed willingly. "Constance's office is down this way, too," she said. "Too bad it's so late. I have a few questions to ask her."

Olivia wanted to go home and hop into the shower, but she patiently followed Spunky. He'd been cooped up all day, and besides, he would be restless all night if he didn't get a walk. Anyway, his fire hydrant was at the end of the block; she could see it. Spunky pulled hard on his leash, and Olivia found herself sprinting toward the hydrant. By the time they reached it, she could feel the sweat dripping down her forehead.

Away from the town square, the growing darkness was more noticeable. While Spunky sniffed eagerly around the base of the fire hydrant, Olivia fanned herself with her free hand. She glanced up and down the street for signs of life. It was Saturday night, and most of the buildings were dark or dimly lit. In one building, however, Olivia saw a brightly lit window. *If I'm not mistaken, that is Constance's office.*

"Come on, Spunks," Olivia whispered. "You've had plenty of quality time with your fire hydrant. Let's go see Constance before she heads home."

Spunky ignored her.

Olivia counted to thirty. "Time's up." She scooped her pup into her arms. Spunky snuggled against her chest. "Good boy," Olivia said. "We are going to pay Constance a little visit." They were a few buildings away

171

when a figure appeared on Constance's porch. Olivia couldn't tell if it was a man or a woman, but it wasn't Constance. That became clear when the figure ran down the front steps and past the Chatterley Heights Management and Rental Company sign. Olivia stopped in her tracks. She glanced up at the window of Constance's office; the room was still lit. Olivia walked forward to get a better look at the retreating figure silhouetted against the sinking sun. Olivia thought the tall, slender figure with swinging hair might be a woman. However, she remembered Constance's new assistant, Craig. His hair had been fairly long. Perhaps Craig had been working late and assumed Constance would answer her own office phone.

Olivia checked her cell. It was nearly nine p.m., but if Constance was still working, maybe she'd be willing to clear up the mystery of the duplicate cookie cutter list. She punched in Constance's office number. The light went out, and the call went to voice mail.

Spunky squirmed in Olivia's arms, so she lowered him to the sidewalk. "You've been a good boy, Spunks. We'll go home soon, but let's wait a few minutes to see if Constance comes down." What Spunky heard was "Start yapping and keep it up until I get the point that you want to run."

Olivia grabbed her noisy, wriggly pup and held him close. "Oh, Spunky, must you make such a racket? It won't do you any good, you know. This is not a residential neighborhood, so there's no one to wake up." Spunky quieted down, but he wriggled so much that Olivia gave up and lowered him to the sidewalk once again. Spunky strained at his leash. Olivia held tight while she watched the Management and Rental Company. Olivia knew there was an elevator to transport Constance's wheelchair to and from the second floor, but it shouldn't be taking so long.

Spunky pulled so hard on his leash that he stood on his hind paws. "All right, I get it," Olivia said. "You want to go home, and so do I. I really need that shower." She could call Constance's cell, but why? The mystery of the copied cookie cutter list would have to wait.

"You must have had a shower," Maddie said as Olivia joined her in the kitchen. "Your appearance has vastly improved. Is it still gruesomely hot outside?"

"Yep, afraid so." Olivia surveyed the kitchen. The last two sheets of lemon cutouts were cooling on racks, but otherwise the room was tidy, ready for another day of baking. "You didn't have to clean up, but I'm grateful. It gives us more time to do some online research on Greta's cookie cutters."

"By 'we,' I assume you mean me." Maddie opened the store's laptop and wiggled her fingers to loosen them, as if she were about to tackle a piano concerto. "Such fun," she said. "I have to admit, I'm glad we're investigating antique cutters and not a murder. I mean, the murder investigating is exciting and all, but it does involve . . ." Maddie's freckled nose wrinkled as she grimaced.

"Murder?"

"Exactly. That would be the downside." Maddie's hands zipped around the keyboard as she pulled up and rejected several auction sites for antiques. "Much as I love and adore cookie cutters, I've never given much thought to their history." A colorful site appeared on the computer screen. "Let's see what CookieCutterSearch.com has to offer," Maddie said. "Ooh, look, an article about the history of cookie shaping in Germany. By the way, I took Greta's cookie cutter list out of our safe so I could use it as a reference." Maddie patted some papers next to the computer. "I read through it. There's lots of German stuff listed."

Olivia moved a kitchen chair next to Maddie and picked up Greta's list. "Tell me what to look for on the list, and I'll see if it's there." She dug to the bottom of the junk drawer for a pencil.

"Okay, this is interesting," Maddie said. "The article is written by Phyllis Wetherill, so it dates from some years back, but she knew her stuff."

"I thought you didn't know anything about antique cookie cutters?"

"Well, I don't really, but Aunt Sadie does," Maddie said. "When I told her what we were doing, she mentioned that Phyllis Wetherill wrote this cool book, which is out of print and pricey to buy used. I'd love to find one in good shape and get it for Aunt Sadie. Anyway, in this article, Phyllis Wetherill says that in the early days, like the sixteenth century, most folks probably used carved wooden molds to shape cookie dough. If there were actual cookie cutters at that time, none have been found so far."

Olivia scanned through Greta's list. "It looks like these cutters — at least the ones that have been dated, which is most of them — date back as far as the 1700s. Some of the dates are marked as tentative. On the

175

last page, some small wooden molds are listed. They are described as 'well worn.' They must be many centuries old."

Maddie leaned back in her chair and stretched. "We'll have to be careful how we describe Greta's cutters to potential buyers. From this article, it seems that dating cutters accurately can be tricky." Maddie pointed at the middle of the screen. "Phyllis, if I may call her Phyllis, says that some German cutters that are a hundred years old might look a lot newer just because they were made with heavier tin. But others that are much younger might fool us into thinking they are really old because they weren't well constructed."

"How will we tell the difference?" Olivia asked. She dreaded trying to find an expert who had no ulterior motives.

"Well, according to Phyllis, the cutter backings might give us clues. The cheaper cutters needed more bracing, and they still didn't hold up well. Sounds fairly subtle to me, but at least it's something. I'll bet Aunt Sadie could help us a lot. We need to find a way to show her Greta's cutters. I'd love to haul the whole collection over to Aunt Sadie's house, but I'm not sure it's safe."

"Maybe we could take photos of the cutters," Olivia suggested.

"No, I'm sure Aunt Sadie would say she has to feel them."

"Well, we'll think of something." Olivia checked the clock over the sink. "It's nearly midnight. I know that doesn't sound late to you, but I want to get an early start tomorrow morning, which is what it almost is. I intend to have a good, long talk with Greta about this list. I need to ask Constance a few questions, too."

"Why Constance?" Maddie closed the laptop lid. "Oh yeah, about the list being a copy and not the original. You know, I'll bet Constance gave you a copy on purpose, so she could keep the original safe in the vault with the collection. It probably didn't occur to her to mention it."

Olivia tried to envision the list as she'd placed it inside the wall safe. "I could have sworn I came back here with the original, but you could be right. Maybe I just assumed . . ." She pushed her chair back to the kitchen table, where it belonged. "I suspect my mind is still on vacation."

"And why not?" Maddie said all too energetically. "We have time before we officially reopen The Gingerbread House. Not that I don't love the place, but I intend to play as much as possible until then. Otherwise, Lucas will bury himself in the hardware store, and our honeymoon will truly be over. You, on the other hand, should get some sleep. Remember, you are two months older than I am."

Olivia yawned. "Tonight I actually feel it."

Olivia cranked her bedroom air conditioner to high so she could burrow under the covers without bursting into flames. After setting her cell phone alarm for seven a.m. and the ringtone to vibrate, she left it on the bedside table, within reach. Her eyelids drooped as soon as she turned off the lamp by her bed. As Olivia's head sank into the pillow, she felt Spunky curl into the curve behind her knees. Their evening walk had worn him out. Soon Olivia heard his light, sweet snore, which sounded to her like a lullaby. She closed her eyes and slipped into a dreamless sleep.

Almost at once, or so it seemed, Olivia's alarm went off with a buzzing sound. Groaning, she pushed up onto her elbow and fumbled for her cell phone. She felt the vibrations and realized she had a phone call. Maddie must have forgotten to tell her something important. Without glancing at her caller ID, she flipped open her phone and let her head sink back on the pillow.

"This had better be important, Maddie.

You woke Spunky. You know how he gets."
The furry subject of Olivia's threat snuggled
against her thigh and went back to sleep.

"Olivia?" said a soft, hoarse voice. "I —"
After a few seconds of labored breathing,
the voice said, "I can't . . . breathe."

Spunky yapped as Olivia shot up. "What's
going on? Who is this? If you're ill, call —"

"Can't get . . . Called 999, but no one . . ."

"999? *Greta?*"

Greta wheezed but said nothing.

"Greta, listen to me carefully. Unlock your
front door right now. Can you do that? It's
really important. I'll have to hang up and
call 911, and they will need to get into your
house quickly. Greta? Can you hear me?"

No sound came through, not even labored
breathing. Olivia hoped Greta had left to
unlock her front door. She ended the call,
then punched 911 as she threw off her covers and slid her feet into the old tennis shoes
that functioned as her slippers. With no
laces to tie, they were floppy but didn't slow
her down at crucial moments. Luckily, her
summer sleepwear consisted of stretched-
out exercise pants and a stained T-shirt, so
she was good to go.

While Olivia explained the situation to the
911 dispatcher, she ran down the hallway of
her apartment to the front door. At the last

minute, she slipped her feet into shoes that would stay on. Spunky followed her every move, wagging his tail with excitement. "No, Spunky, you stay here. No, I mean it," she said as the eager Yorkie stood on his hind legs and tried to push the apartment door open. "Oh geez," Olivia said under her breath. Spunky was quick and determined; he'd be through the door as soon it opened. She envisioned herself chasing Spunky down the stairs, costing precious minutes.

"Okay, hold still." Olivia's voice must have been uncharacteristically convincing because Spunky slipped his head through the harness leash without protest. "Good boy. Keep it up." When she opened the apartment door, Spunky burst through so fast he almost yanked Olivia off her feet. "I'm glad you aren't an Irish wolfhound," she muttered as she stumbled down the stairs. When they reached the foyer, Olivia unlocked the Gingerbread House door and let go of Spunky's leash. He ran eagerly into the store. With a twinge of guilt, Olivia closed the door after him and locked him inside.

Within minutes, Olivia was driving north through the dark, empty streets toward Greta Oskarson's new home. Olivia hoped the ambulance had found Greta and transported her to Chatterley Heights Hospital, if necessary, but she decided to check the house before heading to the emergency room. She felt responsible for Greta's welfare, in part because she'd been given the responsibility of selling such a remarkable cookie cutter collection, and she'd barely started. However, Olivia had a stronger reason to feel involved. Greta had seemed unwell after the Gingerbread House cookie event. What if she had an allergy that their cookies had triggered? Most people with serious allergies were careful to warn their hosts, but Greta seemed proud and secretive. She might have wished to keep such personal information to herself.

Olivia was about a block south of Greta's house when she heard the sirens. As they grew louder, Olivia pulled to the curb. A moment later, she saw the flashing lights and realized an ambulance was heading toward her, on its way to Chatterley Heights Hospital. Olivia waited for it to pass. Her tires squealed as she made a fast U-turn to follow the ambulance. As Olivia straightened her wheels, a dark-colored sedan whipped past her and sped off in the same direction as the ambulance. Olivia got only a fleeting glimpse of the driver, but she thought she'd seen hair blowing in the wind from the open front window. Clouds blocked the moon-

light, but Olivia had the impression the hair
was blond.

CHAPTER ELEVEN

Olivia and two drunks shared the waiting room of the Chatterley Heights Hospital emergency unit. One of the men slept on the rug, curled into a snoring ball. The other drunk slumped in a chair, grimacing as if he might be about to lose his stomach contents. Olivia moved farther away from him.

Olivia hadn't seen any women in either the hospital parking lot or while walking toward the emergency room entrance. She'd seen no women except nurses during the fifteen minutes she had been in the waiting room. Aside from the two drunks, no one had entered or left the emergency room since she'd arrived. The driver who had sped past Olivia hadn't shown up. Maybe she hadn't been following the ambulance after all.

For the umpteenth time, Olivia checked the large clock on the wall. Two-thirty a.m.

Only about twenty minutes had passed since she'd arrived. She forced herself not to irritate the nurse again with another request for updated information. When Olivia had first asked about Greta's condition, the nurse had been willing to share only that Greta was alive when she'd arrived and was receiving emergency treatment. Since she wasn't a member of Greta's family, Olivia wasn't allowed to see her or receive any detailed information about her condition.

Feeling too jittery to sit still, Olivia skirted the drunk on the floor to ask the nurse if the police had been called. The response was a sigh, followed by silence. As she trudged back toward her chair, Olivia heard the loud whine of a siren. She ran outside to the parking lot as a Chatterley Heights squad car passed the entrance and screeched to a halt at another door. Even in the dim light, she recognized Deputy Sheriff Cody Furlow's lanky back as he loped toward the back entrance to the emergency room. At six foot three, Cody was hard to miss, even without the uniform.

If only Del hadn't been called out of town for ex-wife protection duty, Olivia thought. Del would have understood and bent the rules. Greta had called Olivia in desperation because she had no one else to turn to, no one she felt she could trust. Del would have wanted Olivia's help, especially if Greta awakened, frightened. Olivia was well aware that the earnest Deputy Cody Furlow wanted to prove himself, to demonstrate his competence in a crisis. She had always gotten along well with Cody, but she knew he would want to handle this situation by himself. If he did a good job, he might be able to move up to a sheriff's position in another town.

Well then, I'll have to be sneaky. Olivia slid her cell phone from her pocket. Standing under a tall parking lot light, she first called Maddie on speed dial, hoping to leave a message. Maddie answered, and she didn't sound sleepy. "Maddie? Are you actually awake?"

"Sleep is overrated," Maddie said. "Anyway, it's practically morning."

Olivia checked the time on her cell phone. "It's 2:38 a.m."

"That late? Anyway, I'm dressed and ready to pop over to The Gingerbread House for a baking session before the heat reaches its zenith." Maddie paused. "Or do I mean apex? I can never remember, but I'm sure you can tell me."

"Well, either one, I guess, but . . . Geez,

Maddie, I'm calling you from the Chatterley Heights Hospital's emergency room parking lot. It's 2:38 a.m. — definitely *not* 'practically morning' — and this is really important."

"Point taken. Are you okay?"

"Yes, I'm fine, but —"

"Then what's going on? No, wait, I'll call you back in a sec." Maddie hung up instantly.

Olivia paced the emergency room parking lot, unsure what to do. After what felt like an eternity, her cell phone finally vibrated, and she flipped it open. "Maddie, what —"

"Speak to me," Maddie said. "Tell me all."

Olivia gave Maddie a short summary of the night. "I can't get past the guard nurse," Olivia said, "so I haven't been able to see Greta or even get updates about her condition. I'm thinking I might try to call Cody directly on his cell. He probably won't answer, but if he wants to look smart and competent, he really needs to listen to what I know . . . even if it isn't much."

"Do you want my advice?" Maddie asked.

"Desperately."

"Tell Cody what you just said to me: that you have information he needs to hear," Maddie said.

"Yes, but —"

"Don't interrupt. Cody will, of course, want to hear it right away, and he'll expect you to tell him over the phone. So say something tantalizing like . . . Wait, let me think. Ooh, I know, say 'Greta called me in the middle of the night, and she said —' Then cut off the call, as if your cell went dead."

"Cody will just call me back," Olivia said.

"And you will let the call go to voice mail. Cody will try again, and again he'll be sent to voice mail. Then he'll start to worry. He's a cop, so of course he'll be wondering if someone has attacked you, maybe to keep you from telling him what you know."

"But what will that get me?" Olivia asked. "He won't know where I am, and . . . Oh, I get it. Then I pound on the back door of the emergency room as if I'm frantically trying to get away from someone."

"I have an even better idea," Maddie said. Olivia heard squealing wheels in the parking lot behind her. She spun around to see Maddie's little yellow Volkswagen lurching toward her. The car came to a stop a few yards away. Maddie leaped from the front seat and slammed the door. "Did you really think I'd sit at home and miss an adventure? Come on, let's storm the Castille. Wait, that doesn't sound right."

187

"Storm the Bastille," Olivia said. "Remember? The French Revolution?"

"I remember nothing French," Maddie said. "That's your job, and you do it with a lovely accent. Oops, almost forgot." Maddie reopened the car door, reached inside, and backed out holding a paper bag.

Olivia recognized the tumbling gingerbread figures that decorated the white bag. "You thought to bring cookies? Were you hoping to bribe the emergency room nurse? Because I'm fairly certain she won't fall for it."

"I didn't have an actual plan," Maddie said. "I guess I was hoping Greta would be feeling better and might appreciate a cookie. I made these for Aunt Sadie. I felt bad that she wasn't up to attending our event, and she has this sweet little windmill mold she brought back from her trip to the Netherlands. That was decades ago, years before she adopted me and couldn't go off on fun excursions anymore."

"I'm sure she was willing to make the transition," Olivia said.

"We're wasting time." Maddie headed toward the back door of the emergency room. "Come on, call Cody's cell."

Olivia flipped open her phone as she followed Maddie. She scanned through her extensive list of contacts, found Cody's number, and punched it in. After three rings, Olivia was sent to voice mail. She snapped her cell shut without leaving a message. After a few seconds, she tried again, and again she got no answer. "Got any other ideas?"

Maddie frowned. "Dang, that should have worked. Cops ought to be required to answer their phones. Oh well, Plan B." She walked up to the emergency room door and began to pound on it. When the door failed to open, Maddie pounded harder, alternating with kicks.

A latch clicked on the other side of the door, and a sliver of light appeared. "If you have an emergency," said a deep, authoritative voice, "go directly to the front door of the emergency room."

Before the disembodied voice could shut her out, Maddie shoved her foot into the opening. *"Ouch,"* Maddie squealed as the door slammed against her foot. "Now I really need emergency care." She filled her lungs and screamed so loud that Olivia covered her ears. The door opened. A tall, muscular young man in a white uniform stared out at Maddie with a stricken expression on his face.

"What kind of emergency room is this,

anyway?" Maddie grabbed the edge of the open door. "I think you broke my foot."

"But you stuck your foot inside right as I —" The young man's voice had lost its authoritative edge.

"Hey, don't blame the patient," Maddie said. "Let me in; I'm injured. Livie, could you help . . . ?" She wrapped an arm around Olivia's shoulders and leaned against her. Olivia encircled Maddie's waist and guided her through the door. The befuddled young man stepped aside to let them pass. Maddie groaned as she tried to put weight on her foot. The assistant pulled Maddie's free arm over his shoulder and lifted her off the ground. He lead the way to an empty break room, where he lowered her onto a plastic chair.

"Thanks for not abandoning me," Maddie said with a brave smile. "Listen, I can't call you 'Doc.' It sounds disrespectful. My name is Maddie, and this is my friend, Livie. And you are . . . ?"

"I'm . . . well, I'm not actually a doctor, just an orderly. I'm hoping to go to medical school as soon as I can save some money and, um, you know, get admitted."

With a sympathetic nod, Maddie said. "I'm sure you're up to both challenges, Mr. . . ."

"Bill. Some people call me Billy, but I like Bill better."

"Bill it is, then. Would you like a cookie, Bill?" Maddie opened the bag of speculaas so Bill could smell the medley of spices, dominated by cinnamon and ginger.

Bill's expression softened. "My grandmother used to make those cookies. I haven't had them since she died. I can't remember the name, but for some reason I'm thinking of 'speculum.' "

"That is so sad," Maddie said. "We must wipe that association from your mind at once. These are speculaas cookies. Take two, eat them quickly, then say 'speculaas' ten times. That should cure you."

Bill hadn't followed Maddie's quip, but he obeyed her order to take two of the cookies. "Wow," he said after devouring both windmills. "Those are really good. Did they come from that little store in town? You know, the one with all the cooking stuff. I heard it's run by two girls."

As Maddie's eyes narrowed dangerously, Olivia said, "We are, in fact, the two *women* who run The Gingerbread House. Maddie is the genius baker. That's sort of why we are here," Olivia said. "We specialize in cookie cutters. A little while ago, our friend, who is a cookie cutter collector, felt very ill and called me for help. I called 911 and said I'd meet her here. Her name is Greta Oskarson. You see, Greta is an elderly woman, and she hasn't lived in Chatterley Heights for very long, so she doesn't know many people. She was frightened and really wanted us to be with her." Okay, Olivia knew she was stretching the truth a bit, but all for a good cause. "The waiting room nurse won't even tell us how Greta is doing because we aren't related to her, but she doesn't have any relatives nearby. That's why we knocked on your back door. We are all she's got, and we are very worried about her."

The happy smile drained from Bill's broad face. "Oh," he said, barely above a whisper. "I'm really sorry but . . . well, Amanda should have told you. Amanda is the nurse out front. She takes her job awfully seriously, which she should, of course, but —"

"Told us *what*?" Olivia hadn't meant to sound so sharp, but she didn't apologize.

"You said your friend was an elderly woman, right?"

When she heard the past tense, Olivia sank into the plastic chair next to Maddie.

"Uh-oh," Maddie said.

"I'm afraid your friend expired less than five minutes after she arrived," Bill said.

"This is a small hospital, but we have excellent emergency room staff here, we really do. They did everything they could to help your friend, but she was too far gone when she got here. My buddy was one of the ambulance drivers. He sat in back with her, gave her oxygen and everything. She was so weak, barely alive, when she arrived here. She just didn't make it. I'm sorry."

"Is the deputy sheriff still here?" Olivia asked.

"Hang on, I'll check." Bill returned almost at once, shaking his head. "The police just left. The docs figured natural causes, so the police decided there wasn't any crime to investigate . . . unless the docs change their minds. But she was carrying an asthma inhaler, so they figured . . . Anyway, that's what one of the nurses told me. I really am sorry. If I'd known . . ." Bill pointed to Maddie's foot. "Want me to get someone to look at that injury? You won't have to go back to the waiting room."

"No thanks, Bill," Maddie said. "My foot is feeling much better. Just a bruise. But thanks for the offer." Using the arm of her plastic chair, Maddie stood up. She winced as she tried to put some weight on the injured foot. "Nothing is broken, I'm certain of that. So don't worry, and for heaven's sake, don't get yourself in trouble by telling anyone what happened to my foot. There's no lasting harm done."

"Well, okay. Thanks." Bill checked the hallway before beckoning them to follow him to the exit.

While Bill's back was turned, Maddie put her weight on her supposedly injured foot to reassure Olivia that she was fine. Olivia was impressed, in a troubled sort of way. Maddie had managed to extricate them from their situation and keep their visit under wraps by dumping the guilt on poor, sweet Bill. She hoped Maddie remembered to limp on the correct foot.

"Okay, now what?" Maddie asked after they returned from the Chatterley Heights emergency room and settled in the Gingerbread House kitchen.

Olivia poured two cups of freshly brewed, extra strong coffee and handed one to Maddie. While Olivia hunted for cream in the refrigerator, she said, "Next we think about breaking into Greta's house."

Maddie perked up. "Really?"

"Well, maybe not an actual break-in, but I think we'll need to search the house. There's at least a chance a door is unlocked, if Greta followed my instructions on the phone. If not, maybe Constance would give us a key. At any rate, if the police intend to ignore her death, it's up to us to investigate. Thinking back to Greta's call, I can't be sure it wasn't an asthma attack that killed her. All she said was she couldn't breathe. She'd tried to call for emergency help. She only called me because she hadn't realized the number was 911 and not 999."

"But you do think she was actually murdered?" Maddie asked.

"I'm not sure what to think. We need to know more about Greta. During our cookie event for her, it became clear that she'd left behind one or two angry people when she moved to Europe. I want to know what she did to those individuals, or what they thought she did to them. Maybe she kept some papers or letters, anything that would give us hints to her past. If she'd angered folks here in Chatterley Heights, the odds are good she continued to make enemies throughout her life abroad. And don't forget all those stories about her multiple and very rich husbands."

"And their multiple, lucrative demises," Maddie added. "Maybe Greta kept a diary. Would that be too much to hope for?"

"Almost certainly," Olivia said. "Greta struck me as a secretive person. I doubt she would keep anything that might incriminate her. Although people can be unpredictable."

Maddie drained her coffee cup. "Okay, then. Let's get going."

"Right now?"

"There couldn't be a better time," Maddie said. "You said yourself that Greta's house might be unlocked. It's still dark enough to sneak inside without the neighbors noticing. We should get this done. At some point, someone will have to decide what to do with the house and her belongings, and then it will be too late."

"Maybe Greta did die of natural causes," Olivia said. "Who are we to doubt the emergency room doctors? She didn't seem to be in the best of health, especially after the cookie event. We probably shouldn't have pushed her into such a demanding social role."

"Geez, Livie, pretty soon you'll be blaming us for Greta's death." Maddie drank the last of her coffee and delivered her empty cup to the sink. "From what I could tell, Greta was holding her own during her argument with Olaf Jakobson. Greta was out of sorts after that, but she didn't seem exhausted. In fact, I had the impression that the fight energized her, in a cranky sort of way." Maddie pointed toward the kitchen clock, which read 3:50 a.m. "Come on, Livie, it's now or never. The sun will be up in a few hours. Maybe we won't find anything suspicious among Greta's belongings, but at least we won't be left wondering if we should have pressured Cody to investigate her death."

Olivia thought back to her phone conversation with Greta, especially the fear in her voice and her frantic efforts to breathe. *Greta called me for help.* "Okay," Olivia said. "Let's do it now."

CHAPTER TWELVE

Greta Oskarson's backyard was dark when Olivia and Maddie arrived. In lieu of a fence, the previous owners had planted evergreens around the perimeter of the property. The dense trees were now at least ten feet tall and certainly provided a sense of privacy. However, Olivia and Maddie had found it easy to slip between the trees and into the backyard. Olivia wondered if Greta had believed herself more protected than she'd actually been.

"How long until dawn?" Maddie asked.

"We have a couple of hours, give or take." Olivia led the way across the lawn to the back door.

"Maybe we'll luck out and find the door unlocked," Maddie whispered as she reached for the screen doorknob.

"Unlikely."

"Well, you never know." Maddie twisted the doorknob and pulled. The door opened.

"One down," she said. She tried the inner door. "Bingo," she said as it opened inward.

Olivia grabbed Maddie's wrist. "Be careful. We don't know why the back door is unlocked. Someone might be in there."

"Or maybe Greta was more casual about safety than your typical American city dweller," Maddie whispered. She pushed the door wider and slipped through. Once inside, she switched on one of the small flashlights they'd brought along.

Olivia followed Maddie into a neatly organized kitchen. A shiny red kettle rested on a back burner of a gas stove that looked brand new to Olivia. Above the sink and countertop, freshly painted, pale yellow cabinets lined the wall. The glass doors of one cabinet revealed a full set of gold-rimmed china. In the entire kitchen, Olivia noticed only one item that clearly showed wear: a linen tablecloth rimmed with cross-stitched flower garlands. The slight yellowing of the fabric made her wonder if the tablecloth had been handed down through Greta's family.

"What a sweet little kitchen," Maddie said. "Why does it make me feel sad?"

"To me, it feels as if Greta wanted to start her life anew, yet . . ." Olivia smoothed her fingers over the soft, worn tablecloth.

"Maybe she also hoped to recapture a part of her childhood."

"We'd better move on to the rest of the house," Maddie said. "It'll start to get light outside before we know it." She led the way into a small dining room that connected, through an open archway, with a front living room. As in the kitchen, all the furniture looked new and expensive. A built-in hutch in the dining room needed refinishing, but the lead-glass doors shone. "This is a lovely piece," Maddie said as she ran her hand across the wood.

Olivia counted eight boxes in the dining-living room area, all open and partially unpacked. "Now I'm the one feeling sad," she said. "Greta was working hard to set up her new home. It looks like a labor of love . . . and hope." Olivia reached into one of the open containers and lifted out a wooden box. "Look at this, Maddie. The entire surface is covered with little carvings. I think they might be gingerbread figures."

Maddie grabbed the carved box out of Olivia's hands and shined her flashlight on its surface. "That's what they are, all right. I don't have enough light to make out the shapes." Maddie carried the box into a windowless hallway, where she switched on an overhead light. "These carved figures look old," she said. "I think this piece might be a genuine hand-carved antique."

"What makes you think the figures are old carvings?"

"It's hard to see because the carving is so tight and intricate, but look at this one right here." Maddie pointed to a tiny figure on the side of the box. She traced its outline with her fingernail. "See? The bottom part is shaped like a bell with little dots underneath to represent feet. At the top there's the head with another small rounded part on top, like hair gathered in a topknot or a bun. It's a gingerbread woman, but not like the ones we see today. I think these little folks are all minuscule representations of the gingerbread figures you usually find carved into speculaas molds, especially ones from Germanic countries." Maddie grinned. "All that research is paying off." She peered at the front edge of the box. "The carving is worn down here, right around the latch. This piece is old and well used."

"And well loved," Olivia said.

Maddie abruptly handed the box to Olivia and turned away. "Here comes the sad again," Maddie said. "I'm pretty sure I remember Aunt Sadie telling me that Greta's father was a skilled carver. I'll bet he made that for Greta when she was a little girl."

"Mom said Greta was an adored only child," Olivia said. "She was beautiful, brilliant, and much was expected of her. Maybe I'm missing something, but it doesn't sound like an idyllic childhood to me. It sounds complicated and demanding." Olivia lifted the lid of the box. There was nothing inside . . . no photos, no mementoes, no childhood treasures or even adult jewelry. "Greta must have used this box for something," Olivia said, "given the wear around the latch." She sniffed the interior of the box. "Tobacco. I think Greta stored cigarettes in here."

"No!" Maddie snatched the box from Olivia's hands and sniffed for herself. "Yep, cigarettes. What a letdown." Maddie started back toward the living room. "Is this search doing us any good? We already knew that Greta had a checkered past and a number of enemies, but we haven't found any reason to believe she might have been murdered."

"I guess it wouldn't hurt to check the bathroom," Olivia said, "and maybe the bedroom. Greta might have overdosed on a medication, I suppose." They followed a hallway and found a bathroom. "There's no curtain over the bathroom window," Olivia said. It's still dark, so our flashlights might be visible from outside. Let's make it quick."

Maddie opened the medicine cabinet. With a sigh, she said, "Greta's drug habits were profoundly boring. Here's some generic aspirin, unopened. A half-full bottle of Tums, which tells us she had tummy problems, but don't we all. Here's a prescription bottle with a Chatterley Heights Apothecary label that reads, 'Take one at bedtime for sleep. No more than two pills in a twenty-four hour period.' " She pried off the lid and poured the pills into her hand. "According to the label, the prescription was for forty pills, and there are thirty-five left. So . . . two or three nights when Greta couldn't sleep, out of what . . . a week or so since she arrived in town? Not much. I'm guessing it wasn't a sleeping pill overdose that sent her to the emergency room. Not unless she had another bottle, like maybe one she brought with her from Europe."

"When Greta called me," Olivia said, "she couldn't get her breath. I don't think that's a symptom of overdosing on sleeping pills. I suspect she would simply have passed out and never awakened if she'd taken too many of those little guys. We should keep our eyes open for any empty medicine bottles, no matter what the pills were for."

"Apparently, Greta had asthma," Maddie said. "We should look for an extra inhaler or an empty one. Bertha's asthma is much better than it used to be, but she carries an inhaler everywhere. She always has a spare. She says people tend to get themselves murdered around us, and the shock could set her off. I don't think that's fair, do you? Don't answer that."

"This bathroom is disappointingly free of suspicious objects." Olivia closed the medicine cabinet and flicked off the light.

"Let's check the bedroom," Maddie said as she started down the hallway. She hesitated at the open bedroom door. "I think it would be safe to turn on the lights in here. The curtains are really heavy. I don't see so much as a sliver of light coming through. I can't even see the light switches."

Olivia felt along the wall next to the door. "Here we go." When she flipped two switches, a soft yellow overhead light warmed the beige walls. On a small table next to the bed, a reading lamp lit up as well. Next to the lamp, a hardback book lay open, cover up. The bed pillows were pushed up against the headboard, and the tousled sheet and light blanket had been tossed aside. Olivia wondered if Greta had crawled into bed to read when something or someone interrupted her.

Maddie picked up the open book next to Greta's bed. "This is an Agatha Christie mystery," she said. "You'll have to tell me the title. It's in that language I mangle mercilessly, according to you."

"French? Really?" Olivia walked closer to read the book cover. "*Le Cheval Pâle.* Greta was reading *The Pale Horse,* in a hardback edition, yet. Very cool. It looks old. I wonder if it's a first edition." She reached for the book, then changed her mind. "I think I'll leave it where it is for now. There's something about this room that gives me pause."

"Like the sheet and blanket?" Maddie asked. "Maybe someone phoned, or the front doorbell rang."

"Or she might have felt ill," Olivia said, thinking of Greta's desperate phone call to her. "Maybe Greta left the book open and tossed the bedclothes aside to get out of bed quickly. You know what I haven't seen so far? A phone. Did you see a landline anywhere?"

"Nope," Maddie said. "I know she had a cell phone because I have her number."

"Try calling it," Olivia said. "Maybe we'll hear the ring in the house somewhere."

Maddie hit redial and held her cell to her ear. "You listen for a ring, and I'll see if this goes to voice mail."

Olivia stood in the hallway, but she heard nothing. She poked her head back into the bedroom, where Maddie tried redial again. "I just got generic voice mail instructions," she said, "We'll have to wander around the house; the cell phone could be in a drawer somewhere. Or maybe she took it with her to the emergency room."

"Paramedics usually tell patients not to take valuables with them to the hospital," Olivia said. "Anyway, from what Bill the ER guy said, Greta wasn't in any condition to worry about what to bring with her."

With her phone to her ear, Maddie whispered, "How do you know these things?"

"Jason was accident prone when he was growing up." Olivia winced at the memory of watching her younger brother fall past the dining room window on his way down from the roof. Luckily, his clumsy stage had passed before he'd become a mechanic.

Maddie dialed again and again while they paced through the living and dining rooms. As they stepped into the kitchen, Maddie sucked in a breath as if she were about to speak. Instead, she snapped her phone shut. "I think someone answered," she whispered. "Only they didn't say anything. I'm pretty sure I heard breathing, though."

"Are you saying that someone answered Greta's phone and just waited to hear your voice? That's eerie."

"Suspicious, too," Maddie said.

"Why?" Olivia sank onto a kitchen chair. "Maybe Greta stuck her cell phone in the pocket of her robe, and someone at the ER found it. Although you're right, I'd expect at least a tentative 'hello.' Maybe it suddenly went dead, which cell phones have a habit of doing."

"Well, I give up," Maddie said as she slid her own phone into her jeans pocket. "Whoever has Greta's cell also has my number now. Maybe they will call me back at some point. Is it really important that we get our hands on that phone?"

Olivia shrugged. "Honestly, I don't know. It just seems strange to me that the phone isn't in the house. I think Greta might have dropped it while she was talking to me. It cut off, and she never came back on the line."

"But then we'd probably have found it somewhere on the floor already," Maddie said.

Olivia twitched the edge of a kitchen curtain. "It isn't getting light yet. I want to walk through the house again to look for anything that might give us some insight into Greta's past life."

Maddie bounced to her feet. "I'll look for any corners we might have missed our first time through. Ooh, maybe there's a secret room in this house. Maybe that's why Greta decided to buy it." Maddie's emerald eyes shimmered with excitement.

"One can hope," Olivia said. She thought the odds were slim to none, though a secret room might hold some interesting surprises. Unfortunately, they usually turned up only in Nancy Drew mysteries and other novels Olivia had devoured as a child.

Maddie scooted into the living room, where she felt along the floor under the sofa as if she were looking for a trapdoor. Olivia headed back toward the bedroom. She turned on the lights and checked the bed and table, inch by inch. She found nothing, not even a speck of dust.

Next, Olivia began a methodical search of the closet. Greta had organized her clothing by type. The blouses hung at the left side of the closet, skirts in the middle, and dresses at the far end. Sweaters were neatly folded and zipped into plastic storage bags, which covered the length of the top shelf. Greta's shoes stood obediently in rows along the closet floor. Her entire wardrobe appeared to be practical, finely tailored, and exorbitantly expensive. There were no satin gowns such as the one Greta wore in Constance's photo of her. Olivia wondered if Greta had been running low on money, or if she'd made a conscious effort to redirect her life. For her later years, Greta might have longed for quiet, comfort, and understated elegance. No more balls or yachts or wealthy husbands.

In addition to the bed and table, Greta's bedroom contained a cream-colored chest of drawers. Olivia thought the piece might be Scandinavian, perhaps late nineteenth century, but Maddie would know. If so, it had been restored to near perfection. Such loving care lavished on a simple piece made Olivia wonder if it might have been passed down through the generations in Greta's family. The Oskarsons had never been rich — until Greta, that is — so they would have cherished the chest.

Olivia opened the top drawer of the dresser and found lingerie neatly folded in small piles. She touched the fabric of a pale blue slip; it had the liquid feel of fine silk. She felt hesitant to paw through the soft lingerie, and she doubted it would be helpful, anyway.

"Hey, how's it going in here?" Maddie's voice startled Olivia, who spun around so fast she nearly lost her balance. "Whoa," Maddie said. "Were you expecting an ax murderer?"

Olivia pushed her hair off her forehead and realized her hand was shaking. "I'm fine, really. It's just . . . there's something disturbing about hunting through the personal belongings of a woman who was alive only a short time ago."

"If by 'disturbing' you mean 'fascinating,' then I completely agree," Maddie said as she peered into the open drawer. "Those silk undies are gorgeous. I'll bet she bought them in France. Find anything important yet?"

"Not really." Olivia slid the top drawer shut. "The closet is precise, neat, and filled with exquisite and expensive clothing." She opened the middle drawer, which held six elegant summer nightgowns and nothing else. The gowns were all sewn from the same fabric, a thin ecru cotton, but each design was unique, ranging from plain to tucked and beaded.

"Ditto here," Maddie said as she selected the most ornate nightgown and unfolded it. "Wow, the tucking is done by hand. This is incredibly fine stitching. Aunt Sadie would be impressed." She carefully folded the nightgown and returned it to its place. As she slid the drawer shut, Maddie said, "This chest of drawers is a fine piece. Excellent condition."

"Scandinavian, right?" Olivia asked.

Maddie nodded. "Swedish, to be precise. Simple, yet elegant." She ran her fingertips across the top. "Recently restored by someone with a lot of experience."

Olivia knelt on the floor to open the bottom drawer. She found it empty. As she pushed the drawer forward to close it, a small object inside fell. Olivia plucked it out of the drawer.

"What's that?" Maddie asked.

"This must have been stuck to the inside edge of the drawer." Olivia held a folded piece of paper in the palm of her hand. "It's probably just an old bill or something."

"Well, open it up, for heaven's sake," Maddie said. "I'm not a patient woman."

"Tell me something I don't know." Olivia carried her find to the small bureau next to Greta's bed. She switched on the reading lamp and began to unfold the paper.

Maddie's right hand hovered close by, fingers twitching. "You're going slowly just to drive me crazy, aren't you?"

"Yep, out of sheer meanness," Olivia said. "That, plus the fact that this paper is folded so small and tight, it's tough to find an edge.

It would help if I had actual fingernails."

"Can't help with that." Maddie spread her fingers. "I trim my nails really short to keep them from stabbing the rolled cookie dough."

"Okay, got it." When Olivia fully opened the lined paper, it was about three-by-five inches and rounded on two corners. "If this belonged to Greta, she sure had tiny hand-writing."

"Let me see." Maddie slipped the paper from Olivia's hands. "Tiny and shaky," she said. "And some of it is really light, as if the pen ran out of ink and was replaced with another. It looks like a page torn from a small notebook, the kind you might carry in your pocket to write down things you're afraid you'll forget. Can you read this writing? I'm too impatient."

Olivia scanned the faint, scratchy marks on the paper. "It looks like a grocery list with some numbers. There's a line separating the list from a number at the bottom, as if Greta had been calculating the total cost of several items. Except . . ." Olivia squinted at the numbers. "Something isn't right."

"Really?" Maddie grabbed the list and frowned. "I don't think these add up. Or is that my math incompetence talking?" She handed the list back to Olivia.

"No, you're right," Olivia said. "Also, the total is huge, and there's no decimal point or dollar sign. Of course, Greta might simply have left those off."

"Maybe it isn't a total. Maybe it's a serial number, like on a computer or something," Maddie said. "I'll bet it fell into the drawer when she was putting stuff away. Which would make it officially unimportant and boring."

Olivia slipped the paper into her pocket. "We need to get out of here. I'm glad we didn't try to pressure Cody into searching the house. I think we can safely conclude that there's no evidence here that someone facilitated Greta's death."

"Maybe," Maddie said, "and maybe not. I went up to the attic and looked around. Very interesting. If you're wondering how Greta managed to keep the house so free of clutter, I'm here to tell you: she crammed tons of stuff into the attic. She must have sent a zillion crates from Europe. Much of it isn't unpacked yet, but what I saw took my breath away."

"Such as . . . ?"

"Couldn't we go up there, just for a minute?" Maddie took Olivia's wrist and tried to pull her toward the bedroom door.

"Maddie, we really need to —"

"Pretty please with pearlized sprinkles on top? Come on, Livie, I promise you will be amazed. And you never know, we might gain some insight into Greta. Did I mention there are photos? Entire albums of them."

Olivia hesitated. Photos might be helpful, especially if they dated back several decades and identified people by name. Despite the lack of evidence, Olivia couldn't shake the feeling that Greta's death had not been entirely natural. And Greta had called her for help. "Okay, let's take a look at that attic, but we need to make it quick."

"Yay!" Maddie slapped her hand over her own mouth. "Oops, sorry. Excessive enthusiasm." She grabbed Olivia's arm and pulled her about halfway down the hallway to a door. Olivia had assumed it was a linen closet. "Ta-da," Maddie said as the door opened to reveal a staircase, complete with a sturdy railing running up to the top. "Hurry, there's lots to see." Maddie ran up the steps.

Olivia followed at a more conservative pace, remembering her mother's frequent — and, unfortunately, accurate — reminders that she often tripped over her own feet. When she reached the top, Olivia paused, momentarily overwhelmed by the jumble of objects before her. Pale light from a small window caught the shiny sapphire blue bodice of a figure-skimming evening gown that hung on an open rack. Olivia thought of Constance's ten-year-old photo of Greta in a similar gown. All the gowns on the rack, Olivia realized, were shades of blue. Had blue simply been Greta's favorite color, or had she chosen the color because it drew attention to her mesmerizing eyes?

"Well? Isn't this gorgeous?" Maddie giggled like an excited little girl as she lifted the sapphire blue gown off its hanger and held it against her body. "It's just the right length." She twirled around. "Although I suspect it might be a tad tight through the hips. It's sad that Greta won't ever dance in this dress again," Maddie said as she returned the gown to the rack.

"From what I saw of her current wardrobe, Greta wasn't planning to attend any more balls." Olivia saw a stack of albums on a shelf. "These must be her photos." She picked an album with worn edges and opened it to random pages. Every photo showed Greta, in a variety of ball gowns, dancing in the arms of men who weren't facing the camera. Olivia turned page after page. She saw a young Greta smiling, laughing, flinging her head back, looking somber. . . . She was always with a man, but again, the faces of her male companions were hidden. Olivia opened another album and found the same pattern.

"Maddie, did you look at any of these photo albums?" Olivia asked.

"I didn't have time." Maddie picked an album and flipped through the photos. "Wow. Greta was certainly the belle of the ball, wasn't she? She must have had her very own photographer."

"Or maybe Greta kept photos only if she was the center of attraction." Olivia tried another album. "Same thing here. You know, I haven't seen a single photo of Greta standing next to a man, as if they were a couple. Where are those husbands of hers?"

"Sadly and suspiciously deceased." Maddie yanked a battered album from the bottom of a stack. She examined several pages, and said, "These show Greta as a teenager. She was a beauty, I'll give her that." Maddie flipped to the end of the album. "Here she is in Paris, I think."

"Let me see," Olivia said, peering over Maddie's shoulder. "That's Greta standing in front of the Arc de Triomphe. It's on the Champs-Élysées in Paris."

"Show-off," Maddie said. "So maybe this dates from when Greta studied at the Sorbonne? Did I say that right?"

"Perfect," Olivia said. "I suspect you're right about the date, too. She looks quite young."

"She could have been a model," Maddie said. "Look at that tall, willowy figure and the long blond hair blowing in the wind."

"If Greta had been a model," Olivia said, "I'd understand all these photos better. It would have been natural for her to pose for any and all cameras, and photographers would gravitate toward her. Although I'd still expect some photos of her with loved ones."

Maddie closed the album and slid it back on the shelf. "It's sad . . . almost as if Greta never really had any loved ones. Maybe she loved only herself."

"It certainly seems that way." Olivia flashed back to the Gingerbread House kitchen before the cookie event they'd thrown to celebrate Greta's arrival. Greta had struck her as self-contained. She had seemed distant . . . cold. Olivia flipped to the last page of the album she was holding. "Maddie, look at this one." Olivia held the album with one hand and pointed to a photo of Greta sitting in a lounge chair on the deck of a ship. "She looks quite a bit older here, doesn't she?"

Maddie took the album to study the photo

more closely. "You're right. Greta definitely looks middle-aged and not very cheerful. In fact, I'd swear she is sending mental daggers in the direction of whoever is taking the picture. Hey, there's some lettering up high, over to the right of Greta's head. I wonder if it's the name of the ship she was on. Livie, hold this while I shine my flashlight on it." Olivia complied. "The tops of the letters are cut off," Maddie said, "but it looks like 'Alic' to me. What do you think?"

Olivia peered at the letters under Maddie's flashlight. "That's what it looks like to me, too."

"Maybe there's something written on the back of the photo," Maddie said.

"Be careful," Olivia said. "The glue is old on those little photo holders."

"When am I not careful?" When Olivia didn't answer, Maddie said, "Okay, point taken. I'll squeeze the photo really gently, and it should slide out. Ah, there we go." She turned the photo over. "There's some faded, scratchy writing here." She shined her flashlight on the words. "Oh my. Here, tell me what you think this says. It's possible my imagination went berserk." Maddie handed over the photo and flashlight.

"I see what you mean," Olivia said after staring at the words for some time. She even turned the writing upside down to make sure it didn't produce a different message. *"Dead and Buried."* Olivia handed the photo back to Maddie. "That has an ominous ring to it."

"I'll say."

"How old do you think Greta is in that picture?" Olivia shined her flashlight on the photo in Maddie's hand.

"Hard to tell, given the expression on Greta's face," Maddie said. "That scowl might be adding years to her features. I must say, her clothes are downright frumpy. That floral skirt just sort of hangs. Wait, is that a conch shell necklace? I'll bet this photo was taken in the mid-nineties. So Greta might have been in her early to mid-fifties. I wonder if the photographer was her last husband. Do we know his name or what happened to him?"

Olivia shook her head as she slid the photo back in place. "We are woefully ignorant about any and all of Greta's unfortunate husbands. Let's put that information on our computer search list."

"Oh goodie! Isn't it lucky that I excel in computer searches? They are such fun." Maddie took the album from Olivia. Starting at the first page, she flipped through to the end. "Did you notice that Greta aged from maybe early twenties to her fifties through this album? No photos of men, but what do you want to bet this is her husband album?"

"You might be right," Olivia said. "From Greta's expression, she seems irritated with the photographer, yet she kept the photo. It's so odd that Greta never kept photos of the men in her life. Maybe she was left with unpleasant memories of all of them."

"I'd like to know how many of them actually died in questionable circumstances." Maddie replaced the album on the shelf. "I'm betting it was more than one." She wiggled her fingers and said, "I can't wait to get to a computer."

"We'd better wrap this up soon," Olivia said. "Let's look around quickly and get out of here."

"Sounds like a plan." Maddie scanned the remaining shelves.

Olivia peered into partially unpacked boxes until she found one containing two bundles of envelopes, some with foreign stamps, others sent from the United States. She picked up one of the packets and flipped through the envelopes.

"What did you find?" Maddie asked, looking over Olivia's shoulder.

"I'm being idly curious, that's all," Olivia

said. "These letters all seem to have post-marks from the 1970s and 1980s. I was wondering if . . . Yep, there it is."

"There what is?"

"A letter from Clarisse Chamberlain. Then nothing more from Clarisse."

Maddie whistled. "You're thinking about that story Bertha told us, aren't you . . . the one about Greta's European affair with Martin Chamberlain while poor Clarisse was home with her chicken-poxed sons?"

"I am." Olivia picked up another packet. "I'm also thinking that Greta said little about her life. She wasn't with us for long, but still . . ."

"Maybe she had a lot to hide?" Maddie picked up another small box and looked inside. "These are letters, too. Some of the envelopes contain several letters from the same person. For such a reserved woman, Greta sure corresponded a lot."

Olivia shrugged. "In a letter, you can be whoever you want, if you are cunning enough. My impression is that Greta was very, very cunning. I wonder why she decided to come back to Chatterley Heights. She had to know she would encounter people who knew about her past, and maybe even a few enemies." Olivia checked the time on her cell phone. "We've been here

221

too long. How many boxes of letters are there?"

"Just these two, as far as I can tell," Maddie said. "What are you thinking?"

"We need to read them all, and this might be our only chance to get our hands on them. The boxes aren't very big, but I'd rather not risk being seen carting them away. Any idea how we might sneak the letters out of here?"

"Sure," Maddie said. "I've got a bunch of covered cake pans in my trunk. If we're seen, it'll look like we were bringing early morning treats to leave at Greta's door. I'll go get a couple pans, while you get the letters ready. I found some string around here somewhere. Here it is." Maddie handed over a ball of wound twine.

"I'll put a few items inside these boxes," Olivia said. "It might raise questions if we leave them empty. It's obvious that Greta got rid of her boxes as soon as she unpacked them."

"Greta was obsessively neat, so I suppose we should be obsessively careful," Maddie said.

Olivia took a handful of letters from the box and frowned at them. "You realize it's totally outrageous of us to walk off with these private letters."

"Yeah, not to mention illegal and highly suspicious," Maddie said. "It would spoil our fun, but should we leave the letters here?"

Olivia closed her eyes and tried to think. Rationality told her to leave the letters and get out. If Greta's death had been treated as suspicious, she wouldn't think twice about staying on the sidelines. "I don't have an airtight rationale for taking these letters," Olivia said. "But I have such a strong feeling that Greta was murdered. How, I don't know. Why is unclear, too, but she certainly had a few enemies. Her return to Chatterley Heights seemed to rile up some old resentments, and maybe one of them was strong enough to trigger a confrontation. I'm counting on these letters to give us some background. If there's nothing suspicious in them, I'll let it go."

"It's ironic, isn't it . . . Is ironic the right word?" Maddie's freckled cheeks bunched as she frowned in concentration.

Chuckling, Olivia said, "I won't know until you tell me what 'it' is."

"Cody. We were so sure he'd go off on wild police chases to prove himself as a cop, but instead he accepted the emergency room doctor's first explanation of Greta's death. That kid isn't suspicious enough to be a good cop."

"Don't be too hard on Cody," Olivia said. "I'll bet Del would have done the same, although he probably would have waited for the autopsy results before saying anything."

"Do we know if an autopsy is being done?" Maddie asked.

"I assume so, unless . . . Let's try to find out."

"I can do that," Maddie said. "I got on well with that poor, befuddled ER assistant, Bill, plus he owes me for the nonexistent injury to my foot."

"But you should wait a bit," Olivia said. "If it turns out that Greta was actually murdered, you'll have drawn even more attention to yourself."

"You never let me have any fun."

"Let's pack up these letters and get out of here," Olivia said.

"I'll be right back with the cake pans." Maddie paused before heading down the attic staircase. "Livie?"

"Hm?"

"I wish Del were here."

"I know," Olivia said. "Me too."

CHAPTER THIRTEEN

When Olivia's cell phone alarm buzzed at nine a.m., she shut it off and pulled the covers over her head. Her early morning adventures with Maddie, first at the emergency room and then at Greta Oskarson's house, had taken a substantial chunk out of her night. In fact, they had taken most of her night. After a fitful fifteen minutes, however, Olivia conceded that she was too agitated to rest any longer, so she got up.

Olivia's first and most urgent order of business was taking Spunky for a walk. He had been cooped up and abandoned during much of the night; he would want payback, which meant a long, rambling exploration of the park and a variety of side streets, with stops to greet all his favorite fire hydrants. Olivia allowed her pup his heart's desire. Olivia used the time to think about the previous night's adventure and plan her day.

Olivia felt excited, curious, and squeamish

as she thought about the stack of letters that waited on her kitchen table. No doubt about it, she and Maddie should not have taken Greta's correspondence from her attic. In the glare of daylight, her reasons for doing so seemed contrived. Olivia had no solid reason to suspect Greta had been murdered. As far as Olivia knew, the emergency room doctors had found nothing suspicious. Would there be an autopsy? Time would tell. Meanwhile, she had the letters and no covert way of returning them, so she might as well skim through them.

When they'd finished their walk and returned to the apartment, Spunky plunked down on the kitchen floor to rest. Olivia luxuriated in a coolish shower before slipping into fresh shorts and a comfy T-shirt. A rejuvenated Spunky awaited her outside the bathroom door and trotted behind her into the kitchen.

"We're running low on kibbles, Spunks," Olivia said as she measured food into his bowl. "Remind me to put it on the list." Spunky's fuzzy little face disappeared into his bowl. Olivia fixed herself a large, strong pot of Italian roast. While Mr. Coffee finished his brewing cycle, Olivia scrambled and ate her one remaining egg. She really needed to start a grocery list. She loved to plan, but for some reason grocery lists failed to interest her.

"Sorry, that's all for now," Olivia said to her pup, who was staring into his empty bowl as if he were willing it to refill itself. "We're going to work in the living room. Or rather, I'll work, and you may snooze." Olivia broke a Milk-Bone treat in half. "Come on, boy." Spunky abandoned his empty bowl and followed his treat into the living room.

When Olivia tossed the Milk-Bone into the air, Spunky leaped for it. "Oh, well done, Spunks," Olivia said as he caught the treat in his teeth. She threw the remaining piece across the living room, and the little Yorkie sprinted toward it. After his morning workout and a meal, Spunky was ready for a nap. He jumped up on the sofa and snuggled into a corner.

Olivia removed Greta Oskarson's letters from the covered cake pan, and piled them on her living room coffee table. She sorted out any letters written in a language other than English, which accounted for more than about half the envelopes. Olivia's task would not take nearly as long as she'd thought. She stored the non-English envelopes in one cake pan, which she slid on top of her refrigerator as if it contained cookies.

After freshening her coffee, she returned to the living room sofa.

Olivia started sorting the remaining envelopes by year, creating one pile for each year. The earliest legible postmark she could find was dated 1968. The letter would have arrived after the death of Greta's first husband, the count who drowned after falling off their yacht. Olivia resisted the impulse to read the letter immediately. The next earliest date was five years later, 1973. By 1976, Greta was receiving at least one letter a year from English-speaking correspondents, and often three or four more. Olivia wondered if Greta had kept only selected letters.

Olivia paused when she recognized Clarisse Chamberlain's handwriting. Torn between curiosity and sadness, she placed the envelope on the table without opening it. Olivia still missed her friend and their long talks. Clarisse had been forthright and insightful. Olivia was quite curious about what she'd had to say to or about Greta. However, organization first.

As Olivia picked up the next envelope, her cell phone rang. She glanced at the caller ID, and answered. "Hey, Maddie, are you up?"

"I'm up, as well as down . . . downstairs

in the foyer, that is. I am holding a large pizza with everything, so hightail it down here and let us in."

"Us? Do you mean you and the pizza?"

"Okay, the three of us: me, the pizza, and Ellie."

"You brought my mother along?" Olivia groaned as she flopped back against the sofa. "I thought we were keeping this whole episode between the two of us."

"Well, it's the three of us now. Or the four of us, actually. I discussed everything with Aunt Sadie this morning. Trust me, Aunt Sadie and your mom will be really helpful, and both of them can keep stuff to themselves. If Aunt Sadie weren't in a wheelchair, I'd have brought her along, too. However, I promised I'd call her if we need any incisive insights. Come on, Livie, let us in. Cold sausage and pepperoni are not appealing."

"Oh, all right." Olivia closed her phone with more snap than usual. However, she had to admit that her one-egg breakfast was long gone. "You stay where you are," Olivia said to Spunky. "I'll be right back upstairs with two of your best buddies." Either Spunky understood her every word, or he was too drowsy to respond. Olivia made her escape quickly, before he realized she was leaving the apartment.

Ten minutes later, the three women settled on Olivia's sofa with plates of pizza and a roll of paper towels. Spunky yapped happily at Maddie and Ellie before he snuggled between them for part two of his nap.

"I suggest we finish eating before we get to work," Ellie said. "We don't want to drip tomato sauce on these letters. It wouldn't look good."

"It won't look good to who?" Olivia asked.

"Whom, dear," Ellie said. "It won't look good to whom."

"Whatever." Olivia took an extra big bite of pizza.

"If these letters are as important as we think, we will have to turn them over to the police." Ellie selected a second slice of pizza, a narrow sliver with very little meat. "I see you've organized the envelopes by date, Livie. That takes me back to your childhood. You used to arrange your stuffed animals by size, the largest in the middle, the next largest on either side, and then smaller and smaller ones fanning out like wings. So artistic."

"And obsessive-compulsive," Maddie said.

Olivia took revenge by snagging the largest remaining slice of pizza.

Ellie unfolded her small, slender body and stretched. "I feel nourished and refreshed," she said. "I'll wash my hands while you two finish eating. Then I want a look at those letters."

"I'm full," Maddie said, "and tingling with curiosity. Let's get cracking."

Olivia felt guilty about usurping the big slice of pizza, but it didn't stop her from finishing the entire piece. She hadn't realized how hungry she was. After gathering up the empty pizza box and plates, she headed for the kitchen. Maddie followed.

"I'll get Mr. Coffee up and running," Maddie said. "I don't suppose you have any cookies lying around? I promise not to drop buttery crumbs on the evidence."

"As it happens, I froze a whole batch of lemon cutouts before I left on vacation. You know, in case I needed a midnight binge after the drive back. They aren't iced, of course; I sprinkled sparkling sugar on them before I baked them." Olivia reached into her freezer and dug out a covered cake tin. "The cookies will take a while to thaw."

"I like them frozen," Maddie said.

By the time Olivia and Maddie returned to the living room with trays of coffee and cookies, Ellie was already engrossed in one of Greta's letters.

"Not fair, Mom," Olivia said. "You could have waited for us. Reading those letters

231

was my idea, after all."

"Yes, dear, and I'll remember that when we are arrested for possessing stolen property." Ellie selected a bunny-shaped cookie with purple sprinkles, nibbled off the tip of an ear, and returned to her reading. Olivia rolled her eyes toward Maddie, who smirked.

Olivia flopped onto the sofa. "Okay, Mom, how many letters have you already finished and what did they say?"

"Hm?" Ellie's eyes remained focused on the pale gray sheet of stationery in her hand. Her other hand held her cookie in the air, as if the bunny were reading alongside her.

Olivia plucked the cookie from her mother's hand. Ellie's head snapped toward her hand, then to her cookie in Olivia's hand. Ellie's hazel eyes narrowed, a danger sign that her daughter remembered well from her childhood. She was prepared. When her mother's small hand shot out to snatch the cookie, Olivia whipped it out of reach. "Talk," Olivia said, "or you'll never see your bunny again."

Ellie shifted to the lotus position, closed her eyes, and took several long, deep breaths. She opened her eyes and smiled. "Ah, much better. Now Livie, if you wanted to know what I've learned from this letter, you only needed to ask."

"I did ask. You ignored me."

"Oh." Ellie's forehead puckered. "I must have been too absorbed to hear you. Ah well, I shall work on improving my awareness of my surroundings. Now, about this letter . . ." Ellie retrieved the gray paper. "It is written in English, but the syntax is odd. More Germanic than English, I think, though I haven't your gift for languages, Livie. You got that from your father. He was able to decipher entire bird conversations."

"Yes, Dad was awesome," Olivia said. "Now, about that letter . . . ?"

"This letter is signed 'Gerhard,' " Ellie said. "That's all, just a first name. At least, I assume it's a first name. Anyway, it sounds German to me, although I suppose it could be Scandinavian."

"Ellie, I'm perishing of curiosity," Maddie said. "What does the letter actually say?"

"Well, it reads like sort of an angry love letter. Hopeless love, that is . . . and very, very angry." Ellie twirled a lock of long, gray hair around her index finger. "It's such a shock when someone turns out to be so very different from the person she appears to be."

Olivia wished she'd snatched the letter, rather than the cookie, from her mother's hand. "Agreed, Mom, but what does the letter —"

"I'm getting to that, Livie. Give me a chance." Ellie skimmed through the letter again. "It begins rather abruptly by telling Greta to be patient, that her gift is on the way. That seems an odd way to offer a gift to a lady, which is why I sensed anger. Maybe Gerhard sent Greta a gift right before she broke it off with him, and there was no way he could stop it from arriving. Then there's more about how valuable the gift is, and he hopes Greta is happy with it. So odd to harp on the value of a gift to a loved one. Usually one emphasizes the sentimental value."

"Maybe Greta wasn't really a 'loved one' to Gerhard. Can I see that?" Olivia held out her hand, and her mother gave her the letter. "You're right, this reads oddly. German isn't my language, but I don't think this phrasing results entirely from syntax issues. There's some odd word usage, too. Listen to this: *'I trust the value of this trinket will be of satisfaction to you. And that it will be the end of the matter.'* It sounds a bit . . ."

"Like code!" Maddie bounced on the sofa and clapped her hands before grabbing two more envelopes.

"I was going to say it sounds a bit formal,

234

not what you'd write to a loved one," Olivia said.

"Here's another one." Ellie waved a sheet of blue paper. "This letter says, 'I am enclosing the item you desired so much. Though I assume I will never hear from you again, yet a part of me does not regret our time together.' "

"I might have one like that, too," Maddie said as she skimmed a page of crisp, white stationery. "Listen to this: 'Words cannot express my disappointment and my feeling of betrayal. You had only to ask, and I would have given you anything. Nevertheless, I am sending, under separate cover, the gift you crave.' "

"There's a distinct theme in these letters," Olivia said. "It sounds to me as if the mysterious Greta Oskarson obtained her considerable wealth from more than just a series of wealthy husbands. I suspect she was also a prolific blackmailer."

"Ooh, blackmail," Maddie said. "Now things are getting interesting."

"Our visit to the ER wasn't interesting enough?" At once, Olivia wished she hadn't opened her mouth.

Ellie's eyes widened. "The emergency room? Why? What happened? I thought you called 911 for Greta. Are you two all right?"

"It's nothing, Mom. We're fine."

Ellie sprang off the sofa and glared down at her daughter. "Olivia Greyson, you told me all you did when Greta called was to call 911. What else happened last night? Tell me at once."

"Oh, all right, Mom, but we're wasting time. I went to the emergency room because . . . well, Greta's phone connection went dead while I was talking to her, and I didn't know what had happened. So I called 911 and then hopped in my car. I heard the ambulance and followed it to the emergency room. I kept trying to get an update from the nurse or receptionist or whatever she was. She stonewalled me, never mind I was the one who called 911. I wasn't a relative."

"I'm sure that was frustrating," Ellie said, "but they do have their rules. They can't be giving out personal information to someone who has no strong ties to the patient. I mean, what if Greta had been a celebrity, and you were a reporter angling for a scoop for some gossip magazine?"

"Mom, why on earth . . . Never mind. I wanted to know if Greta was okay, let's leave it at that. Here, eat your cookie." Olivia returned the cookie she'd snatched from Ellie's hand.

Ellie nibbled on her cookie and frowned.

"So what was the excitement about?"

"No excitement. I called Maddie, and she came to meet me."

"But Livie, somehow you found out that Greta had died, and you became suspicious that she might have been murdered. Otherwise, you and Maddie wouldn't have gone to her house and collected her letters." Ellie sounded genuinely puzzled and worried.

"That was my fault," Maddie said. She quickly summarized her sneaky assault on the back entrance to the emergency room, her faked foot injury, and how she'd duped a gullible attendant into revealing Greta's death. "Livie and I weren't satisfied," Maddie explained. "It sounded as if the doctors figured Greta was an old woman who just up and died from a breathing problem or something. We were afraid there wouldn't be an autopsy because of her asthma. Plus we'd assumed Cody Furlow would want to investigate just to prove himself, but apparently he isn't experienced enough to know a suspicious death when he sees one."

Ellie chewed on her lower lip, which Olivia recognized as a sign of nervous concentration. "Well, we'll have to hope for the best," Ellie said finally. "There may yet be an autopsy, especially if the doctor suspects an overdose, even an accidental one. If they find any evidence of something like poisoning, there will be an investigation. Cody will search Greta's house."

"But we've already searched her house," Maddie said, "and we found absolutely nothing that looked like evidence of poisoning."

"Uh-oh," Olivia said as she flopped down on the sofa. "If the police do get suspicious later, they will dust for fingerprints. We didn't think about that. Our fingerprints will be everywhere and on everything, including her bedroom furniture. That will be hard to explain." Olivia grabbed a sofa pillow and hugged it. "I can't believe I didn't think of that."

"Now, now," Ellie said. "Don't be too hard on yourself, Livie. You were awakened in the middle of the night with a crisis, which you had to handle. You felt personally responsible. One thing led to another . . ."

"What's my excuse?" Maddie asked.

Ellie patted Maddie's arm, and said, "You are Maddie. You are impulsive, excitable, and adventuresome." Ellie arose from the sofa and stretched. "We needn't assume the worst will happen, but we must be prepared. I know you won't like my advice, but here it is: Go immediately to the police station and tell Cody everything you have told me. Emphasize your concern that Greta might have been murdered and your fear that her death was being written off as natural. And share these letters with Cody. I'd say there's plenty in them to indicate that Greta might have been a blackmailer."

"And blackmailers," Olivia said, "tend to get themselves murdered."

By evening, Olivia and Maddie had read most of Greta's letters and discussed possibilities for hours. They had decided to delay telling the deputy sheriff about their search of Greta's house. They couldn't provide any clear, indisputable evidence of either blackmail or murder, either in the house or in the letters. If an autopsy pointed to murder, they would come clean.

The unrelenting heat plus her interrupted sleep the night before had left Olivia longing for rest, so she crawled under the covers at ten p.m. Spunky hopped up onto the foot of her bed, more than ready to snooze. Before Olivia would be able to fall asleep, however, she had one more task to perform, and she wasn't looking forward to it. She propped up her pillow and leaned back against it. One envelope lay on Olivia's bedside table, under her reading lamp. She picked it up with reluctance and stared at the familiar handwriting. It had belonged to her dear friend, Clarisse Chamberlain. Maddie and Ellie had agreed that Olivia alone should read Clarisse's letters.

Olivia took a few moments to remember her friend, who had given her, in addition to friendship, untold hours of invaluable advice. Without Clarisse's business acumen and unwavering belief in her, Olivia doubted she'd have had the courage to buy her sweet little Queen Anne home and open The Gingerbread House. She dreaded finding out that Greta had uncovered a reason to blackmail Clarisse.

"Might as well get it over with," Olivia said to Spunky. Olivia lifted the torn flap of the envelope and drew out the contents. She held three sheets of Clarisse's familiar, pale lavender notepaper. The pages were folded separately. Olivia unfolded all three and discovered each was a separate letter, written in Clarisse's favorite blue-black ink. Two were dated six months apart. The third had been written only a few months before Clarisse's death. Olivia realized all three letters had been composed during her own friendship with Clarisse . . . and long after Martin Chamberlain's affair with Greta.

Olivia's curiosity finally overcame her

reluctance. She picked up the earliest letter and began to read. The distinctive handwriting was firm and elegant. Clarisse's confident, gently humorous communication style brought her back so clearly that Olivia could almost hear her voice. The letter's content appeared friendly and made no reference to Greta's brief affair with Martin. From Bertha's account, Clarisse would have known about the incident for years by the date of the letter in Olivia's hand. She assumed Clarisse had forgiven and moved on, which would have been typical of her.

When Olivia turned the page over to read the end of the letter, she was startled to see her own name. Feeling voyeuristic, she skimmed through an entire paragraph that sang her praises. Clarisse had described her young friend Livie as "smart and focused, yet also creative" and "possessed of a strong business sense, which she uses to pursue a dream that transcends profit." *Yikes!* Olivia was touched, yet also glad Clarisse hadn't said those words directly to her. She would have felt overwhelmed.

Clarisse's second letter read much like the first. She never mentioned her husband or sons, but she did recount an evening she'd spent with Olivia. The episode had taken place more than a year before the date on

Clarisse's letter. She and Clarisse had discussed antique cookie cutters for hours, while they'd gone through Clarisse's extensive collection. Olivia remembered feeling spellbound as Clarisse lovingly recounted the story behind each cutter, including its history, as far as she knew it; where she had come across the cutter; and what the cutter meant to her personally. They had never discussed monetary value. The collection had been evaluated and insured, of course, but that hadn't been important, not to Clarisse.

Olivia smiled as she refolded the second letter and put it aside. She opened the third and final letter. It was dated shortly before Clarisse's death. At once, Olivia sensed unsettling differences in this letter. Clarisse's normally neat handwriting looked looser and darker, as if she'd been pressing harder and writing faster than usual. Olivia noticed several strike-outs on the paper. As she read, her heart began to thump in response to a sense of urgency that emanated from the page.

The letter read:

Congratulations, Greta, you have accomplished a rare feat. You unerringly sensed my weak spot and bored your way into my trust. I should have known better. Martin was not a perfect man, but he was virtually impervious to the wiles of other women. Virtually. I forgave him — and you, as well — for your indiscretion. Your radar picked up my own discomfort with anger and resentment, so you couldn't resist stoking them again. They are enervating emotions, and I avoid anything that deters me from fully enjoying my life and my work. However, don't think you have won, that you have destroyed another happy life. My anger will be gone very soon. You, on the other hand, must continue to live with yourself. I'm sorry for you. You were raised to expect that life would be your servant, fulfilling all your dreams and desires. When that doesn't happen, you lash out. You hurt others to fill your own emptiness.

I don't know everything that you have done, but I can find out. And I will use what I find to hurt you, if you try to hurt me through those I care about. Do not ever contact Olivia or anyone who knows her. I can only imagine through what sordid means you obtained the bulk of this antique cookie cutter collection you've been bragging about, and I will not allow you to involve Olivia in your attempts to profit from it. Stay in Europe. You are not welcome here.

"Wow," Olivia said, loud enough to awaken Spunky. He tilted his furry head and studied her, as if he were trying to gauge her mood. "I'm okay, Spunks," Olivia said. "It's just a mild case of shock." Not for the first time, Olivia wished she could pick up the phone and call Clarisse, who had often stayed up late to work in her home office. But Olivia would never be able to call Clarisse again, so she did the next best thing: she called the phone in the Gingerbread House kitchen and waited for the answering machine to click on. "Maddie, it's me," Olivia said. "I found out something startling this evening. We should definitely discuss this before we consider confessing to Cody, so if you come to the store early to bake, and I know you will, call my cell right away. Keep calling until I wake up. I'll throw on some clothes and join you in the kitchen."

Olivia doused the bedside light and slid under the covers. Her eyes wouldn't stay shut. Clarisse's warning to Greta hurtled around her mind like an endless roller coaster. Olivia decided to use her never-fail sleep aid: she took a deep breath and pictured herself snuggled inside a soft gumdrop canoe, floating slowly down a river of molten milk chocolate. One of her hands hung over the side of the canoe. Her fingers trailed through the warm, thick liquid, while blue, pink, and purple sugar crystals sparkled in the moonlight as they fell around her boat. Eventually, Olivia slipped into sleep, but only after she'd banished the piranha-shaped cookie that bobbed dangerously close to her chocolate-dipped fingers.

CHAPTER FOURTEEN

"Livie? Yoo-hoo, Livie, wake up."

That's Maddie's voice, Olivia thought. *Why am I dreaming that Maddie is trying to wake me up?* Olivia felt a hard object pressed against her ear. Her cell phone . . . She must have answered Maddie's call and fallen right back to sleep.

"Livie, you told me not to give up until you were awake, and I always do as I'm told . . . at least, when it promises to be amusing. So here's the thing, Livie. I am prepared to whistle into the phone, if that's what it takes to wake you up. You know how much phone whistling irritates you. The beauty of it, from my point of view, is that you can't whistle, so you won't be able to take revenge on me. Although I suppose you could take revenge some other way, but that wouldn't have the same satisfying sym-metry."

Olivia groaned.

"Oh good, you're alive," Maddie said. "I was beginning to wonder."

"What time is it?"

"Well, as you know, Livie, when I get the urge to bake, it's usually predawn. However, vacation made me lazy, so I didn't get here until now, which is 5:37 a.m." When Olivia made no comment, Maddie asked, "Are you sure you're okay? Because the message you left on the kitchen answering machine got me worried. In television mysteries, when a character says she has found out something really important, it usually means she is about to get, you know, terminated."

"Maddie, I have no idea what you are talking about, but keep going. I'm starting to wake up." With her free arm, Olivia pushed herself to a sitting position. "I'm also remembering why I told you to wake me up," she said.

"Good. Tell me before I burst."

"Give me ten minutes to shower and dress. Then I'll come downstairs."

Maddie sighed audibly. "You're torturing me, but okay. Bring along some eggs, and I'll scramble up breakfast."

Olivia ran her fingers through her tangled waves and wished she had time to wash her hair. "Um, I think I ran out of eggs."

"Of course you did," Maddie said. "For a

super-organized businesswoman, you sure have a hard time keeping your own kitchen adequately stocked. We ran out of eggs down here in the store kitchen, too. However, no worries, we'll have cookies for breakfast. And coffee, lots of it, very strong. See you in ten. And I expect an awesome revelation after all your hype."

"You took twenty whole minutes," Maddie complained when Olivia showed up in the Gingerbread House kitchen. "I made the coffee and put out cookies almost fifteen minutes ago."

"Sorry." Olivia headed straight for Mr. Coffee. "I couldn't stand my hair, so I washed it. I didn't take time to blow-dry it, so it will dry in strings, but they will be clean strings." Olivia stirred cream and sugar into her cup. "Spunky insisted on coming downstairs with me. He's in his chair, staring out into the park." Olivia took several gulps of her coffee, and said, "Ah, elixir of the gods. Where are those cookies you promised for breakfast?"

"I ate them." Maddie avoided Olivia's gaze. "I got hungry, okay? And I don't want to hear a word about how much weight I've gained since my wedding." She took a cake pan from the freezer and slid off the lid.

Olivia watched warily as her best friend since age ten refilled the cookie plate. "Honestly, Maddie, I haven't noticed that you've gained any weight. In fact, you look a bit slimmer to me. Anyway, since when have you started obsessing about a pound or two? Lucas hasn't made any insensitive comments, has he?"

"Lucas? Of course not. He is the soul of sensitivity. Besides, he thinks I'm gorgeous. That's the problem; I want him to keep thinking of me that way. So I weighed myself. I gained two whole pounds over less than a week of vacation! All we did was hike and swim. At this rate, I'll be a blimp in a month."

Olivia laughed so hard she spilled her coffee. As she mopped up the spill, she noticed Maddie wasn't laughing. *Oops.* "Maddie, my friend, don't you know that muscle weighs more than fat? You gained two pounds of muscle from all that exercise."

Maddie's eyes narrowed to emerald slivers. "You made that up to make me feel better."

"No, really, Mom told me. Mom would never lie about anything related to health and/or well-being."

Maddie's balled-up fists relaxed. "You're right, she wouldn't. Not Ellie." Maddie reached toward the plate of cookies and snatched a daisy with blue sprinkles. "What was so important you made me go through the agony of trying to wake you up early?"

Olivia reached into the back pocket of her jeans and produced the envelope that held Clarisse's letters to Greta. "Read these in order," Olivia said as she handed over the envelope. While Maddie read, Olivia fixed herself another cup of coffee and selected an apple-shaped cookie. Now she could report to her mother that she'd had an apple for breakfast.

"Whoa." Maddie dropped the papers on the table as if they had burned her hands. "This third letter . . . I would love to know what Clarisse discovered about Greta. I wonder how Clarisse came by the information. Would Bertha know anything about this, do you think?"

Olivia sank onto a kitchen chair and hugged one knee to her chest. "If Bertha knew, wouldn't she have said something to us? She told us about the affair between Martin and Greta. Anyway, that happened when Clarisse's sons were little boys. As you can see in the first letter, Clarisse had known about that for some time, and she had forgiven both Martin and Greta."

"Which I wouldn't do," Maddie said, "but

that's just me."

Remembering her friend, Olivia said, "Clarisse hated betrayal. She must have been in anguish. I suspect she needed to forgive Greta and . . . well, if not forget, at least put aside the whole episode. Maybe Clarisse focused on their mutual interest in cookie cutters so her friendship with Greta would feel safe and normal again. Anyway, I got the impression from Clarisse's third letter that she was referring to something more than Martin's fling with Greta. She sounded so shocked and angry, as if she'd only just found out about what Greta had done. Whatever it was, I can't tell if Greta actually told her about it, or if Clarisse heard about it from someone else."

"Livie, you don't suppose . . . What if Clarisse found some evidence that Greta was murdering her husbands for their fortunes?"

"Oh, I doubt that," Olivia said. "How would Clarisse come across that information when, apparently, the police could never prove anything? Unless . . ."

"What? What? Livie, I can see your brain clicking away. Have pity on me, at least think out loud."

Olivia frowned and shook her head. "Clarisse wasn't easy to dupe," she said. "It

251

would take more than gossip to make her this angry. Someone had to give Clarisse convincing evidence that Greta was not to be trusted, or she wouldn't have tried to protect me so fiercely." Olivia refolded the letter and slid it into the envelope. "Bertha doesn't seem to know about this letter. We need to talk to Mr. Willard. He was Clarisse's attorney, and he knew her well." She glanced at the clock over the sink. "It's 6:24 a.m., and Mr. Willard usually gets to his law office not long after six a.m., so he should be firing up his cappuccino machine about now. Come on, let's go."

Maddie unplugged Mr. Coffee, stowed the uneaten cookies in a tin, and scurried to follow Olivia out of the kitchen. "Hey, maybe Greta died of shock when someone she'd wronged in the past showed up at her new home. Wouldn't that be a lot like justice?"

"Maybe too much like justice to be true," Olivia said. Spunky leaped off his chair and pranced toward Olivia as she entered the sales floor. She scooped him into her arms, and said, "Let's take Spunky with us. Mr. Willard loves him. And let's leave through the kitchen. I'd just as soon keep this outing less than public." They cut back through the kitchen, where Maddie unlocked the back door leading into the alley. While Maddie locked the door from the outside, Olivia said, "I truly hope this will all blow over before Del comes home."

Maddie was first to reach the end of the alley. She checked the street and signaled Olivia to follow her. "You'd think that by now Del would realize you can take care of yourself and stay safe," Maddie said quietly.

With a chuckle, Olivia said, "Are you kidding? I'm still not convinced that Del can keep *himself* safe. Look what he's gotten himself into with his ex-wife."

"Point well taken," Maddie said. "Let's use my car, and we won't park in front of the bookstore. We don't want to advertise our location. My little yellow VW is almost as easy to spot as your PT Cruiser. Those tumbling gingerbread creatures are a dead giveaway." Maddie unlocked her VW and slid behind the wheel. "We'll park in back of the bookstore. BookChat doesn't open until nine, so we'll have to get him to come down and let us in the back door. We can throw pebbles up at his office window."

"Or we could simply call his office number from one of our cell phones," Olivia said with perhaps a hint of sarcasm.

"What fun would that be?"

In the end, neither maneuver proved

necessary. As soon as they'd parked behind the BookChat Bookstore, Spunky spotted a squirrel. He leaped from Olivia's lap as she opened the car door and chased after it. He got only as far as the end of his leash, but his ferocious yapping brought Mr. Willard's tall, reed-thin figure to the open, upper-story window of his law office. Olivia and Maddie waved up at him and pointed toward the back door of the two-story building. Mr. Willard seemed to nod at them before he disappeared.

"I hope he understood our hand signals," Maddie said.

"Mr. Willard understands everything." Olivia tugged on Spunky's leash to draw him closer.

The back door opened a few minutes later, and Mr. Willard appeared. Spunky took advantage of his mistress's momentary distraction to yank the leash from her grip. Olivia turned back to look for him. "Spunky!" she yelled, but he was gone from sight.

"Livie, it's okay," Maddie said. "Turn around."

Olivia obeyed. Spunky hadn't run off; he had broken free to race toward his buddy, Mr. Willard. "Okay, fine," Olivia said, "but I almost had a heart attack."

Maddie laughed in a way that Olivia found less than sympathetic. "Bertha told me that Mr. Willard is so taken with Spunky he now carries dog treats in his suit pocket. He's been sneaking them to Spunky whenever he visits Bertha in The Gingerbread House."

"That little con artist," Olivia muttered under her breath. "No wonder he's been gaining weight." But when Mr. Willard — holding Spunky to his chest with one long, bony arm — greeted them, Olivia didn't have the heart to insist he stop indulging her already-spoiled pup. For all she knew, Gingerbread House customers were habitually feeding extra treats to Spunky. The little guy was too irresistible for his own good. Maybe she should adopt a companion for him . . . a nice, big cat. Except the cat would have to stay upstairs, because Bertha was allergic.

Mr. Willard led the group up the narrow back stairs to the second floor. He didn't release Spunky to Olivia's arms until he needed both hands to unlock and unstick the ancient, swollen door to his office. Spunky snuggled against Olivia's shoulder and fixed melting brown eyes on her adored face.

"You cunning little creature," Olivia said lovingly. "Don't think I'm not on to you."

255

Mr. Willard's outer office held a well-used desk, no chair, and floor-to-ceiling bookcases filled with law books. The only object on the desk was a dusty Underwood typewriter. Olivia smiled. The first time she had ever entered the outer office, she'd seen an old electric typewriter in the same spot. It seemed appropriate that Mr. Willard had decided to replace it with an even more antiquated, yet more appealing, typewriter. A secretary had once occupied the room, but not since well before Olivia's return to Chatterley Heights. Mr. Willard skirted the abandoned desk and opened the door to his private office, where he spent many of his daytime hours. His antique maple desk and a deep chair occupied nearly a third of the small room. Piles of paper and books, some of them open, surrounded Mr. Willard's laptop computer. A smaller table nearby held a printer, and two visitors' chairs faced the desk.

"Have a seat," Mr. Willard said, "while I whip up some cappuccino for us. Would Spunky like a blanket to nap on?"

"He's fine on my lap," Olivia said. Spunky agreed. He curled into a circle and closed his eyes.

"I love visiting your office, Mr. Willard," Maddie said. "It almost makes me want to shoplift, just so I can spend time here."

When Mr. Willard grinned, shallow wrinkles curled around the corners of his mouth. "As I've mentioned before, Maddie," he said, "I am not a criminal attorney. Perhaps it would be wise to visit my office merely for the cappuccino machine." Mr. Willard distributed tiny cups filled with the frothy mixture. He settled behind his desk, and asked, "Now, what brings the two of you to my office at such an early hour? Has it perhaps something to do with Greta Oskarson's death? Don't look so surprised, Livie. Bertha and I met for breakfast yesterday at Pete's Diner. Word had spread quickly. Are you wondering what to do about Greta's cookie cutter collection? It will take some time to determine the location of any living relations, if they exist. If she made a will, she did not discuss it with me."

Olivia exchanged a quick glance with Maddie. "At the moment," she said to Mr. Willard, "I'm not too concerned about the collection. It can stay where it is until we know what to do with it. Right now we're more in need of information and advice. So consider us on the clock as of now."

Mr. Willard nodded and pulled a notepad from his desk drawer. "Have the police released any new information about Greta's untimely death?"

"Not that we've heard," Olivia said. "However, Maddie and I have been wondering if there's more to it than our deputy sheriff seems to think."

Mr. Willard's deep-set eyes widened as his eyebrows shot up. "When you say you've been wondering, do you mean that you've been investigating?"

"Would that be a bad thing?" Maddie asked. "I mean, what if we felt we needed to know Greta better, so we did some investigative, um, exploration?"

"Exploration?" Mr. Willard's sparse, gray eyebrows nearly disappeared into the creases that formed across his forehead. "Perhaps you should simply tell me what you have done that you fear might have crossed the legal line."

With a pleading glance toward Olivia, Maddie withdrew into the depths of her chair.

Olivia took a deep breath. "After we found out Greta had died, we sneaked into her house to find out more about her. We wondered . . . well, we had so many questions about Greta's history, and we thought it possible that her return to Chatterley Heights had stirred up some old resentments. We wanted a look around her house. Let me assure you that we did not break in. The doors were unlocked."

"Is that all?" Mr. Willard asked.

"Well, we did borrow some old letters . . . and a mysterious note we found."

Mr. Willard's forehead wrinkles reformed themselves as he frowned in puzzlement. "Letters? A note? Why? As far as I know, Greta Oskarson died of natural causes."

"We think she might have been murdered," Maddie blurted. "We were afraid Cody would screw up and not investigate."

"And now," Olivia said, "we're not sure what to do with what we've got. From the content of the letters, it looks to us like Greta was blackmailing a lot of people. Also, we found some correspondence from Clarisse Chamberlain that implies Greta did something unforgivable, something beyond her fling with Martin."

"Ah." Mr. Willard sipped his cappuccino. "That is disturbing. And you believe that others, perhaps citizens of Chatterley Heights, might have suffered at Greta's hands?"

Olivia nodded. "We're also wondering if the rumor that she expedited her wealthy husbands' deaths might be true."

"All this makes Greta sound like a master

criminal," Mr. Willard said with a faint smile. "Perhaps I can put your minds at rest, at least a bit. I was concerned when I heard Greta was moving back here. I was aware of her brief relationship with Martin Chamberlain, and I was not surprised. Greta was stunning and ruthless, even in her youth, and I was afraid she might take advantage of people I cared about . . . including you, Livie. So I touched base with several of my legal contacts in Europe. I learned that, contrary to rumor, the deaths of Greta's husbands were thoroughly investigated and found to be due to either natural causes or, as in the case of her first husband, accident. The only exception was her last husband, who was also reported to have died by drowning, but only because there wasn't sufficient evidence to draw a different conclusion. Greta was not a mass murderer, at least."

"At least?" Maddie shifted her chair closer to Mr. Willard's desk. "Does that mean she was something else . . . like a blackmailer?"

Mr. Willard's bony shoulders lifted in a shrug. "It is possible. According to my contacts, blackmail allegations couldn't be proven. The authorities received blackmail complaints from second parties — wronged wives, for instance. They accused Greta of conducting affairs with their husbands for the express purpose of blackmailing them. The descriptions of Greta's technique were remarkably consistent, but the authorities were never able to obtain sufficient evidence. The victims themselves invariably refused to cooperate."

"Wow," Maddie said. "Greta must have found some really good dirt on those guys."

"She was clever, obviously," Olivia said. "We read some letters she'd received. Several of the victims hinted that Greta was blackmailing them, but the letters were so guarded in their phrasing, it's hard to see how they could be used as evidence. The victims must have been terrified of exposure."

"Ah yes," Mr. Willard said. "The Greta I knew had a penchant for wealthy, prominent men."

"I'll bet," Maddie said. "Wealthy, prominent men make perfect blackmail victims."

"Until one of them decides to fight back," Olivia said. "Then it's —" Her cell phone blasted out the first two lines of the Blood, Sweat & Tears version of "You've Made Me So Very Happy." Olivia glared at Maddie, who gave her a sheepish look.

"Sorry, sometimes I, um, energize Livie's ringtone," Maddie explained to Mr. Willard.

When the raucous music began again, Olivia grabbed her phone. "I'll turn it off," she said.

"No, don't," Mr. Willard said. "Any call before nine a.m. is likely to be important."

"Or it's a scammer from some island in the Pacific," Maddie said.

"Nope, it's my mom. I suppose I should answer." Olivia opened her phone and put it to her ear. "What's up, Mom? Everything okay?"

"Livie, I'm so glad I caught you. I'm just heading off to an early yoga session, which I sorely need, but I . . ." Ellie's voice grew fainter, and Olivia guessed she was speaking to someone else. "Sorry, Allan wanted to know where his clean shirts had gotten to, and I had to explain that shirts don't get clean if they aren't transported to the laundry room. Oh, and before I forget, come to dinner here this evening. Jason will be there."

"Okay. Any special reason?"

"Just that I need a family dinner. Now, where was I?"

"Heading for yoga," Olivia said. "Beyond that, I haven't a clue." She glanced at Maddie and rolled her eyes. "Mom, what's up? Why are you going to yoga at this hour of the morning? Are you okay?"

"I'm a bit distracted, that's all." Ellie's sigh came through clearly. "Hang on." Seconds later, Ellie said, "If you must know, it's Calliope. I'm at my wit's end."

"Wait a sec, Mom." Olivia held her hand over her phone, and said, "I'll be right back, I promise, but there's something going on with Mom. She's usually so cool and calm about people. However, Calliope rattles her." Olivia lifted her drowsy pup and handed him to Maddie.

"By all means, speak with your mother," Mr. Willard said. "Use the outer office for privacy. If Ellie is flustered, something must be wrong. Maddie and I will chat until you return."

"Thanks." Olivia hurried to the outer office and closed the connecting door. "Okay, Mom, tell me what's going on with Calliope. Cal, I mean. Aren't you afraid she'll hear you talking about her?"

"I'm outside now, on my way to yoga, but I'm taking the slow way. I'm not in a terrible rush, for once," Ellie said. "I will never get used to calling her Cal. I don't know why, but every time I look at her, I think 'Calliope.' She's so . . ."

"Horse-like?"

Ellie giggled. "Such a terrible thing to say, dear, but I'm afraid it's true. It wouldn't be nearly as noticeable, I think, if her personality were less . . ."

"Pushy?"

"I was going to say 'forceful,' which isn't much nicer, when you think about it. I do feel compassion for her, of course. She isn't terribly attractive, which can be a burden for a woman, and her forcefulness doesn't help. Difficult personality traits do seem more acceptable in beautiful women. So unfair, but it's the way the world seems to work, even when a woman has other —"

"Mom, did you and Calliope come to blows or something?"

"Oh, no, dear, so far I've maintained my ladylike demeanor, but my control is slipping. I'm worried about Jason."

Olivia began to pace around the empty desk in Mr. Willard's outer office. "I'm getting confused, Mom. Jason is usually so easygoing, in a snarky sort of way. Has Calliope upset him?"

"No, not at all," Ellie said. "They are planning to move in together."

Olivia's thigh hit the corner of the desk as she turned too sharply. "Did you just say 'move in together'? I'm having trouble wrapping my mind around that concept."

"Livie, for heaven's sakes, I didn't mean move in together as in *move in together*. You

264

see, Jason so wants to buy a little house of his own."

"I'm aware of that," Olivia said. "It's all he talks about lately."

"That's the problem," Ellie said. "This morning before work, Jason came to the house for an early breakfast. Calliope was there, of course, and Allan, and me. Everything seemed to be going fine. Then Jason began talking about buying a house. Well, you know how excited he gets when he focuses on a goal."

"Normal people get excited, Mom. Jason gets obsessive. So I'm guessing it was Calliope's idea that she take up residence in this fantasy house?" Olivia remembered how insistent Calliope had been that the Gingerbread House cookbook nook would make a perfect little apartment.

"Yes," Ellie said, "and it isn't a fantasy house. Jason wants to buy the house where Greta Oskarson died."

"Whoa. That's just wrong, on so many levels. First, Greta *died* in that house, or at least would have if I hadn't called 911 for her. And second, it has only been about a day since her death. Has Jason been inhaling gasoline? Why would he want that particular house, anyway?"

"Oh, he got it into his head that he might

265

be able to buy it cheaply because . . . you know."

Olivia hiked herself up onto the empty desk and rested her free arm on the sturdy old Underwood typewriter. "Jason thinks no one will want that house because Greta became ill in it and then died at the ER? That's a stretch, even for Jason."

"I'm now inside the band shell in the park," Ellie said. "It's still too early to arrive for yoga, so I think I'll sit on the bench for a bit. It's so lovely and cool in here. I need a calming environment. Where was I?"

"You were about to tell me that Jason liked the idea of Calliope moving into Greta's house with him, which only confirms my long-held belief that Jason is not my actual genetic sibling. Does he believe Calliope will help him pay the mortgage? Because it's my impression that Calliope is a professional moocher. She wants to have her own space without paying for it."

"Yes, that has puzzled me, too," Ellie said.

"I wouldn't say I'm puzzled by it. Calliope is broke, probably always has been, so mooching has become a way of life for her." Olivia sneaked a peek at the time on her cell. "Mom, I really have to go now. Could we —"

"But Calliope isn't broke," Ellie said.

"She's got scads of money. She could buy Chatterley Heights outright, yet she doesn't want to pay for so much as a room."

"But —"

"Yes, I know, Calliope lived in Europe for years, which isn't cheap. From what she has told us, she was always a guest in someone's villa or castle or whatever. It puzzled me beyond endurance, so I dragged Allan away from his beloved computer and insisted he tell me Calliope's life story. Allan knows all about it, of course, because Calliope is his cousin on his mother's side, and his mother was the kind of person who kept track of every family member . . . even ones she hadn't met or never wanted to see again."

Olivia had to admit, at least to herself, that she was curious. "Okay, I'm sure I'll regret this, but what is Calliope's story?"

"I'm glad you asked, Livie, because I still have ten minutes to wait before my yoga session, and talking helps calm and center me."

"So glad I can help," Olivia said. "And I promise not to interrupt unless absolutely necessary. I'm hoping it will take well under ten minutes."

"You see," Ellie said, "Calliope's parents, unlike poor Allan's folks, were incredibly rich. Calliope's mother and Allan's mother were sisters, both of them very attractive. Of course, Allan is quite good-looking, in a male sort of way. Although he isn't tall. Everyone else in Allan's family is tall, even his sister."

Olivia cleared her throat.

"As I was saying," Ellie said with a hint of sternness in her tone, "Calliope's mother, whose name escapes me, was considered a great beauty. She caught the eye of an extremely wealthy German businessman . . . although, according to my mother-in-law, theirs was truly a love match. Calliope was their only child. They adored and pampered her. Calliope wasn't a beauty like her mother. You see, she looked like her father."

Ellie paused a moment to let that sink in. "All was well until Calliope was nine years old, when her adoring parents died in a small plane crash. Calliope was left alone with piles of money, all of it tied up until she turned eighteen. Someone had to raise her, but none of her relatives really wanted her, only because they couldn't get their hands on her money. Young Calliope was passed around until she finally reached eighteen and inherited her fortune. Since then she has lived a nomadic life, much like her childhood. She often stayed with ac-quaintances, and she does, as you put it, mooch. Her hosts must have known she was wealthy and hoped she would eventually reward them for their hospitality. So very sad."

"I don't know, Mom. It seems to me Calliope might have had lots of friends if she'd paid her own way. She could have bought a villa of her own and provided hospitality to others. She made choices that drove people away."

Ellie was silent for so long that Olivia wondered if they'd been cut off. "Mom? Are you still there?"

"I'm not sure I agree with you, Livie." Ellie sounded sad. "I think about how Calliope grew up after their parents died. Being passed among resentful relatives must have felt awful, as if she would never again be loved for herself. Maybe that's all she wants. Maybe mooching is her way of testing people to see if they accepted her presence only in hopes of being paid. I suspect I've already failed that test, which is why she's so eager to leave our home."

"No, Mom, never. Besides, even if Calliope is purposely testing people, how were you to know? I mean, let's face it, she can be a pain in the —"

"Oops, I only have two minutes to get to yoga. But don't hang up, Livie, I can sprint and talk at the same time. I still haven't told you the real reason I called." Ellie's voice began to fade in and out, so Olivia assumed she was jogging. "It's about Greta Oskarson. What did Cody say when you told him about the letters you and Maddie took from Greta's house?"

"Um, well . . ."

"Oh, Livie, was he really angry?"

"Not exactly." Olivia slid off the desk and began to pace. "We haven't quite gotten around to telling him about the letters." Olivia heard a moan across the phone connection. "Does it really matter at this point? Cody hasn't tried to contact me. We've been speaking with Mr. Willard, and he hasn't heard any rumors that Greta was murdered, so I assume —"

"Well, you and Mr. Willard assume wrong."

From her mother's agitated tone, Olivia decided silence might be the wisest choice.

"Livie, I am standing at the door to the yoga studio, and I really, really need yoga, so I'll say this quickly. I wish you had told Cody earlier about Greta's letters. It would have looked so much better. You see, I have a good friend who volunteers at Chatterley Heights Hospital. I ran into her during my morning jog. She told me that Cody decided to check with the Howard County crime lab about whether Greta should be autopsied, and they urged him to transport her body to them immediately. They performed the autopsy last night."

Uh-oh.

"Apparently, it's complicated, but there's a chance Greta did not die from natural causes," Ellie said. "That's all I know except my friend said something about the police searching Greta's house. She didn't know if they'd already conducted the search, or if they were planning to do so."

Maddie's and my fingerprints are all over Greta's house. "Okay, Mom. Thanks for telling me. And don't worry. My attorney happens to be in the next room, chatting with Maddie."

"Ah, dear Mr. Willard," Ellie said. "At least you are in capable hands."

"We'll be fine, Mom. Only just to be on the safe side, you might want to double up on those yoga sessions."

"Exactly what I was thinking, dear."

CHAPTER FIFTEEN

The Gingerbread House would reopen in one day, and Olivia felt more than ready. The store, on the other hand, looked as if a gang of sugar-crazed children had used it as a playground. There was serious cleaning up to be done.

Olivia stood in the middle of the cookbook nook, envisioning a new display design, when she heard the front doorbell ring. Since most of their customers knew the store was closed on Mondays, Olivia considered ignoring the bell and staying where she was. She began to sort through her latest shipment of cookbooks, which she had deposited on a side table. As Olivia scooped up an armful of books, the doorbell rang again. Maybe it was her mother. It wasn't Maddie. Lemon-scented air had begun to drift into the cookbook nook, which meant Maddie was busy baking in the kitchen.

Olivia unlocked and opened the front

door, half expecting her mother to tap-dance past her into the foyer. To her surprise, the visitor was the young blonde with the exotic first name — Desirée. She was dressed for the heat in khaki shorts that showcased her long, shapely legs. A tight, pale-blue tank top molded itself to her slender, yet curvy, upper torso.

"Hello, welcome to The Gingerbread House," Olivia said. "The store is closed today, but you are welcome to come in for a visit, if you wish. Let me find a place for these cookbooks, and I'll show you around." She deposited her load on an empty display table near the cookbook nook entrance and hurried back to the main floor, eager for a chat with the young woman who had looked so familiar to Greta Oskarson. Olivia found Desirée gazing through the glass doors of the locked cabinet, where they displayed the more valuable vintage and antique cookie cutters. Desirée was so engrossed in her examination of the cabinet's contents that she started at the sound of Olivia's shoes on the tile floor.

"Oh, sorry," Desirée said with a light laugh. "I'm just so fascinated by these old cookie cutters that I go off into a dream world, you know?" She offered her hand to shake. "I'm Desirée Kirkwood, by the way. I attended your cookie event last Saturday, but you probably wouldn't have noticed me."

As Olivia shook the slender, perfectly tanned hand and gazed into her violet eyes, she thought how hard it would be not to notice Desirée.

Desirée turned back to the cookie cutters and said, "This display makes me think of my mother and my grandmother. During the holidays, I used to sit on a stool in the kitchen and watch the two of them make gingerbread cookies. They didn't have really old cookie cutters, like, you know, antiques or whatever. I think my grandmother used to have some old ones, but they were long gone by the time I came along. After that, I think she collected box tops or something and sent away for some cheap ones. I think those cookie cutters were too flimsy to make it all the way to antique, you know?" Desirée's sneering tone implied that inexpensive plastic or box-top cookie cutters were invariably worthless, though Olivia knew that cutter collectors searched long and hard for that elusive 1970s-era plastic cutter of Snoopy sitting on a pumpkin.

With a shrug, Desirée said, "The cookie cutters didn't really matter to me, you know? At that age, I just cared about the cookies. I mean what kid doesn't?"

"I know what you mean," Olivia said. "I was grown up before I became fascinated by the history and stories behind vintage and antique cutters."

"Yeah." Desirée nodded her head so vigorously that a curtain of long blond hair escaped from behind her ear and fell across her right eye. She swept it back with her index finger. Up close, Desirée looked older than she had during the store event. Olivia guessed her to be in her mid-thirties, despite her teenager-like manner of speaking. She was almost certainly a natural blonde. Olivia noted the roots, which ranged in color from pale to golden yellow, with some light brown mixed in. Those subtle variations in shading would be tough to create and maintain with dye.

"Say, I heard at your open house about some super-old cookie cutters that old lady collected." Desirée clasped her hands together like an overexcited child. "You're the one who's supposed to be selling them off, right? Boy, would I ever love to see those. Are you going to, like, put them out on display or whatever?"

Increasingly, Olivia had the sense that Desirée was putting on an act. But why? Olivia had ceased to be charmed, but she pasted a smile onto her face and played along. "We haven't yet decided how to handle the situation," Olivia said. "The owner's death has complicated matters. I believe the police are looking for her heirs." Olivia had no idea if the police had even thought of searching for Greta's heirs, or if there were any, but it was a good excuse for delaying the sale of her collection.

"Oh, of course, it's so sad." Desirée tilted her head and put on a mournful expression. "I saw her at your party, but I didn't get to talk to her. Between you and me, she looked kind of old and tired. Maybe she sort of slipped away in her sleep?"

Olivia responded to Desirée's probing question with a light shrug and a sad smile. Desirée's expression shifted to neutral. She glanced at her watch, and said, "Well, if you do decide to show those antique cookie cutters, I'd really like to know about it. I'll stop in again."

"Do you live in the area?" Olivia asked. "I could put you on our email list."

Desirée's violet gaze darted sideways. "I'll be around town for a while," she said. "I like to come to Chatterley Heights now and then to shop at Lady Chatterley's, you know? I just love their clothes."

Lady Chatterley's Clothing Boutique for

Elegant Ladies was a popular destination for women of the wealthy variety. Olivia hadn't pegged Desirée as a member of that elite shopping demographic, but she certainly had the figure to pull off even the slinkiest of Lady Chatterley's silk gowns. Olivia could picture Desirée at one of the many balls Greta had attended. Perhaps there was a reason Desirée had looked familiar to Greta.

Maddie poked her head around the kitchen door. When she saw Desirée, she hesitated. Olivia sent the message, with a slight tilt of her head, that she wanted Maddie to join the conversation. Maddie nodded. She retreated into the kitchen and reappeared almost at once, carrying a plate of wildly decorated, daisy-shaped cookies.

"Hi," Maddie said as she offered Desirée a cookie. "I didn't get a chance to talk with you at the event on Saturday. I wanted to tell you how much I coveted that gorgeous outfit you were wearing. Although you looked much better in it than I would."

Desirée waved a dismissive hand. "Naw, you'd look terrific in that dress. I'm too scrawny, or that's what my mother always used to tell me. You'd fill it out better."

"That's one way of putting it." Maddie put the plate of cookies on a nearby display table, within reach.

"Maddie is my business partner, and she's also the baking genius," Olivia said. "Maddie, this is Desirée Kirkwood. She has been asking about Greta's cookie cutter collection."

"Cool," Maddie said. "Do you live nearby?"

Desirée shrugged. "I move around a lot for my job. I was in the area, so I crashed your event on Saturday. Fabulous cookies! Do you ever make cookies with really old cookie cutters . . . you know, like super-antique ones?"

If Maddie was caught off guard by the question, she hid it well. "My cutters do start to look like antiques from constant use, but no, I don't use the really old ones. They can be fragile."

"Yeah, they're probably too valuable to risk breaking them or something, right?" When Maddie didn't answer, Desirée added, "Well, anyway, these cookies are great, and I loved all those interesting foreign ones you served on Saturday."

"I hope you had a good time," Maddie said. "You seemed to be getting along well with Olaf Jakobson."

Desirée snorted in derision. "That arrogant old jerk? I can spot his type a mile off. Thinks he can casually mention how rich he is, and women will throw themselves at him. Guys like him get really riled when a woman turns them down, so I played nice and made myself scarce." Once again, Desirée checked her watch. "Well, I'd better let you get back to work. I'll stop by again, before I leave town, to see if you're going to sell that collection. It might be fun to find a cookie cutter or two that remind me of my mom and grandma, you know?" Desirée glanced back at the antiques cabinet. Her shrug implied the contents weren't all that important to her. She spun around and headed toward the front door before Olivia could renew her offer to add Desirée's name to the store's mailing list.

In silence, Olivia and Maddie watched through the large front window until they saw Desirée walking across the Gingerbread House porch. As Desirée bounced down the front steps, Maddie said, "That was an interesting little interlude. I wonder what she really wanted."

"I could hazard a guess," Olivia said. "To start with, I suspect she is a lot smarter than she wants to appear. She was really pouring on the young dumb blond stuff."

"Didn't your mom think Desirée is about our age?" Maddie asked. "She sure doesn't act like it. Did you notice how she slipped out of character now and then?"

Olivia nodded. "Before you came out of the kitchen, Desirée was pumping me for information about Greta's collection. I'm wondering if she has some personal interest in it. Or maybe she is a collector pretending to be ignorant."

Maddie shook her head. "I could see Desirée's face when she took that last look at the cookie cutters in our cabinet. I think her interest is personal. For just a split second, she looked like she was going to cry."

Olivia pushed the "start" button for the dishwasher and began to fill the kitchen sink for the few items that required hand washing. "Need any help decorating those cookies?" she asked Maddie, who was sliding a pan of cutout cookies into the oven.

"I'm mostly just baking now." Maddie set the timer and began to gather up the cooled cookies, which she packed carefully in two covered cake pans. As she stowed the second pan in the freezer, she said, "We have plenty of decorated cookies to last us a while, even if we suddenly have busloads of customers. The ones I'm freezing should supply us for the rest of the week. We can decorate those when we need them. So now we should add some serious computer research to our agenda, or we'll never figure out who helped Greta Oskarson to her grave. I realize the actual cause of Greta's death is confusing, but I think someone got the process started. I want to find that someone."

"As do I." Olivia sank onto a kitchen chair. "I feel bad about Cody, though. I like him, and I know Del thinks he has what it takes to become a good sheriff, but he needs to make quicker decisions. As you said, it's a confusing case, and I suspect Cody is trying too hard to do everything right."

"I have an idea," Maddie said. "What if we figure out who is responsible for setting Greta's demise in motion, and then we somehow hand the pertinent information over to Cody? Was that applause I heard?"

"Actually, the timer for the oven just dinged," Olivia said.

"Close enough." Maddie grabbed an oven pad and rescued the cookies before they browned too much.

"I'm not sure how we would accomplish your plan, but I like the thought." Olivia opened the lid of her laptop. "I'll fire up the computer."

"Goodie!" Maddie clapped her hands. "It's about time." But before the screen had finished waking up, a raucous buzzing sound in the kitchen signaled that someone was leaning on the front doorbell. "What wretched timing," Maddie said when the irritating noise finally stopped. "Well, maybe it's your mom. We can bring her back here to help."

"I'll check." Before Olivia had reached the kitchen door, the buzzer went off again. It occurred to her that her mother would never press the front doorbell with such indelicate force. Olivia was glad she had left Spunky snoozing upstairs in her apartment; she had a feeling their visitor was the sort who might send Spunky into a protective yapping fit. Calliope Zimmermann came to mind. A second later, Olivia knew she had wronged Calliope. She saw the impatient visitor's figure through the large front window that provided a view of the store's front porch. Olivia pretended she hadn't seen Olaf Jakobson's face glaring in at her, but she knew he had seen her, so she had no choice. She had to answer the door.

"Most businesses are open on Mondays," Olaf said. "Most businesses know they need to keep their customers happy."

Olivia ignored his snide tone. With a faint smile, she said, "May I help you, Mr. Jakobson?"

"I'm here to buy a cookie cutter," Olaf said. "Money is no object."

Olivia tightened her lips to keep from laughing. "Cookie cutters tend to be affordable for most people." She could tell that Olaf wasn't planning to give up and leave, so she stepped aside to let him enter the foyer. Olaf was a tall man, on the husky side. Olivia had to move quickly to avoid being knocked backward as he pushed past her into The Gingerbread House.

"That isn't the type of cookie cutter I have in mind." Olaf planted himself in the middle of the sales floor with his back to Olivia. "I want the kind of cookie cutter that isn't affordable for most people, and I'll need it at once, gift wrapped. Show me what you've got. Better yet, just pick an expensive one and wrap it right away." When Olivia didn't rush to do his bidding, Olaf turned around and scowled at her. "I'm in a hurry, and I'm not accustomed to waiting."

Olivia allowed herself an inward sigh as she closed the store's door behind her. "Mr. Jakobson, I really don't know what you have in mind. Even our most valuable antique cookie cutters aren't terribly expensive." She pointed toward the locked cabinet where their vintage cutters, and a few antique ones, were on display.

Olaf tossed a disdainful glance toward the antique mahogany cabinet with glass doors. "Not those," he said. "She told me about those things, but they are nothing."

"She?"

Olaf's expression said clearly that he considered Olivia dense beyond belief. "Desirée, of course. I'm sure you noticed her here during your little cookie party. Stunning girl." Olaf's tone had softened. "She certainly stood out in *that* crowd. I am taking Desirée to dinner tonight at Bon Vivant. It's the best restaurant Chatterley Heights has to offer, but it will have to do."

Since Bon Vivant, with its fine food and extensive gardens, was a destination for folks from both DC and Baltimore, Olivia had no doubt Desirée Kirkwood would be impressed. She was certainly moving fast in her quest for valuable cookie cutters. It had only been a few hours since she had visited the store herself and described Olaf Jakobson as an arrogant jerk. Desirée had also insisted she didn't know anything about antique cutters. Olivia had to wonder what had changed since then.

"Well, I'm afraid the cutters in that cabinet are all we can offer you, Mr. Jakobson. You might want to try Anita Rambert, a local antiques dealer. If anyone might have antique cutters more valuable than ours, it would be Anita. Or you might ask Desirée what type of cutter she would like." At the very least, Olivia thought, Anita would charge him more.

"You don't get it," Olaf said. "I don't have time to dig up some flea market junk dealer, and I certainly don't have time to waste arguing with you. Desirée doesn't know I'm getting her a gift. She mentioned Greta's cookie cutters, so I want the most valuable item in Greta's collection. I know you have it in your possession, so just take one out and sell it to me. Right now. I am running out of patience."

Her mother always did breathing exercises when she was upset, so Olivia took a deep breath. Then she took another. Deep breathing, Olivia decided, was overrated. "Mr. Jakobson, Greta Oskarson's cookie cutter collection is locked in a secure storage facility, and it will stay there while her death is being investigated and any remaining family located. Those cutters are not for sale." Olivia strode toward the front of the store, opened the door, and held it for Olaf. "The store is currently closed."

Olaf's face turned dangerously red. His upper arm muscles bunched, as if he wanted to hit her. Olivia felt her hand shake, but she kept hold of the doorknob. She gave deep breathing one more try, and this time it worked, at least enough to slow her thudding heart. Olaf must have sensed Olivia's resolve, because he strode through the open door and into the foyer. Olivia stayed by the door, her hand clutching the knob. She was afraid she might fall over if she let go. When Olivia heard the front door slam behind her, she exhaled and sank to the floor.

Maddie poked her head out the kitchen door. "Livie? I thought I heard someone yelling out here, so I . . . Why are you sitting in the doorway?"

"Well," Olivia said, "it seemed like a good idea at the time."

Olivia fixed herself a cup of coffee and relaxed on a chair in the kitchen. "Whew. Olaf Jakobson's tirade wore me out. It's only ten o'clock Monday morning, but I feel as if I've lived through a full week since I returned home from vacation."

"You have, in a manner of speaking," Maddie swirled pale lemon yellow icing on a daisy-shaped cookie. "First, we threw together an event for Greta. Then she woke you up in the middle of the night, gasping for breath. You called 911, raced to the emergency room, hung around with a couple of drunks, tried to wring information from Nurse Ratched about Greta's condition . . . Then I arrived — ta-da!" Maddie flung out her arms, along with a glob of yellow icing. "I decided it was time to speed things up a bit, which involved feigning a sprained ankle and charming poor Bill the ER guy into letting it slip that Greta had died. I'm not bragging, you understand, but merely stating a series of facts." Maddie bowed her head modestly, as befit a heroine. "Of course, there was more, but I won't summarize since I played a lesser role."

"Uh-huh," Olivia said. "I do remember that I've spent very little time actually asleep since Greta called me. And I especially remember the part where we sneaked into poor Greta's house, went through her belongings, and made off with her correspondence, which we spent yesterday perusing. I'm not sure that was my brightest idea ever, given Greta's natural death has morphed into possible murder. Thank goodness Mr. Willard reassured us that the police would expect our fingerprints to be in Greta's house, since she had asked me to handle the sale of her cutter collection."

"Never mind that Sunday morning was the first time we had ever actually been in

Greta's house," Maddie said. "That little fact will probably emerge eventually, but let's not dwell on it. Mr. Willard isn't a criminal attorney, as he so often tells us. Can the police make him tell if he knows if and why we searched Greta's house after her death? I don't get how that works, exactly."

"I don't think so, but I don't really know." Olivia yawned as she stretched her arms toward the ceiling. "Anyway, Mr. Willard knows lots of cutthroat criminal attorneys, should we need one."

Maddie mixed a hint of red into purple royal icing before transferring it to a pastry bag. "I'll bet Mr. Willard would be feeling less nervous if Del were handling the case, and so would I. Del would be furious with us, of course, but he wouldn't turn us in to the authorities."

"Maybe not immediately, anyway," Olivia said. "Pass me a cookie, would you? I'm starving." Maddie handed her a pink daisy with a red center. Olivia bit into it at once.

"Don't bother to admire the artistry, Livie, not on my account."

"Sorry," Olivia said with a grimace. "Interrupted sleep makes me hungry. You know how much I love your cookies, Maddie. Anyway, I plead distraction. I was thinking

288

about that third letter Clarisse wrote to Greta. . . . You know, the angry one. I'd love to know what Clarisse found out about Greta that was so awful. I was really hoping Clarisse had confided in Mr. Willard, but no such luck." Olivia noticed the open laptop on the kitchen desk. "No wonder you weren't listening in on my little contretemps with Olaf out on the sales floor."

"You're slipping into French again, Livie."

"Was not."

"Were too."

"Maddie, I promise, 'contretemps' is used as an English word, too. Look it up."

"I am." Maddie's fingers sped around the computer keyboard. "Oh. Well, how was I supposed to know that?"

Olivia chuckled. "Maddie, friend of my childhood, you are the best darn web surfer I've ever known. I am a mere web plodder who can speak French. Also, you are better coordinated than I am."

"True, that." Maddie closed the laptop lid and sat next to Olivia. "I have to admit, though, I mostly struck out searching for relevant information about Greta, Olaf, Desirée, and anybody else I could think of who might be connected with Greta's death."

"Really?" Olivia took their empty cups to the counter and filled them with Mr. Coffee's remaining brew. "You mean even Olaf, with his gigantic ego, doesn't have an online presence?"

"Oh, Olaf is featured online all right, and he is *so* photoshopped. I suspect he has a full-time image fixer, some first-rate hacker who quickly wipes out anything uncomplimentary as soon as it appears."

"Okay, then, what about Desirée?" Olivia asked. "She is young, beautiful, and a classy dresser. She has the money to hang out in Chatterley Heights solely to buy expensive outfits from Lady Chatterley's Clothing Boutique for Elegant Ladies."

"I did find Desirée Kirkwood online, mostly decorating the arm of powerful men inside the beltway." Maddie began to pack the remaining lemon cutouts, fully cooled, in a covered cake pan. "I wouldn't be surprised if Desirée is somebody's mistress, but I found nothing to confirm that. Her address is in a tony neighborhood, so she either inherited money or has a fabulous job . . . or again, there's the mistress thing. Desirée doesn't do Facebook or any of the other favorite social network sites. Contrary to popular opinion, not everyone feels compelled to tell all on the Internet." Maddie tried to wedge the last cookie-filled cake pan into their well-stuffed freezer. "I didn't check to see if Desirée had a criminal record. That costs money, which I draw the line at spending unless it's on fun."

"Are you sure Desirée isn't a fashion model, past or present?" Olivia asked.

"Positive," Maddie said. "Her photo would be everywhere, even if she hadn't modeled in a while. There are some really obsessed guys out there. Scary." Maddie gave up on the freezer and put the cake pan in the refrigerator.

"What about Greta?" Olivia asked. "She was well known in European social circles."

"Aside from the interest in her first husband's death, society news is all I could find," Maddie said with a sigh. "And not much of that. After her last husband died, Greta seemed to disappear, more or less. The Internet doesn't function like a history book; it doesn't go back and fill in all the blanks from years before its own existence. Someone has to care enough to find the missing data and post it on some website, or maybe start a website dedicated to a relevant subject, such as 'Society Balls in the Last Millennium.' Greta wasn't exactly posting cruise photos on Facebook."

"Well, I guess we'll have to find other sources," Olivia said.

"Like what?" Maddie capped her pastry

bag and hoisted herself up onto the kitchen counter. "What's left?"

"It's a long shot, but Bertha might know what Clarisse was referring to in her letter, when she said she knew what Greta had done. Bertha worked for the Chamberlain family forever, and I know Clarisse often confided in her." Olivia checked the clock. "Bertha did offer to help us get the store ready to reopen tomorrow morning. We could call and see if she's still free."

"Except we don't need any help," Maddie said. "I've finished many batches of cookies, so we are good to go for the whole week."

Olivia shrugged. "I think I'll call her in to work anyway. She might have to cancel other plans for her day, so I'll definitely pay her. It would be worth every penny."

As she swung her legs back and forth from her countertop perch, Maddie said, "Remember, Bertha has been known to gossip a bit. She's the one who told us about Greta's affair with Martin Chamberlain. What if she lets something slip about Clarisse's letter?" Maddie fiddled with her emerald and diamond engagement ring and her brand-new wedding band. "Granted, I can get a kick out of being the subject of gossip. On the other hand, I'm not thrilled by the thought of being arrested so soon after my nuptials. Maybe in a month or two . . ."

Olivia laughed, and said, "I'll take the rap, if it comes to that. I'll say I duped you when you were exhausted from lack of sleep."

"Yeah, like anyone will believe that."

"Anyway," Olivia said, "I think we can trust Bertha. She kept the secret of Martin's affair with Greta until long after both Martin and Clarisse had died. I'd say Bertha is a pretty restrained gossip, especially since she started seeing Chatterley Heights' only attorney."

Maddie shrugged. "At this point, I'm willing to try anything or anyone, even if it means executing another illegal search. My curiosity has overtaken my fear of incarceration."

CHAPTER SIXTEEN

"I'm so glad you called me in to work, Livie," Bertha said as she mopped her forehead with a paper towel from the kitchen dispenser. "The air-conditioning in my little house simply isn't up to this heat, and I sure didn't cool down on the walk over here. Poor Mr. Willard is buried in research for a client he'll be meeting with later today so we can't go to an afternoon movie like we'd planned." Bertha smiled as she examined the kitchen table. "Are all these cookies for the reopening tomorrow? My, they look lovely. I noticed new displays out on the sales floor, too. What's left for me to do?"

Olivia exchanged a quick glance with Maddie. "Well, first we wanted to chat with you. It's about Greta Oskarson." Olivia hesitated, trying to come up with the right approach.

Bertha's round face puckered, as if she

felt uneasy. "I really didn't know Greta well," she said. "She and Clarisse were friends, for a time. After what happened between Greta and Martin, well . . . I probably shouldn't have told you two about that unfortunate episode."

"Don't worry about that," Olivia said. "The more we hear about her, the more certain we are that Greta harmed a number of people here in Chatterley Heights."

"And now Greta has been murdered." Bertha sounded less than heartbroken. "It just goes to show you, doesn't it? At least I know my dear Clarisse can't be accused of anything, bless her soul. Mind you, there was a time when she was mad enough to have murdered that woman. I wouldn't have blamed her, either." Bertha sighed. "But she wasn't like that. Forgive and move on, that was my Clarisse. Martin was truly contrite about the affair, I'm sure of that. He followed Clarisse around like a puppy. He could hardly stand to see how much he'd hurt her. Honestly, I don't think he understood how or why he ever got involved with Greta. I mean, she was beautiful and cultured and all that, but he'd met scores of beautiful, talented women, and he'd never showed much interest in anything but his businesses."

Olivia relaxed and listened. Now that Bertha had put aside her qualms, she seemed eager to share her memories. Maddie quietly left her own chair, retrieved a pitcher of lemonade from the refrigerator, and filled three glasses. She selected six decorated cookies and arranged them on a plate. Before delivering the treats to the kitchen table, Maddie winked at Olivia over Bertha's head.

"Clarisse threw herself into her work for several months," Bertha said. "I was worried at first, but then I saw she was getting better, more cheerful. Martin paid more attention to her than he ever had, even before the boys were born. Good thing, too. Clarisse was strong-minded; she wasn't about to put up with any more shenanigans." Bertha picked up a pink daisy, trimmed with red, and took a bite without her usual gushing admiration of the cookie's beauty. "Clarisse was a true lady. Would you believe she actually forgave Greta?"

"Really?" Maddie's expressive eyes widened. Olivia held her breath, hoping Maddie hadn't overdone the surprise act.

"God's honest truth," Bertha said. "I know because Clarisse started writing to Greta again, like she used to before she found out about the affair."

Olivia decided it was too risky to ask leading questions about Clarisse's letters to Greta. Maddie was right; if Bertha suspected they had the letters in their possession, she might not be able to keep it to herself. Maybe there was a less direct approach. "How did Clarisse find out about the affair in the first place?"

"Well, now that you ask, that's why I was so surprised when Clarisse forgave Greta." Bertha appeared to sink into her thoughts as she nibbled her cookie.

Maddie looked dangerously close to shaking Bertha to make her elaborate on her comment. Olivia shot Maddie a warning glance. After several seconds had passed, Olivia said, "I'm not sure I could forgive a woman who'd had an affair with my husband, especially if he'd never betrayed me before she came along. I mean, I'd be furious with him, of course, but if he'd never strayed before, I might figure the woman led him on."

"Oh, Martin had never cheated on Clarisse before Greta, or after her, either. I'm certain of that. It was Greta who pursued Martin, not the other way around. And it was really more of a brief fling. I know because Clarisse told me." Despite the air-conditioning, Bertha's cheeks had reddened. She brushed a lock of gray hair off her forehead before taking a long drink of lemonade.

Bertha had been like a mother to Clarisse. Olivia was having second thoughts about forcing her to revisit such an upsetting episode. If Bertha showed any further signs of distress, Olivia would stop questioning her. Meanwhile . . . "Clarisse was an amazing woman," Olivia said. "I can't imagine forgiving Greta if she'd initiated an affair with my husband. How did Clarisse find out about it? Did Martin feel so guilty that he confessed?"

"Oh my, no. Not at first, anyway. Martin broke off the affair and tried to keep the whole episode hush-hush. Then some time later, Clarisse became very concerned about you, Livie. I'm not sure why, exactly. All I know is, after Martin's death, Clarisse told me to keep an eye on you and let her know if I felt someone might be trying to take advantage of you. She didn't explain what she meant. That was before I worked here, of course, but Clarisse knew I loved to visit The Gingerbread House. She mentioned the name Greta Oskarson, but I think Clarisse was using her as an example."

To give herself a few moments to think, Olivia left her chair and walked over to the refrigerator, where she pretended to search for something in the freezer. Carrying the pitcher of lemonade, Maddie joined her. "Clarisse's third letter," Maddie whispered. Olivia nodded. Maddie reached into the freezer for a tray of ice cubes. She twisted the flexible tray to loosen the cubes before adding a few to the pitcher of lemonade.

When Olivia and Maddie returned to the kitchen table, they found Bertha lost in thought. Unpleasant memories, Olivia guessed from Bertha's tight frown. "I'm confused about one point, Bertha," Olivia said. "If Clarisse didn't ask you to look after me until after Martin's death, what triggered her concern?"

"Oh my," Bertha said. "I hadn't thought about that. I don't know exactly why Clarisse got so worried about you, but . . . well, all I do know is it happened sort of suddenly."

"Suddenly? Why do you say that?" Maddie asked.

"Well, let me think now." Bertha sipped her lemonade. "You know, I don't remember anything out of the ordinary happening that day, except . . . Well, there was a phone call, but now I think on it, that came before lunch, and it was just about business." Bertha lapsed into silence.

Never a patient woman, Maddie drummed her fingers on the table. Olivia shot her a warning glance, which silenced the tapping. Maddie grabbed a fuchsia, tulip-shaped cookie and bit off the violet petal tips, one by one.

"Clarisse mostly worked at home in those days," Bertha said. "After Martin died, she wasn't feeling up to being on the road much. You know, visiting her businesses, chatting with everyone . . . When Clarisse was feeling sad about Martin, work could distract her, but she needed the quiet of home to help her concentrate. So I'd fix her lots of strong coffee, and she'd go into her office and close the door."

Olivia had assumed that Clarisse's workload was the only reason she would seem, at times, to withdraw into herself and stay home to work. Maddie popped the last bite of the tulip cookie into her mouth and reached for a two-toned yellow, rose-shaped cookie. Olivia took pity on her impatient friend and tried to speed up the questioning. "Bertha, try to think back. What happened right before Clarisse became upset and warned you that someone might somehow take advantage of me? Did Clarisse get a phone call that afternoon? Or perhaps she received a letter that seemed to change her mood?"

"Now, let me think." Bertha closed her eyes for a moment. "Not another phone call, I'm certain of that. I remember because we still had just the one landline in the house. During our lunch together in the kitchen, Clarisse asked me to answer the phone if it rang. She was planning to go over some important papers and didn't want to be interrupted. But the phone didn't ring all afternoon." Bertha swept a few strands of fine, gray hair off her forehead. "I'm sorry," she said. "I don't seem to be helping much."

"Have a cookie," Maddie said. "It's a proven fact that decorated cutout cookies stimulate the brain." She shifted the plate closer to Bertha.

"Oh, you . . ." Bertha said with a girlish giggle. "I shouldn't, not with a few pounds still to lose, but perhaps just one more." She selected a pansy with grape and lilac petals. "This shouldn't do too much damage. It's so little. And so pretty." Bertha took a dainty bite and closed her eyes as she chewed. "Heavenly," she said.

"You're doing a great job, Bertha," Olivia said. "Do you remember if Clarisse received a letter or a package that day?"

Bertha's eyes popped open. "The mail . . . The post arrived as we were finishing lunch in the kitchen," she said. "Clarisse was heading back to her office when the doorbell rang, so she answered it. The mailman gave her a special delivery letter or a package — I didn't see it, so I can't say exactly — and then she went straight to her office. She took the mail with her." Bertha's eyes moved as if she were watching Clarisse walk away. Olivia and Maddie sat motionless, trying not to distract her. Bertha suddenly straightened in her chair. "Oh, and I just remembered . . . When the doorbell rang, Clarisse forgot to take along her coffeepot. After lunch, I always gave her a fresh pot of coffee to take with her to her office. Anyway, I was washing up and didn't notice the pot for ten minutes or so. I dried my hands" — Bertha wrung her hands as if she were drying them — "and I brought the pot to her office myself. I just knocked quick and went in. Clarisse was sitting at her desk, holding a sheet of stationery. Only she wasn't reading it. She was staring at the fireplace, which was odd because it was a hot day."

Maddie snapped to attention. "Ooh, I'll bet Clarisse was thinking about burning the letter to hide the evidence from her sons."

"Down, girl," Olivia said. "Bertha, did you

notice anything about the letter? What color was it? Was it typed or handwritten?"

"The paper was white, I think, with a deckle edge. I think deckle edges look so classy, don't you? I also remember there was an opened envelope on the desk, next to Clarisse's elbow. I never saw the letter or that envelope again."

"Maybe Clarisse *did* burn it," Maddie insisted. "Bertha, do you remember if she started a fire that day?"

Bertha laughed. "Goodness me, I surely would have noticed that! The fireplace was always closed off during the summer to keep the heat from coming inside through the flue. Clarisse knew better than to start a fire; she'd have filled the house with smoke. Anyway, she had a paper shredder right there beside her desk, so that's what she would have used."

"Prosaic," Maddie said, "but effective. I don't suppose you heard the shredder?"

"I wouldn't have paid attention, Maddie. I emptied that shredder every day, sometimes twice. I swear, Clarisse shredded everything, as long as it wasn't important for taxes or such. She hated clutter."

"She did indeed hate clutter," Olivia said, remembering Clarisse's nearly paper-free desktop. "I think we can safely assume she would quickly have hidden or shredded anything she felt was too private."

As Olivia stood up to stretch, Maddie began to clear the table. In a tentative voice, Bertha said, "I don't like to take pay when I haven't done any work. It doesn't feel right. Shouldn't I be out in the store cleaning or stocking the shelves or . . . ?"

Olivia patted Bertha's soft shoulder. "There really isn't much to be done that can't be fit into the workday tomorrow. Are you meeting Mr. Willard for lunch?"

Bertha sighed unhappily. "Poor Willard is so busy right now, and I do hate sitting at home with nothing productive to do. Livie, when was the last time the store got a thorough dusting from top to bottom?"

"Um, never?"

"Well then, now is the perfect time. I just love cleaning a room until there isn't a single speck of dirt or dust anywhere." Bertha clasped her strong hands together as if nothing could possibly excite her more than the thought of deep cleaning. "Mr. Willard won't let me dust his office. It hurts me to walk in there without a dustrag in my hand."

"I'm not sure we have any dustrags," Olivia said.

"I don't even know what a dustrag looks

like," Maddie said.

"Oh, you two. Just give me an old towel, and I'll do the rest. I am so looking forward to making the store shine! Not that I don't love working with customers, you understand, but there's no satisfaction greater than cleaning a whole room to perfection."

"If you say so." Maddie dug through the clean kitchen towels until she found one with a frayed hem. "Don't you need a bucket or something?"

"Goodness, no. I don't want to get everything wet. I'll use that spray in the little storage closet. It picks up dust and dirt so they don't just settle back down on a surface. And it leaves such a nice shine."

"Spray?" Maddie asked. "I don't remember a spray can in the storage closet."

"Really? I put it in there long ago, so you could use it if you wanted to do some cleaning. My goodness, didn't you girls even notice it?" Bertha looked genuinely distressed by the thought.

"I guess we're usually in a hurry when we're restocking the shelves," Olivia said.

"Oh, not that storage closet," Bertha said. "I meant the little one out on the sales floor. Although I guess it's too small to be called a closet. You know, it's behind the table where we serve the coffee and cookies every day. Such a convenience. When I need to spot clean a shelf, I just take a napkin from the coffee table, and then I reach inside the cabinet for the spray."

"That little hole in the wall? It isn't even big enough to hold supplies for the coffee," Maddie said.

The three women trooped out onto the sales floor, where Olivia and Maddie moved aside the table that usually held cookies and the coffee urn. The "closet," as Bertha had called it, was actually a small, shallow cabinet built into the knee wall that supported the long, deep shelf Olivia had commissioned when she'd turned the ground floor into The Gingerbread House. The coffee and treats table usually hid the little enclosure. Maddie reached under the table and opened the door. Inside, the space resembled a medicine cabinet. "Well, I'll be," Maddie said. "There really is a spray can in here. Who knew?" She removed the can and handed it to Bertha.

"What's this?" Olivia asked as she reached into the cabinet.

"Oh, I forgot all about that," Bertha said. "I left a pen and a little notebook in there, in case I needed to remind myself that we were running low on coffee or paper napkins. I never think to write in it, but we might as well leave it. Maybe now I'll remember it's there."

Olivia retrieved the notebook and pen from the cabinet. As Maddie watched, Olivia opened the notebook and found the first page ripped across the middle. The top half of the sheet was missing. "I think I'll keep these, if you don't mind," Olivia said.

"Of course," Bertha said. "The pen is probably dry by now, though. It's just an old ballpoint I got for free." She held her beloved can of cleaning solution against her chest, and said, "I can't wait to get started on this room."

Maddie threw her arm around Bertha's broad shoulders and guided her away from the coffee table. "And I, for one, can't wait to see the results. For all we know, these shelves are an entirely different color under those layers of grimy dust. If you need us, we'll be in the kitchen."

Bertha didn't answer. She was already dusting display items one by one as she cleared them off the shelf. While Bertha hummed cheerfully, Olivia and Maddie headed toward the kitchen.

As soon as Maddie closed the kitchen door behind them, Olivia reached for the antique spice rack that hid the store's wall safe. She lifted the rack off the wall and handed it to Maddie. Olivia's hand shook with excitement as she worked the combination and opened the heavy door of the safe. She reached inside to remove the small scrap of paper she and Maddie had found in Greta's bedroom dresser drawer.

Maddie nestled the spice rack on the table before picking up the pen and notebook Olivia had taken from the small cabinet behind the treats table. "It sure looks like the same type of paper to me," Maddie whispered as she opened the notebook to the first page and placed it flat on the kitchen counter, centered under a light.

Olivia smoothed open the folded fragment of paper that had been wedged into the seam of one of Greta's bureau drawers. When Olivia laid the torn edge of the paper against the notebook's torn first page, they matched perfectly.

Maddie picked up the pen she'd brought in from the storage cabinet and tried to write on a page in the notebook. She compared the result with the scratchy letters at the bottom of the mysterious note. "Another match," Maddie said. "I wonder how Greta found this notebook and pen. Maybe she'd been searching the sales floor for something to write on while Bertha stuffed her cookie cutters into our wall safe. That's a creepy thought."

"It might explain how the sparkling sugars got rearranged," Olivia said. "Greta must have been in a hurry." Pointing to the note, Olivia said, "Part of this note looks sort of like a grocery list, although I can't make out the words. It's written with a different pen."

"I'm confused," Maddie said. "What does this mean? If Greta was so frantic to jot down those numbers, why would she use the same paper to make an indecipherable grocery list? It's indecipherable to me, anyway, though Lucas thinks I need glasses. Then she folds the paper into a tiny lump and stuffs it into the seam of a bureau drawer. Was she mentally unhinged?"

"In some ways, maybe she was," Olivia said. "But in this instance, I'm guessing there was method in her madness. Maybe the grocery list is a cover, in case someone found the note."

"But why? Why would Greta go to all this trouble for some scratchy numbers that don't mean anything?"

Olivia stared at those scratchy numbers. "I think they do mean something. I think Greta was writing down the combination for our safe."

"Well, then she got it wrong. Look at this."

Maddie slapped her index finger underneath the first number. "Our combination starts with a seven, and Greta wrote a four. If she had a plan to steal her own antique cutters for the insurance money and then blame us for the loss, it wasn't going to work. She had the wrong combination. Maybe that's why the cutters were still in our safe when we moved them to the secure storage facility."

"I don't think so," Olivia said. "I think the cutters remained in our safe simply because Greta didn't take them out. Why, I don't know. She did have the right combination, though. That first number is a European seven, which has an extra line through it about halfway down. This seven looks like a four because Greta was writing in a hurry with a bad pen. Even if Bertha was whispering the numbers to herself, like she usually does, Greta would probably have been watching the dial spin to make sure she didn't miss a number. That's a lot to do at one time."

Maddie flopped onto a kitchen chair. "Okay, you've convinced me, more or less. Greta stole the combination to our wall safe. But again I ask, why? If she was planning an insurance scam, why would she wait? Once we moved the whole collection to more secure storage, it was too late. We gave Greta a key to the storage vault, so she would have become a suspect."

"I don't know, Maddie." Olivia put the paper and notebook in her jeans pocket and sank onto a chair next to her best friend. "Greta was cunning. Maybe she changed her plans for some reason. Whatever she had in mind, it died with her. I hate to say this, but I can't help feeling relieved that we won't have to work with her. Greta was ruthless and diabolical, and I'm quite sure she had plans that included leaving the two of us in a dangerous spot."

CHAPTER SEVENTEEN

After a light lunch of salad and iced tea, which Maddie had volunteered to pick up from the Chatterley Café, Bertha insisted on continuing her cleaning in The Gingerbread House. Maddie and Olivia remained in the kitchen for a planning session.

"I haven't checked on Aunt Sadie today," Maddie said as she drank the last of her iced tea. "Her air-conditioning pooped out during the night, and Lucas sent someone over to fix it. It's such an old system, I'm afraid it might be unfixable."

Olivia removed the last clean item, a serving plate, from the dishwasher and wiped off any excess water before putting it away. "Maybe we should rescue Aunt Sadie," she said. "If her air conditioner is out, we could bring her here for cookies and lemonade. Besides, I have lots of questions to ask her about Greta."

"Ah, so your offer isn't entirely altruistic?"

Maddie moved out of range before Olivia could whack her with a wet kitchen towel.

Olivia slid their used lunch plates into the dishwasher's lower rack. "I prefer to think of it as a win-win," she said. "I'm almost finished here. Then we can leave Bertha to her cleaning frenzy. I left Spunky upstairs. We'll bring him along with us."

"Oh good," Maddie said. "Aunt Sadie adores Spunky, so —"

A hallelujah burst from Olivia's cell phone. "The 'Hallelujah Chorus', Maddie? Really? Why can't I have a nice, generic ringtone, like other boring cell phone users?" Olivia reached for her phone as it sang out again.

"Because that would be, as you so accurately put it, boring," Maddie said. "Who is it?"

"Del," Olivia said.

"I'm out of here." Maddie headed for the door. "But as soon as you hang up, I expect you to tell me everything that Del says."

"Scram, Maddie." Olivia waited for the kitchen door to close before cutting off the song. "Del?"

"Hi, Livie!"

"You sound chipper," Olivia said. "Has Lisa's situation been resolved?"

"Nope," Del said, "but it cheers me up to

hear your voice. What's going on at your end?"

"Um, has Cody been in contact?" Olivia didn't feel any obligation to protect Cody's reputation . . . if it needed protecting.

"He was, finally, a little while ago," Del said. "He sure took his time. I gave him a lecture for not contacting the medical examiner immediately after Greta Oskarson's death. He should have searched her house, too. By the time he got around to it, someone had gone inside. Although they might have been there right before Greta called 999 instead of 911. Who knows?"

Olivia's heart doubled its usual pace. "Why does Cody think someone might have been in Greta's house when she got sick?"

Olivia heard a snorting sound before Del said, "Very belatedly, Cody decided to test for fingerprints on the doorknobs. He'd found all the doors unlocked."

Olivia gulped hard. "Greta called me when she felt sick, you know. I told her to unlock the doors so the EMTs could get to her. Their fingerprints would be on the front door, at least. Her line went dead while I was talking to her, so I called 911 and sent an ambulance to her house."

"Cody forgot to tell me that, too. Why did Greta call you in the first place?" Del's tone sounded curious, rather than suspicious.

"She had my cell number. Maddie and I were working with her to sell her antique cookie cutter collection, remember? I'm sure I told you that." Olivia shook her head at Maddie, who poked her head into the kitchen. Maddie shrugged and withdrew.

"Oh yeah," Del said. "I remember that much, at least. Hang on a sec." A scratchy sound told Olivia that Del had his hand over his phone. "Okay, I'm back. Here's the weird thing about Greta's house," he said. "There weren't any fingerprints at all on any of the doorknobs, inside or out. Most other surfaces had been wiped clean, too. That would have taken some time."

All the fingerprints were wiped clean?

"Well, right now it's Cody's problem," Del said. "Too much going on here."

"Speaking of which, what's happening at your end?" Olivia asked.

"You wouldn't believe." Del's sigh came through clearly.

"Try me. I'm gullible."

"Sure you are, Livie. I'm beginning to wonder if I'm the gullible one. Lisa . . ." More quietly, Del said, "Well, to be blunt, I'm not sure anymore that she didn't shoot her husband on purpose. Lisa swears up and down she never knew the gun was

315

loaded, that she only intended to scare him off. She expects me to back her up."

"What are you going to do about that?"

Del chuckled. "Don't worry, Livie, I won't lie for Lisa. There's no way I can corroborate whether or not the gun was loaded. I didn't even know she had access to a gun. How could I? It's not as if we kept in touch."

Olivia was surprised by the depth of her relief. "So what can you do, besides give Lisa moral support? Are you going to investigate on your own?"

"Probably."

"You sound halfhearted," Olivia said.

"I am." Del was quiet for several seconds before adding, "I only half believe that Lisa is innocent. I have the feeling I never really knew her. She married this jerk twice, you know."

"You were the sane guy in the middle."

Del chuckled. "I was the boring guy in the middle. I made Lisa feel safe, at least for a while, and then she wanted a more exciting relationship. She dumped me, and here I am, thinking I'm supposed to rescue her."

Olivia paused to measure her words. "Del, do you *want* to rescue Lisa, or . . ."

"I've asked myself that same question, Livie. The answer is a resounding 'No!' I do not feel a driving desire to be Lisa's rescuer. If anything, I'm tired of her shenanigans. On the other hand, I don't want to see her convicted of murder if she isn't guilty. I'm in the process of finding her a better lawyer. The last one was useless."

"If I were in Lisa's shoes, I'd be grateful for any support," Olivia said.

"I'll stick around for the trial, if it comes to that." Del sounded tired. "Then I want to come home."

"You are needed here, Del," Olivia said softly. "In more ways than one. . . ."

"I was hoping you'd say that." Del cleared his throat, as if he felt nervous. "Livie, I'm worried about the situation in Chatterley Heights. It's not that I don't trust Cody; I think he's got a lot of potential. He needs more seasoning, that's all. His instincts aren't honed enough. That's partly my fault; I haven't ever let him take the lead. Besides, the Oskarson case is a tough one. The evidence is confusing. It isn't entirely clear if Greta died because someone tried to strangle her or . . . well, never mind. I could call in someone to help Cody, but I want to give him a chance to show what he can do. Livie, I shouldn't ask you this . . ."

"Ask."

"Would you keep me up-to-date on the

317

case?" Del asked. "I've checked with the medical examiner and crime scene folks — behind Cody's back, I'm afraid — but it would help if I knew what's going on in town. You know the drill: who's saying what, any history that might be helpful, that sort of thing."

"The gossip, in other words," Olivia said with a laugh. "Sounds like fun. Do you have time to hear what Maddie and I have heard so far?"

"I'm just sneaking off for a cup of coffee, so now is a good time," Del said.

"Wait, do I hear a car door closing? You're driving off while talking on your cell, aren't you? I refuse to be an enabler."

"As I keep telling you, Livie, it's — hang on a sec . . ." Del's voice disappeared for a time, though Olivia thought she heard the blare of an angry car horn. "Okay, what was I saying? Oh yeah, I'm a cop, so it's okay for me to use a cell phone while I'm driving."

"Even when it isn't an emergency?" Olivia asked.

"Something tells me you've already decided the answer to that question. Okay, I give up. I'm pulling off the highway right now." Del didn't speak for a minute or two, but Olivia heard the highway noise begin to fade. "I have no idea where I am," Del said, "except that I'm in an empty parking lot. The engine is off. Satisfied?"

"For now," Olivia said. "And of course I'll keep you informed, if you'll reciprocate by sharing some information with me, if you have any. After all, you aren't assigned to the case. Also, you're sort of asking me to keep tabs on your deputy sheriff, which is above and beyond my duty as a citizen."

"Point taken," Del said with a chuckle. "Okay, my squad car will remain at a full stop, engine turned off. I'm locked inside without a cup of coffee and a bit of time on my hands. Tell me everything you've heard about Greta and her death."

"Okay," Olivia said, "I've heard Greta might have died from an asthma attack. Maddie heard from a waitress at the Chatterley Café that Greta had been poisoned. I even heard someone speculate that she'd been frightened to death. What's up with all that?"

Del laughed, a welcome sound to Olivia. "Well, I did say that the evidence is confusing. However, it isn't unusual to hear all sorts of wild rumors after an unexplained death, especially in a small town. People have a natural tendency to fill in the blanks. I'm hearing the same stuff here about Lisa's husband's death," Del said. "However, I'll tell you what I do know about Greta's death, but you must absolutely keep it to yourself."

"You know Maddie will worm it out of me." Olivia figured she had a duty to warn Del.

"Excuse me while I sigh heavily," Del said. "Yes, I am well aware that Maddie will find out, as will the rest of Chatterley Heights and surrounding areas, but she might just as easily hear it from a hospital employee or a patient or an intern's girlfriend, or . . . You get the picture. So I'll fill you in, anyway . . . not because it's a good idea, but because this isn't my case, and I want you to be informed if you are going to be my eyes and ears. My only caveat is please, I beg of you, stay out of danger. Don't take risks, and don't confide in anyone, if you can help it. Make sure Maddie understands the dangers. Despite the fuzzy evidence, my instincts tell me there's a murderer out there."

"Heard and understood," Olivia said.

"I can't believe I'm doing this," Del said.

"Me neither."

"Okay, here's what the coroner has pieced together so far," Del said. "Technically, Greta died of a heart attack, though she did have other problems that can't have helped."

"Greta was gasping for breath when she called me," Olivia said. "She sounded as if she might be having an asthma attack."

"Right," Del said. "The rumor about poison isn't true. Greta did show signs of coronary disease, but her heart wasn't on the verge of ceasing to function, according to the medical examiner. And she did have some bruises on her neck. The ER doctor didn't think they were significant enough to have caused her death. Another ER doctor took a later look and decided the bruises might be ligature marks, though it was hard to tell."

"This is getting complicated," Olivia said. "Were they ligature marks or not?"

"Probably, but the M.E. couldn't say definitively that Greta hadn't clutched her own throat in panic, maybe because she was having trouble breathing," Del said. "The full autopsy revealed that Greta had, in fact, died of heart failure, possibly due to attempted strangulation and/or simple terror. Or not. The M.E. is leaving open the possibility that someone helped precipitate Greta's death, but so far there's no clear evidence. Also, they have no suspects."

"So is it possible that someone assaulted Greta?" Olivia asked.

"Possible," Del said, "but bear in mind that Greta lived long enough to call you, unlock her doors for the EMT guys, get transported to the hospital, and survive there for a short time."

"Oh. I see." Olivia didn't see at all, but she hoped it would become clearer soon. It crossed her mind to wonder if the attacker, if there was one, might have been outside Greta's house while she and Maddie were searching it. A shiver ran down Olivia's spine as she imagined a shadowy figure watching the house, waiting for them to leave before returning to wipe off finger-prints.

"As you can see," Del said, "the problem here is that they don't know exactly what to call Greta's death. Attempted murder? Natural causes? A combination of the two? So they are holding back information until they can figure out what they are looking at. The crime lab is going over everything as we speak."

"Del, what do your instincts tell you?"

Del sighed audibly. "I try to be suspicious of my own gut hunches, but I'm inclined to suspect that someone else was in that room with Greta when she became ill."

"For what it's worth," Olivia said, "I have the same feeling."

"Now," Del said, "tell me everything you and Maddie have been up to, because I'd lay odds you two have been investigating on your own. Which I still don't like, as you well know. It scares me."

"I know," Olivia said. "Let me make sure we are alone. Don't you dare start driving again." Olivia peeked out the kitchen door to the sales floor. Bertha was near the kitchen door, wielding her can of dust spray with enthusiasm. She would be working her way across the room, but slowly. Maddie was also near the kitchen, arranging display tables in preparation for reopening The Gingerbread House. Olivia made a quick decision to head up to her apartment for more privacy.

As soon as Olivia inserted her key in the door, she heard Spunky's happy yap from inside her apartment. He leaped into her arms before she could close the door behind her. "Okay, Spunks. Something tells me you're thinking about Milk-Bone treats, as if you don't get plenty of those from every-one else." The little Yorkie wriggled out of her grasp and raced toward the kitchen.

"You only want me for my Milk-Bones," Olivia muttered as she followed Spunky into the kitchen. She broke two treats in half and threw one piece across the kitchen floor.

Spunky skidded over the linoleum toward his reward, giving his mistress enough time to call Del again. He answered as Olivia threw another Milk-Bone half. It slid under the kitchen table, and Spunky dove after it.

"I'm in my own kitchen," Olivia said, "so I can talk freely. Spunky won't tell. He knows who has the key to the Milk-Bone treats."

"Wise lad," Del said.

"You won't like what I'm going to tell you."

"We've established that, Livie. It is what it is."

Olivia took a couple of deep breaths and plunged ahead. She told him about the cookie event she and Maddie had hosted to welcome Greta. She related verbatim, as best she could remember, the conversations she deemed potentially relevant to Greta's murder. She repeated her telephone conversation with Greta, her call to 911, and her visit to the emergency room, though she failed to mention how she and Maddie had come by their information about Greta's death. After more deep breathing, Olivia confessed that she and Maddie had searched Greta's house for anything suspicious, and finally, that they had absconded with Greta's correspondence. Del said not a word during her recital.

"One more thing," Olivia said. "There were letters from Clarisse to Greta. Del, Clarisse had found out something awful about Greta. Clarisse's letter wasn't specific, but she was furious. She ordered Greta to stay away from me."

"Interesting," Del said.

"Interesting? That's all? You mean you aren't angry with me?"

"All I said was 'interesting.' Don't push your luck." Del's tone wasn't nearly as stern as it might have been, or so Olivia told herself.

"I suppose I should give Greta's letters to Cody?" Olivia asked. "Although I doubt he'd have found them himself."

"Probably not," Del said. "If Cody had thought to search the attic, he would first have asked the crime lab to lift fingerprints. They would have found yours and Maddie's. The crime lab would have called me. They don't quite trust Cody, so they've begun running their own findings past me. I'm caught in the middle, and I hate it. I can't believe I'm saying this, but don't turn those letters over to Cody just yet. From what you've told me, he won't find clear evidence of blackmail in those letters. At this point, they would only confuse matters.

Clarisse was the only person those letters might have incriminated, and I think we can safely eliminate that possibility. Let's wait and see if the letters become relevant and not a confusing distraction. However, the instant you find anything definitive, give it to Cody. I don't agree with the M.E. that he isn't competent, and I want him to have the chance to prove himself."

"Understood," Olivia said. "Del, I'm sorry about all this. I can't even pass the blame to Maddie. Searching Greta's house was my idea," Olivia said.

"I really can't leave you on your own, can I?"

"Apparently not. However, I'm fairly set in my ways, so all you can do is accept me as I am. Or not." Olivia held her breath.

"I kind of like you the way you are," Del said. "Besides, I'm certain you have the capacity to learn from your mistakes."

"Thanks. I think." Olivia realized Spunky was at her feet, staring up at her hopefully. She hadn't thrown the last two Milk-Bone halves. As she tossed them both across the kitchen, Olivia heard Del's voice but didn't catch what he'd said.

"Sorry, Del, I was on dog-treat duty. What did you say?"

"I was saying that I have to go meet with

Lisa's attorney. I'm late already. I'll be in touch soon. Try to be safe, okay? I lo—" The rest of his sentence drowned in the roar as his engine started up.

CHAPTER EIGHTEEN

Spunky trotted happily behind Olivia as she reentered The Gingerbread House after her phone confession to Del. "You stay out here with Bertha, okay?" Spunky waved his fluffy tail and yapped. Olivia wanted to believe that he fully understood her, but she suspected he was angling for another treat.

"Oh, what fun," Bertha said. "Come sit in your chair, Spunky, while I polish the front window for you." She patted the wooden arm of the antique chair in which Spunky held court daily.

Olivia noticed that the chair's soft, embroidered seat looked, for once, free of the silky strands of hair Spunky often left behind. During her vacation, Olivia had spent extra time on his grooming regimen, but she'd slacked off since her return home. She hadn't worried about it because Spunky didn't seem to need the frequent grooming that other Yorkshire terriers required.

"Spunky's chair looks great, Bertha," Olivia said. "Thank you! I need to give the little guy a good brushing later."

"I'd be glad to brush him as soon as I've finished sprucing up the sales floor," Bertha said.

"Don't bother," Olivia said. "The grooming tools are upstairs in my apartment, and —"

"Oh, I have everything we need in my handbag." The size of Bertha's handbag was legendary in Chatterley Heights. "I bring grooming tools along every day, just in case I get a chance to brush Spunky. We have such a good time, don't we, little one?"

The enthusiastic tone of Spunky's yap gave Olivia the distinct impression that treats were involved in the grooming regimen. Bertha, Mr. Willard . . . Olivia knew that her stepfather, Allan, kept doggie treats in his desk drawer. How many other Chatterley Heights residents were sneaking extra food to Spunky? No wonder he had gained half a pound. Not that she should talk, Olivia told herself. Everyone else seemed to have lost weight or gained strength on their vacations, while she and Spunky had gained weight and, in Olivia's case, lost muscle tone by planting herself on an outdoor reclining chair with a stack of books. Well, heat or no heat, she and her pup would be taking more walks together.

"Then I'll leave Spunky with you for the moment, Bertha. Thanks. I'll be in the kitchen with Maddie for a bit, if you need us."

Bertha aimed her spray can at a dusty shelf, and said, "We'll be fine. Maybe you two should take a break. We'll all be back to work tomorrow, and I'll bet folks will start dropping by early to find out if you know anything about Greta's death."

"You're probably right," Olivia said. "Do you have your store key with you?"

"I always bring it along," Bertha said. "I can lock up if you and Maddie decide to go out. Just let me know."

Olivia thanked her again and reached for the kitchen door. She could already hear the intermittent bursts of song that usually meant Maddie was wearing her earbuds and baking. "I thought we were all baked up for at least a week," Olivia said as she walked into the kitchen.

Maddie pulled out her earbuds. "Just prepping another batch of dough, that's all," she said. "You can never have too much cutout cookie dough in the freezer. That's some sort of immutable law. Besides, I go to sleep if I'm not moving. What's up?"

"Are you at a stopping point?" Olivia made sure the kitchen door was securely closed behind her.

"Give me a sec," Maddie said. "I need to finish up this dough and put it in the fridge to chill."

"Sure," Olivia said. "I need to make a phone call, anyway." While Maddie wrapped her cookie dough in waxed paper and a towel, Olivia used the kitchen phone to call Constance at her office. Constance answered on the first ring.

"What happened to Craig?" Olivia asked.

"Livie," Constance said. "It's a good thing I excel at identifying voices. Since you ask, Craig is taking a late lunch. Shall I take a message?"

Olivia ignored the sarcasm. "I have a quick question," she said. "I can't remember. . . . Did you mean to give me the original of Greta's cutter collection list?"

"Your memory is crashing," Constance said. "Yes, the original is for you. Why? Is something wrong? Hang on a sec." The line went on hold. A short time later, Constance said, "Okay, everything is fine. I just checked in my safe, and I have a copy, not the original. I can tell because our copier makes a line on the sheet; it needs cleaning."

"Constance, were you working at your office last evening?

"Nope, why?"

"Spunky and I were out for a walk, and I saw your light on. Someone came out the front and walked away. I thought it might be Craig, but your light was still lit. I tried to call your office. No one answered. It just struck me as odd."

"Don't worry about it," Constance said. "Craig is still learning the ropes, so sometimes he stays late. He's a go-getter. My office light goes off after a period of time, if it doesn't detect movement. Anything else?"

"That's all. Thanks." Olivia hung up. She still felt vaguely troubled, but she couldn't figure out why.

"Well?" Maddie asked. "Did Constance accidentally give us the copy?"

Olivia shook her head. "We both have copies."

"Where's the original?" Maddie asked.

"Good question. But we'll let that go for now," Olivia said. "I thought we'd go on a field trip."

"Goodie! Whose house will we search this time? How about Olaf Jakobson's? He had that big fight with Greta at the cookie event, so I'm nominating him for suspect of the day." Maddie put the used mixing bowl and utensils in the dishwasher. "Kitchen chores can wait," she said.

"No more house searching," Olivia said. "I promised Del."

"That's right, you talked to Del. Tell me about it. And I mean instantly."

"Patience, my friend, all will be revealed," Olivia said. "Well, almost all. Right now, I want to make that visit to Aunt Sadie. In case she doesn't want to come back with us, we'll bring along Greta's collection list. I think we should stop at the storage facility, too, and select some cutters. I've marked the ones I want to show her. Aunt Sadie is a fund of knowledge, especially about people. She knows her cookie cutters, too. She's the place to start."

Everyone loved Sadie Briggs, who had raised her niece, Maddie, from the age of ten. She was known as Aunt Sadie to so many Chatterley Heights citizens that many had forgotten her surname. Middle-aged men and women remembered her as a kind and fun babysitter, and most of the women in town had sought her out for her compassionate listening skills. Many folks knew how to sew, knit, and embroider, among other handwork skills, because Aunt Sadie had spent patient hours teaching them. Best of all, she had a long memory and impressive powers of observation.

"Aunt Sadie will know all," Maddie said as she and Olivia stepped out of The Gingerbread House and into a wall of heat. Only Spunky showed any enthusiasm when they entered the northeast corner of the town square. They cut diagonally through the park, where a thick canopy of trees protected them from direct sunlight, until they reached the southwest corner. The treeless Chatterley Heights Public Library parking lot felt like a desert, but they endured and finally reached the dense tree cover provided by Cherry Blossom Lane.

"Whew," Maddie said. "Even I, sun lover that I am, must admit this is a bit much. Spunky must be roasting under that thick coat of his."

Spunky had slowed down a bit, Olivia thought. She scooped him up and held him against her side, where he hung like a dishrag. Spunky was too pooped to yap. Olivia and Maddie followed Cherry Blossom Lane as it led them to Aunt Sadie's small house, where she had lived for over fifty years.

"It won't be long, Spunks," Olivia said. "And Aunt Sadie has trees, water, and air-conditioning. Won't that be nice?"

"Aunt Sadie is sitting out on her porch,"

Maddie said. "She is a tougher woman than I am." As they walked up the short front walk, Maddie waved to her. "Aunt Sadie, how can you stand the heat? It must be a million degrees on that porch. Don't tell me your air conditioner pooped out again." Maddie reached into the pocket of her shorts for her cell phone. "I'll call Lucas right now. Business at the hardware store has been slow lately with so many folks out of town. He could come over right —"

"Maddie, don't fuss," Aunt Sadie said. "My air-conditioning is working fine. Lucas did an excellent job of fixing it. In fact, I have it going right now, even though no one is inside to enjoy it. There's a breeze out here, and the trees keep the sun out of my eyes."

"But aren't you hot?" Maddie asked as she sank onto a porch chair. "Are you sure you're feeling okay?"

"Maddie, for heaven's sake, I'm fine. It's just that . . . well, lately everyone is being so careful of me, keeping their visits short, making sure they don't tire me. If I stay inside the house, people think I'm resting, so they won't even ring the doorbell. No one asks for embroidery lessons anymore. No children stop by to tell me about their day." Aunt Sadie shook her head and sat up straighter in her wheelchair. "That's enough of that, now. You girls and Spunky are here to visit, and that makes me happy."

Maddie produced a Gingerbread House bag. "We come bearing cookies," she said as she handed the bag to her aunt.

"Yum," Aunt Sadie said. "Let's eat some right away. There's lemonade in the fridge. Maddie, would you go pour us some?"

"Sure," Maddie said.

Aunt Sadie smiled as she watched her niece hop up and go inside to fetch lemonade. "Maddie is always so enthusiastic and full of energy. I hope that never changes. She seems happy with her marriage to Lucas. She is, isn't she, Livie?"

"She is, indeed. She's so blissfully happy that sometimes I can't stand it."

"Good, good. I'm relieved to hear that," Aunt Sadie said.

Olivia felt uneasy, as if Aunt Sadie might be anticipating her own death and was anxious to know her beloved niece would be okay.

Aunt Sadie lightened the mood at once. "Now, hand over that tired little creature in your lap. It's my turn to spoil him." Spunky reached his front paws toward Aunt Sadie as Olivia passed him to her. "How's my little pup?" Aunt Sadie cooed. Spunky ate it up.

He snuggled against her stomach and gazed up at her with huge brown eyes. "Next time I'll have some treats for you, sweetie."

Olivia smirked as she watched Spunky twist Aunt Sadie around his paw. *That little grifter. If he could wander around town on his own, he'd weigh twenty pounds in a week.* "Spunky gets more than his share of illicit treats," Olivia said.

Maddie reappeared with a tray holding a pitcher of lemonade and three glasses, each filled to the brim with ice cubes. She'd also brought three small plates, paper napkins, and a small bowl of water for Spunky. "This ought to cool us down," she said as she served the lemonade.

Aunt Sadie took a sip and put her glass on a table next to her. "Now," she said, "tell me what I can do for you. It's clear there's something on your minds. You haven't gone and gotten yourselves involved in an investigation of Greta Oskarson's death, have you?" Aunt Sadie grinned. "Well, of course you have. I'll bet you're here because I know a great deal about Greta, some of it less than flattering."

"You are scary, Aunt Sadie," Maddie said.

Aunt Sadie's delighted grin knocked twenty years off her apparent age. "You've known that for a long time, Maddie. Well, ask away. Unlike some, I freely admit my love for a good gossip session. Although some folks deserve being gossiped about more than others."

"I'd say Greta falls into that category," Olivia said. "Maddie and I have been racking our brains trying to figure out a list of suspects . . . in case it turns out she really was murdered, of course. Del is out of town, and it's not that we don't trust Cody, but . . . Well, he doesn't seem to be doing anything."

With a gentle smile, Aunt Sadie said, "Cody Furlow is an earnest boy. I used to help him study for math exams. That boy couldn't add two and two, but nobody ever tried harder. That's what got in his way. He overthought every problem, and sometimes he'd talk himself into the wrong answer. Luckily, math isn't police work. Cody will be a fine officer once he gets enough experience and stops second-guessing himself."

"Maddie is right," Olivia said. "You really are scary."

"Enough of that, now." Aunt Sadie took a long sip of lemonade. "Let's talk about Greta, poor lamb. Oh, I know she could be arrogant and selfish and just plain mean. No denying that."

"No kidding," Maddie said. "She was awful to Clarisse Chamberlain."

"Ah, well, Martin played his part in that episode," Aunt Sadie said. "Is that what you wanted to ask about, Livie?"

"That, and more." Olivia opened the Gingerbread House bag and offered it to Aunt Sadie, who reached inside and snared two daisy-shaped cookies, one pink and the other purple. Olivia passed the bag over to Maddie.

"Clarisse is gone now, rest her soul," Aunt Sadie said. "It won't hurt her if I tell you what she told me in confidence." She bit off a pink daisy petal and sighed with contentment.

"Clarisse actually discussed Martin's affair with you?" Olivia asked.

"Oh, Livie," Maddie said. "You know perfectly well that everyone tells Aunt Sadie everything."

"Poor, dear Clarisse." Aunt Sadie put her cookies on a plate. "Martin was a good man, a fine businessman, and he adored Clarisse. But he was so naive when it came to women. Most of the women he met were wives of other businessmen, and he didn't take them seriously. Clarisse told me it drove her crazy. When they had dinner parties, Martin would talk to the men and ignore the women."

"Which meant Clarisse was stuck with the wives," Olivia said. "In those days, all they talked about were kids and how hard it was to get good help. At least times have changed."

"There were plenty of interesting women in those days, Livie," Aunt Sadie said with gentle sternness. "Clarisse enjoyed having a chance to meet many of them. Martin paid so little attention to women that he ignored the ones who were business partners with their husbands, even though Clarisse was his business partner. That wasn't wise, of course. Clarisse was left the job of placating them, which she did with grace and pleasure."

"Point taken," Olivia said, with a contrite smile. "My mom tells me the same thing all the time. But back to Clarisse and Martin . . ." She relayed to Aunt Sadie the content of Clarisse's last three letters to Greta, along with Bertha's memories. "Apparently, Clarisse had forgiven Greta for her affair with Martin, but then Clarisse got some sort of communication — we think it was a letter — that made her angry again. Aunt Sadie, do you know anything that might help me understand what was going on? Do you have any idea who sent that letter and what might have been in it?"

With a sad smile, Aunt Sadie said, "I'm afraid I do. She asked me never to speak of it, and I never have, but given the circumstances . . ."

Maddie refilled the lemonade glasses while Aunt Sadie nibbled her cookie, apparently gathering her thoughts and memories. "Bertha's information is correct, as far as it goes," Aunt Sadie said. She stroked the silky hair on Spunky's head. "Martin swore that his dalliance with Greta was short, and Clarisse believed him. Anger and resentment were such uncomfortable emotions for Clarisse. She forgave Martin and Greta both, perhaps too quickly. She so wanted to feel content again. If a business partner had betrayed her, Clarisse would have required absolute proof that the offender had confessed everything and was genuinely contrite. But Martin was the love of her life. So she accepted his story without question, and she moved on."

"Are you saying that the letter Clarisse received later . . . the one Bertha saw her holding . . . ?" Olivia felt light-headed and realized her breathing had become shallow.

"Clarisse showed me that letter," Aunt Sadie said. "It was indeed from Greta. Thinking about this makes me so sad . . . and angry."

Maddie lightly touched her aunt's arm. "If it's too hard for you, Aunt Sadie, please don't risk —"

"I'm fine, sweetheart." Aunt Sadie patted Maddie's hand. "I've wanted an excuse to get this off my chest ever since Greta Oskarson showed up again in Chatterley Heights. My heart will be stronger for it. You see, Greta Oskarson was a blackmailer of the worst kind. She was so greedy, and she had not one ounce of compassion for the innocents she devastated along the way. Martin, poor soul, had lied to his wife about the length of his affair with Greta. More than once, Martin returned to Europe alone for business. The two of them met again at least one time, although Martin had sworn to Clarisse that they'd had only one brief fling. Greta included a photo with her letter to Clarisse. It showed an older Martin with Greta at an outdoor café in Paris. Clarisse said that Martin did not appear to be aware of the photographer. Martin wasn't doing anything improper in the photo, but the fact that he had lied about seeing Greta again was enough to convince Clarisse he had betrayed her."

"But why would Greta send such a letter?" Olivia asked. "Martin was dead. What did she hope to accomplish?"

Aunt Sadie sighed and shook her head. "Wounded pride," she said. "You see, when Clarisse wrote that she had forgiven Greta, she happened to mention Martin's assertion that the affair had ended quickly. Greta was enraged. To her, it seemed as if Martin had taken the relationship lightly. She took it as a personal insult, and she wanted revenge. She bided her time, waiting for Clarisse to let down her guard . . . to be more vulnerable again."

"Are you saying Greta wrote that letter out of sheer spite?"

Aunt Sadie nodded. "Greta didn't want forgiveness from a wronged wife. She believed she'd been able to seduce so many men because she was superior to their wives. To Greta, forgiveness felt belittling. Her revenge on Clarisse was carefully timed to do the most damage."

"Yikes," Maddie said.

"Greta took such awful vengeance on Clarisse because Martin had downplayed the affair." Olivia felt a surge of anger that made her shiver in the heat.

Aunt Sadie nodded. "Of course, by downplaying the affair, Martin had made it easier for Clarisse to forgive Greta."

"Martin wasn't always smart about people and I don't understand how he could do something like that to the wife he seemingly adored," Olivia said. "But what Greta did was . . . It was incredibly cruel." Olivia thought about Clarisse, about how betrayed she must have felt. "It's so hard to fathom."

Aunt Sadie slowly shook her head. "It was very, very cold. Greta was self-obsessed, to put it mildly. I fear some of the fault belongs to her parents. You see, they treated her like a princess. They made her believe she was better and more deserving than everyone else. Greta's father was an impoverished Swedish immigrant. Her mother was a first-generation Swedish American, and her family had been middle class in Sweden. However, their status declined after they emigrated. They were older when Greta was born. She was their only child, angelically beautiful, as well as brilliant and talented. They doted on her."

"Lots of kids get spoiled," Maddie said, "but they don't automatically turn vicious."

"Of course not, dear heart." Aunt Sadie patted Maddie's arm. "Frequently such children grow up when they have to face the world. Reality has a way of puncturing illusions about oneself."

"Clearly, reality didn't have that effect with Greta," Olivia said.

"Oh, I think Greta did become disillusioned, but it hardened her. She wanted revenge on the world when it failed to provide the rewards she had been taught to expect." Aunt Sadie sipped her lemonade. "I think I need another cookie, if you don't mind."

Maddie held open the Gingerbread House bag, and Aunt Sadie selected another daisy, decorated with emerald green polka dots on pale green icing. Maddie took a random cookie, which turned out to be dark blue with pale yellow polka dots. She passed the bag to Olivia.

Before taking a bite of her cookie, Aunt Sadie said, "Livie, I regret not warning you about Greta as soon as I heard she'd asked you to handle the sale of her collection. I so hoped she had come home because she'd had a change of heart and wished to make amends. I suppose that's my weakness, wanting to believe that people can change for the better."

Olivia reached over and patted Aunt Sadie's hand. "That isn't a weakness," she said.

The three women sipped lemonade and munched their cookies in silence. When she'd finished her cookie, Olivia asked, "Aunt Sadie, could we impose upon you awhile longer?"

"Stop fussing, Livie. How else can I help you two?"

Olivia reached into a quilted bag her mother had made for her. She retrieved several sheets of paper and handed them to Aunt Sadie. "This is a list of the cookie cutters in Greta Oskarson's collection. I brought along the ones I've marked on the list. We haven't shown this to anyone else. At the moment, we aren't sure what will be done with the collection. It might be taken out of our hands at any time, but so far no one has even talked about what is going to happen to it." Olivia found herself feeling grateful to Cody for his hesitancy. If Del were in charge, by now he probably would have taken the list and the collection for evidence.

Aunt Sadie took the list and scanned the first page. "Fascinating," she said. "How can I be of help?"

"Aunt Sadie, please don't mention this to anyone," Olivia said. "The collection has been in one of the bank's secure storage units. I picked out some of the older, presumably more valuable ones to show you. But before we do that, we'd like your first impressions of that list. You know your antiques, including cookie cutters."

Aunt Sadie's eyes lit up. "What fun. I will

need my reading glasses, however. Maddie, would you . . . ?"

"Sure," Maddie said. "Any idea where you left them?"

"Not a clue, I'm afraid."

Maddie chuckled. "Okay then, I'll check the usual places. Be back in a sec."

While Maddie searched for her aunt's glasses, Olivia said, "We aren't trying to test you, Aunt Sadie. We don't even know what we are expecting you to say. We just want to hear anything that strikes you as you read this list and look at the cutters. I have a strong sense that this collection is somehow connected to Greta's murder."

"Do you think the collection is truly valuable enough to kill for?" Aunt Sadie asked.

"I honestly don't know," Olivia said. "Greta's collection seems quite impressive, but it would be unusual for cookie cutters to be valuable enough to make someone commit murder, at least in sheer monetary terms. But there's something about this collection . . ." Olivia quickly told Aunt Sadie about their discovery of Greta's hidden note containing the combination to the Gingerbread House safe. "Frankly," Olivia added, "I'm still not sure why Greta chose me to sell her collection. Aunt Sadie, am I making a big deal out of nothing?"

Aunt Sadie frowned in silence until Maddie burst out of the front door with altogether too much energy. "Sorry it took so long to find your reading glasses," Maddie said. "Honestly, I think you invent new hiding places just to give me exercise." She handed the half-glasses to her aunt. "I found them under your pillow this time. You'd made the bed, too."

Aunt Sadie took the glasses and absently dropped them on the table.

"Are you feeling okay, Aunt Sadie?" Maddie asked. "Can I get you anything?"

"What? Oh no, dear, I was just thinking." Turning to Olivia, Aunt Sadie said, "No, I don't think you are imagining things. I knew Greta rather better than many. She and I were close in age, though she was a couple years younger. I was always interested in people, as you know. I couldn't help but watch Greta's behavior. She looked like an angel, but I certainly wouldn't have crossed her. She used to steal boyfriends from other girls, but not because she really wanted them. She did it to show that she could. I began to realize how carefully she planned each conquest."

"Like the way she punished poor Clarisse?" Maddie asked.

"Exactly," Aunt Sadie said. "Greta worked

out intricate plans to achieve her purpose. She thought about everything, including what to do if her plans went awry."

Aunt Sadie settled her reading glasses on her nose. "Now, let's have a look at this cookie cutter list, shall we?" She read through the pages in silence, her frown deepening. When she'd finished, Aunt Sadie slid her glasses halfway down her nose to look at Olivia's face. "Did you say you'd brought along some of the cutters?"

Olivia dug into her satchel and drew out two plastic bags, each containing six cookie cutters. "I wasn't sure which ones to show you, so I brought the oldest, along with a sample of newer ones, though they would all seem to qualify as antiques." She slid the zippers at the tops of the bags and put them on the table next to Aunt Sadie.

Aunt Sadie picked up the bag containing the oldest cutters. She carefully removed the cutters, one by one, and placed them on her lap. Olivia handed her back the list describing Greta's entire cookie cutter collection.

"I marked the older cutters with black ink," Olivia said, "and the younger ones with blue. I'm not sure what I'm looking for, Aunt Sadie. Maybe just your first reactions or instincts . . ."

Aunt Sadie picked up the first cutter, a six-pointed star, and held it in her palm as if testing its weight. She ran her finger along the surface and the cutting edge, feeling for nicks. Finally, she pushed her glasses closer to her eyes and examined the cutter, inside and out. Olivia and Maddie remained silent as they watched Aunt Sadie work through all six cutters, giving each the same careful attention. Without speaking, she replaced them in their bag and went through the same process with the younger cutters in the second bag.

Olivia's shoulders felt stiff from the intensity of watching Aunt Sadie's examination . . . and from her own building curiosity. "Aunt Sadie, I'm about to explode. What do you think?"

"Well . . ." Aunt Sadie frowned. "It's so difficult to know anything for certain. Remember, I am not an expert on antique or even vintage cookie cutters. I would feel better if you consulted someone more knowledgeable. Maybe you could speak with someone at the National Cookie Cutter Historical Museum? They know so much more than me, and they have Phyllis Wetherill's writings, which I can only dream of owning."

With a pleading look, Olivia said, "Aunt

Sadie, that museum is in Joplin, Missouri, and we are in Chatterley Heights, Maryland, where we're pretty sure there's a murderer wandering around free. At least, *we* are convinced Greta's death wasn't entirely natural, even if the medical examiner is hedging his bets. I can't risk shipping these cutters to the museum. What if they got lost or smashed in the mail? Besides, it would take too long. Aunt Sadie, you know so much more about cutter history than we do, and you've seen and held lots of vintage and antique cutters."

"Or talk to Anita Rambert," Aunt Sadie said. "If it's experience you want, she's got more than I do. Anita knows more about the monetary value of antiques, too."

Olivia hesitated. She couldn't yet justify her concern about Anita, but she decided to take the risk. "Aunt Sadie, I suspect Anita might be planning to take over the collection. I know it sounds far-fetched, but . . ." Olivia told Aunt Sadie about the disappearance of Greta's original collection list.

"Have you asked Constance if she knows where the original got to?" Aunt Sadie asked.

"Not directly," Olivia admitted, "but I do know that Constance had Craig make one copy for her files, and she thought she was giving me the original. When I called Constance, she confirmed that she has a copy, as do I. So where's the original?"

"Oh, my," Aunt Sadie said. "Well, sometimes Anita does get carried away. She isn't selfish and mean, though. She probably had the best intentions. Did you say the name Craig?"

"Craig Evans, I believe," Olivia said. "He is Constance's office manager."

Aunt Sadie shook her head and said, "Dear, dear. Craig is also Anita Rambert's cousin. Anita got him the job with Constance. Now, Livie, don't look like that. Craig got that job well before Greta Oskarson made it known she would be returning to Chatterley Heights. My guess is Anita was worried you weren't knowledgeable and experienced enough to get top dollar for Greta's cutters, so she twisted her cousin's arm to get hold of that list for her. He probably took the original by mistake."

Olivia had to admit, at least to herself, that Aunt Sadie was probably right. Anita was an antiques expert, and she could play rough when it came to business, but she wasn't known as a cheat. She fought fair. Still . . . Olivia recalled the swinging hair of the slender figure she'd observed walking away from Constance's building. "I'll get

Anita for this," Olivia said.

Maddie offered a quick distraction. She sank to her knees in front of her aunt's wheelchair, and said, "Aunt Sadie, I'll bake all your favorite cookies and deliver them weekly if you'll only tell us what you think about the antique cutters. I'll bring you a kitten and clean the litter box every day. I'll name my firstborn after you."

Aunt Sadie laughed and kissed the fluffy top of her niece's head. "Maddie, please, I beg of you, do not saddle a child with the name 'Sadie.' But all right, I'll tell you my impressions." While Maddie settled back into her chair, Aunt Sadie gathered her thoughts. "I do have a few reservations about some of the cutters you've shown me," she said, "but there is no smoking gun, as they say. They are all in excellent condition with no rust or breaks, and I didn't see any signs they'd been repaired. I suspect they were German-made because most of them do not have backs, as American-made cutters do." Aunt Sadie picked up the two bags and glanced at the contents. "Two of the cutters have braced backs, and another two of the larger ones have rectangular backs that aren't quite big enough to cover the backs. Those are all signs of German-made cutters. Even the designs are typical classic German ones, like the pig, a circle, a six-pointed star. The heart shape has a thinner tail than you'd see in an American cutter."

"So far, so good," Maddie said.

Aunt Sadie nodded slowly. "There's more. Some of the cutters identified as older feel a bit heavier, at least to me, which makes sense since heavier tin was used in the earlier years. There's more use of solder in the later cutters because it became less expensive over time." After several moments of silence, Aunt Sadie picked up one of the older cutters, the star. She took the same design from the bag of younger cutters. Holding one in each hand, Aunt Sadie closed her eyes and leaned her head against the back of her chair. She lifted her hands, apparently testing the weight of each.

"What is it, Aunt Sadie?" Maddie asked. "You've noticed something, haven't you?"

Aunt Sadie opened her eyes. "Maybe."

"What did I tell you, Livie? She's the best!"

"Now, Maddie, it might be nothing, and it's far from scientific. There's probably a reasonable explanation. Anita would know." Aunt Sadie peered closely at the two star cookie cutters. Holding up the older one, she said, "This cutter is darker, which is characteristic of the older cutters. However, I would expect this older cutter to be heavier than the younger one. Instead, by my estimation, the younger one feels just a bit heavier."

"Maybe because there's more solder in the younger star?" Olivia suggested.

"Not enough to make it feel noticeably heavier," Aunt Sadie said. "Maddie, remember I told you that Greta's father was an expert carver?"

Maddie nodded. "We found a beautifully carved box in Greta's house. I figured her father probably made it for her."

Aunt Sadie's smile was gentle and sad. "What I think I never told you is that he worked with many materials, including metals. He was an accomplished tinsmith. I know he taught Greta how to carve. Her mother thought it unladylike to work with metal, but I wouldn't be surprised if Greta picked up the skill by watching her father work. She was a clever girl."

"Golly," Maddie said. "You think these cutters are all fakes? Greta made these cutters herself, to look like antiques? But how would she have been able to make the older one look darker? Oh wait, I've seen ads online for antiquing solutions that age all kinds of stuff, like wood or metal."

"But wouldn't that leave a paper trail?" Olivia asked. "If a customer paid for valuable antique cookie cutters and then tried to have them authenticated, the truth would probably come out."

"No need for fancy chemicals," Aunt Sadie said. "Plain old vinegar will do the trick. Spray it on the metal and leave it in the sun for however long you want. You can control how dark it gets. Greta's father would have known that."

Olivia's mind raced through the various messes she and Maddie had avoided due, unfortunately, to Greta's death. It would have been an honor to represent such a promising collection, but it might have turned into a disaster.

"Livie?" Maddie asked. "It's a million degrees out here. Why has the blood left your cheeks?" When Olivia didn't answer, Maddie said, "Earth to Livie. Asteroid approaching."

"It just occurred to me," Olivia said. "That asteroid could have wiped us out. What if we'd brokered the sale of Greta's collection and found out later that we'd sold fake antiques?"

"I guess it would have been messy," Maddie said. "But everyone knows we aren't super experts on the subject."

"Right." Olivia closed her eyes and took a deep, calming breath. Her mother would have been proud. "Don't you see? That is precisely why Greta Oskarson chose me to represent her. Anita Rambert would have spotted the fakes quickly, before they got sold for exorbitant amounts of money, which they aren't worth. Greta intended to rake in all that money . . . and then disappear, leaving me on the hook."

CHAPTER NINETEEN

"Isn't this lovely?" Ellie smiled at everyone seated around the dinner table — Olivia, Allan, Jason, and Calliope — as if they had been separated for decades. "The family is all together for the evening meal. I've been so looking forward to this."

Since everyone else was eyeing the food on the table, Olivia took pity on her mother. "Thanks for arranging this get-together, Mom. I've been so busy today preparing the store to reopen tomorrow, I haven't had a chance to complete a sentence."

"Hah!" Allan's booming voice caused Ellie to drop her fork. "Don't expect to finish a sentence at this table. The more we eat, the more we talk."

"I almost forgot the wine." Ellie scraped back her chair. "I know we don't usually have wine with dinner, but I thought it would be . . ." Ellie blinked rapidly, as if she were trying to remember what she was going to say.

"Are you okay, Mom?" Olivia asked. "You look flustered. Flustered isn't like you. Should you be scheduling more yoga classes?"

"I attended two yoga sessions today, Livie, but thank you for caring. Now, who would like a nice glass of Chardonnay? Everyone? Excellent." Ellie filled all the glasses as close to the brim as she could.

Olivia watched her mother with growing concern. Ellie wasn't behaving normally. She was the people handler, the calm one who always appeared to float above the fray. Now she seemed rattled, even agitated.

Ellie caught her daughter watching her, and said, "Livie, dear, aren't you hungry?"

"Hm?" Olivia glanced at the table. The platters of grilled salmon, steamed green beans, fresh sliced tomatoes sprinkled with basil, and rosemary bread had all piled up next to her plate. "Looks great, Mom. You've been busy." Olivia understood at once. Her mother had created a special meal, which meant a special announcement. Olivia glanced at Jason and Calliope. Was it her imagination, or did they look chummy?

Belatedly, Olivia filled her plate. As she slid the platter of sliced rosemary bread closer to her brother, she asked, "So Jason, are you still thinking of making an offer on Greta's house if it goes on the market?"

"Nah, not anymore." Jason reached toward the plate of salmon. "Push that closer, would you, Olive Oyl?"

Calliope guffawed, and a bit of tomato leaked out the corner of her mouth. No one seemed to notice except Olivia.

Jason grinned as he slid a hefty serving of salmon onto his plate. "I got a much better idea." He handed the plate to Calliope, who took a smaller, though still generous, portion. "That house isn't really right for me," Jason said. "I talked to Lucas about it. He did all the refurbishing for Greta, so he could describe the place to me. It's too small and dark and old-fashioned. Too girly for my taste. Anyway, Lucas told me about this place just south of town, out past the Nightshade Motel."

"Oh, there's a great neighborhood," Olivia said. The Nightshade Motel had a shady reputation, especially at night.

"I said *past* the motel, Olive Oyl. Geez. Maybe you forgot, but there's farms south of the motel. They're being sold off for developments, but there's this one I looked at about two miles down the road. The farm fields are small, and most of the land is hilly, so the developers don't want it. The farmhouse is in decent shape, just needs some renovation."

"And he can get the whole parcel for a song," Calliope added. "House, two barns, fields, woods, everything."

"Well, yeah, I can now," Jason said with a grin. "Cal charged right in and wrangled a deal with the owner. Man, can she ever negotiate." Jason bumped fists with Calliope, who looked happier than Olivia had ever seen her.

"That's great news, Jason," Allan said. "Is Lucas going to help you with the renovation work?"

"I don't need Lucas," Jason said. "I've got Cal." Jason took a generous slice of rosemary bread and managed to fit half of it into his mouth. He showed no awareness of the silence around the table.

Calliope noticed, however. Her long jaw tightened, giving her a belligerent look. "I like working with my hands," Calliope said. Her tone sounded defensive. "I'm good at it. I used to do lots of repairs when I stayed with . . . friends. I wanted to earn my keep. And I'm strong, too."

"She sure is strong," Jason said. "She almost beat me at arm wrestling."

Olivia noticed that Calliope didn't downplay her near-victory over a man who was perhaps twenty years her junior. Jason was a full-time mechanic, and worked out regularly. Calliope, in fact, looked rather pleased with herself.

With surprise, Olivia realized she was feeling more kindly disposed toward Calliope. Olivia could admire a physically strong middle-aged woman who could actually fix things. However, one quick glance at her mother told her that Ellie did not share her admiration. Ellie's hazel eyes stared at her untouched plate as she braided a strand of her long, gray hair. Not a good sign.

Allan wolfed down a second serving of salmon, happily unaware of his wife's angst. Jason and Calliope both reached for serving plates and helped themselves to more food. It was up to Olivia to help her mother. But first she had to figure out what was going on. "Mom," Olivia said quietly, "is there any more of that Chardonnay? It hit the spot."

"Oh." Ellie released her braid as she twisted in her chair to view the kitchen counter. "The bottle is almost empty. I have another in the little refrigerator downstairs. I'll go get it."

"I'll go with you." The others paid no attention as Olivia followed her mother through the kitchen to the basement stairs.

Olivia said nothing until she and Ellie were downstairs and well out of earshot.

As Ellie reached for the refrigerator door, Olivia said, "You don't really need to open another bottle just for me. That was a ruse to get you out of the room so we could talk."

"Well, I could use another glass," Ellie said as she reached for a bottle.

"It's that serious? Mom, what's bugging you so much?" Olivia took the wine bottle from her mother, who couldn't be trusted to remember it was in her hand.

"Livie, weren't you listening just now? Calliope has found a way to move in with Jason, and he fell for it."

"It sounds like a win-win to me," Olivia said. "Jason will probably be footing the bill, but Calliope clearly wants to help with the renovation work. I've never seen her look so happy. Come to think of it, I've never seen Calliope look happy at all, ever. And Jason seems content with the arrangement. The two of them get along like . . . like . . . I was going to say brother and sister, but Jason and I get on each other's nerves. Anyway, Jason and Calliope might actually be good for each other. Jason works during the day, so he'll get a break, and I'm reasonably certain Calliope truly wants to work on house renovations. What am I missing?"

Ellie leaned against the refrigerator door and crossed her strong, slender arms over her tiny rib cage. "Maybe I'm being an overprotective mother."

"In what way? Are you afraid Calliope will start to take over Jason's life or drive him crazy or something? Because it's my observation that Jason likes and respects Calliope for her skills. I don't think her bluntness phases him. In fact, he doesn't seem to notice it." Olivia wished she could open the wine bottle and sit down with her mother, but the damp, badly lit, unfinished basement wasn't exactly a calming environment.

"Honestly, Livie, I'm not sure what I'm afraid of." Ellie sighed heavily. "For all I know, they will be perfect for each other."

"That might be going too far." Olivia felt relieved when Ellie laughed, however briefly. "This is a wild guess, but are you worried that having Calliope around will prevent Jason from finding another girlfriend?"

Ellie's shoulders slumped. "Yes, I am. Calliope has driven me to the brink of madness. I'm so worried that any young woman Jason brings home will run for the mountains as soon as she meets Calliope. I'll never have any grandchildren." Ellie slapped her hand over her own mouth. "Oh Livie, I'm sorry, I didn't mean to —"

"It's okay, Mom. Jason and I are a bit on the slow side, but don't give up on us yet."

Ellie chuckled. "I do think of Spunky as sort of a grandchild."

"I'm glad you do," Olivia said. "There are times when I would happily give him to you."

"No, you wouldn't."

"Yes," Olivia said. "I would. However, I always get over it. He crawls on my lap, and I remember what a tough, loving little guy he is. Mom, remember Jason's toast to Maddie at her wedding? Jason likes strong, competent women. He knows what he wants; he just hasn't found her yet. When he does, it's my guess that she and Calliope will get along fine."

Ellie smiled at her daughter, and asked, "How did you get so smart?"

"Not a clue." Olivia looped her free elbow through her mother's and guided her up the basement steps. When they reached the dining room, Olivia and Ellie witnessed a domestic miracle: Allan and Jason were clearing the table. Calliope was fitting plates and silverware into the dishwasher. She had piled the sharp knives and cookware next to the sink for hand washing.

"Hello, sweetheart," Allan said as he dipped down to give his wife a kiss. "We thought the wine might go well with dessert. We can always have coffee after that, if we're feeling loopy."

"You mean you aren't slipping back to your office to work?" Ellie asked.

"Not tonight, I think," Allan said. "This has been such a delicious and pleasant family dinner. I'd like it to continue it for a while."

"Who are you," Ellie asked, "and into what closet did you stuff my husband?"

Allan laughed and kissed Ellie on the forehead.

Olivia wondered if they'd all wandered into an alternate universe.

After dinner, the Greyson-Meyers family gathered in the living room for dessert. With the temperature still hovering around the mid-eighties, everyone preferred air-conditioning to the screened porch. Olivia was relieved to see her mother looking more relaxed. Ellie beamed as she brought in a large serving plate piled with fresh fruit and tiny herbal cookies. "I bought the cookies at the Chatterley Café," Ellie explained. "I couldn't bear to heat up the house with cookie baking right before we all gathered for a family dinner. Besides, the café had such a lovely assortment of cookie flavors.

These little pink ones have peppermint leaves in them. The darker pink ones are rose geranium; so delicious. I'll let you guess the other flavors."

Jason and Calliope dove into the colorful arrangement, filling their dessert plates with raspberries, blueberries, cantaloupe chunks, and as many cookies as they could grab with one hand. Olivia was relieved to see her mother looking pleased, rather than alarmed.

"This reminds me of being on a cruise ship," Calliope said. "The food was great, and there was lots of it. Good thing we had plenty of activities, or we'd have gotten fat enough to sink the ship. Of course, some folks just made the rounds of bars, lounges, restaurants, cocktail parties . . . but most of us tried out the activities, like swimming and dance classes. You could dance every evening, if you wanted. I'm not much of a dancer. Don't like to dress up."

"Me neither," Jason said. "I'm happiest in my greasy work clothes."

"Anyway," Calliope said with her mouth full of cantaloupe, "there were always ways to fill up the day. You'd love all the craft classes, Ellie."

"Where did you go on your cruise?" Olivia asked.

"Cruises," Calliope said with her mouth full of blueberries. "I took three cruises, all on the same cruise ship, the *Alice Springs.* It's Australian, makes stops all over the place, so we were always meeting new people. I got to be friends with folks I'd meet on that ship. Many of us took more than one cruise, so we'd see each other over and over. It felt like coming back home, only a lot more interesting. Although some people I'd rather not see again. When you spend a couple months together on the same ship, you get to know each other . . . for better or for worse." Calliope popped two rose geranium cookies into her mouth. "Not bad," she mumbled.

Olivia snapped to attention. In Greta's attic, she and Maddie had found a photo of Greta lounging on the deck of a ship. Olivia remembered the letters that appeared in the photo: ALIC. She was willing to bet The Gingerbread House that those letters were part of the ship's name, and that name was almost certainly *Alice Springs.* What were the odds that Calliope and Greta Oskarson had been on the *Alice Springs* at the same time?

"But you must have met some interesting characters," Olivia said.

Calliope shrugged. "Some, yeah. On a

ship, it's a lot like living in a small town. You get to see the people you like nearly every day, if you want, but you're stuck with the jerks." Calliope restocked her plate with pineapple slices, bing cherries, and more cookies. "I didn't mind the colorful jerks," she said. "You know, the ones who'd drink all night in the ship's bar and stand on a table reciting Shakespeare. That was fun to watch when the weather was rough. In the morning you'd find them snoring in a deck chair, still dressed in tuxedos."

Jason exploded with laughter. "Got any photos of those guys?"

"Sure," Calliope said. "I put together a whole slide show. I'll email it to you." She spit the pit of a cherry onto her plate. "I couldn't stand the rich ladies who looked down their noses at the rest of us."

Olivia hesitated a moment, hoping Calliope would elaborate. When she didn't, Olivia plunged ahead. "When you mentioned those rich women, I immediately thought of Greta Oskarson," she said. "Were these women like her?"

Calliope's broad cheeks reddened. "I was talking about Greta Oskarson." Calliope glared at her empty plate as if she were replaying a scene on shipboard. "When I saw her again in your store, Livie, I couldn't believe it. You know, she was on all three of the cruises I took, and I never once heard her mention cookies or cookie cutters. As far as I could tell, she was only interested in her ball gowns and how many men she could steal away from their wives or girl-friends." Calliope snorted. "We used to call her 'the viper' behind her back. She was vicious. She used to 'hold court' with a group of other ladies who thought they were better than the rest of us. When one of us passed nearby, Greta would say something insulting about us in French or German, and her ladies-in-waiting would titter like stupid girls." Calliope grinned. "Greta didn't know I speak both French and German fluently. I use whatever language the people around me are speaking, and I'm pretty good at picking up accents and slang. It helps me get along with people. One day I ran past Greta and her minions because I was late for a poker game. I heard Greta say, in German, that I galloped like a plow horse. I didn't mind that so much, but then she said I was ugly because my father had been ugly."

"Geez, that's cold," Jason said. "I don't suppose you punched her in the nose?"

"I did better," Calliope said. "I shouted at her, in German, that at least I wasn't a black widow, killing husbands for their money. You should have seen her face, all their faces. Nobody insults my father and gets away with it."

"Well done, cousin!" Allan said, toasting her with his glass of wine.

"She deserved it. Greta made it her business to dig up everything she could about other people. She loved having that power." Calliope selected one grape from the serving plate and ate it. "That was the last time I traveled on the *Alice Springs*," she said.

"And you said you'd met Greta on previous cruises?" Olivia asked.

Calliope nodded. "Greta and I were both on the *Alice Springs* the year before that last one. Greta was traveling with one of her husbands. One night he fell overboard and was never found. Greta claimed he'd been having trouble sleeping and went for a walk on deck, while she stayed in bed. Nobody could prove anything different. You know, it's funny you should ask that. That cruise popped into my mind at your cookie party. I saw someone there who was a dead ringer for another woman who was on the *Alice Springs* when Greta's husband drowned. Can't be, though. She was too young."

"Who was too young?" Olivia tried to sound casual.

"That silly blond girl who wasted her time talking to that old guy. I forget his name."

"Olaf Jakobson?" Olivia asked.

"That's the one. She has hair like a woman I saw on the ship. I remember because she and Greta had a big argument. I never found out what it was about."

"Was this woman French, by any chance?" Olivia asked.

"No, I'm almost positive she was German. Anyway, it couldn't be her because she would probably be in her late fifties by now." Calliope shrugged. "Blondes all look alike, anyway."

While Allan, Jason, and Calliope lingered in the living room and finished up the dessert tray, Olivia followed her mother into the kitchen. As Olivia washed and Ellie dried the items Calliope had set beside the dishwasher, Olivia recounted Maddie's and her visit with Aunt Sadie. Ellie was unusually quiet during the recital.

"What's up, Mom?" Olivia asked. "You haven't made a single comment."

"Oh, I was just thinking how confusing this whole episode has been. I had no idea Greta had made so many enemies in her lifetime, and I still can't fathom why she would want to return to Chatterley Heights.

We might never know for sure why or how she died. I'm particularly disturbed by what Aunt Sadie said about Greta's cookie cutter collection. If I'd even suspected Greta was sucking you and Maddie into a scheme to defraud collectors, I'd have —"

"Don't even say it, Mom. Luckily, somebody else beat you to it."

"Well, there are plenty of suspects, that's for sure. Livie, I want you to do something for me. Go talk to Anita Rambert. Now, don't do that loud sighing thing again. I mean it. You and Maddie will both be on the suspect list, if there ever is one, and you need to be prepared. You need to make it clear that you were suspicious of the collection, not Greta's partners in a scheme to defraud collectors. If you act quickly, the police are less likely to think you might have killed Greta to take control of her collection."

"Mom, that's a stretch."

"Please call Anita," Ellie said. "For me."

"How can I trust Anita after she stole a copy of Greta's list?"

"If Anita really did get the list from her cousin, I'm sure she had her reasons." Ellie planted her fists on her slender hips, and said, "Get your cell phone out and call Anita right now. I mean it."

"But —"

"No 'buts.' Call her."

Olivia knew when her mother meant business, and this was one of those times. Anyway, it would be helpful to talk to Anita. Olivia reached into her pocket for her cell and selected the number from her phone book. She wasn't surprised when Anita answered on the first ring.

"Livie," Anita said. "Good. We're running out of time."

"You and my mom have been conspiring behind my back, haven't you?" Olivia arched an eyebrow at Ellie.

"No time for that," Anita said. "And don't blame Craig. I asked him to copy the list for me, since you wouldn't let me anywhere near it. We're a tight family. Craig accidentally took the original instead of the copy. Livie, I've been suspicious of that collection ever since Greta came to town. Remember, she was here for a week before you and Maddie returned. The heat doesn't bother me, so I stayed here. I tried and tried to talk to Greta, to convince her that I could make more money for her if she'd let me sell her collection, but she stonewalled me. It didn't make sense. Greta was not a sentimental person, and from what I'd heard about her, she didn't care about trust and honesty. So why would she be so insistent that *you* sell her collection?"

"Thanks so much," Olivia said.

"Look, Livie, whether you believe it or not, I like and even respect you as a businesswoman. The Gingerbread House brings antique-hungry customers to Chatterley Heights, which helps my business."

"All right then," Olivia said. "Tell me what you learned from reading Greta's list of cookie cutters."

"Without having seen and held the cutters, I'd say there are more fakes in that collection then there are genuine antiques. Aunt Sadie called me after you and Maddie showed her a sample of Greta's cutters."

"Et tu, Aunt Sadie?" Olivia sighed.

"Never mind that," Anita said. "From what Aunt Sadie told me about the cutters you showed her, it wouldn't have been long before someone began to question their authenticity."

"Okay, I admit that I came to the same conclusion," Olivia said. "It also occurred to me that Greta had tried to set me up to take the fall, if there was one." She told Anita her suspicion that Greta had a backup plan to steal her own collection from the Gingerbread House safe.

"Yup. Quite the old darling, wasn't she?

375

Livie, we're all worried about you."

"Who's 'we'?"

"Well, me and your mom . . . Aunt Sadie, of course, and Constance. Constance called me after you called her to ask about who got Greta's original list. She got the impression that you might not have it, and then she remembered that Craig is my cousin, so . . . I confessed my perfidy and told her why I wanted to see the list. Constance and I are kindred spirits: shrewd yet honest businesswomen with suspicious natures. We know a con when we smell it."

"Constance is more forthright than you are," Olivia said, and then wished she hadn't.

"I deserved that." Anita chuckled. "Heck, I earned it. The point is that we see danger ahead unless you make it very clear that you, too, are suspicious about the authenticity of Greta's collection, and you divorce yourself from its fate."

Olivia went silent, her mind filled with questions she was struggling to put into words. She agreed she might be in some danger of becoming a suspect, but what if the medical examiner couldn't definitively determine how Greta died? What if everyone was wrong about the authenticity of Greta's collection? Had Anita convinced everyone that her own intentions were honorable simply so she could take over the sale of the collection? Might someone else lay claim to the cutters? Olivia was increasingly convinced that the only way out of this incomprehensible mess was to plow through it.

"Olivia, are you still there?" Anita asked.

"Thanks for telling me all this, Anita, and I'll do some thinking. You are officially forgiven, more or less, for swiping Greta's original list. Come to The Gingerbread House tomorrow morning at eight a.m. I'll let you know what I've decided. Bring the list back, too." Olivia hung up without waiting for a response. If she knew Chatterley Heights, rumors would be flying soon enough. In fact, she was counting on it.

CHAPTER TWENTY

When Olivia returned from dinner with her family, the foyer of her Queen Anne smelled like ginger and cinnamon. Maddie was at it again. "That woman can't keep her hands out of the cookie dough," Olivia said under her breath. Spunky stood on his hind legs, his front paws against the Gingerbread House door, and gave his happy yap. "I'm glad, too," Olivia said. "Maddie and I have some planning to do, and we'll be needing cookies for what I have in mind. Come on, Spunks." She lifted her eager Yorkie into her arms. "You can snooze in your chair until Maddie and I finish in the kitchen." Olivia entered the store's sales floor, locked the door behind her, and flipped on the overhead lights. Aunt Sadie had given them a thick curtain that she wasn't using, so they could now cover the front window at night. Olivia had to turn on the overhead lights to help her navigate around the displays without crashing into them. On the plus side, Binnie and Ned would no longer be able to spy on her so easily.

After settling Spunky in his chair, Olivia headed toward the kitchen. She paused after opening the kitchen door, hoping not to startle Maddie as she eased an unbaked speculaas cookie from its mold. "Nicely done," Olivia said when the cookie was safely settled on a baking sheet. "Better you than me. I always mangle them."

Maddie performed a quick curtsy. "It does take a bit of practice and, of course, natural talent. You know, I always wondered what an unnatural talent would look like."

"Wonder later," Olivia said. "Right now, we have work to do. We need to finish before dawn."

"So you texted. I took it as a cue to start baking again. Your brilliant plans always seem to call for dozens of cookies."

"Except when they involve breaking into houses." Olivia rinsed Mr. Coffee's carafe and filled it to the limit with fresh water.

"Ooh, are we going to break into another house? Although I'm not sure we can claim that we actually broke into Greta's house, since the door was unlocked. It was more like 'entering.' Anyway, can it wait until I've finished this batch of speculaas?"

"No breaking and/or entering tonight." Olivia poured the carafe of water into Mr. Coffee's reservoir. "I do have a plan, though." Olivia paused as she measured ground Italian roast into the basket. "Our first order of business is to announce that we will be closed for one more day. I'll make an announcement on our website and to everyone on our email list, if you'll put a note on the front door. We are going to have a private showing of Greta's cookie cutter collection. I told Anita to come."

"That's totally exciting," Maddie said, "but why the hurry? We won't have time to contact collectors."

"We aren't inviting collectors," Olivia said as she pulled up the Gingerbread House website. "We'll be inviting murder suspects. We need Greta's murder solved quickly, so we can deal with her cutter collection. Specifically, I mean the fact that it contains fake antiques. We need to separate ourselves from that collection, for our own protection. I'm virtually positive Greta's death wasn't entirely natural, and her collection is involved somehow. While the M.E. has been pondering the technicalities of Greta's demise, our deputy sheriff, bless his earnest heart, has missed opportunities to gather evidence while it was fresh."

"Oh," Maddie said. "Didn't you hear the news, Livie? I can't believe your mother didn't get to this first. Although, to be fair, I was on the phone with Polly while she was reading her emails, so she told me right away."

"Polly told you what?"

Maddie frowned in concentration. "She said the medical examiner consulted with someone, don't ask me who . . . an expert on something or other. I'm not good with exact details. I was hoping your mom had filled you in."

"She didn't. Give me the gist."

Maddie brightened. "I can do the gist. The M.E. decreed that the bruises on Greta's neck, plus the fact that someone later came to the house and wiped off fingerprints, imply she was probably attacked at some point before her death. At any rate, even if Greta did die of natural causes, an attack probably wouldn't have helped. All things considered, the M.E. decided that her death warranted more investigation."

Olivia felt the blood leave her face. "Maddie, that means Cody will dust Greta's house more thoroughly for fingerprints, doesn't it?"

"According to Polly, he already did that.

You know Cody, once he finally decides to act, he does it yesterday."

"But aren't you worried? He'll have found our fingerprints in the attic, remember?" Olivia heard Mr. Coffee spit his last drops, but she ignored him.

"He did find them," Maddie said. "But, according to Polly, he didn't think anything of it. He figured Greta had taken us to the attic to show us photos. Cody is earnest about his police work, but between you and me, he hasn't quite honed his instincts. He isn't nearly suspicious enough."

"Knowing Cody, he will now become overzealous," Olivia sank onto a chair and reached for a cooled speculaas cookie. "I'm not looking forward to that."

"Oh, Livie, don't fuss." Maddie poured two cups of coffee and gave one to Olivia. "You and I will unmask Greta's attacker tomorrow. That's what you meant when you said you had a plan, right? I hope it's a good one."

"Me too." Olivia added cream and sugar to her coffee and gulped down most of it. "We need to gather our suspects together before they disappear. I'll work on that, and it won't be easy."

"It's lucky I decided to beef up our cookie supply, if I may mix food references." Maddie waved her hand toward the cooling speculaas cookies.

"The catch is that I don't want too many people to know about the showing."

"Ha," Maddie said. "Good luck with that."

"Sometimes I long for the anonymity of the city." Olivia refreshed her coffee and opened the lid of her laptop. Offering Maddie her chair, she asked, "Is there any way of checking a ship's manifest online? I'm thinking specifically of passenger lists."

Maddie slid onto the chair and wiggled her fingers. "What ship?"

"The *Alice Springs,* in 1995," Olivia said.

"Ooh, you figured out the name of the ship Greta was on, the one we saw in that photo."

"I have Calliope to thank for that," Olivia said.

Maddie produced rapid clicking sounds, while Olivia waited for the next batch of speculaas to finish baking. When the timer dinged, she replaced the baked cookies with a pan Maddie had already prepared.

"Not having much luck," Maddie said. "There are some historic passenger lists available, but they are for lots of different ships. Availability is spotty, and so far I don't see anything as late as 1995. These records are meant for people who are interested in tracing their ancestors. I could apply for the information through official channels, but that would take time, and there are no guarantees. I also see posts from people trying to find names and email addresses for others who were on the same cruise. Looking through all those would be really labor-intensive. Want me to keep looking?"

"Maybe you could search for references to someone on the ship who might have fallen overboard in 1995."

Once again, Maddie's fingers bounced around the keyboard. "Okay, I found one small notice in an Australian paper about a male passenger who fell overboard and drowned. All it says is that the guy was elderly, walking alone on deck at night, no one saw him go over . . . His death was declared an accident. Given his age, the authorities assumed he experienced vertigo and lost his footing. The ship wasn't near a port of call when it happened. No more details." Maddie twisted in her chair. "Do you want me to keep searching?"

"No, this is taking too long. We'll find another way. It might be a wild-goose chase, anyway," Olivia said. "Hand over the laptop. I need to shoot off some emails to our customers."

"Good." Maddie hopped out of the chair as the timer dinged. "I've got baking to finish. It's okay to chatter at me about what you're doing. I'm an excellent multitasker."

"Well, multitasking is not one of my gifts, I'm afraid," Olivia said. "Anyway, now I'm finding various sneaky ways to invite a select group to the store tomorrow morning. I'm giving out a few assignments . . . starting with my mom. She needs to get Calliope to come. I'm also asking Mom to pick up Anita and to park in the alley behind the store, just in case folks start gathering on the porch. Could you pick up Mr. Willard?"

"Sure," Maddie said. "What about Bertha?"

"We won't need her," Olivia said. "I don't want too many people around. I'll let Mr. Willard know. He'll be just as glad that Bertha won't be in any danger." When she had finished the email to her mother, Olivia emailed Bertha to ask a question and to tell her not to come to work in the morning.

The oven timer dinged, followed at once by another ding telling Olivia that she had an email. "Excellent," Olivia said. "Mom promises to be mum. Cute. She will bring Calliope with her. Oh, and Mom had a great idea for getting Olaf and Desirée to show up tomorrow."

"If there's anyone who can accomplish that feat, it's Ellie," Maddie said.

"Mom says Polly called her with some gossip. Polly had just gotten home after she and her boyfriend celebrated their one-year anniversary with dinner at Bon Vivant. They saw Olaf dining with 'that gorgeous blonde' who came to our cookie event. I think we can assume the woman was Desirée. By the end of their meal, according to Polly's friend, the two of them were acting mighty lovey-dovey. Polly is good friends with their waitress, who said that she heard Olaf and Desirée make a date for early breakfast at Joe's Diner tomorrow morning." Olivia paused for a sip of coffee.

"How very convenient," Maddie said. "Isn't small-town gossip wonderful?"

"Sometimes," Olivia said. "I'll drop by their table in the morning and simply tell them we're showing some of Greta's cookie cutters tomorrow. They aren't likely to tell anyone else. Olaf will want to buy something for Desirée, and he won't want competition."

"What if they don't show up?" Maddie asked.

Olivia shrugged. "Something will come to me." Her computer dinged to announce the arrival of another email. "It's Bertha," Olivia said. "She is up late emailing her sister. Oh, that's interesting . . ."

"What? What's interesting?" When Olivia didn't respond, Maddie shoved a pan of cookies into the oven, closed the door, and set the timer. Casually, she said, "Livie, the kitchen is on fire. Where did you put the fire extinguisher?"

"It's over near the door," Olivia said. "Wait. What did you just say?"

"I asked what you were reading that was so interesting." Maddie handed Olivia a cooled speculaas. "Eat," she said. "I suspect your sugar level has dipped into the danger zone."

Olivia laughed as she took the cookie. "Somehow I doubt that. Anyway, I was reading Bertha's email. She told me why Greta stayed in the Gingerbread House sales area while Bertha stuffed her precious cookie cutters into our wall safe. Greta insisted she was feeling tired and a bit faint. She preferred to rest in the cookbook nook until Bertha had finished. That didn't seem odd to Bertha, so she didn't think to mention it to us."

"That *is* interesting." Maddie pulled a chair next to Olivia. "But what does it mean?"

"It means, my friend, that our Greta had

a plan from the beginning. She'd covered all the bases. If anyone questioned the authenticity of her cutters while they were in our store, she had the combination for our safe. She could take them back and pretend they'd been stolen. Also, since she wasn't in the kitchen when Bertha put the cutters in our safe, no one would suspect Greta. She could accuse us of being negligent and then claim the insurance money."

"You know," Maddie said, "it's hard to imagine Greta sneaking in here at night and robbing our safe."

"Greta wasn't as weak as she pretended, despite her fatal heart attack. I'm willing to bet that she was, among other things, a cunning thief. However, there are other scenarios I can think of offhand. She could have accused us of substituting fakes for her originals. We'll probably never piece together Greta's entire plan, but I'm sure it was thorough, covering every contingency with several alternative escape maneuvers. That woman was an experienced con artist."

"Yikes," Maddie said. "I'm beginning to realize what a gigantic bullet we dodged."

"Well, we aren't out of the woods, yet, my friend." Olivia returned to her email program.

"Now for Mr. Willard's email, which will be complicated. I sure hope he has time to help out. He's the only one with the expertise and the contacts. If Del were here . . ."

"Yeah," Maddie said, "except if Del were here, he would tell us not to do what we are about to do."

"Ah, but Del would know we intended to do it anyway, and he would end up riding shotgun," Olivia said. "I probably should try to lure Cody here tomorrow morning. He's our only hope of protection, should our plan go awry."

The oven timer dinged, and Maddie popped up to rescue her pan of cookies. "Our plan is wonderful," she said. "What could go wrong? Don't answer that." She placed her pan on a rack to cool. "Why are you asking Mr. Willard to be here tomorrow morning?"

"It's a long shot," Olivia said, "but I'm hoping Mr. Willard can get some information for me, especially about Greta." When she finished, Olivia glanced up at the kitchen clock. "It's two a.m. Are you about done with the baking? I'll be getting up to shower before I head to Pete's Diner at six-thirty a.m."

"You go on to bed," Maddie said. "I'm starting some cardamom tangerine shortbread. I'll clean up when I'm finished."

Olivia hesitated with her hand on the kitchen doorknob. "I just have one worry left about tomorrow morning," she said. "I'm afraid Binnie and Ned might get wind of our plan and hang out on our porch. We can keep the curtain closed, but knowing Binnie, she'll pound on the window. She won't let up, either."

Maddie smiled, not unlike a cat hovering over leftover tuna salad. "I've been thinking about the Binnie-and-Ned dilemma. I have a cunning scheme in mind. Don't fuss, Livie. Run along and get a good few hours of sleep. Let me take care of the local press."

"I have a feeling I should be terrified by your offer, but I'm too tired." When Olivia left the kitchen, Spunky awakened instantly, jumped off his chair, and met her at the door. Neither uttered a sound as they trudged up the stairs to the apartment. Olivia opened the door, and Spunky went straight for the bedroom. "Sometimes," Olivia called to her pup, "I think you are more human than dog."

Before joining her pooped pup, Olivia checked her kitchen phone. Her cell phone had run out of juice. She'd have to remember to charge it overnight. She had two messages on the old kitchen answering machine.

Both were from Del. She punched the "play" button.

"Livie? I've been trying to call you for hours. I suppose you left your cell plugged in upstairs again. Anyway, it's nine p.m., and I wanted to let you know that I'll be out of touch for a while. Things are happening here. Can't explain. More later." Olivia left the machine going to hear the second message. "Hi Livie, Del again. Just hoping to catch you. Getting exciting here, more than I like, but . . . Okay, I'll try again." *Click.*

CHAPTER TWENTY-ONE

Olivia awakened before six a.m., already thinking through the details of her plan to determine who had triggered Greta Oskarson's death. She'd had only a few hours of sleep, but it was enough to convince her she'd been crazy to even think about gathering potential murder suspects in The Gingerbread House.

"Who do I think I am, Miss Marple?" Olivia asked herself. Spunky answered with a sleepy yap. Olivia ruffled the silky hair on his head. "I agree with you. We should get up at our usual time and open the store at nine, like any other day." She rubbed her eyes and sighed. "But it's too late for that. I wish Del were here." Olivia swung her legs over the side of her bed and slid her feet into her comfy, worn-out, lace-free tennis shoes. Spunky watched her through slitted eyelids. "Lucky dog," Olivia whispered, "you get to stay in bed all morning, while your mama makes herself look like she's lost her mind." That plan appeared acceptable to Spunky, who curled into a ball and went back to sleep.

After a quick shower, Olivia dressed in her lightest blouse and work pants. She had decided to go through with her plan to tempt Olaf Jakobson and Desirée Kirkwood to come back with her to The Gingerbread House to discuss Greta's collection. Even if she couldn't unmask Greta's attacker, Olivia figured she might learn more about Greta's past in Chatterley Heights, which could lead to more suspects.

Since she would be eating breakfast at Pete's Diner, Olivia decided to skip making a pot of coffee. However, Spunky would be alone all day. She went to the kitchen to leave him some dry food and found the little guy waiting expectantly beside his empty bowl. "You didn't have to get up so early," Olivia said. "I wasn't going to forget you." She poured an extra-generous portion in his bowl, which he instantly attacked with gusto.

"I'm running late," Olivia muttered as she noted the time. *Okay, what do I need? Cell phone, where's my cell phone?* She saw it on the kitchen counter, poking out from under a stack of dishes she'd forgotten to put away the night before. Olivia grabbed her phone and flipped it open. It didn't light up. "Oh no, I meant to charge it. Honestly, that vacation messed with my brain." She plugged in her phone and left it to charge.

Feeling flustered and impatient, Olivia hurried out of her apartment and down the stairs. She unlocked the foyer door, stepped out, and dropped her keys. *Okay, Livie, take a deep breath like your mother taught you.* Olivia knew why she felt so agitated. She didn't have a firm plan in mind for the coming confrontation with suspects. She wasn't even sure they were the right suspects. Whoever attacked Greta could be long gone by now. Well, she'd just have to wing it. And she wouldn't be alone; she had help. After one more deep breath, Olivia left The Gingerbread House, proud that she had remembered to lock the front door.

Olivia walked through the well-shaded park, feeling more focused as she approached Pete's Diner. No, she wasn't Miss Marple, but she knew she was a good observer of people . . . not as good as her mother, but still pretty good. Olivia began to understand that her curiosity about Greta's fate was tempered by a lack of enthusiasm for the woman herself. Greta hadn't been a likable person. She had used people, hurt those who were foolish enough to love her, and possibly killed a husband or two. Greta had been a cold, cruel, entirely self-obsessed woman. She had created what was almost certainly a collection of fake antique cookie cutters, which she'd intended to sell to eager fools. Olivia and Maddie were among those Greta had duped; she had set them up to take the blame if her cookie cutter scheme failed.

Despite her reservations about Greta, Olivia entered Pete's Diner feeling clear about her mission. Someone had triggered the chain of medical events that led to Greta's death. That same someone had left Greta to die. Olivia couldn't look the other way.

At six-thirty a.m., Pete's Diner was filling fast. Most of Pete's early morning customers wanted to enjoy their breakfasts before trudging off to work. Olivia saw Olaf Jakobson and Desirée Kirkwood occupying a booth against the wall, where they read the newspaper in silence as they waited for their meals to arrive. Perhaps the relationship wasn't going well. Wealthy as he was, Olaf hadn't been successful with women, at least not for long. He always failed the charm test, and he didn't seem to notice or care.

Pete's oldest and most acerbic waitress,

Ida, appeared at Olivia's table. "You're up early, for a change." Ida plunked a cup next to Olivia's elbow and filled it halfway. "Plenty of room left for all that junk you put in your coffee." To Olivia's surprise, Ida pulled over an empty chair and sat down. "Saw you eyeing those two lovebirds, if that's what they are. Hard to tell at the moment. Earlier they were gazing into each other's eyes like a couple of soppy teenagers."

"I'm curious about them," Olivia said. She polluted her coffee with cream and sugar, as expected. Ida didn't comment. "Ida, do you know anything about Desirée Kirkwood?"

Ida, an experienced gossip, did not look toward Desirée and Olaf's booth. "She's an odd one," Ida said. "Looks to me like she got her hooks into Olaf, which most women couldn't do. Right now, she doesn't seem all that interested in him. I suppose that's how she intends to string him along. She's a pretty thing, I'll give her that. Don't know much about her, though. She's not from around here. I'd know it if she was."

"She dropped by The Gingerbread House the other day," Olivia said.

Ida slapped her rarely used order pad on the table and clicked her pen. "Tell me what you want for breakfast. We can talk while I'm writing. Gives me a chance to get off my poor feet for a few minutes."

Olivia always ordered the same breakfast: scrambled eggs with cheese, bacon, and toast. Ida knew that, of course, so Olivia suspected she wanted a gossip break. "I'll have my usual," Olivia said. "Have you heard Desirée say anything about where she came from or why she's here in Chatterley Heights?"

"Nope," Ida said. "Not a word. She doesn't talk much."

"She did mention to me that she was interested in Greta's antique cookie cutters," Olivia said. "Of course, I can't sell them yet, but I was thinking of getting a few private bids . . . you know, in case Greta's heirs, should she have any, want me to put them on the market."

Ida stuffed her unused pen in her apron pocket. "Want me to drop a hint? From what I've heard, those two are the only folks I know who might be able to come up with enough cash to afford those cookie cutters. Olaf can, anyways, and he needs to give that girl a big gift soon, or she'll be gone."

"I guess you could mention that I'll be back at the store after breakfast," Olivia said. "Only wait until after I've finished my breakfast and left. I'd rather not talk about the cookie cutters in public, if you know what I mean."

Ida nodded. "Most people gossip too much."

"I'll be in the store kitchen," Olivia added, "so they could come through the alley to the back door, and I'll let them in."

"I'll get your breakfast. More cream and sugar, too." Ida frowned at the cream and sugar levels. Olivia felt an urge to point out that both levels had been low when she sat down, but she held her tongue. Ida was co-operating nicely, and Olivia didn't want to spoil that.

While planning her strategy, Olivia munched through her eggs and bacon without tasting them. The early morning diners had begun to clear out and head for work, but Olaf and Desirée lingered over coffee and what looked like the *Baltimore Sun*. Neither spoke. When Ida offered to refill their coffee cups, they looked briefly at her, but not at each other. They looked like a bored married couple . . . until Desirée reached across the table and ran her index finger along Olaf's hand. Olaf looked up and nearly smiled. The interchange was over so quickly that Olivia wondered if she'd imagined it.

Ida arrived at Olivia's table and topped off her coffee. "I'll be taking off soon, Ida," Olivia said, "but I do have one question for you."

Ida dropped wearily onto an empty chair and pushed a gray curl back under her hairnet. She was over seventy and looked every day of it, but she refused to stop working. "Things are slow right now. Ask away."

The diner was quiet, so Olivia lowered her voice. "Remember a few days back, when Constance and I met here for breakfast? You stopped by our table as Constance was showing me a photo of Greta Oskarson. She was in a ball gown."

"She looked a lot younger, too," Ida said with a snide grin.

"I remember what you said when you recognized her." Olivia glanced over at Olaf and Desirée, who appeared engrossed in the newspaper. "You said she'd better not show her face around here again. What did you mean by that?"

Ida slid her chair closer to Olivia. "I knew a lot about that woman. We were about the same age, you know. We went to school together. Greta was trouble from the beginning. She had some sort of evil power over men, even in high school, and she used it to get what she wanted. The stories I could tell you . . . But all it takes is one story. Did you notice how much Olaf Jakobson hated Greta?"

"It was hard to miss," Olivia said. "He had an argument with Greta at our cookie event in her honor. I know they were once engaged."

An older couple came through the diner door and selected a table. "I'll make this quick," Ida said. "The second wave is about to begin. Anyway, Olaf says he broke it off with her, but Greta said she did the breaking off. Fact is, neither of them officially broke their engagement. Olaf gave Greta a big ring, they'd planned a huge wedding, and then . . . well, no one knows what really happened. Right before the wedding, Greta just up and left, ring and all. She took all the wedding gifts that had arrived, too. Said they belonged to the bride. I heard from a lot of folks that Greta never even thanked them for the gifts. She just walked off with them, like she deserved to keep them." Three more customers entered Pete's Diner and settled at a table by the window, which looked out on the town square. The elderly couple closed their menus and stared at Ida.

"Gotta go," Ida said. "The natives are getting restless. I'll pass along your message to Olaf once you've headed back to your store." She shuffled toward the older couple to take their order.

Olivia counted out cash for her breakfast bill, including a generous tip. As she left the diner, one thought stuck in her mind: Olaf Jakobson wasn't the sort of man to forgive and forget a very public betrayal.

Despite the building heat, Olivia walked briskly through the park to the alley behind The Gingerbread House. She caught a glimpse of the store and was relieved to see that the front porch was empty. She assumed the peace wouldn't last. If past experience was any indicator, Binnie and Ned would get wind of the rumor that Olivia would be showing some of Greta's antique cutters to a few select buyers.

Olivia found her mother's aging Toyota parked down the alley, which meant Calliope must have arrived as well. Using her key, Olivia unlocked the alley door. When it didn't open, she realized it was bolted from the inside. She knocked and waited. No one responded. She'd have to go through the front door.

After relocking the kitchen door, Olivia walked briskly toward the front of the Queen Anne. She rounded the corner of the house to find her worst fear realized: Binnie and Ned were crouched on the front porch, apparently trying to peek through an opening in the heavy curtain covering the window. Ned's camera flashed rapid-fire. A faint yapping sound told Olivia that her mighty protector, Spunky, must have heard noise on the porch and slipped under the curtain to confront the intruders. *Uh-oh. What is Spunky doing in the store?* Olivia didn't recall whether she had locked the foyer door when she'd left for breakfast, but she was positive she had locked her apartment door. Spunky must have pulled his old puppy trick, a skill acquired most likely during his escape from the puppy mill and subsequent time he spent on the streets of Baltimore. After Olivia was lucky enough to adopt him, there was an adjustment period. Whenever Olivia left her apartment, Spunky would slip out while she was busy with her key. He'd hide quietly behind the door until she left. Olivia learned always to check the shadows to make sure Spunky wasn't there, biding his time.

Focus, Livie. Spunky is safely in the store. From her position, Olivia could see most of the town square. As she scanned the park, she recognized Olaf Jakobson and Desirée Kirkwood. They strolled from tree to tree, following the shade. They were approaching the band shell, heading in the general direction of The Gingerbread House. They appeared to be in no hurry. Olivia drew back behind the corner of the Queen Anne and thought furiously. If Ida had followed her instructions about what to tell Olaf and Desirée, they would probably head directly for the alley behind the store. Binnie would be on the lookout for anyone coming toward The Gingerbread House, and she would undoubtedly be suspicious when she saw Olaf and Desirée enter the alley. She would, of course, follow them. If Binnie came upon Olivia apparently lurking in the alley, it wouldn't be long before she figured out that a secret meeting must be going on inside.

Binnie was relentless, and Ned's camera, once it started flashing, never stopped. Intending to call Maddie to warn her, Olivia reached for her phone and realized it wasn't in her pocket. At the same time, she took several steps backward to stay out of sight. Her foot hit a small rock. Thrown off-balance, Olivia teetered backward, flailing her arms. She felt herself fall. With dread, Olivia waited to feel her head crack on the hard surface of the alley; instead, she fell into someone's hands. Luckily, they were strong hands. They had caught her, under her arms, less than a foot from the pavement.

"Livie?" asked a concerned and familiar voice. "Are you hurt?"

Olivia hung suspended backward. She arched her neck and looked into the handsome, upside-down face of Maddie's new husband, Lucas Ashford. "Hey, Lucas," Olivia said. "Nice catch." Lucas pulled her upright and made sure she was stable before he released her. "I'm in a bit of a pickle," Olivia said.

Lucas stroked his chiseled chin. "Maddie called the hardware store and told me the two of you might need help. She wants to keep Binnie and Ned from hassling your guests. She also said you had sent some folks over here to the store, but she realized those two reporters were already on the porch. As I understand it, you and Maddie need to get folks inside before Binnie and Ned can pounce on them."

"Exactly," Olivia said. "If you two have figured out a plan, I suggest we implement it fast. The people I sent over have nearly arrived." She peered around the corner of The Gingerbread House. "Thank goodness, it looks like they are taking their time. I can see them walking up the band shell steps. Of course, there's no telling how long they

404

will stay inside the band shell. Right now, Binnie and Ned are focused on trying to see through the curtain covering the front window, but if they turn around as Olaf and Desirée walk toward the store . . ."

Lucas flashed his shy, endearing smile as he whipped out his cell phone. He pressed a button, and said, "Okay, now." He hung up and punched again. As his cell rang, he said to Olivia, "Wait at the alley door. I'll tell Maddie to let you in." As Olivia obeyed, she heard Lucas say, "Hi honey, the truck should be there in seconds. You do? Okay, I'll go along, just in case." Olivia ran down the alley to the Gingerbread House door, which opened as soon as she arrived.

"I was watching for you," Maddie said as Olivia wedged through the barely open alley door and into the kitchen. "Livie, I'm so sorry I had to lock you out, but I was afraid Binnie and Ned might follow you and get inside the store. Everyone is here except Desirée and Olaf."

"They are heading this way," Olivia said. "Lucas said —" She noticed the kitchen table was covered with an embroidered tablecloth and set with small plates and coffee cups. In the center of the table were two serving plates heaped with decorated cookies. Maddie was dressed for action in pale green shorts and a matching T-shirt that read COOKIES R ME. Her hair was a mass of red frizz, as if it had caught her excitement.

"Lucas said you have a plan to keep Binnie and Ned away from us," Olivia said. "How do you expect to — ?" At that moment, brakes screeched outside in the alley behind The Gingerbread House. "What was that?"

"Our plan." Maddie grabbed Livie's wrist and pulled her toward the door that connected the kitchen to the sales floor. "Come on, we have quick work to do."

"But what's that truck doing in the — ?"

"Just follow orders," Maddie said. "As soon as you go into the store, run for Spunky and grab him. Try not to let more than your hands show through the window. The curtains should fall back into place. Bring Spunky back to the kitchen. We're moving the guests in there until we're sure Binnie is gone." Maddie flipped open her cell phone.

Olivia frowned. "But what about the Health Depart— ?"

"We'll scrub later. Just do it, now." Maddie whispered into her phone as she followed Olivia out to the sales floor.

Olivia reached through the curtains and got a firm hold on Spunky's middle.

Startled, he yelped as Olivia yanked him away from the window. She felt awful about frightening her pup, but she trusted Maddie. It helped to know that Lucas was involved. As Olivia held Spunky against her chest and hurried back toward the kitchen, she was aware of growing confusion on the sales floor. Spunky yapped frantically, while Maddie gathered the others into a group. Olivia saw her mother open the store's front door for a repairman, who was carrying an armload of impressive tools.

Olivia pushed open the kitchen door with her shoulder and carried Spunky inside. She settled at her kitchen desk to comfort her rattled little Yorkie. Spunky recovered quickly, showing he was no sissy. However, he did squirm in her arms when the kitchen door burst open and a herd of people invaded the quiet space. Olivia watched the procession from her chair. Her mother, she noticed, had confined her long, wavy hair to a bun at the nape of her neck. Ellie wore her one and only summer suit, a rich purple seersucker outfit that she wore to weddings and funerals, though only if she wasn't well acquainted with the happy couple or the unfortunate deceased.

With professional decorum, Ellie guided the few guests to their seats at the kitchen table. Anita Rambert took the seat closest to the coffeepot. She poured herself a cup before anyone else had a chance to sit down. Olivia thought Anita seemed tired, although she was as stunning as ever with her sleek black hair and perfect figure. Mr. Willard was his usual cheerful, cadaverous self. He, too, reached for coffee as soon as he sat down. He added generous amounts of cream and sugar. Olivia felt a twinge of jealousy, knowing that not one of those calories would linger on his gaunt frame.

Ellie joined Olivia and quietly said, "Calliope is helping Jason with some questions relating to his house offer. Don't ask me for details; neither of them thinks I can comprehend the simplest information. Calliope promised to arrive as soon as possible."

"I hope so," Olivia said.

"Repairs shouldn't take long," Maddie said to their guests. She lifted a plate of cookies from the kitchen counter and handed it to Mr. Willard, who took three. "We invited only a few select people to this gathering," Maddie said, "so we'll wait a couple more —" A sharp rap on the alley door interrupted her.

"Ah, two of our special guests," Ellie said as she peeked through the peephole in the alley door. She unlocked the door and quickly ushered Olaf and Desirée into the kitchen. Olaf panted as if he were over-heated, though he wore light seersucker shorts and a T-shirt. Desirée gave the impression that she was immune to heat. Her silky, pale pink outfit looked as fresh as it had when Olivia saw her earlier at Pete's Diner. Her walk across the park had failed to produce even a hint of that oily sheen Olivia battled every summer.

Ellie poked her head outside to check the alley. After relocking the door, she gave Olivia a reassuring nod, which she hoped meant that the coast was clear. Olivia longed to know how Lucas and Maddie had tricked Binnie and Ned into leaving the porch, but the story would have to wait. If she hoped to figure out who had attacked Greta and precipitated her death, it was now or never. Maddie met her eyes over the heads of the seated guests. Olivia nodded. Spunky had settled down on the seat of Olivia's chair, so she left him there. At once, Maddie lifted a box from the kitchen counter. With a slight jerk of her head, she indicated that Olivia should join her in the store.

Maddie led the way to the cookbook nook, where she deposited the box of Greta's cutters on a table. "The kitchen won't work," she said. "Way too crowded. I'll set up on the sales floor, and you can bring everyone out later."

"What about Binnie and Ned?" Olivia asked.

"They are long gone, and I hope this is a lesson to them." Maddie smiled at Olivia's pucker of confusion. "Lucas and one of his guys picked them up in the alley and offered to help them follow the truck our guests were supposed to be in as they headed to an undisclosed location to broker a deal with you. I know it sounds like a plot from a B-grade movie, or worse. But honestly, it worked like a charm. Binnie and Ned fell for it. I'm guessing they got caught up in the moment and saw themselves as heroic reporters following a juicy story. Anyway, they are out in the country somewhere following a truck driven by another of Lucas's guys. He's paying them double their hourly wage."

"Brilliant," Olivia said, "and totally satisfying. I haven't worked out exactly how —" Footsteps on the sales floor startled her into nervous silence. When Mr. Willard poked his head into the cookbook nook, she slumped with relief.

"I should get back to the kitchen, but I want to hear this." Maddie sat on the edge of Olivia's armchair so Mr. Willard could have the other one.

"I'm glad to catch you both alone," Mr. Willard said. He glanced back at the sales floor before entering the cookbook nook. "I wanted to let you know what I found out when I talked to a couple contacts of mine in London. Understanding the urgency, both men did some immediate research and called me back within hours."

Olivia felt a stab of guilt as she noticed dark circles under Mr. Willard's deep-sunk eyes. "I'm so sorry I cost you a night's sleep."

Mr. Willard's thin lips stretched into a smile that was paper thin, yet somehow charming. "Nonsense. I enjoy the hunt, and it was pleasurable to reconnect with old friends abroad. I will have to take Bertha on a trip to Europe so she can meet them. But time is of the essence, as we legal types are fond of repeating. My contacts both work regularly with the French police, and they were able to do some quick checking for me." Mr. Willard stopped to listen for foot-steps.

Maddie sighed. "Oh, all right. I really hate to miss all the fun, but I'll volunteer to stand out on the sales floor and keep guard. If someone comes through the kitchen door,

I'll call out a greeting and a name." She picked up the box of cutters. "And you will tell me everything Mr. Willard says, Livie. Or else."

Olivia watched as Maddie positioned herself at an empty table on the sales floor, where she began to put out a selection of Greta's cutters. Olivia rejoined Mr. Willard in the cookbook nook. "What did you find out from your contacts?" Olivia asked.

Mr. Willard cleared his throat. "To begin with, Greta was not unknown to either the British or the French police. The French were more inclined to give her the benefit of the doubt, although when a second husband perished by falling overboard, they became more suspicious. However, they were unable to prove Greta's involvement in those deaths. My London contact was kind enough to check with the Australian maritime authorities, as well, concerning the second death by drowning."

"Are you saying that no one on board saw anything at all suspicious about that death? Even though the body was never found?" Olivia's voice sounded too loud in the quiet space. She lowered it. "Did they question anyone?"

"They questioned quite a number of people. There was some sense that many who knew Greta felt loyal to her, or perhaps somewhat afraid of her." Mr. Willard hesitated, clearing his throat several times. Finally, he said, "There was only one informant who cast doubt on Greta's innocence, but the authorities were inclined to disbelieve her."

"But why?"

Mr. Willard cleared his throat once again. "They seemed suspicious of her motives. Apparently, Greta had been particularly cruel to her, in a public way, by insulting her parents and drawing attention to her, um, looks."

"Oh, no, you mean . . . ?"

Mr. Willard inclined his head. "Yes, I'm afraid her name was Calliope Zimmermann."

"Rats," Olivia said. "This isn't good."

"No, it isn't," Mr. Willard said, "but that isn't the only information I was able to gather."

"I'm hoping that means we have other viable suspects?"

"I believe so," Mr. Willard said with the merest smile. "However, let's begin with Greta herself. One of my contacts in London told me that Greta had at one time been suspected of insurance fraud. I wasn't able to glean the details, I'm afraid, since she was never charged."

"Interesting," Olivia said. "That helps confirm my suspicion that Greta might have had a backup scheme to steal her own cookie cutter collection, in case someone questioned its authenticity. That woman was scary. I must learn to be more careful."

"Indeed, you must," Mr. Willard said with unmistakable firmness. "I do have one more tidbit to share with you. It's about Olaf Jakobson. I'm astonished that this information was kept successfully under wraps for decades. I only found out through my lifelong friendship with the Jakobson family attorney. He is no longer retained by the family due, sadly, to ill health and age. Normally, he would never reveal such information, but he is concerned that it might be evidence in a murder case, and he appears to be the only one who knows."

Olivia glanced toward the entrance to the cookbook nook. "Mr. Willard, you understand that I might not be able to keep this information confidential, right?"

Mr. Willard nodded. "I understand that. My friend was the only one bound to silence, and frankly, he hasn't long to live. He asked that the information be considered a deathbed confession, and we attempted to cover the legal issues involved. Here is what he told me: The Jakobson family is extraordinarily wealthy. Shortly before Greta and Olaf were to be married, the family settled a sum of money on Greta, as a wedding gift. The sum was half a million dollars."

"Half a million?" To Olivia, this seemed an incredible gift, especially since it had been given over fifty years earlier. "And?"

"And," Mr. Willard said, "immediately after she received the gift, Greta left the country, taking the money with her. The Jakobson family tried to get it back, but they were unsuccessful."

"Wow. No wonder Olaf hated Greta so much. She stole more than their wedding gifts. I very nearly feel compassion for him."

Mr. Willard chuckled softly. "I'm afraid it caused a rift in the family, which was unfair to Olaf, but families can be . . ." Mr. Willard shrugged. "After that episode, Olaf's younger brother became the favored son. Olaf has never —"

"Hi, Mr. Jakobson." Maddie's cheerful voice easily reached the cookbook nook. Olivia and Mr. Willard exchanged glances in silence. "I've nearly finished setting up the cutter display out here on the sales floor. It's less cramped than the kitchen. We thought all of you might enjoy having a private look at some of the oldest and most valuable cookie cutters from Greta Oskarson's collection."

Olaf growled something unintelligible in return.

"Sure," Maddie said. "Bring Desirée on out. In fact, let's go get everyone. Let the fun begin."

Olivia waited a few seconds before she looked out at the sales floor. Maddie saw her and waved her into the room. Olivia motioned to Mr. Willard to follow her. "I'm still unsure how to handle this situation," she whispered to Mr. Willard. "I'm rather nervous."

Mr. Willard patted Olivia's shoulder, and said, "I always find it best to read the signs and go with the flow, as they say. The correct procedure will emerge on its own. I only wish I could have provided you with more information. I do, however, have some advice for you, Livie."

Olivia heard concern in his voice. "I hoped you would."

"Tread lightly. Listen, observe, but avoid showing suspicion. Then leave the rest to the authorities."

Olivia nodded in agreement. There was nothing she would like better than to hand the whole mess over to the police, as soon as possible. And then, she vowed, she would never, ever involve herself in another crime investigation.

CHAPTER TWENTY-TWO

Olivia donned her businesswoman smile as she welcomed the select group of potential buyers, otherwise known as suspects, onto the Gingerbread House sales floor. "Feel free to handle the cookie cutters," she said. "They've endured many decades of use, and they have survived." Maddie had divided a selection of Greta Oskarson's cookie cutters among three tables, so the participants wouldn't be too close to one another. The display included all the cutters whose antiquity Aunt Sadie had questioned, along with a number of cutters she'd thought to be authentic.

Fresh coffee and more cookies awaited on the refreshment table, where Ellie had stationed herself. Olivia chose to stand behind the sales counter, where she could pretend to do paperwork. Maddie stayed closer to the front of the store, where she could watch the proceedings and look busy reorganizing displays.

Olivia had relaxed after Mr. Willard's advice to simply observe. She began with Olaf. He barely glanced at the cookie cutters as he followed Desirée around the display tables. Olaf's obvious boredom and impatience made Olivia remember the bruises on Greta's neck. Over the years, Olivia hadn't interacted much with Olaf, and even less with his family, but she couldn't recall a time when he'd appeared relaxed or content. From what Mr. Willard had told her about Olaf and Greta's breakup, she could understand his sour outlook on life. He must have hated Greta for publicly humiliating him and causing his demotion from favored son. Olivia could easily envision Olaf, flushed with pent-up rage, lunging for Greta's neck. Would he have released her and let her live? Maybe, if he'd realized in time that he might also be sacrificing his own life. Or would his swollen ego have convinced him he could get away with murder?

"Livie, dear . . ." Ellie's voice startled Olivia so much that she jerked sideways. "Careful, dear, remember your balance." Ellie placed a steadying hand on Olivia's arm.

"My balance is fine, Mom."

419

"Of course it is, dear. I only wanted to let you know I'll be in the kitchen. If you need me, just pop your head in and let me know. I won't be long. Calliope is quite late, and I do feel her presence would be useful."

"Me too." As her mother headed toward the kitchen, Olivia shifted her attention to the lovely, puzzling Desirée Kirkwood, who had arrived in town at a convenient moment if she was truly interested in antique cookie cutters. For someone who had denied any real knowledge of antique cookie cutters, Desirée appeared to be fascinated by Greta's collection. She moved slowly around the tables, examining each cutter from all angles. Desirée's eyes widened as she picked up the very cutter that had escaped from the Gingerbread House safe when Olivia tried to open it upon her return from vacation: a tin heart shape with an elegant narrow tail. Aunt Sadie had said it might be a genuine antique due to its weight and pattern of wear. Desirée peered at the inside edge of the heart cutter and smiled as she put it back on the table. Olivia was curious to see what Desirée had found inside that cutter, but that would have to wait until their guests had left.

As far as Maddie had been able to determine, Desirée wasn't active on the Internet.

She had no website or Facebook account, wasn't on Twitter, didn't blog, at least not under her name or anything close to it. Maddie hadn't located a domain name owned by any Desirée Kirkwood. On the other hand, Desirée was older than she tried to appear, so maybe she hadn't yet jumped onto the Internet bandwagon.

Olivia wished Calliope would show up. Maybe it was truly coincidental that she had appeared in Chatterley Heights at the same time Greta moved back to town. Or maybe not. In her favor, Calliope had admitted to having run-ins with Greta on board the *Alice Springs.* On the other hand, Olivia couldn't dismiss Mr. Willard's discovery that Calliope had been the only one on the ship to accuse Greta of murdering her husband. What if Calliope's accusation had merely been payback for Greta's public abuse of her, as the police concluded? Could any of Calliope's stories be trusted?

Maddie took her cell phone from the pocket of her shorts, as if she'd felt it vibrate. With a shrug, she let herself into the foyer and closed the store's front door behind her. Olivia assumed Lucas must be checking in with her. With any luck, he had transported Binnie and Ned to another state.

421

When Olivia returned to her covert observation, she saw Anita Rambert frowning at a cutter she held in her hand. With a glance toward Olivia, Anita took the cutter with her to stand directly under a ceiling light as far away from the tables as possible. Olivia abandoned her post and signaled Anita to join her inside the cookbook nook.

"Have you had any of these cutters authenticated yet?" Anita asked quietly.

"We showed them to Aunt Sadie," Olivia said.

Anita nodded. "She undoubtedly warned you that some of them are fake antiques."

Olivia shrugged. "She said they might be, but she couldn't be sure. She did suggest that you might be a better judge of their authenticity."

"I'll bet she did. Is that why I'm here? Or did you suspect I finished off Greta to get at her collection?" Anita handed Olivia the cutter, a heart shape. "If Greta created this so-called antique, she was either completely ignorant or, more likely, insufferably arrogant. It's one of the worst fakes I've ever seen. She didn't even bother to add some variation to the antiquing job. And it's made of very lightweight tin. It wouldn't have held up to use for a week, let alone decades."

"Maybe it was one of Greta's early attempts," Olivia suggested.

Anita dropped the cutter on a bookshelf. "I found several other cutters that are more skilled fakes."

"Greta should have known the difference," Olivia said.

Anita's dark eyes narrowed. "Or maybe she was arrogant enough to believe that only she could identify a fake. Look, Livie, what's going on? Some of those cutters are genuine antiques, and some are even signed. But they aren't familiar to me, by which I mean they've probably been out of circulation for a very long time. Did Greta steal somebody's collection and then spend years expanding it with fakes?"

"Your guess is as good as mine," Olivia said with a shrug.

Ellie glided through the cookbook nook entrance, startling Olivia and Anita. "Livie, you should probably get out there. Your guests are becoming restless." Olivia and Anita quickly followed Ellie back to the sales floor. Maddie had not yet reappeared. Mr. Willard was chatting with a bored Desirée, while Olaf paced in a circle, muttering under his breath. When he saw Olivia, he said, "Are you interested in unloading this bunch of stuff, or aren't you? I don't have all day."

"Perhaps I haven't been clear," Olivia said. "I wasn't intending to —"

"I wasn't born yesterday," Olaf said. "You need to unload these trinkets, which is why you gave us a message through that old waitress at the diner. As far as I'm concerned, this is all junk. If you're smart, you'll get rid of it fast. I'll give you five hundred for the whole lot."

Olivia was momentarily struck dumb. Anita, on the other hand, charged forward until she was inches from Olaf's face. Olaf took a step backward. He recovered quickly, however. His fleshy face tightened and flushed with rage. Olivia edged aside. She decided to let Anita do what she did best: outright intimidation.

Anita's willowy body straightened, making her slightly taller than Olaf. "Sir, that offer was ridiculous," she said. "If you genuinely wish to negotiate for this priceless collection of antique cookie cutters, then start with a reasonable offer. Otherwise, we have nothing to say to each other. I am accustomed to dealing with serious clients." When Anita turned her back on Olaf, her sleek hair swung over her shoulder. Anita sent Olivia the slightest of winks.

Desirée touched Olaf's arm and nodded her head in the direction of the kitchen. Olaf followed her as she wove around the store displays until she reached the coffee and treats table, which Ellie had abandoned. They began a whispered conversation that looked intense.

Maddie appeared at Olivia's side. "What the heck is going on here?"

"Obviously, Olaf wants to buy Greta's collection for Desirée," Olivia said, "but I can't tell if that was his idea or hers. How about you? Is everything okay?"

"Why shouldn't it be?"

"Didn't you sneak out to the foyer for a phone call?" Olivia said. "I figured it must be from Lucas. Please don't tell me Binnie and Ned are on their way back here."

Maddie snickered. "Not a chance. Lucas knows how to lead women astray. It'll be dark before Binnie realizes she's been had. My phone call was —"

Olaf had Desirée by the wrist and was pulling her back toward Olivia.

"I'll just be slinking along now," Maddie murmured. "Good luck." She strolled over to the refreshment table, where she checked the coffee supply before heading toward the kitchen.

Olaf's color had returned to normal for an out-of-shape, hard-drinking older man with anger issues. As they passed the display tables, Desirée's gaze lingered on one section of Greta's collection. Olivia thought the grouping contained some of the cutters that both Aunt Sadie and Anita suspected might be genuine antiques. Might Desirée actually be a knowledgeable collector or antiques dealer masquerading as a nostalgic novice? As Olaf approached Olivia, Anita drifted toward the display tables, where she examined the cutters that had interested Desirée.

"Okay, here's my offer." Olaf's thinning gray hair was damp with sweat, despite the air conditioner.

Olivia chose not to remind Olaf that the collection was not for sale. She wanted him to keep talking.

"Desirée says she's only truly interested in a small selection of these things." Olaf flung his arm in the general direction of the cookie cutter display. "They look old and beaten up to me, so they can't be worth all that much."

"They are antiques," Olivia said. "They are supposed to be old."

Olaf shrugged, and said, "I'm offering five hundred dollars, but this time it's for only five particular cookie cutters. Those are the ones Desirée wants. They remind her of her childhood."

Behind Olaf's back, Anita gave a slight shake of her head to warn Olivia not to agree to Olaf's terms. Olivia had no intention of doing so. "I'm sorry, Mr. Jakobson, I really am," Olivia said, "but I can't offer these cutters for sale at the moment." She glanced toward Mr. Willard, who had been watching the proceedings in silence.

Mr. Willard cleared his throat, which caught everyone's attention. "Livie is correct," he said. "At present, she is legally required to keep the collection intact. It will take some time to locate Greta's solicitor in England, where she last lived, and to determine whether she had signed a will. We must also determine whether she had any living relatives, who would, of course, inherit her estate. It is a complex, time-consuming process."

Olaf spread his arms in a gesture of defeat. He turned away without further argument and returned to Desirée's side. When Olaf tried to put his arm around Desirée's shoulders to comfort her, she turned away.

"Well, she knows her antiques," Anita said. "I took a good look at the five cutters Desirée was so interested in, and they are almost certainly genuine. I could sell those for five hundred dollars apiece, at the very least. However, I won't hold my breath."

Anita checked her watch. "I need to get to work soon. Is my assignment here completed?"

Before Olivia could answer, her mother emerged from the kitchen with Calliope in tow. "Look who's here," Ellie said before withdrawing back into the kitchen.

Calliope headed straight for the coffee and cookies. Olivia suspected their guests were ready to leave soon, and she hadn't made any progress. Maybe it was time to give up. Cody would be investigating Greta's death more thoroughly now that the medical examiner had determined her bruises were at least relevant to her death. Let Cody have the glory, Olivia thought, as long as Maddie and I don't become his prime suspects.

Carrying a full cup of coffee, as well as a plate piled with decorated cookies, Calliope headed for the cookie cutter display tables. Olivia thought she ought at least to introduce Calliope before the gathering broke up. As Olivia approached the tables, Calliope bit off half a cookie and had to put down her plate and cup in order to avoid dropping chunks of cookie on the cutters. Olaf snorted derisively at Calliope, who stared at him. She looked from Olaf to Desirée, who was standing beside him. Desirée said something to Olaf that made him laugh.

Olivia held her breath, remembering Mr. Willard's story that when Greta ridiculed Calliope's looks, on board the *Alice Springs,* Calliope had taken revenge by accusing Greta of murdering her husband. Desirée, however, was not Greta. Instead of joining in Olaf's laughter, Desirée shushed him. Calliope's angry scowl dissolved, to be replaced by puzzlement. "I know you," Calliope said as she stared at Desirée's face. "I've seen you before."

"I'm afraid I don't remember meeting you," Desirée said. "You might have seen me around town. I don't live here, but I've been shopping quite a bit."

Calliope shook her head. "Nope, not here." She stared so intently that Desirée moved closer to Olaf, as if she wanted protection. Olaf put his arm around her shoulders.

"I promise you, we've never met," Desirée said.

Olivia heard a familiar clicking sound and saw Spunky on the sales floor. How on earth . . . ? Of course, she'd put him in the kitchen after he'd sneaked downstairs earlier. He must have squeezed through into the sales area when someone opened the kitchen door. She caught sight of his furry little body entering the cookbook nook.

Good, he'd be safe from human feet in there.

"Now I remember," Calliope said as she peered closely at Desirée's face. "Wow. You must have had a lot of plastic surgery."

"Excuse me?" Desirée turned to Olaf. "Let's get out of here."

Olaf nodded and spun her around. As they maneuvered around a display table, Calliope called after them. "It was on the *Alice Springs,* wasn't it? You probably don't remember me, but I remember you. I remember that light blonde hair. You had a fight with Greta. I thought you were going to punch her. Boy, did she let you have it."

Desirée broke free of Olaf's protective arm and turned to face Calliope. "Look, I don't know who you are or what you're talking about. I'm twenty-five years old; I haven't ever needed plastic surgery. My hair used to be white blond, but it has darkened over time. I've never been on a ship. And you are crazy."

Calliope shrugged. "Well, you sure look like a woman I met on the *Alice Springs* back in 1995. Your hair is just like hers was, except maybe lighter, and really, how many women have hair like that? Either it's natural, or you dye the roots every morning. You do look older than twenty-five,

430

though. Maybe thirties. Plastic surgery can only do so much, you know."

"Okay, so I'm thirty-three. Now, for the last time . . ." Desirée was standing near the five cookie cutters she had wanted so badly. She picked them up one by one, then put them back on the table, clustered together. A tear trickled down her cheek.

"I remember now," Calliope said "That woman who fought with Greta . . . she had a daughter with her. That was you, wasn't it?"

Olivia's heart began to race. Disconnected facts swirled around chaotically in her mind. They were all connected, but she didn't know how. Those five antique cookie cutters, an abandoned child, an argument between Greta and a blonde on the *Alice Springs,* baking cutout cookies with a mother and grandmother, hair blowing in the wind as a car races past, following an ambulance . . .

"It was you in the car behind the ambulance." Olivia thought the words a split second before she heard them come from her own mouth.

Desirée heard her, too. With a last, longing glance at the cutters on the table, Desirée reached under her silky jacket to a pocket in her slacks. When her hand reemerged, it was holding the smallest gun

Olivia had ever seen. Not that she had seen many guns. Compared with Del's service revolver, Desirée's gun looked like a toy. Nevertheless, Olivia had no doubt it could kill as effectively. And it was pointed directly at her.

No one moved. Olivia heard a clatter as someone dropped a plate.

"All of you," Desirée said, "slide your cell phones across the floor and under the tables. You too," she said to Olivia.

Olivia pulled out the pockets of her slacks to show they were empty. "I left mine upstairs, charging. I'm . . . always forgetting to charge it."

Desirée hesitated, but she accepted Olivia's explanation.

"Desirée, why?" Olaf gulped loudly as if he were trying not to cry. "I wanted to marry you."

"I know, Olaf." Desirée sounded sad. "Only I didn't know that when I first met you. That would have been the perfect revenge, wouldn't it? You and me? Greta ruined both our lives." With her free hand, Desirée grabbed the five cookie cutters, one by one, and stuffed them into her pocket. "Those are *my* cookie cutters." She took a step away from the table, keeping watch on the entire group.

"Yes, I believe they are," Olivia said. "You must have been looking for familiar scratches when you examined the insides of those cutters."

"You understand." Desirée swiped at a tear with her free hand. "My mother taught me to do that. She used to show me which scratches went all the way back to my grandmother's time. She talked about my grandmother often. I felt like she was with us. She wasn't, though. She killed herself before I was born."

"I'm so sorry," Olivia said, and she meant it.

"We only had two of my grandmother's cutters," Desirée said. "They weren't valuable, so we were able to keep them. These cutters belonged to my grandmother, too." Desirée patted the five antiques in her pocket. "They have the same tiny initials inside . . . my grandmother's initials. My grandfather took them when he left her. And do you know why? Because *she* wanted them for her precious collection. Greta wouldn't even allow my grandmother to keep her own cookie cutters. She was evil."

Olivia was acutely aware that her own mother might walk out of the kitchen at any moment.

"And do you know why my grandmother

433

killed herself? Because of that witch, Greta Oskarson. She seduced my grandfather and stole him away from her. He was a count in France, you know. Real royalty. And rich. When he met Greta, he divorced my grandmother and abandoned his daughter, my mother, when she was only ten years old. The last thing he did for them was send them to the United States to protect them from the scandal. I think he was really just protecting himself. He cut off all contact with them." Desirée took a breath that quivered with repressed tears. "My mother always missed him. That's why she was on the *Alice Springs.* He was her father, and she wanted so much to see him again. When she did, she discovered he was old and sick, but he wanted her back in his life. He was going to tell Greta he was leaving her to reconnect with his daughter and meet his grandchild . . . me. But Greta killed him first. My mother couldn't take it. She killed herself a year later. I was sent to live with a foster family until I was eighteen."

"Well, it all makes sense then," Calliope said. "Greta killed your grandfather and caused your mother and grandmother's deaths, so you killed Greta. I'd do the same thing in your place."

"No, it wasn't like that. I just wanted my

cookie cutters back." Desirée patted her pocket. "They held my best memories of my mother. Greta laughed at me. She wouldn't let me hold them, even once. She called me a stupid girl. I was so angry. I grabbed her around her scrawny neck and squeezed, but . . . She started to wheeze. I got scared, so I left. I left her to die."

"But you followed the ambulance to the hospital, didn't you?" Olivia said. "You wanted to make sure she was taken care of, right?"

Desirée hesitated as if she were pondering the question. Finally she shook her head. "No," she said. "I wanted to make sure she was dead." Desirée's gun had dropped lower as she talked, but now she raised it and pointed it at Olivia again. "You are going to get me out of here," Desirée said. There was no longer any softness in her voice. With her gun steadily aimed at Olivia, Desirée quickly skirted the end of the table. No one was close enough to intervene. She grabbed Olivia's wrist, twisted her arm behind her back, and used her as a shield as she inched toward the front door.

Everyone in the room appeared frozen like pieces on an abandoned chessboard. Only Olivia noticed that Calliope was edging sideways, closer to a display table, whenever

Desirée turned her head. When Calliope was near enough to the table, she scooped as many cookie cutters as she could hold in her large hands. With the form of a professional pitcher, Calliope raised her arm to throw the cutters.

A movement at the cookbook nook entrance caught Olivia's eye. Desirée saw it, too. It was Spunky, trotting out to see what all the fuss was about. Olivia felt her heart sink to her feet. She willed her little dog to retreat back into the nook, but Spunky wasn't that kind of guy. He saw the gun, now aimed at him. That didn't seem to bother him. However, one look at Desirée's stance and her grip on Olivia told Spunky that his beloved mistress was in danger. He issued a warning in the form of a low, menacing growl. When that didn't work, Spunky's little muscles bunched as he prepared to attack.

"No, Spunky," Olivia cried. "Stay!"

Spunky hesitated for a moment, then stiffened. He had heard fear in Olivia's voice. He couldn't know the fear was for him. Spunky burst from the nook entrance and ran directly toward Desirée and her gun. Olivia tried to struggle, but Desirée was remarkably strong. She straightened her arm, aimed. Spunky growled.

Olivia's peripheral vision perceived movement to her left. She shifted her head slightly, enough to see Calliope raise her arm like a baseball pitcher. A moment later, a flock of cookie cutters flew across the room. Along their flight path, the cutters jostled several cookie cutter mobiles that hung from the ceiling. The tinkle of tin against tin momentarily distracted Desirée, who froze like a terrified animal. Unfortunately, Spunky froze, too. Desirée recovered first. She aimed again at Spunky.

A clear, three-note whistle pierced the air. Olivia saw Spunky's ears perk. At once, he leaped into the air and began to run around in circles. Desirée's gun tried to follow his movements. As a two-note whistle sounded, two events happened at the same time. Spunky raced toward Mr. Willard, and a second volley of cookie cutters flew through the air, aimed accurately at Desirée. This time Olivia managed to shove her elbow into Desirée's ribs and break free.

Calliope leaped onto Desirée's back. The gun clattered on the tile floor as Desirée's feet slipped out from under her. She fell flat on the floor, face down. Calliope smoothly grabbed both of Desirée's wrists and twisted them behind her back. Calliope glanced up at the gathering, and asked, "I don't suppose one of you has a length of rope in your pocket?"

Mr. Willard reached in his trousers pocket and pulled out an old-fashioned men's handkerchief.

"That'll do," Calliope said. Mr. Willard handed her the handkerchief. As Calliope lifted Desirée upright, she said, "You've got some delicate bones there. Hope I didn't break any of them."

Olivia joined Mr. Willard. "You sure can whistle," she said. "You've been training Spunky to do tricks, haven't you?

Mr. Willard's thin lips spread even thinner as he grinned. "Spunky is a smart boy," he said. "Besides, teaching him tricks gave me an excuse to feed him treats."

The door to the Gingerbread House kitchen opened. Maddie poked her head into the sales area, a puzzled look on her face. "I just got back," she said. "It was so quiet out here, I thought everyone had left." Maddie caught sight of Desirée, her hands now tied behind her back, safely in Calliope's strong grip. "Did we miss something?"

"We?" Olivia asked.

Maddie opened the kitchen door, and out walked Deputy Sheriff Cody Furlow, all six foot three of him. He was in uniform.

"Cody!" Olivia said. "We were just going to call you." She beckoned to Calliope, who escorted a dejected Desirée across the sales floor and turned her over to the deputy. Olaf Jakobson followed behind.

"I suspect Mr. Willard would like his handkerchief back," Calliope said. "Besides, I think handcuffs would be a safer bet. This girl is stronger than she looks. This is Desirée Kirkwood, and her hands made those bruises on Greta Oskarson's neck."

Cody looked stunned, but he quickly recovered his professional demeanor. He fitted his handcuffs around Desirée's wrists before removing the handkerchief. Tears streamed down Desirée's cheeks. Olaf stood as close to Desirée as Cody would allow.

"I'd better get the prisoner safely locked in our jail," Cody said. "I'll have to interview all of you as soon as possible."

"Sure," Olivia said. "But Cody, how did you know to show up here?"

"Oh, I . . ." Cody turned to Maddie.

"I'll explain later," Maddie said. "For now, just assume that Deputy Sheriff Cody Furlow knows all and sees all."

CHAPTER TWENTY-THREE

On Wednesday evening, Maddie and Lucas, toting plenty of wine and tangerine cardamom shortbread, joined the Greyson-Meyers family for a home-cooked meal that required as little actual preparation as possible. Ellie had declared her independence from cooking and baking for the duration of the August heat wave. She was willing to use the microwave, but that was it.

"We can serve ourselves from the kitchen," Ellie said. "Then we'll move to the dining room. I've got the ceiling fan at its highest setting, and the air conditioner has been going all day." Ellie pointed to the kitchen counter, which was lined with pots and serving plates. "I hope you're all starving, because I got meatloaf and mashed potatoes from Pete's Diner; coq au vin, arugula and tomato salad, fresh corn, and sourdough rolls from the Chatterley Café; and three different pasta salads from Bon Vivant."

"Wow," Jason said. "I might almost get enough to eat this evening."

Calliope snorted and socked Jason in the upper arm. Maddie wedged her large dessert platter and wine selections into the remaining space at the end of the counter.

Everyone returned to the dining room with their plates piled high. All conversation ceased for a time while they dug in to the feast. As they slowed down, Ellie asked, "What do you think will happen to Desirée? So much pain in her young life. She didn't strike me as a cold-blooded killer."

"Not like Greta, anyway," Maddie said. "I still think Greta knocked off a rich husband or two."

"Me too," said Calliope. "That's why I asked Mr. Willard to find Desirée a first-rate defense attorney. He has one in mind."

Ellie put down her uneaten forkful of meatloaf. "That was kind of you. But does Desirée have the money to pay for that level of representation? Would Olaf help, do you think?"

Calliope speared a hunk of potato with her fork. "Olaf and I worked it out. He's rich, and I'm rich, so why not? We're going to split the cost. No big deal. Olaf really fell for her."

"Yeah, it almost made him human," Maddie said.

Jason was first to clean his plate. He always went back for seconds, but this time he remained at his place for several minutes. He took a sip of wine, and said, "So I bought the farm."

Ellie's head popped up. "Excuse me?"

"The farm, Mom. You know, the one Cal and I told you about. I got it at a great price. Cal helped me with the deal from start to finish. It's vacant right now, so we can move in as soon as I close next week."

Ellie tried to exchange glances with her husband, but Allan was busy spearing a hunk of coq au vin. "So, by 'we,' I assume you mean yourself and . . . ?"

"Cal, of course," Jason said. "She's going to be really helpful with the renovations. The place needs a lot of work, but Cal says the structure is sturdy."

"I'll be out of your hair in a matter of days," Calliope said to Ellie.

"So, do you two think you can live in the same house without killing each other in an arm-wrestling contest?" Olivia asked.

"Sure," Jason said with a wicked grin. "Cal is the fun sister I never had."

Maddie quickly grabbed her wineglass and held it high. "Here's to Jason's first house."

The others raised their glasses, though Ellie was on the slow side, and she put hers back down without taking a sip.

"Mom, are you feeling okay?" Olivia asked. "You look tired. Is the heat getting to you?"

"Oh, no, Livie, I'm fine. Jason, I'm very happy for you. And you, Callio . . . I mean, Cal."

"Heck, just call me anything you want," Calliope said. "I like Cal, but Calliope is the name my parents gave me, and it keeps them closer to me. I don't think I'll ever stop missing them." She stuffed a large forkful of pasta salad into her mouth.

"I guess I have been feeling a bit down lately," Ellie said. "And before you ask, Livie, I've been to plenty of yoga sessions. It isn't enough. I miss all the classes I used to take. During the worst of the recession, we had so many arts and crafts teachers who were more than willing to come to Chatterley Heights. It was wonderful. Now the economy is doing better, and those folks are finding jobs, or at least they are able to teach classes closer to home."

"Why don't you travel to other towns or a nearby city where you can still find classes?" Olivia asked.

"That's not the same at all, Livie. I so enjoy sharing the experiences with all my

443

friends and neighbors, walking to classes . . . Driving to a city for a class with people I'll probably never see again isn't nearly as much fun."

"Hey, I have a great idea," Calliope said. "We could start an arts and crafts school right here in Chatterley Heights. Then you'd have a place for instructors to come to, plus a ready-made clientele."

"Calliope, it isn't that simple," Ellie said. "We'd need a building and supplies, and I'm afraid we could never come up with the money to start such a school, let alone keep it going."

"That part's easy," Calliope said. "I'll put up the money. I've got way too much of it lying around doing nothing. I can find workers, too. Heck, I'll help build the place. I helped build a school in Africa once. Or we could renovate some old building that Constance can't unload."

Ellie put her hand on Calliope's arm. "But what about Jason's farm?"

Did her mother sound a bit hopeful? Olivia was wondering if she should intervene when she was saved by the doorbell.

"I'll get it," Jason said.

"I can work on Jason's farm and a school at the same time," Calliope said. "I get bored if I'm not cutting boards and pounding nails."

"Hey, look who I found hanging around," Jason said as he returned to the dining room. "It's our missing sheriff."

"Del!" Olivia jumped up and threw her arms around him. "Welcome home!"

"Ooh, public show of affection," Maddie said. "I like it."

"Pull up a chair, Del," Allan said. "There's plenty of food in the kitchen."

"I can't stay." Del brought over an extra chair and sat next to Olivia. "I'll just eat Livie's leftovers. Oh wait, she cleaned her plate."

Olivia whacked his shoulder. "What happened with Lisa? Is she out of the slammer?"

"Delicately put, Livie. Yes, she's a free woman. You'll never guess what little tidbit Lisa forgot to mention to me. She has a boyfriend. Or had, I should say. He took her place in the slammer. It turns out he's the one who shot Lisa's husband in the back. He wiped off Lisa's gun, but he didn't think about prints on the bullets, which were Lisa's, of course. To do him justice, he finally turned himself in when it seemed clear that Lisa would be going to trial for murder."

"Well, that's something," Olivia said. "So

what will you do the next time Lisa calls you in need of assistance?"

Del grinned at her. "I'll suggest she ask her current boyfriend for help, and then I'll wish her luck." Del checked his watch. "I need to get back to the station. Cody has been briefing me on the Greta Oskarson case."

"Speaking of which," Olivia said, "I'm still puzzled by what happened to Greta's cell phone. Maddie and I kept calling it to find out where it had gone to, and finally someone answered. They didn't say anything, just listened a moment and hung up. Did Desirée take it?"

Del nodded. "Desirée desperately wanted her family's cookie cutters. She went to Greta's house intending to break in while she was asleep. When she found the back door unlocked, she went inside and began to search the house. She became frustrated and decided to confront Greta. However, Greta was a poor sleeper. She didn't like to take sleeping pills, so she was reading in bed when she heard Desirée searching in the attic right above her bed. Greta panicked, began to hyperventilate, and her asthma kicked in. That's when she tried to call 911 and finally called you. Unfortunately, Desirée's anger and frustration had gotten the better of her. She burst into the bedroom while Greta was struggling to talk to you. Desirée demanded the return of her family's cookie cutter collection. She saw Greta with her cell phone, grabbed it, and put it in her own pocket. Then she turned away to leave the bedroom and continue her search."

"But didn't Desirée try to strangle Greta?" Olivia asked.

Del nodded. "Desirée figured Greta was too weak to be a threat and, besides, she no longer had a phone. But Greta recovered enough to get out of bed and go after her. That's when Desirée put her hands around Greta's neck. Desirée claims she was so horrified by her own actions that she let go and ran from the house. She insists Greta was alive at that time, wheezing but alive. Unfortunately for Desirée, she almost certainly triggered Greta's heart attack."

"It's all very tragic," Olivia said. "I am sorry we didn't confide more in Cody. We weren't sure whether Greta was murdered."

"It was a messy case, I agree." Del swiped Olivia's half-eaten sourdough roll from her plate. She passed him the butter. "I should have been here to help Cody take the lead. It's time he did so."

"Well, at least he was there to arrest poor,

sad Desirée," Olivia said.

"Do you know why Cody went to the store?" Del asked. "Because I asked him to find out if you were okay, Livie. I couldn't seem to get you on your cell, and you didn't respond to my messages. I was beginning to worry."

"Oops," Olivia said. "Sorry about that. Lots going on."

Del finished his roll and pushed back his chair. "Walk me to the door?" He stood and held out his hand toward Olivia.

"Yes, she will," Maddie said before Olivia could utter a word.

Olivia took his hand and held it as they walked across the living room to the front door. Del opened the door and pulled her outside. "How about dinner tomorrow evening?" he asked. "If you say 'no,' I'll have to cancel the reservation I made at Bon Vivant. No one cancels a reservation at Bon Vivant. It would be humiliating."

"I couldn't put you through such an embarrassing experience," Olivia said. She kissed him on the tip of his nose. They were about the same height, so she didn't have to reach.

"Thank you for saving my dignity. And for the kiss, which I feel honor bound to return." And he did. "To be continued," Del said. "Livie, I got worried when you didn't respond to my calls. I missed you so much and I found I really enjoyed talking over the Lisa situation with you. Well, enjoyed might be too strong a word to use about discussing Lisa. I guess what I'm trying to say is . . . I like being with you and I like talking things over with you. Maybe we could . . . do that more? I mean . . ."

Olivia laughed gently. "Does this mean you'll share more with me about your cases?"

"Well . . ."

"That's articulate enough for me." Olivia smiled and hugged him tight.

RECIPES

Tangerine Cardamom Shortbread
1 cup unsalted butter, soft
1/2 cup sugar
1 tablespoon freshly grated tangerine zest, chopped (Use organic tangerines and scrub well.)
1/2 teaspoon tangerine flavoring (or orange flavoring)
1/2 teaspoon vanilla
2 1/2 cups flour
1/2 teaspoon cardamom (or up to 1 teaspoon, if you like a stronger flavor)

Heat oven to 350°F.

In a large mixing bowl, combine softened butter, sugar, tangerine zest, tangerine flavoring, and vanilla. Beat at medium speed until creamy. Add flour and cardamom. Beat mixture until coarse crumbs form.

If you are using ceramic shortbread pans, follow directions or divide the dough evenly and press into two 9-inch, ungreased round baking pans. Bake for 20 to 25 minutes or until edges are a light golden brown. Cool for 10 minutes, then cut into 16 wedges per pan. Cool in pans for 1 hour.

The employees of Thorndike Press hope you have enjoyed this Large Print book. All our Thorndike, Wheeler, and Kennebec Large Print titles are designed for easy reading, and all our books are made to last. Other Thorndike Press Large Print books are available at your library, through selected bookstores, or directly from us.

For information about titles, please call:
  (800) 223-1244

or visit our Web site at:
  http://gale.cengage.com/thorndike

To share your comments, please write:
Publisher
Thorndike Press
10 Water St., Suite 310
Waterville, ME 04901

CPSIA information can be obtained
at www.ICGtesting.com
Printed in the USA
FFOW03n0337030415
12387FF